HEREAFTER

AURORA WILDEY

Printed in: U.S.A.

First Edition: Infinite Ink Press (2018)

Contact Information:

Infinite Ink Press

infiniteink@yahoo.com

www.infiniteinkpress.com

www.aurorawildey.com

Cover design by: Deranged Doctor Design

Paperback:

ISBN-13: 978-0692103449

For:
Penny Cross, Jim Bayles,
Kevin Jones & Piotr Grudziński
You are gone from this world but not forgotten.

CHAPTER ONE

NOW THAT THE wind had shifted, the acrid smell of wood smoke hung heavy in the air, even inside the confines of the small diner. There was no mandatory evacuation order yet, though the locals were well aware it could come at any moment. If the brushfire reached the edge of town, a good fire break and some garden hoses weren't going to be enough to take the force out of the fire that was burning on the other side of the ridge. All the residents could do was hope the river would be wide enough to keep the flames from jumping across.

Mid afternoon carried the darkness of dusk, with an even more eerie blood-orange glow on the horizon. The sun was only a vague light through the thick wall of smoke that followed the direction of the whipping wind.

Serena had wiped down the same table three times now as she stared, lost in thought, out the window. She'd rather be home instead of wasting her time in a nearly empty diner, but she needed the job just a little too badly. She intended to use her all-too-short break, before the dinner rush began, to go home and gather her few most precious possessions. At least that way, she'd have them in her trunk in case they had to high tail it out of town before her shift ended.

"Miss, where is my peach pie? I ordered it ten minutes ago." A rather annoyed looking bleached blonde woman, in a grey-pinstriped pantsuit, shot a steely glare from where she leaned against the counter.

Kendall, should have been minding the counter, but was nowhere in sight. Serena was already on double duty washing dishes and bussing tables, since part of the staff hadn't come in that morning.

"I'll check for you, just a moment, sorry," Serena muttered, trying to put on her best chipper, happy to help face as she stashed the rag and spray bottle back into their place next to the sink before washing her hands. If she weren't in full view of the dining area, she'd be tempted not to bother with the pleasantries.

Kendall had apparently forgotten to note the pie was for a to-go order. The cook had served the slice up on a plate, instead of in a to-go box. Serena busied herself transferring the pie to a box, careful not to damage the slice much more than it already was. She made the customer's caramel mocha, giving her a large instead of the small she had ordered to make up for the inconvenience.

Serena made sure that everyone's coffee was topped up before going in search of Kendall. She found her sneaking a cigarette inside the freezer, shivering while trying to hide behind the boxes. Kendall stomped the butt out fast when she'd seen the door open, only to grumble in frustration that she'd been busted, but thankfully not by the owner.

"Didn't you get enough smoke outside on the way in?" Serena muttered, pulling the door shut quickly. Hopefully, it would give the air a minute to clear before she re-opened the door. Otherwise, everyone in the kitchen would smell it and know what Kendall had been up to. "Come on, quit goofing off, I need to take my lunch soon."

Kendall re-stashed her lighter in the pocket of her apron and straightened her long, dark curls before she brushed past Serena. The door slammed shut with a resounding thud behind her, not four inches from Serena's nose. Serena didn't have time to make as much of an issue out of it as she would have liked to. The owner's wife was coming back from her own dinner break and an order needed to be brought out to the corner booth before another customer got the urge to start complaining. The boss wasn't going to care about their petty bickering, or their pissing contest over what the fire-induced lack of customers was doing to their tips, or better yet, lack of them.

Now that his wife was back to mind the few occupied tables, instead of sending just Serena on a break, the boss had tossed them both out, until the dinner crowd would normally be about ready to roll in. Serena did all she could to keep from rolling her eyes as Kendall coughed when she breathed in a good breath of the smoke in the air outside. She pulled her shirt collar up over her nose to keep from breathing it in herself.

"Think I'm going to head home and get some things done," Serena called as she was already quickly rounding her old, beat-up hatchback to climb inside. She prayed it would start, and not give her problems starting the way it often did when it had been sitting for a while.

Kendall, predictably, climbed into the passenger seat without even asking, propping her feet up on the dashboard and pulling off her shoes. "You're not leaving me here, Walt will forget I'm on lunch in ten minutes and have me filling salt shakers."

Serena breathed a sigh of relief as the engine roared to life. She backed out of the parking space, careful to turn on the headlights. The drive home wasn't far and, thankfully, took her in a direction that wasn't overrun with smoke. Grayness hung in the air and the smell seemed to permeate everything in the car, even with the windows up.

Serena had barely put the car in park, before she'd made a dash for the door of her building. The smoke made her lungs burn from running even more than usual. Kendall followed in her wake, complaining the whole way about her being in such an ungodly hurry. Serena's eyes were burning as she cleared the stairs. After one failed attempt she got her key into the lock and opened the door, not bothering to even kick her shoes off, as she normally would have, as soon as she got inside. For the moment she had other more important things on her mind.

Serena had already grabbed the old, beat-up suitcase that had belonged to her grandmother, out of the closet. She'd thrown it onto the bed by the time Kendall had managed to drag herself inside.

Serena didn't say much as she watched her come in. She busied herself digging through her dresser and closet, finding the things she wanted to toss inside. The first things to go in were the obvious, her photograph album, jewelry, and important personal papers, followed by her spare work clothes and her favorite clothes that she didn't want to be without if she had to be gone awhile. Thankfully she didn't own much, and could fit nearly all of it in the suitcase and a good-sized tote bag. Her furniture was clearly another matter, not that any of it besides her bed, couldn't be replaced by hitting up a few garage sales. If the fire did sweep through, it wouldn't be the first time in her life Serena had to start all over again with nothing.

Kendall, as usual, decided to hang around and voice her annoyance in the way only she could get away with, by rummaging through what was left hanging in Serena's closet.

"So, if you're not taking this, can I have it?" She quipped, holding up the Kelly green halter dress Serena had almost worn as a bridesmaid to what was supposed to be a co-worker's wedding. It had mysteriously been called off last minute a couple years ago.

"Maybe, I don't know." Serena shrugged, trying to lean on the top of the suitcase so she could get the latches to close. "It wasn't a cheap dress, but where are we ever going to find a place to wear something that dressy around here?"

"New Years maybe?" Kendall replied, holding the dress against her stomach to check the size. Then she held the dress up to admire it, and herself, in the full-length mirror on the back of the closet door.

"Damn you're annoying," Serena mumbled. She dug out the ugly matching shoes and threw them at Kendall only to watch her laugh and stuff them into one of the plastic shopping bags she kept for trash in the kitchenette. Kendall tossed the bundle next to her purse to take with her when they left.

They had been best friends since the seventh grade, not that many people would be able to tell by the way they talked to one another. In a way, it was more like a sibling relationship, than a friendship. There were times they couldn't stand each other, and fought like cats and dogs, but girls from the wrong side of the tracks had to stick together.

"I think I might shorten it and put a slit in the side. How do you think that will look?" Kendall asked almost teasingly.

"Well with that shade of green and that many sequins, at least you will look like a rather shiny lot lizard."

Kendall tossed a throw pillow at her head, which Serena barely avoided before watching it ricochet off the side of the dresser, sending a pair of small resin ducks scattering to the floor with a clatter, breaking one into pieces.

"Smooth move," Serena said, picking up the scattered pieces and setting them back up where they had been, without bothering to try and find where the glue was. "You sure you don't need to go home and pack?"

"Nah, I already have a bag stashed in Mom's car, just in case." Kendall shrugged, plopping down on the bed and waiting for Serena to finish packing. It was about the only advantage still living at home with her mother had, not that there were many to speak of, especially when her mother was on a good bender. She and Kendall had considered getting a place together, but in the end, saner minds had prevailed. They realized that too much togetherness would probably prompt them to end up shooting one another.

Not much else was said, and they couldn't have held a conversation down the stairs due to the smoke. Kendall helped to carry the second bag and a laundry basket down to toss into the back of the car. Serena made it a point to stop and fill up the gas tank, even if the wait in line at the pump ate up most of the rest of her break time. They listened to the radio, unable to do more than stare at the back end of the car in front of them until it was their turn at the pump.

After paying for gas, Serena had just enough cash to buy a two liter bottle of generic soda and a box of granola bars to keep in the car in case she did have to drive for a while before she had a chance to stop for food. She stashed them on the back floorboard under her blanket and pillow. The car would be uncomfortable to sleep in, but she'd manage it somehow if she really had to for a couple days.

The smoke became thicker the closer they drove back toward the diner, forcing Serena to turn on the headlights just to see where she was going. The wind seemed to have shifted, having picked up even more so in the time they had been gone. Traffic had slowed, making Serena hope they wouldn't be later than they already were getting back.

Eventually slow traffic had given way to the flashing of lights from the sheriff's cruisers blocking the intersection just a block shy of the diner. A deputy in a dust mask stood directing traffic and sending it another way after stopping each car and speaking briefly with the driver. It didn't take them long to find out that the voluntary evacuation for their area was now a mandatory one. In the distance, she watched Walt complaining all the way as he and the few remaining diners were escorted to their vehicles. She turned the corner and was steered in what she hoped was a well thought out evacuation route.

Halfway out of town they hit a snarl, the on-ramp to the main highway gridlocked, with seemingly half the people in town and school buses loaded with kids, all trying to leave at once. Impatient with the wait, she turned onto a back road to take another route. Once past the city limits, she floored it with Kendall griping all the way for her to slow down.

She had no idea where they were going to go. Neither of them had family outside of their own small town. The radio talked of a shelter that had been set up for evacuees at a couple of sites in the next county over, so she started driving in that general direction. The smoke was still making it hard to see, at some times harder than others, depending on which way the wind blew strongest.

Serena almost didn't see the curve due to the smoke until they were on it. She slammed on the brakes only to have the car lose its footing on the loose gravel at the edge of the pavement. They skidded through the ditch and toward the trees. It all happened too fast for them to do much more than scream, and then there was silence.

CHAPTER TWO

"KENDALL, YOU OKAY?" Serena heard herself calling, barely registering her own voice. Her vision blurred as she opened her eyes to find herself lying in a bed, somehow having gotten out of the car. Blinking eventually cleared her sight enough for her to study the dimly lit room. The air was clean and smoke free. Oddly she wasn't in any pain, even if she was sure she had been knocked unconscious by the impact when her car had hit the tree.

She tried to sit up, and was surprised to find that she could without any difficulty. Pulling the blankets back, she found herself dressed in a clean, soft nightgown with a pink rosebud print. Soft, pink terrycloth slippers with a satin rose stitched on top waited next to the bed for her to slip her feet into, almost identical to the pair she had worn when she was only about seven years old.

She slid her feet into the slippers, and crept across the wooden floor, it didn't so much as make a groan as she made her way toward the door. There was no light switch, but on top of the dresser next to the door, there was a small oil lamp with a carrying handle. She lit it with the matches that lay beside it, and held it up to see the room come into better view. Serena turned back toward the bed where she had been sleeping only a couple of minutes before.

Even in that light the room looked eerily familiar. An old-fashioned canopy bed stood against the far wall, covered with a homemade patchwork quilt. A hope chest sat at its foot, with hand sewn rag dolls perched upon it. She remembered a room very much like that one. The memory was bittersweet, even if she had been happy there.

"Hello?" she called out as she opened the door, only to find a silent and darkened hallway. She stepped out the bedroom door, leaving it slightly ajar, to help her find her way back again. No one answered as she explored the other bedrooms only to find them furnished but completely empty, the beds perfectly made as if they hadn't been slept in recently. If Kendall had been there at all, she wasn't there now. The house reminded her greatly of her grandparent's home, where she had been raised the first twelve years of her life after having been abandoned by her mother, even before she was old enough to remember.

The master bedroom contained a large, four-poster bed, covered in a white chenille bedspread, much like the one in her grandparent's bedroom. The bathroom smelled of lemon soap, and the faucets turned with an all too familiar groan before the water flowed, pipes protesting and sputtering before a steady stream came. It was then she noticed something was definitely not right. Her gaze fell on the orange colored tiger-striped toothbrush in the holder next to the sink. She'd loved that toothbrush, and had one just like it until they had stopped making them. Her grandmother had decided she was too old for children's toothbrushes anyway.

An icy chill ran down her spine as she finally glanced into the mirror. It wasn't her reflection that greeted her, but only the ruins of the room in which she stood. There was only broken glass where the window should have been. Everything was covered in filth and peeling paint littered the floors and broken fixtures. She screamed, turning to find the room just as she had previously seen it. Only the mirror contained the horrifying apparition, and blinking this time failed to make it go away.

Heart pounding in her ears, she ran into the hallway, careful not to drop the lamp from how badly her hands were shaking. She ran for the stairs, but stopped in her tracks when she saw a little girl standing there. The girl's starched white apron was almost glowingly bright against her brown and blue gingham prairie dress. Her hair was pigtailed and tied with thin cords of leather under her hair ribbons instead of elastic bands.

"You just looked in the mirror, didn't you? It's scary the first time you see it, I know," the girl said, canting her head and kicking the toe of her old fashioned laced up leather boots against the bottom of the rail next to where she stood.

"What is that... why?" Serena was able to gasp, trying to catch her breath and calm herself. She looked at the child, feeling no less un-nerved. "Do you live here? Is your family Amish?"

"No." The girl laughed, even if she looked sad all at once. "I saw you had come, so I came to help you. It takes some people time to figure out they are here, and it's harder for those people. Once you understand, it's really not that scary here, it just is until you get used to being here."

"Where are we exactly?" Serena asked, knowing they hadn't driven far before everything became a blur. It had been a half hour at most. Maybe the girl was the daughter of a member of one of those odd fundamentalist cults she'd heard about on the news before.

"I wish I knew," the girl said, letting go of the rail and stepping closer while fixing her dark brown eyes on Serena's. "We all seem to come here differently, but the story is very much the same, none of us know how to get back to where we were before."

"What do you mean?" Serena asked puzzled to watch the girl brush past her and toward the room she had been sleeping in. She wondered if the girl had been watching over her until she woke.

"By the way, I'm Lucy Miller," the girl called as she stopped short in the open doorway, waiting for Serena to follow. "You'll want to get dressed before we go see the others."

Lucy waited for Serena to go inside before closing the door softly behind her. Serena's memory came back as she approached the dresser on which the lamp had been waiting. She put it back where it had been before she opened the dresser to find clothes that seemed to be the right size within: well broken in and comfortable jeans, and a shirt identical to her old favorite grey sweater with the rainbow stripes running across the chest and the sleeves. It was odd and un-nerving to be standing in a near replica of her old room, surrounded by what had once been most of her favorite things, ones she'd had to leave behind long ago.

Serena had dressed as quickly as she could without looking into the mirror on the dresser. She kept her head held low, until she managed to find an old bed sheet in the closet and tossed it over the top of the mirror to hide the reflection within, or worse yet, the lack thereof. Serena unbraided her hair, pulling the brush through it as best she could without being able to see herself. She was hoping she'd wake up from what she had at first taken for only a nightmare, but when she opened the bedroom door again, Lucy was still there waiting for her impatiently.

She'd almost forgotten to ask until then, but suddenly remembered Kendall had been with her, her stomach knotted. There was a catch in her throat when she asked, "The friend that was with me, is she here?"

"Not that I am aware of. You have been the only person to come in a while now. If she were here, she would have gone to her own place. We all find the place here that we most consider home, and when we leave in time, it goes with us. On nights when the fog comes, it means changes, and that is how we know someone new is here."

"We aren't dead, are we?" she asked. When she glanced out the window, instead of fields like she remembered, there were trees, as far as the eye could see.

"No, do I look dead to you? I'm as real as you are. We all are," she grumped, reaching out and pinching Serena's arm for good measure. "See?"

"Ow! All right, but was that really necessary?" Serena hissed, rubbing her arm as she followed Lucy toward the stairs.

"Don't call me a ghost again."

"Fine."

"Are you ready?" Lucy asked before turning toward the stairs again, this time not waiting for her but simply expecting to be followed. Serena did her best to keep up, following her downstairs and through the living room to the foyer, where her grandfather's old, well-patched work coat hung, right where it always had.

Serena stopped just short of going out the door, halting to admire it and running her fingers over the roughness of the canvas-like fabric.

"Are my grandparents here?" She asked, calling after Lucy before she was all the way off the porch and down the front steps.

"No, they've been gone a long time, you know that."

"Yes, I know. I don't understand. How is any of this possible?"

"No one here knows. Most of us wish we did, a few of us don't." She shrugged, waiting for Serena to close the door and follow before she resumed leaving, this time at a leisurely pace. "Some of us have been here longer than others, and even they don't know."

"Years?"

"Decades. So long, they've grown young again and even gone," she said with a look of worry crossing her face. "We'll have to explain, but maybe not so much right now. It's going to be a lot to take in."

The walk was silent after that, and even though it was a lengthy walk of what she surmised to be close to an hour, the sky never darkened any further. The homes along the way made no sense. Some of the homes were modern, some older, and also from differing places. An old thatched roofed cottage or log home, was as likely to be next to a tract home as they were a Victorian gingerbread, or an old brick farmhouse.

"I took you the long way around so you could see." Lucy finally broke her silence as she led her down a path toward the river to a summerhouse near the shore, where several other people were gathered around a fire together.

The people there were both old and young, male and female, and their manner of dress varied just as greatly as the homes that they seemed to occupy. The older women fussed over the small children, who seemed well behaved and sat quietly with the others, who had turned their gaze upon both Serena and Lucy as they approached.

"I see you found her, Lucy dear, come sit down," a nearly middle aged, dark haired woman who vaguely reminded Serena of June Cleaver in her manner of dress said, waving them toward where the others were gathered on old wooden chairs and cushions on the floor.

Lucy allowed Serena to take the last rocking chair, setting down on the floor nearby only to have a toddler curl up on her lap, where he usually did most evenings. She nodded, not waiting for Jane to speak again before telling them, "She was in the new farmhouse. I don't know her name yet."

"I'm Jane," The dark haired woman said, setting back down in her own chair and not waiting for the others to speak. "May I ask your name, dear? I see you and Lucy are already acquainted."

"Serena Heller," she answered, already feeling a little uncomfortable under Jane's gaze. She reminded her of her grandmother's disapproving neighbor, who was often fast with a lecture when Serena wasn't careful to stay off of her lawn and keep her dog from digging in the garden.

"Well, Serena, I guess we should welcome you to wherever we are. I am sure this is difficult for you, as it is for the rest of us, but we carry on and make the best of it," Jane replied in a no nonsense tone, which was grating, even if Serena could sense she didn't mean to be unkind. It seemed that Jane was not the sort of person who sugar coated things, even when to do so may have been kinder.

Serena nodded, looking around at the two or three dozen people gathered, over half of them children, though only a few were younger than Lucy.

"Is this everyone?" she asked, studying their faces while at the same time trying not to stare longer than was kind at one particular person.

"No, there are others, not all of us are together at the moment."

Jane didn't strike Serena as someone who thrived on fantasy. Jane was direct and matter of fact in both her speech and her mannerisms. She seemed like someone who had lived a hard life, one that didn't allow her to show a softer side. She'd known people like that in the past, and while they usually meant well underneath it all, it was very difficult to get past their tough façade.

"And what is all of this exactly?" Serena asked, knowing that question alone was the stereotypical elephant in the room. It seemed to be the question everyone wanted to know, but no one had any concrete answers to.

"Well, we shall see, won't we?" Jane muttered, as she turned away. Her look of annoyance was clear, in not even herself knowing the answer. "We'll talk more later, for now we have other things to tend to."

Serena watched as she took some of the others with her and walked slowly down the footpath that followed the river before disappearing into the mist.

The mood lightened almost as soon as Jane left them. The children especially had gone from serious to almost playful. The tiny boy in Lucy's lap had drifted off to sleep there, and Lucy seemed not to be in any hurry to disturb him, letting him rest there until one of the older children, a girl in her late teens, came to take him to wherever his bed waited for him.

"Is she his mother?" Serena asked Lucy, noticing the sadness in her eyes at that question as she watched him be gently carried away.

"No, none of the children have parents here, the old ones, or even the ones that really are children," she said, registering the look of confusion on Serena's face at her words. "You'll understand in time, there's much to be explained, and so much we still don't know, but soon you'll understand."

The crowd seemed to be thinning as those gathered returned to their homes. Serena and Lucy were silent for most of the now short walk back to the old farmhouse, its familiar silhouette comforting as much as the memory brought sadness.

Lucy didn't follow her inside, but stopped, pausing at the foot of the porch steps, leaving her with one final warning, "Rest, but no matter how tempting it may seem, please don't be drawn into watching the mirrors. Some people never get past it. I think their minds end up trapped in a world we may never return to."

With that, Lucy turned and vanished across the lawn and into the shadows and mist at the edge of the tree line, only the lantern she carried showed which direction she had gone.

It took Serena several moments to gather the courage to go inside. Her feet led her to her old room almost on autopilot. She curled herself under the covers of that old canopy bed, a now returned, but once long left behind teddy bear clutched tightly against her, still smelling of cedar as he always had. She closed her eyes, hoping that when she opened them again, she would find all of this had been only another strange dream, but it proved to be one she could not awaken from.

CHAPTER THREE

IT DIDN'T TAKE her long to fall asleep. Her sleep, unlike in her life before, was near dreamless save for the voices near the moment of awakening. She awoke and slept again several times. The dim, twilight-like light outside never faded to darkness, nor turned to daylight, in all the hours she had lain there. There were only the changing hands of the old fashioned Swiss clock on the wall across the room to tell her that nearly ten hours had passed, as she finally drew the covers aside with a heavy sigh.

Serena was careful not to disturb the sheet she had thrown over the mirror as she brushed her hair doing the best she could to look presentable under the circumstances. Vanity it seemed, would no longer be a luxury she would be afforded here, not that she had ever thought of herself as beautiful by any stretch of her imagination. Maybe if she'd had the money for the right clothes, or a good stylist, she'd thought, almost laughing at herself for thinking of all the good any of those things would do for her. She rummaged through the dresser, happening upon her old dip-dyed jeans, and a neon rainbow tie-dyed tee shirt.

Of all the ridiculous memories to find here, Serena thought to herself. How old had she been when she'd found this shirt at the county fair and thought it was the greatest thing ever? Had she been ten, or maybe eleven? This whole place, and everything in it, seemed to revolve around her memories, things appearing when she gave them the slightest thought. She had however; been unable to conjure anything but what had truly been a part of her life before. She couldn't summon jewels, or that expensive jacket a girl at school had worn that she had coveted.

"They were never ours to own," Lucy said quietly as they walked the path toward the summerhouse in grey twilight again, once she'd come to walk her to the summerhouse. "We can only have what was really part of our world. Our homes are filled with things that belonged to us, and the things that belonged to our loved ones. Maybe they are there to remind us, or to comfort us as we pass the days, to wherever we're going when we leave here."

"So there is an end to all of this?" Serena asked, touching Lucy's shoulder to stop her. She turned so she could look into Lucy's eyes, her stomach tying up in knots to see her unease at having been asked the question.

"Yes, we grow younger the longer we stay in this place, and in time we forget ourselves." Lucy shivered as she uttered those words, for once seeming to truly be like the small child her appearance belied, and not one with wisdom well beyond her years. "We are cared for by the ones that come after us, until in time, we all become only babes, then one day we're gone, we don't know where."

There was no mistaking the fear in Lucy's eyes. Serena staggered as if struck, feeling like ice water had been poured into her veins. She could hear her heart pounding in her ears, her head swimming as she tried to wrap her head around the words that made no more sense than any other part of that nightmare had since it had begun.

"How? Why?" Was all Serena managed to utter, panic almost setting in. She wanted to run, fast as she could, back to the farmhouse, and back to that damned canopy bed, pull the covers over her head, and will herself to awaken in the real world again.

"I don't know, none of us do." Lucy sighed quietly, feeling sad for her. This talk was one she knew would be soon in coming anyway, and better Serena hear it from her than in Jane's rough manner. "I was a great-grandmother when I first came years ago. I've been here so long that I'm a child again, and I'm afraid even I will forget my life before. I don't want to forget."

Lucy's tears finally fell, and Serena knew, she dared not ask a thing more, as she just stood quietly hugging herself. She was unsure if Lucy would have allowed a hug, even if she had tried to embrace her. For the moment, Lucy truly did look the part of a weeping child, drying her tears with the sleeve of her prairie dress as she fought them back.

They were jolted from their thoughts by the deep bellow of a foghorn that seemed to make the ground below their feet rumble, though not enough to send them tumbling to the ground. Tears momentarily dried, a mild look of alarm spread across Lucy's face as she grabbed Serena's hand.

"Hurry, move, go faster," Lucy almost squeaked, pulling Serena into a near blind run down the path again, going as fast as her feet could carry her.

"What's the hurry? What the hell is going on?" Serena gasped, doing her best to keep pace with her and not be dragged along or lose her footing on the fast-dampening earth, as the grayness they had wandered into quickly began to thicken.

"We have to get to shelter before the fog rolls in, or we'll never find our way. I don't want to get caught wandering blind in this, I don't even want to think about where we would end up."

The fog was closing in on them, trees becoming only vague shapes outside of the reach of the light of the lanterns they carried in their hands. Serena spotted the glow of a fire down a narrow side path and steered them toward it, one she did not believe that Lucy had taken her down before. Lucy dragged her feet, protesting loudly when Serena dragged her towards it as if she were suddenly more afraid of what would be at the end of that path than the fog.

They could see no sign of a dwelling until they came closer; the sod-roofed home seemed to be built into the side of the hill itself. There were no windows and only a door that stood slightly ajar with a dim glow of candlelight coming from within. Near the house a bonfire roared, the glow the only thing that seemed to push back the darkness.

Serena and Lucy both stopped near the fire, trying to catch their breath and ease the pounding of their hearts when they were blinded by a beam of light that swept through the darkness as the lighthouse next to the sea to the West of the summerhouse came to life. The rumble of the fog horn grew louder as they staggered to the ground, screaming as the beam of light ceased its sweeping and fixed upon the clearing in which they stood for what seemed like a small eternity. Then, just as suddenly as it had come, the beam of light had gone, leaving them near blinded and stunned as the fog slowly began to fade away.

"I told you, we should have gone faster, nothing good ever happens in the fog," Lucy stammered, her voice almost a whisper.

Serena shook as they sat in the dewy grass trembling and catching her breath for a moment before she could speak without her voice failing her.

"Is it always that way? What just happened?" Serena finally asked, her voice still quivering. She hugged her knees to her chest to try to calm her shaking.

"No," Lucy replied, "the fog has come many times, it and the lighthouse mean changes, but this is the first time I've seen it happen. I always hide inside when the fog comes. I'm afraid if I get lost in the fog, I may not find my way back again."

The bonfire did little to take the chill out of their bones as they huddled next to it, staring silently into it, mesmerized by its dancing flames. A twig snapped behind them. Lucy turned and jumped to her feet.

"Run, Serena, run!" Lucy screamed as she bolted toward the trees, her pigtails flying behind her, screaming all the way without looking back.

Serena almost didn't see the tall unkempt bear of a man until it was too late. She rolled away just as he tried to seize hold of her. She clamored to her feet, bolting after Lucy, only to find him undeterred and on her heels. He dragged her to the ground before she reached the edge of the clearing.

"Run, get help!" Serena screamed after Lucy while struggling to get free. The wind whooshed out of her lungs, and her head swam as she gasped for air. She struggled not to lose consciousness as her hands were bound, and the man flung her over his shoulders. It was a fight that she lost as she was carried inside the house she and Lucy had stumbled upon only moments before. The man dumped her unceremoniously onto the floor and into a pile of straw in the corner of the room. She curled into a ball hoping, and something close to praying, that Lucy had managed to slip away as she lost the fight to stay awake.

Lucy ran blindly into the fog, her lantern lost in her haste to run away. The only thing there was to guide her, was the glow of that awful lighthouse that she presently cursed with every ounce of her being, even if for now it was all she could follow. The summerhouse was in that direction, and hopefully so were some of the others. She didn't know who that man was, but he was the most frightening thing she had encountered in decades.

Lucy ran through the woods as quickly as her short legs could carry her. The fog had not yet completely lifted. The further she got from the cottage the more it receded. At first she had been screaming, but she only had the breath to either run or scream, unfortunately not both. She stumbled often, but managed not to do more damage than a skinned knee. Once she finally got to the beach, she tried to pick up her speed for the last stretch of the run.

Jane was where she always was, holding court for the evening in the summerhouse despite the fog. The fire in the hearth crackled loudly as the children huddled close to it, looking alarmed when Lucy barged in still at a run. She looked disheveled, with bleeding, skinned knees, and scratches from thorns.

"Well, aren't you quite a sight?" Jane chuckled before she caught the frightened look in Lucy's eyes.

Lucy fought for breath to tell her what was happening.

"What's the matter, Lucy dear, did you take a spill in the fog and hurt yourself?"

"Help," was all Lucy managed to get out at first, much to Jane's amusement. Once she caught her breath she'd blurted out, "There's someone in the woods, at the new house. He attacked me and Serena; she's in trouble."

Now that Lucy had gotten the words out utter panic was setting in, and she dropped to her knees. Jane barked orders for a party to be sent to search for Serena made up of their strongest men and women.

"Show us, Lucy, take us there," Jane ordered sternly, grabbing her firmly and helping her rise to her feet. She handed Lucy another lantern. Jane left some of the older children and young women in charge of the small ones, as she and most of the adults followed Lucy back down the path. The fog was only just clearing to mist as she led them back towards where she'd last seen Serena, as quickly as she could under the circumstances.

"We were coming from Serena's house, and a new house appeared just as the fog came," she told Jane as they did the best they could to try to move safely down the trail. "Something happened, something terrible..." Lucy's voice trailed off, half cursing herself for not being able to go any faster. She looked for the section of trail she'd taken with Serena, straining her eyes to see that telltale bonfire in the woods. The only landmark she could think of to guide anyone faster than her through the darkness.

Serena awoke moments later to the loud crashing of the home being ransacked. She tried to curl up with her back against the wall in the shadows, staying as still as she could trying to remain un-noticed. The man she was watching seemed nothing like the rest, he spoke not a word as he tore through possessions that obviously were not his own. He broke and tossed aside things that did not please him. What else was this man capable of?

A few moments later, seemingly satisfied with his plunder he approached her. She tried to back away from him, only to find herself firmly in a corner with nowhere to go. It was only then she saw another man emerging from a loft above. He was nearly as tall as the first man, almost as hairy, but cleaner and more mindful of his movements. He raised a hammer and struck the man hard across the back of his shoulders. The blow barely missed the bear-man's skull. Undeterred, the man staggered briefly before turning to face his assailant. Serena breathed a sigh of relief that, for at least that moment, his attention was turned in another direction.

As the two men fought, Serena did her best to try to edge her way to the door, staying close to the wall, and trying to keep clear of the battle that neither man at that time seemed to be decidedly winning. She managed to scoot to the door and struggled to crawl over the threshold before rolling onto the soft, damp earth once again. She did her best to get from her knees to her feet without using her hands. Her only thought was to hide herself among the blackness of the fog and the trees until Lucy could return with help.

Unfortunately, Bear-man seemed to have other ideas, having noticed her slipping away. He turned his back on the battle to pursue her. She screamed as she ran, attempting to put some distance between them, though he gained on her using an unnatural speed. She stumbled and hit the ground hard just as she reached the bonfire and tried to roll away. All she could see was Bear-man's face as he crept towards her, with a wild look in his eyes. She had nowhere else to go but into the roaring fire behind her.

A sickening thud sounded as the hammer met its mark this time. Bear-man crumpled to the ground groaning and snorting, but still very much alive.

The fair-haired man with the hammer let out a roar as he raised the hammer over his head and swung downward with all his might, as the beam of light from the lighthouse once again swept over them. It would have been a finishing blow. The air shimmered and the hammer struck nothing but bare earth. The beam of light vanished, and the Bear-man was gone.

CHAPTER FOUR

As the lighthouse's beam swept away, Serena once again found herself on the ground, this time face down and shielding her eyes. She tried to crawl away, her screams still echoing in her ears. Bear-man was gone, but there was still the other stranger looming near her. His weapon had crashed to the earth far too close to her for comfort. Her only thought at that moment was to scramble for the trees and hide herself. She had no desire to find out who this second man was. All she wanted was to get far away from there.

His back to the beam of light, the man was not as stunned by the brightness as Serena might have hoped. Still enraged that his enemy had eluded him, he instead turned his attention to her. He was at first puzzled at the strangeness of her clothing. He would have taken her for male, were it not for the bright colors of her clothing and the shape of her body. He reached out to seize hold of her before she could crawl away from him. All he had to do was roll her onto her back and raise his weapon to subdue her. Even though Ardal had eluded him, it amused him that he managed to steal his quarry away from him, and she was a pretty thing indeed.

Serena could do little more than stare up at him with fear in her eyes as he loomed over her, straddling her waist. One hand went under her chin to turn her face to his. He kept his weapon at the ready with the other. She shivered as his hand reached to brush the hair back from her eyes. Then he grasped her firmly by the hair at the nape of her neck and began to rise to his feet, pulling her to her knees after him.

"Come, you are mine now," The man said sternly, as he pulled her to her feet, keeping a firm grip on her hair. He guided her toward the house they had left only moments before. She struggled to stay upright against his grueling pace, and the man paid no mind to Serena's screams, or her pleas for him to let go of her.

Serena stumbled as he pulled her across the threshold, but he quickly tugged her to her feet again, before pushing her into that same pile of hay that Bear-man had tossed her into moments before. Only then did he let go of her, moving back to the door to close it with a heavy thud, and sliding a heavy beam into place to bolt it closed.

Once the stranger's back was turned, Serena did her best to struggle with the ropes that still bound her wrists tightly. They had already cut into her skin from her sorry attempts at crawling, but still held fast. The more she struggled with them the harder they seemed to bite into her skin; blood began to trickle down her arm.

It did not take long for the man to turn his attention back to her, the fear in Serena's eyes plain to see as he watched her struggle with the bindings. It was obvious she had too much fight in her to be a common slave girl. She seemed determined to resist, which told him Ardal had little, if any time to break her, and she had likely only just been stolen.

Serena flinched as he approached her, bringing a knife with him and unsheathing it. She was too afraid to move away and risk angering him. He knelt, grabbing her wrists to examine the ropes. To her surprise, he cut them loose. He, however, did not loosen his grip on her, even as he sheathed the blade. The man's eyes almost seemed to burn right into her, as she looked up at him, too afraid to look him in the eye.

"What is your name, girl?" he asked, his other hand moving to rest upon the back of her neck. His voice was softer but carried that same stern tone as it had moments ago. He left no doubt that he expected answers and, if she valued her life, truthful ones.

"Serena," she answered, starting to shiver. She tensed, trying to stay as still as she could, not that she felt she would ever be strong enough to break the seemingly iron grip with which he held her. The last thing that she wanted was the terrifying rage she had seen moments before directed at her.

"I am Rune. Tell me how you came to be in my home, how a slaver such as Ardal happened upon you, and just who you belong to?" Rune said quietly, waiting for her answer. He was almost amused to see her tremble, and satisfied for the moment that she was most likely far too afraid of him to consider deceiving him.

Serena took a deep breath to steady her voice before replying, "I was passing on the road nearby when the fog came. I saw your fire outside and walked toward it. Once I reached the fire, he attacked me, and the little girl I was traveling with. I live near here, and I don't belong to anyone but myself." The last part of her answer was said with as much of a tone of defiance as she probably dared to use considering the circumstances.

"Well, now you belong to me, do you understand?" Rune replied, meaning it more as a statement of fact than a question. He saw the fear well up in her eyes and tightened his grip on her; only then did Serena try to squirm free. She flinched and let out a soft cry when he pulled her closer. "Calm yourself. If I wished to harm you, rest assured that I already would have done so."

"Please let me go, I need to go home. You don't understand what is happening here," Serena pleaded as he lowered his face close to hers, his eyes narrowing. She shuddered when she saw her words displeased him even if they had to be said. "The others will be coming for me soon. Lucy would have told them what has happened by now, and before long, they will be coming to rescue me."

"Is that what you presume of me?" Rune growled, tightening his grip on her hair to hear her scream. He lowered his face to look straight into her eyes, not caring for the moment if there was little other emotion but fear in hers. "I am nothing like Ardal. Do you hear me?" He kept his grip on her until she nodded in reply, and only then did he loosen it. "I lost my wife to the clutches of Ardal, and now I wish to take another. It is fitting I should take the woman that I have saved from him."

"You know nothing about me," Serena said sheepishly, feeling no less afraid. Rune seemed to have far less bad intentions for her than she had first bargained for. Her stomach sank, he seemed to not be the slightest bit deterred, and he did not release her, but his iron grip on her eased and became almost gentle.

"I knew nothing of Kitta either before the day I wed her, but the marriage was good, our parents arranged it." Rune, for the moment, wore a look of sadness instead of anger. "Need I ask your father? I will do so, gladly."

"I have no father, I never knew my parents; my grandparents raised me," Serena answered. It never occurred to her to lie, even though it would be more likely to get her free of him. The truth would come out eventually, and he did not strike her as the sort to take kindly to being misled. "I lived on my grandparent's farm for most of my childhood, but they died a long time ago. I have been on my own since then."

"Who cares for you? No woman lives alone," Rune asked, confused. "All women must have someone to look after them."

Serena shook her head, puzzled by his confusion when she replied, "I have no one. I take care of myself, or at least until recently. Now there is nothing for me to do, I'm lost here." She sighed, not as frightened as before, but still uneasy to have him so close.

"So, I need to ask no one to have you?" Rune stated. It was news that pleased him, his hand loosening its grip on her hair to instead raise her chin. He pulled her lips toward his, only to be interrupted by a loud pounding at his door. "Stay here," he ordered, releasing her to stand and retrieve his weapon before moving toward the door cautiously. "Ardal may have returned, and he will not have you."

"There is one person, who may object," Serena said quietly. Rune opened the door cautiously. Confusion etched his face when he saw the crowd gathered outside his door.

"I believe you may have a young woman here that belongs with us, where is she?" Jane asked in her usual forceful tone. She and the others were unarmed but had come in numbers, and they had more than a sporting chance of subduing him.

Rune blocked the doorway but sat aside his weapon as he observed the strangely dressed peasants, most barely more than children. Though, several of the young men looked strong enough to make a skilled fighter. It was clear to him that the woman that spoke did so with authority.

"She is here, Ardal has gone, and the girl has not been harmed."

"Then send her home." Jane motioned toward the door, more than hinting to him that they intended to push past him if her request wasn't honored. "You will let her go with me now, if we are to believe that you have good intentions."

Rune turned back to Serena, gesturing for her to come to him. He watched as she rose from the floor and cautiously approached him. He drew her next to him before he opened the door further. "As you can see she is well and no harm has come to her, nor will I allow it," Rune answered Jane in an equally stern, but far more quiet voice.

"Are you all right?" Jane asked Serena, showing what for the moment, seemed vaguely genuine concern. Serena could do little but nod in reply. Jane nodded toward the far side of the clearing, where Lucy stood waiting, still looking terrified. "Off home with you then, we will speak later."

Rune reached to pull her back to him as she began to step away, leaning in to press his lips to her ear before whispering, "Soon, I will come for you."

Rune stood in the doorway watching as Jane and the others led Serena down the path that vanished into the trees. It did not surprise him that some of the group lingered at the edge of the clearing to watch him while the rest vanished from his sight into the last lingering traces of the mist. The twilight glow was returning to the sky. Given time, once he was no longer being watched closely, he would set out in search of her. He wanted her, and she would not elude him that easily.

CHAPTER FIVE

JANE HAD SCARCELY SPOKEN a word other than an order to be followed. Serena and Lucy followed her down the path, Lucy clinging closely to Serena's side as they walked. The child looked as badly shaken as Serena felt as they walked, keeping to Jane's determined pace, and not the run at which Serena wished to flee. Jane would never have allowed running in fear, you walked away with your head held high, or you didn't walk away at all.

The winding path led them through a stand of willow trees that gave way to a grove of ancient oak trees, their branches heavy with Spanish moss. Only as they rounded the last bend did they see the small utilitarian tract house hidden behind large magnolia and lilac trees. The lawn, small but well manicured with a sizable vegetable garden, was surrounded by a white picket fence. The back gate creaked softly as they passed through along the narrow flagstone pathway toward the house.

Jane ushered them inside, leading them to the kitchen table to have a seat. She asked the others to leave, or wait for her in the back garden. She closed the door softly, puttered about putting the kettle on the stove, and then joined them at the table. She set a selection of mismatched cups and saucers in front of them along with a jar of instant coffee on the table. Each cup got a carefully leveled spoonful before she returned the jar to the cupboard. The tiny kitchen was cluttered but immaculately clean, built obviously more for function than style or comfort.

"Well, now that we've had a moment to calm ourselves, would you both mind telling me what went on this evening?" Jane asked, filling the cups with steaming water. She put the kettle back onto the extinguished burner before she joined them at the table with a dampened cloth. Her manner did not seem harsh as usual, but a mild look of anger still lingered in her eyes as she washed the cuts on Serena's wrist. She bandaged it gently, wrapping Serena's wrist in clean cloth and using safety pins to hold the bandages in place.

"I don't really know," Serena replied, trying not to wince, or let herself fall apart and cry as Jane went about her work. "Lucy and I were walking to meet the others at the summerhouse when the fog came. We could barely see anything. We went toward what looked like the closest place to wait for it to pass. There was a bonfire, we sat down next to it, and then out of nowhere, a man attacked us. Lucy ran, but I couldn't get away."

"The man in the doorway, was he the one that did this?" Jane asked with a grave tone, wanting to know just what and whom they were dealing with. It would tell her how much they had to worry and how leery they had to be of this new stranger.

"No," Serena answered quietly. Jane could tell he made her uneasy. "No, the man in the house came after. He fought the man that was was hurting me, then a light came, and the first man disappeared. I don't know where he went."

Jane looked to Lucy, where the child shivered in her chair, her coffee untouched. "This man, did the fog bring him, was this the change?" Jane scowled in disapproval when Lucy only nodded in reply. "Speak, child, words?"

"Yes," Lucy stammered, acting as if she wanted to sink into her chair and disappear. "That house was not there before the fog came, I am sure of it. I go that way almost every night, and it's never been there until now." It was obvious there was more Lucy wanted to add, but didn't, starting and then stopping herself from saying whatever it was she wanted to say next.

"Out with it child," Jane said, her tone softening, trying to coax it out of her. Maybe a softer hand was what was needed to get the girl to tell her what she needed to.

"That house, that place, it's where..." Lucy's voice trailed off again. She fought to gain her composure before she continued, careful not to let any tears fall, not in front of Jane, who she was certain would only mock her for them. "That house, it sits where Charlie's was, before he went away."

"I am aware of that Lucy," Jane said quietly, trying not to be as hard as she often felt she needed to be. She nudged Lucy's coffee toward her, hoping to get her to calm herself and take a sip. "I know you and Charlie were great friends. He cared for you when you first came here, but he has gone. That place could not have remained empty forever. When we leave this place someday, others will come to take our place as well. It's the way of things. By now you know that as well, if not more than I."

Lucy nodded, but it was obvious by the tears brimming in her eyes that she could say no more about the matter. Serena thought she should have known from the beginning that more than the fright of what happened had been bothering her. Now that the rest of the story had come out, so to speak, she could not help but feel badly for her.

Jane was satisfied that Lucy had told her all she could for the moment, and she sighed and took a sip of her coffee before turning back to Serena. Other more pressing matters were on her mind than whose home used to sit nestled inside that clearing. She was, for the moment, more concerned with the man who seemed to reside there now.

"Did the man that was in the house harm you?" Jane asked Serena seriously, unsure of what she could do, but she would consider her options based on the circumstances.

"No, but he frightens me," Serena added, shuddering softly as she thought of the last few moments alone in that house with him. If Jane and the others hadn't come what would've happened next? "He told me that since he saved me from the other man, that he believes I belong to him. He wants me to marry him because of it, if I understood him. What man thinks that way?" Serena chuffed, not quite managing laughter at the thought of it.

"A man born well before our time when that would have been the outcome, and a woman's wishes carried very little weight in our world," Jane answered quietly, this being one subject she was well accustomed to. "Life as you knew it as a woman is a far more recent invention than you realize, my dear. In my youth, women did little more than stay at home; we cooked, we cleaned, and we raised the children. We did as we were told, and we had very little choice in the matter. Life stayed that way until the men went off to war, and once they came home, it was back into the kitchen. It likely would have been your mother's, or grandmother's generation that rebelled and changed all that. Feminism as you know it, didn't exist until I was quite older than I appear now, too late for my generation I'm afraid."

"So what do I do?" Serena asked, still unsure of how to deal with what happened. She had been through worse as a child who had gone through the system, far worse, but she was still at a loss for how to handle things from here.

"For now, nothing. Carry on as you would otherwise. I don't believe this man will harm you," Jane answered, finishing off the last of her coffee. She let out a heavy sigh before continuing, "Do be direct and honest when you speak to him. If you don't want him, that fact must be made clear, and I cannot be the one to tell him this."

They sat in silence for several more minutes before Lucy folded her arms and rested her head sleepily on the table. Jane reached out to stir her. "Go home for now, both of you, and sleep. I doubt he will trouble either of you any more tonight. I have posted a watch, if he wanders far I will know."

Jane handed them a lantern before sending them out the back door the way they had come in. The fog had cleared by then, and the moon hovered near the horizon looking as though it were almost close enough to touch, so much bigger than it had ever appeared before in any sky Serena could remember.

"Lucy, see she gets home, but pass nowhere near that house, do you understand?" Jane said as she showed them to the gate, stopping to close it behind them before she turned, disappearing back inside the house before they made it to the grove of oak trees.

As they walked, the woods seemed a far more menacing place than it had only a short while ago. Fortunately they did not have to pass the same way to make it to Serena's farmhouse. The house was silent and still as they made their way inside, and though Serena had not bothered to lock the door the night before, she would tonight as soon as Lucy departed.

"It will be okay," Serena told her, saying it as much for her own assurance as Lucy's when she saw how hesitant the girl appeared about going back out into the woods alone to make her way home.

"I know. I'm just worried. What if the other man is out there?"

"He's gone, the light came back and took him away again, or at least I hope it did," Serena answered, crossing the room to pull aside the curtain and look out the window. There was nothing but the meadow and trees. No one seemed to be lurking. "If you're too scared, you can stay here tonight, there are plenty of other beds upstairs. It's up to you."

Lucy nodded, looking relieved for the moment. Serena walked to the door and locked it, disappearing to lock the back door as well. Lucy sat at the foot of the stairs and waited for her to return. She studied the photos and paintings that seemed to line almost every wall, far more colorful than any photographs that she remembered.

"This way," Serena said, brushing past Lucy and continuing up the stairs. She waited for her to follow, and led her toward what would have been the guest room at the end of the hall. It was the one her cousins would have slept in when they visited. It had pale yellow wallpaper, and twin beds covered with daisy printed bedspreads. Toys and dolls adorned the tops of the dressers and the window seat. Lucy seemed quite overwhelmed by it all, looking around the room before sitting down on the bed furthest from the door to take everything in.

Serena did not know why she had thought to show her to that

room and not the other guest room. She had almost forgotten that Lucy was quite old, and not the small child she seemed to be.

"Is this all right?" Serena asked, hoping she hadn't upset her. Lucy studied the room looking a little dismayed by it.

"Yes, it's fine," Lucy answered, at last looking back at her. "It's just so strange, all of this in a child's room, so many things, and a bed of your own. My sister and I shared a room, and even a bed until we married and left home. This is quite different than I imagined."

"You make it sound as though we had everything," Serena said, helping to turn the covers down for her. She had to fight the urge to tuck her in. She knew very well she could manage it herself. "It seemed like we had so little, far less than many other people I knew then."

"Far more than the children of a poor man scratching his living out on a land claim he won in a poker game." Lucy laughed softly. "Times were different then, sometimes we need to remember that. People here come from so many times, and places, and we need to see things through their eyes, to learn how to live together. Goodnight, Serena."

Without another word, Lucy curled up under the blankets and closed her eyes. Serena closed the door softly as she left the room; she only stopped to gather a nightgown before making her way into the bathroom. She sat on the side of the old claw foot tub, sighing to herself as she waited for it to fill while thinking of all that Lucy and Jane had said to her. She was still frightened and worried about how to handle the days ahead in this strange new place that she still knew so little of.

Serena didn't fully relax until she had undressed and lowered herself into the water, careful not to wet the bandage on her wrist. She sat with her eyes closed until the steam had all but gone from the water. Only then did she wash what was left of the mud away, doing the best she could to manage with only one hand. She kicked the drain plug loose with her foot and climbed from the tub, shivering as she dried herself with those old, familiar fluffy pink rose printed towels that had been her grandmother's favorite.

She brushed her hair as best she could after towel drying the ends of it. Looking in mirrors was no longer an option. She'd already covered the bathroom vanity with shoe polish that morning, lest she forget and glance into it. Seeing what was on the other side was not something she felt she would ever get used to.

She was half in a sleepy daze as she slipped into her nightgown, bare feet making not a sound on the floor but the faint creaking of the wood as she crossed the hall. She wound her fingers through her hair, in a half-hearted attempt to braid it. Her mind was elsewhere as she entered her room. She fished through a basket on her dresser searching for a hair tie to fasten it. The door closed behind her and the lock clicked into place. She froze, turning slowly to see Rune standing there, waiting for her.

CHAPTER SIX

"WHAT SORCERY IS THIS?" Rune asked before moving quickly to cover her mouth to keep Serena from screaming. He kept her pinned between himself and the dresser until she stopped resisting him. "Answer me quietly, but do not scream," he added, slowly removing his hand, but keeping Serena held firmly in place.

Serena fought to calm herself enough to answer him, more afraid of what he would do if his question went unanswered than any anger a response to his question might provoke. He was right about one thing, she wanted to scream, loudly enough to wake half the woods, but she knew he would never let her. He would stop her before the sound had time to reach anyone.

"I don't know, I wish I did," Serena stammered, seeing the anger in his eyes focused on her. She fought to catch her breath. "I did try to tell you. You weren't where you thought you were anymore, none of us are. We don't know how to get back, or even if we can go back."

"This is all a lie, nothing but trickery," Rune growled, roughly seizing Serena by her hair and pushing her into the corner between the dresser and the wall. She feared he would crush her beneath the weight of him. He jerked her head back so she had to look into his eyes. His other hand wrapped firmly around her throat, keeping her head held in place as he lowered his face within an inch of her own. "You will tell me the truth, woman of mine. I will not be made a fool."

"It is the truth, I swear," Serena cried, only to have it quickly stifled when the volume exceeded a level Rune apparently deemed acceptable.

Rune turned to glance at the door, listening silently for a moment before he turned back to Serena, satisfied that all seemed quiet and still. "I told you to answer me quietly, unless you want to disturb the child. I have no wish to make your daughter fear me more than need be." That said, his hand slipped from her mouth to grip her chin again. "Quietly now, tell me."

"Lucy is not my child," Serena answered, half stammering over the words as she shuddered. Her fear was nearly impossible to hide as she stared wide-eyed back at him. "She is only a little girl trapped here as we are. No one knows how we came to be here, or why we are here. I only arrived not long before you did, and some of the others have been here many years. If they knew how to leave, I am sure they would have done so by now, and so would I."

"One way or another, we shall see, yes?"

Rune was by no means a giant of a man, but he still stood over a head taller than Serena. Even his stature did not belie the outsized strength he seemed to possess for a man of his size. Struggling against him had proven futile, once he had a firm grip on her. Try as she may, she could not wriggle free. The more she struggled, the firmer his hold on her became. The next several seconds passed in silence, and she began to wonder if her feeble attempts at a struggle had only begun to amuse him. It was a suspicion that seemed to be confirmed, when Rune let go of her long enough for his hands to move lower. One firmly wrapped around her waist, and the other slid to her backside, nearly crushing her against him as he kissed her forcefully, not giving her time to protest or scream. The harder she pushed against him and pelted his back with her fists, the more excited he seemed to become, pushing himself harder against her.

"No!" Serena gasped, only to have his grip warn her to quiet herself again. His face drew into an icy glare, his displeasure more than apparent, only to be met this time with more anger than fear from her. "I'm not your wife. I won't have sex with you unless I decide to marry you. If you try to force me to I will fight you, even if you kill me."

"If I truly meant to take you, do you honestly believe you could stop me?" Rune chuffed, almost laughing at the thought. His expression turned devilish. He gripped her backside with both hands and lifted her from the floor, laughing low in his throat at her screams and shocked expression as he turned to pin her firmly between himself and the wall astride his waist, kissing her deeply yet again, to stifle her cries.

Serena thrashed against him, her fingers tearing furiously at his clothing and hair. Her nails dug deeply into his skin, more than hard enough to have drawn blood from him as she clawed at his back and his arms. Her futile attempts to free herself did little more than fan the flames, as anger yet again gave way to fear. Fear turned to blind panic as he tore her nightgown away as if it had been made of paper. The tattered pieces fell to the floor. He grasped her with his iron grip again to turn from the wall, and he lowered her onto the floor to lie on the rug beneath him in the center of the room.

Rune wasted little time pinning her hands above her head, using his weight to keep them held fast. Only then did he stop the kiss. He slid his free hand over her mouth, hushing her as he did so. His face flushed as he stared at her wild-eyed.

Serena lay naked and helpless beneath him. Tears started to fall from her eyes. Only then did he begin to still, he could have her easily, but he didn't want her that way.

"Quiet yourself, woman of mine. If you wish this game to end, cease your struggle and I will free you," he said, waiting to make sure Serena understood his words before he lowered his hand from her mouth and set her wrists free. He lowered his lips to hers, and kissed her once again. This time the kiss was gentle. "If that was all I wished of you, pretty one, make no mistake, I would have you this moment. I have no wish to harm you, but if you fight me and tear at me as if you are wild, I will tame you." He tore away the tatters of what remained of his shirt, tossing it near the door by what was left of her gown. "Since you were so kind as to relieve me of my clothing, I thought it only fair to remove yours. You will gain nothing trying to harm me."

Serena shuddered uncontrollably as she lay there staring up at him, more afraid than she had been in many years. She feared more of his wrath and struggled to find any shred of defiance and courage she could muster as she answered, "And you will not win my heart by forcing your will on me."

"We shall see, my little fierce one, won't we?" Rune replied, the faintest smile crossing his lips as he kissed her. He lowered himself ever so slowly downward, brushing his lips against her breasts before rising to his knees. His hands pressed on her thighs, as he felt Serena shiver, as she lay there bare under his gaze. He made no attempt to hide what he wished to see, or what was on his mind as he whispered, "But if you were willing, what a night we would have."

Rune tugged Serena to her feet, and wrapped her in his arms without saying another word. His lips brushed hers softly before kissing her neck.

Serena could do little but whimper as his hand curled into the hair at the nape of her neck. The kiss went from almost gentle to hard as he undoubtedly meant to leave his mark, and she could do little to dissuade him. She had not registered the source of the sound of the rest of his clothing falling softly to the floor until she felt the heat of him pressed tightly against her belly.

"I would give myself to you," he whispered, nudging her backward toward the bed. He sighed with disappointment at Serena's resistance when she pushed against him. He kept hold of her wrists but stepped away from her. She stood frightened and shivering as she looked back at him. "As you wish, woman of mine, as much as I do not wish to wait, I will return another night."

Serena stood stunned as he released her. She said nothing when he dressed himself. She pulled a large, colorful silken scarf from where it sat folded atop the dresser to cover herself. It proved fruitless as he came close again, unfurling it and using it to pull her against him and into a kiss that took her breath away.

"You will not be needing this." He smirked as he slid the scarf off her. He released her with what could only be described as a look of satisfaction, and wrapped the scarf around his shoulders, taking it with him as he unlocked the door and vanished down the hall.

Serena stood frozen, unable to move until she heard the front door open and then close. Only then could she stop shaking enough to shut the bedroom door and lock it.

She sat with her back to it, curled up into a ball, and finally fell apart. Even without the events of that evening, it had been a long time coming. She struggled with what seemed to be a nightmare to which she had no solution. She was alone now, in that place that knew neither day nor night, surrounded by people and places that made no sense. Escape was all she could think of as she sat there on the floor, hugging herself until she fell into an exhausted and fitful slumber.

She awakened sometime later, swearing she heard voices, and her neck aching. It was the first pain she had felt in days and it jolted her back to reality.

Serena sat up feeling stiff. She pulled on the first clean nightgown she could find in the dresser. Then she held her breath as she pressed her ear against the door, listening until she was satisfied that the hallway was empty. Serena unlocked the door and crept quietly down the hall, unable to breathe a sigh of relief until she'd wandered the rest of the house, checking each room to make sure they were empty, and the door he'd left through was locked and bolted. She made sure to look in on Lucy, only to find that she had thankfully slept through everything.

She would not return to her room that night. Instead, she curled up under the blankets of the other twin bed, in the same room Lucy slept in. She spent hours watching the girl before sleep finally returned. All she could think about as sleep overtook her was escaping back to the other side of the mirror.

CHAPTER SEVEN

Serena stared blankly at Lucy all through breakfast, absent-mindedly chewing on a piece of toast that may as well have been cardboard. She had been that way since coming downstairs that morning to find Lucy standing on a step stool in front of the stove, cooking eggs that had since gone cold on her plate. It was hard not to register the worry on Lucy's face. Serena kept tugging uncomfortably at the neck of the cowl-neck sweater she had dressed in, in a sad attempt to cover the angry looking marks that she was certain covered a good portion of her neck. Without benefit of a mirror she had no other means of concealing them, and the last thing she wanted was for anyone to notice it.

Serena was not ready to talk about what had happened, especially with Lucy. Even reminding herself of Lucy's true age did not make burdening her with her troubles feel any less wrong. Lucy still looked the pigtailed image of a little girl in a calico Sunday dress. Her neatly braided hair was tied up in matching ribbons that had been borrowed from the drawer of the vanity in the spare bedroom they had slept in. It was likely an old homemade dress that had once been Serena's mother's, the embroidery along the smocked collar unmistakably her grandmother's handiwork. It was not a dress she had ever recalled wearing as a child.

Her grandmother had always made a point of not burdening her with stories, or the things that her mother left behind. She was her mother's child in name only; the old woman had made that abundantly clear to her. Her early childhood had, for the most part, been a happy one despite the fact that she had been born addicted to the drugs that only a few years later her mother died from. Occasionally though, she still wondered what her mother must have been like, at least before addiction took its toll on her.

She tried to push the thought from her mind and put on a brave face, noticing the worried expression Lucy was wearing. "It's a lovely dress, Lucy, where did you find it?" she asked, though she already likely knew the answer.

"In the back of the closet. There's a whole row of them there. Some of them are made of old flour sacks, like I made for my girls when they were younger," Lucy answered, tugging at the fabric. "This one looked like it would fit, I hope you don't mind."

"No, not at all." Serena sighed, attempting a bite of the eggs, which were by then stone cold, not that it mattered. Even if it had bothered her, she never would have told her so. The eggs had no more taste than the toast she had nibbled at before, but she was trying to at least give the appearance that all was well, and that she was only tired.

Inside, Serena was doing her best not to go to pieces again. She for once could not fathom what frightened her the most; Rune, or the strange world she and the others were trapped in. It seemed that finding the way home was the only solution to both those worries. Avoiding Rune forever seemed impossible, and Serena could only hope that this infatuation he had with her was short lived. Until it ended, all she could think to do was avoid being alone with him, something that now appeared unlikely if he really set his mind to it.

She'd been relieved to leave the house as soon as breakfast was finished. The walk through the woods calmed her for once, even though the paths were not yet completely familiar. The woods were silent, the leaves not even stirred by the faintest of breezes. The sound of the river was heard long before it was seen through the trees as the path drew near it. The summerhouse lay not far ahead in the distance, near where the river met the seashore.

It was easy to follow the sound of the waves and the smell of the salt water, even before the trees parted. She almost hadn't seen him, until she was directly under him, looking up to find Rune perched in a tree at the edge of the clearing, watching the others at the summerhouse milling about. She reached for Lucy's shoulder, drawing her finger to her lips to silence her before making her aware of him, and trying her best to quietly creep past him, skirting the tree line in the other direction coming out on the beach, down the shoreline from where he seemed to be watching.

She wasn't sure she could handle seeing him again, certainly not that quickly after what happened between them only hours before. He was strange, determined, frightening, and nothing like any man she had ever met before. Any resistance she showed him, only seemed to be met with the sheer iron force of his will, which as of then, she had no solution to thwarting.

She knew they could not reach the summerhouse without being seen. There was a long stretch of beach and the pier in between them and what felt the closest thing to safety. She tried not looking back as she walked, holding onto Lucy's hand, determined to not give into the fear and run away. She had already shown him far more fear than she ever should have. Fear had a way of making you a target, and if Rune had not already he now had his sights fixed on her. Her hair stood on end. Rune was watching her; she could feel it. She gave into the urge and looked over her shoulder.

Rune was no longer in the tree where she had last seen him, but instead, had been silently following up the shoreline only steps behind her. Her heart pounded in her chest so fiercely she could barely breathe. He was gaining on her, his long strides becoming faster now that he knew that she had seen him. As terrified as Serena now was, she was more resolved than before not to run. He closed the distance and walked silently behind her, his hand brushing against the back of her hair.

Lucy was also unnerved; even if she did not understand the reason for Serena's fear, she could sense it. Whoever this strange man was that had come to take Charlie's place, she struggled to welcome him as she had the others. He'd come so quickly, leaving her almost no time to mourn or prepare. She had been fooling herself to think that she would ever have been ready. Her eyes turned to that cursed lighthouse, her face burning with how much hate she felt for it even if it was, at the moment, dark and silent.

Jane awaited them at the end of the pier, turning to watch them as they came. Children darted back and forth, playing contentedly in the sand, splashing as they waded joyfully in the water. Jane left them under the careful gaze of a woman named Martha, who had already been helping her to look after them.

"Lucy, go help with the little ones." Jane nodded, waving her toward the beach to get her out of earshot.

Lucy had not been happy with being sent away, but she let go of Serena's hand and did as Jane asked. There was nothing Lucy disliked more than being treated as if she actually was a child, but eventually in the not so distant future, she would need to be.

"I see our newcomer has found his own way," Jane stated, turning her attention to where Rune had sidled up behind Serena. The way Serena shuddered when he laid his hands on her shoulders did not escape her, or the sigh of relief that she seemed to breathe when she held her hand out for her. "I will speak to Serena alone for now, you are welcome to wait by the fire in the summerhouse with the others, and I will speak with you after."

Rune was not in favor of this notion, but relented as Jane led Serena down the beach and away from him.

Serena could have cried with relief, not that Jane would have ever tolerated such behavior. Jane led her to one of the many mounds of large rocks that dotted the shoreline, out of the man's line of sight, unsurprised when Serena looked behind them to assure herself they were not being followed.

"Am I to assume you and our guest have had dealings with one another since we spoke last?" Jane asked, sitting her down on a rock, if for no other reason than to get Serena's legs to stop shaking when she had asked her the question.

"How did you know?" Serena stammered, the alarm on her face would have been plain for anyone to see as she stared up at Jane nervously, hugging herself and making more than a concerted effort not to bite at her nails.

"An educated guess, that's quite a mark you have there," Jane said, trying to offer her a warm smile as she tugged the collar of her sweater further away to examine it. "This man, he seems to be a determined one. Did you tell him?"

"I tried," Serena replied, doing her best to fight back tears, a battle she was nearly losing. "No matter what I say, it doesn't dissuade him. Last night he was there..." Serena's voice trailed off, almost afraid to tell Jane what had happened. She was just too ashamed.

"He was where?" Jane asked her voice calm but direct as she watched the girl start to shiver. "Tell me. I won't know how to deal with this man until you do."

"When I went home last night, and went up to my room, he was already waiting there." Serena answered her voice trembling. "I don't know how he got inside, or how he managed to find me."

"Did he rape you?" Jane asked bluntly, viewing it as the most obvious question considering Serena's present demeanor. She reached her hand down to rest on Serena's shoulder before she knelt in front of her, trying to comfort her.

"No," Serena whispered, finally letting the tears fall, turning her face to look at the waves crashing onto the sand, unable to look Jane in the eye. "But I was very afraid that he would. He doesn't seem to take no for an answer."

"If he did not, given that chance, I do not believe that he will," Jane assured her. "That sort of honor is rare to find from a man of his time, my dear, but whatever you do, do not make yourself his enemy."

"What would you have me do? Give into him? I don't want him, he is a nightmare," Serena cried, trying hard not to let the others down the shore hear her, afraid more than anything that Rune would be among them.

"No," Jane replied sternly, warning her to quiet herself. "Do as you already have, be direct, and be consistent, do not waver. If you do, he will be waiting. Keep in his good graces. He is the sort of man who would kill and even die for you."

"Why me?" Serena asked, flustered at Jane's reaction; understanding, but not quite as sympathetic as she had hoped for.

"I'm not the one you should be asking that question," Jane said, standing and nodding down the beach to where Rune stood waiting at the end of the pier like the stubborn ox of a man he was proving himself to be. "That man is the only one who can give you that answer, but until you stop fearing him and make him listen to you, you aren't going to get the answers you are looking for. Mark my words, he will be a thorn in your side until that happens."

CHAPTER EIGHT

LUCY HAD BEEN furious when Jane waved her away, pouting almost like the child that she was as she watched her disappear down the beach with Serena. She hated the turn that her life was taking, even though she knew it was only the way of things. The thought of what was coming for her in the near future terrified her enough, without Jane and the others taking charge of the community that she had worked so hard to build the last several decades. Were Charlie still by her side, he would never have allowed her to be walked over that way. Lucy still believed she was more than competent to make choices for herself and the others. Unfortunately, the others no longer seemed to have the same confidence they'd always shown in her before then. It stung her heart more deeply than she would ever let on to any of them.

It was clear to her, at least in her own mind, that she was not needed, either to help with the children at that moment, or even it seemed, for her knowledge. Instead of walking to the water's edge as she had been told, she made her way to the far end of the pier, taking off her shoes and knee socks before dangling her feet over the edge and into the water. The horizon looked like an ocean without end,

save for that awful lighthouse that she'd somehow never outgrown
her hatred for.

She knew that Charlie would tell her it did no good to hold on to
that sort of emotion, and that it would only fester and rot the good in
her days away. For now, she failed to find the optimism that had come
so easily in the days she had spent with him, growing younger
together, and wishing more than anything, they'd been able to grow
old together again as well. Sadly, life in this place did not work that
way. He had faded away only days before, cradled gently in her arms
as she had promised him he would be. He had always tried to assure
her that they were only going on to a new life, something better, but
she'd been told the same story in the life she knew before. This was
nowhere near the heaven she'd been raised to believe was awaiting
her.

Tears burned her eyes as she took her feet back out of the water,
hastily trying to pull the socks onto her legs when she saw Jane and
Serena coming back up the beach in the distance.

Jane was not going to give her another lecture for crying. She'd
barely pulled her shoes on before racing back up the pier, brushing
past Rune, and making a break for the tree line before anyone had a
chance to stop her.

She ran as fast as her feet could carry her, the tears clouding her
vision causing her to stumble. Pulling herself back to her feet again,
she ignored the scraped knees and elbows and continued to run. She
did not know where she was running to, or more so, what imaginary
nameless monster she was running from. After a while, the paths all
seemed to run together, and she reached far beyond what were
usually their borders. The trees grew back on themselves, blocking
the view of the sky overhead.

She only stopped when she stumbled upon an overgrown gate in
an ancient stone wall, that guarded the path that led to the lighthouse.
Even at her old age, she'd heard only stories of that place. It was out of
bounds and forbidden. Many of those that crossed that border never
returned again, or at least, that was the legend. She wasn't sure she
believed in fairy stories anymore.

Despite her unease, anger clouded her judgment and she made her way through the thicket. The brambles and thorns tore at her dress and snagged on her hair. Her hands tore at the vines that wound around the gate, paying no mind to the scratches as she screamed with frustration trying to push her way through it. She pushed it inward enough that she could barely squeeze through it; tearing off a sizable piece of the pretty dress she wore in the process. The path on the other side was overgrown as well. She climbed over the rocks as the path made its way up the steepest of hills that existed in this place.

The climb was formidable, but she hadn't been more determined in many years to undertake anything. She wanted answers, and she wanted the truth, more than she had ever wanted anything.

Stunned beyond words at the sight as she crested the hill, she found herself crawling outward onto the softest grass she had ever encountered. The brush gave way to a rolling lawn so green, it looked as if it belonged on a picture postcard. Before her was a garden, overflowing with flowers she could scarcely have dreamed of, fragrant and almost glowing as they danced in the faintest of breezes.

She knelt there for several moments, stunned by their beauty before rising to her feet and making her way quietly across the lawn until she was among the beds of flowers. She followed the sound of a fountain that stood at the center of an elegantly carved, iridescent, marble pavilion surrounded by a small pond. The water was still and tranquil, dotted with shimmering lotus flowers and koi carp that twinkled like diamonds as they swam calmly beneath the surface.

Lucy knelt next to the pond, unable to resist cupping a handful of the water and bringing it to her face to wash the burn of her tears away. She took her handkerchief from her apron, saturated it, and rubbed the cool water over the blood that had dried on her scratches, offering her soothing comfort where there once was the sting of the thorns.

The flowers that grew around her smelled heavenly. Their scent washed over her the longer she sat there until she was unable to remember what she had come there for. All she knew was, she was overwhelmingly sleepy. Her body sank down to rest in the softness of the flowerbed, asleep before she'd had a chance to wonder why it had so rapidly overcome her.

She was still lying there when the old man found her, lifting her gently up into his arms to cradle her. The old woman was not the first child to have been ensnared in that bed of slumber flowers.

Sulwyn had planted the flowers there for that purpose, to keep the little ones away from far too many other things in his realm so close to their own. In so many years, this child had been the first to come, to seek him, as they sometimes did.

The answers they sought from him were not often the answers they wished to hear from him. The child had done well, and would soon be on her way to approaching her transition. Most accepted that time, but others, like her, came to him seeking the truth that it seemed kinder to protect them from. The life she knew before was gone, and her return to innocence in that realm was all but inevitable.

Sulwyn stood, carrying Lucy gently in his arms to a soft bed of moss under a silver rain shower tree. He laid her down upon it, carefully arranging her dress and her hair before a soft shimmering rain of its flower petals fell to cover her like a blanket. He stooped down to kiss her forehead softly before leaving her to slumber there, and turned to make his way back to the lighthouse.

The others would soon come to find her there, and she would lie there sleeping until they did. Only someone who took her hand and called her name could now awaken her.

CHAPTER NINE

THE EVENING GATHERING began in an uncomfortable silence. Serena did her best to avoid Rune, only to have him shadow her, coming closer each time she moved away. It was all a game to him. By the time the nightly fire was lit and crackling within the hearth, they were gathering the children together to be accounted for.

Serena watched as Jane paced nervously back and forth outside the door as the last of the stragglers made their way inside. It had distracted her enough that she didn't notice Rune standing behind her. She jumped with a start when he leaned down to kiss her neck gently, in the same place he'd left his mark the night before. His arms encircled her belly to keep her from pulling away.

"What troubles you so, mine? Do I frighten you?" He whispered into her ear.

"Yes." Serena nodded, unable to lie. She shivered at his touch.

"Do not fear, you will know me well in time." Rune replied. His lips brushed against her ear softly before he turned her to look at him.

Rune didn't have time to draw her close again. Jane re-entered the building, making her way to him at a determined pace. Serena had never seen this much concern on Jane's face. Until that moment she had seemed utterly unflappable.

"Lucy, the little girl that was with you, have you seen her?" she asked Rune directly. Her face wore a grave expression of concern, awaiting the results of another search of the beach and pier which, as of yet, had proved fruitless.

"Not in some time," Rune answered, nodding toward the door, "she was on the pier for a short time, but she left just as you returned, that way into the forest. I can show you."

Rune made his way out of the door of the summerhouse; drawing Serena with him as he crossed the beach and indicated which path she had taken.

"Could she have gone home?" Serena asked Jane, though it seemed doubtful. Someone had already gone to look for her there and had returned empty handed.

"Where could the girl be? She knows her attendance here every evening is a rule. She's the one who made it," Jane said far more loudly than she knew she should have, and in a tone she wasn't at all proud of. "We'll have to split up and search the woods for her. Where else could she be?"

Jane left Martha in charge of the children and was gathering a team of searchers when Rune stopped her, stepping between Jane and the others to get her attention.

"Wait, listen," he said, even if he felt he was the last person on her mind. She seemed far too emotional to him, and he didn't believe that she was thinking clearly.

"You have ten seconds. Talk," Jane replied in an annoyed tone. She crossed her arms and prepared to step around him if she had to.

"You must have more care, think wisely. If too many go searching for her, all they will do is cover her footprints. Which among you is a skilled tracker? That person must go first with a small group of others following behind to help. They must not walk in front of him."

Jane looked confused, searching her mind for what she knew of those gathered there. They were good men and women, all of them, but she did not believe any of them quite had the skill he was calling for.

"That is one thing I do not believe we have among all of us," Jane answered, not exactly fond of admitting this was a weakness.

"I will do my best," Rune answered, "I do it while hunting, and while at war, but I have never done it to search for a child as small as this one. She will be like trying to find a feather on the wind, next to a grown man."

"What will you need?" Jane asked, willing to take a chance on him for lack of other options.

"I will need a knife, an axe, a length of rope, and a small group of others to follow me with at least one other strong young man among them," Rune answered.

"You will have what you need, but I am going with you," Jane answered, waving a young man that stood nearby to gather the things that Rune requested.

"Then you will need to follow my direction, just as the others will, and do as I tell you."

"So be it," Jane replied in a not so comfortable tone of voice. She was used to giving orders more than taking them, especially from a man she knew so very little about.

They stood in silence until the young man she sent away came back with the items Rune had asked for. The knife was easy enough to obtain, but he was able to find him little more than the axe they used to chop the firewood they burned inside the summerhouse.

"Adequate," Rune said, testing the heft of the axe in his hand. "Now we can go."

"This is Robert," Jane said, nodding to the young man who had brought them the supplies. "He will be coming with us, he is one of the finer young men among us."

Rune nodded and tugged at Serena's hand, walking toward the woods. "Come."

"Why am I coming?" Serena asked, feeling she would be next to useless. She knew nothing about tracking, or even what to look for.

"Just humor him," Jane said sternly, prodding Serena to follow after him. The tone of the conversation in the summerhouse was eerily silent as the four of them disappeared across the clearing and into the woods.

Their pace was not nearly as rapid as Jane would have preferred it to be. Rune took each step carefully but confidently, his eyes peeled for any sign of prints.

The footprints in the soft, leafy dirt of the path showed that Lucy had not been walking, but running when she passed that way. In more than one place, he also had found evidence that she'd fallen, and then kept going.

The woods became thicker, and the path narrower the further in they ventured. Broken twigs showed where she had passed, Rune could only guess some time ago.

"Wait, she can't have come this way, she knows she shouldn't be here," Jane said, reaching her hand to stop Rune from turning down another path, one they had all been told a hundred times was forbidden.

"The trail does not lie," Rune answered, reaching to pluck a small scrap of calico fabric from a thorn bush growing next to the path. "This is the way she has gone, if you wish to find her you will follow me."

Without another word, Rune turned and took the path, using the axe to cut back the branches for them to pass through in places where the brush was overgrown.

Serena tried to stay a good distance behind him, wanting to stay well clear of where he was swinging. Her stomach knotted as she watched him, unable to deny just how strong he was. Rune was swinging that axe as if it were no heavier than a child's toy. He landed skillful blows exactly where he intended them.

Jane became more and more nervous, the closer that the stone wall loomed. It was too tall to climb, and the gate was overgrown with vines. It opened, if ever so slightly, just enough for the girl to have crawled through, judging by another piece of her torn dress that hung from the frame holding the heavy iron gate in place.

Rune and Robert went to work with their knives, doing their best to cut away the weeds and small branches that wound through the gate and the frame.

Serena stood next to Jane a short distance away, and watched them work with a worried expression. Looking up as she waited, she saw what appeared to be a large barn owl swoop overhead and perch itself on the wall, observing them.

Serena could not take her eyes off the owl, meeting its gaze, and watching it curiously. The crack of Rune and Robert pushing against the gate drew her attention away. They widened the gap enough for one of them to fit through. Rune held it open, his face reddening from the sheer force of the exertion, before Robert managed to slither through. Rune handed him the axe, and there was nothing more to do than to wait while he cleared more branches that were jammed against the gate on the other side.

Even with the branches cleared, it still took all their might to pull the gate open, not completely, but wide enough that they could pass through it sideways with little effort, even with Rune's broad shoulders. Already drenched with sweat, he and Robert rested briefly before waving the women to join them as they continued.

"There is only one way she could have gone from here, and that is upward," Rune nudged Serena onto the path ahead of him, easily reading the fear in her eyes at the height. He was unsure of her skill at climbing and wanted to stay close behind her to steady her.

The path was rocky and steep. Serena's feet slipped more than once, sending her screaming and sliding back into Rune's arms where he waited to catch her.

"Stop standing, walk with your hands as well," Rune told her, nudging for her to bend, and following her downward. "If you feel yourself begin to slip, flatten yourself against the path and dig in your feet until you are no longer sliding, then continue upward. Do not trust branches or small rocks to hold your weight."

Serena crept ahead ever so slowly, trying her best not to look down, or even think of her discomfort of having Rune so close. He genuinely seemed to be trying to help her, sticking close behind her until she crested the hill and crawled on her hands and knees out of breath. It took her a moment to rise as far as her knees, shaking as she tried to catch her breath. Rune slid up behind her and wrapped her in his arms while they waited for the others to complete their ascent.

"You have done well, my dear one," he whispered in her ear, his breath warm on her neck, before gently kissing her cheek. "You are afraid, but still you are brave, this pleases me."

She was far too tired to protest having him so close, not that she believed anything she said would make a difference to him. Rune seemed to want far more than she felt she could give him. She was grateful that he had saved her from Ardal, but she did not love him. Serena did not know if she ever would, she barely knew him.

Rune did not move away until the others came up. He reached his hand out to help them up the last few feet of the climb. He waited for them to catch their breath and rest a moment. They took drinks of water from a canteen that was passed among them before he led them through the stand of trees ahead. The long grass obviously trampled by someone who had passed a short while ago.

They were all taken aback, much as Lucy was, by the stunning sight that met their eyes. Their small group spilled onto the unearthly green lawn and garden stretching out before them, so bright it almost glowed. It was the most colorful thing any of them had seen in all their days there, even despite the still eternal twilight.

"This way," Rune said. Looking around he saw no one, but he was certain that someone had to be living in this strange place.

They hurried along, following the trail Rune was tracing through the soft grass to the fountain. It was clear Lucy had stopped there; the flowers were trampled down where she had been lying.

"Here, another set of footprints, a man, quite tall," Rune said, finding that those footprints continued on from that place, but Lucy's did not. "Whoever this man is, he has carried her from here."

Jane and Serena looked at him with silent alarm at the realization that they were not alone. Someone else was in the garden, and whoever he was, he'd taken Lucy.

Serena saw nothing as she looked around for any sign that they were being watched. The same barn owl still followed them, circling overhead. It then swooped low over their heads flying in the direction Rune was leading them.

Rune kept Serena close to his side, one arm around her, and the other firmly gripping the axe he still carried, ready to swing it, should the need arise.

The owl flew ahead until it landed in the branches of the silver rain shower tree, trilling at them as if to point the way.

It was all Serena could do not to dash ahead. She stayed by Rune's side as they hurried quickly but carefully ahead to kneel by Lucy's side.

Serena and Jane knelt next to her as Rune and Robert stood watch over them. It frightened them to find her in so deep a sleep. Lucy's hair was outspread, and her body covered with flower petals; it was obvious to them that someone had watched over her and ensured her safety when she ventured so far and fell into her slumber.

Serena scooped Lucy up onto her arms; terrified she had come to harm until she stirred when they called her name.

Lucy looked confused and frightened when she opened her eyes. She was unable to remember where she was, or how she had come to be there.

All Serena could do was stare up at the owl where it ruffled its feathers as it sat in the branches. As if satisfied its work was done, it took to the air and soared in direction of the lighthouse.

Too exhausted to walk, Lucy instead rode on Rune's back the entire walk back to Serena's house. Jane refused to allow her to be alone, and Serena had gladly offered to look after her until morning.

Lucy had not said a word until Serena helped her out of the tattered dress and into a nightgown, tucking her into the same bed she had slept in the night before.

"I'm sorry I ruined your beautiful dress," Lucy whispered before snuggling down further under the covers, her voice far more child-like than it had been before that night.

"I'm just glad that you are all right, we can make another dress, okay?"

"Uh huh," was the last thing Lucy said before she fell into a deep slumber. Serena struggled to hold back tears as she sat there for several moments watching over her. She knew that she should leave Lucy to sleep, but it was so very hard to take her eyes off of her.

CHAPTER TEN

SERENA'S BODY felt heavy and weak as she closed the bedroom door and stepped out into the hallway, not surprised to find Rune there waiting. Damn Jane for leaving her alone with him.

He rose from where he had been perched on the railing at the top of the stairs, moving to close the distance between them. Just the sight of him there made her breath catch in her throat. The smell of dust and sweat clung to him as he drew her close. She found herself exhausted, and for once, far too tired of arguing to pull away from him.

"You care for her well, like a mother. I feel that in you," Rune said, reaching to lift her chin to look at him. "Your children must have been happy ones."

"No," Serena whispered, sadder than she felt she would have been to say that word. "I have never had children. I always thought that someday I would, but I never met anyone. It's too late now."

"You are young, and we could have many, if you would have me," Rune replied, looking into Serena's eyes with a look that was all but tearing her heart in two. She didn't have the strength to fight him when he leaned down to kiss her, a kiss not broken until he noticed the tears falling from her eyes. Damn him, Jane had been right, she'd left him an opening, and here he was turning it into a chasm.

"Why are you crying?" Rune asked, his expression confused that for once Serena was not pulling away, and she seemed to have fallen into his kiss almost willingly.

"Because it can never happen," Serena whispered, her bottom lip quivering. She hated the thought of the truth she had to tell him. Even she didn't want to accept it. "In this place we don't grow older, we grow younger. This world we are in isn't a new life. It's nothing but un-life. Nothing can grow here, especially not a child."

"You do not know that for certain," Rune told her, his expression doubtful as he held her tighter. "To know anything for certain, you must try, many times. Wishing without effort will never result in what you desire. You already know that I am willing."

"You barely know me." Serena blushed, stunned by his words. She felt much too close to him for comfort, but at last admitted to herself that the disquiet inside her would have been the same no matter whose arms she was wrapped in.

"I know all I need to," Rune stated plainly. He kissed her forehead softly and reached to cup her face in his hands. "What must I do, woman of mine, to prove that I mean no harm to you? You are a gift sent to me by the Gods, and if we now dwell in Hel's realm together, there is no shame in this. If you will accept me, I will stay with you through the end of this world and all the others."

"Rune, I am afraid," she answered, the words leaving her lips before she realized she had spoken them aloud.

"There is no need, I will not harm you." Rune drew her close again unable to understand the worry in her eyes as she stared up at him.

Serena drew a deep breath, her hands resting on his chest, trying to find the words to what she wanted to tell him. There was no good way to say what she needed to say. "Rune I have never done what you are asking from me. I have always been afraid to try."

"What makes you fear it?" he asked, relieved to now understand at least that much. "There is no reason to be afraid. I will be gentle until you wish otherwise."

Serena nodded, but saw the look of confusion in his eyes when the tears started falling again. She leaned her head against his chest for a long moment, trying to hold the tears back long enough for her voice not to tremble.

Rune did not push her away, but much to her surprise, held her tighter while stroking her hair.

"There is something I must tell you," Serena said when she finally gathered the courage to speak. Her body trembled with the thought of the memory. "Long ago, when I was a child, I became an orphan after my grandmother died. I was sent to live with a family of strangers I had never met before. I had only lived there a few days when their son, who was older, tried to harm me. I fought him, but he touched me, and kept trying whenever I was left alone with him. I ran away to keep him from doing more than that. I got into trouble because of it, and they locked me away for a few days. But I didn't care by then, because I was safer that way."

Serena shuddered to see the look of anger in Rune's eyes. His body stiffened against her. She was frightened to think of what was going through his mind, and wondered what he must think of her now that she had told him.

"What was done to him?" Rune asked, his jaw clenching as he spoke. He tried to calm himself. There was, however, no hiding his anger; even if he now understood just why she feared him.

"Nothing. I tried to tell his parents and the social worker, but no one believed me. After that, I went to live with another family. When I was old enough, I moved away, and since then I have lived alone."

"I believe you," Rune said, leaning down to kiss her softly. He drew her closer and rested his head atop hers. "You are no longer alone, I am here. I will be patient, but you must be brave. Come."

Rune stepped away and took her hand, leading her quietly toward the stairs, canting his head when she hesitated, and watching her look back over her shoulder.

"Where are we going?" Serena asked, hesitant to leave with him. "We shouldn't go far, what if Lucy wakes up?"

"She will be all right," Rune added, tugging at her again until she gave in and began to follow him down the staircase. They both stepped carefully, listening to the creaking of the boards beneath their feet, trying not to let their exit wake Lucy. "We will only be going as far as the river; we will be back long before she wakes."

They said not another word as she followed him downstairs. Rune only paused long enough to take a blanket from the laundry basket before he led her out the back door, and into the night. He closed the door behind them with a soft click.

The woods were silent at that hour, the moon looming large and low overhead as they walked. Rune kept her close to his side. They saw a few lights burning in the windows of the houses they passed. It seemed late; even though time had a strange way of running together in this place, were it not for the routine those living there had made for themselves.

Rune led her down a path she had yet to explore. It was upstream from the way she and Lucy had traveled to the summerhouse. It led to a smaller branch of the stream that seemed both calmer and shallower. At the end was a pool that shone as clear as glass, reflecting the light of the moon overhead.

"Here," Rune said, letting go of her hand and spreading the blanket out on the grass next to the water. "This place reminds me very much of the tide pools near my home in the summer."

Serena could only look around in silence, taken aback by the beauty of the scene before her. Rune peeled off his clothing as if he had not a care in the world that she would see him. She was already blushing deeply long before he reached to pull her close to him.

He tugged her sweater over her head before she had a chance to offer an ounce of resistance. The rest of her clothing was pulled down and off as he slid to his knees in front of her, kissing her belly as he pulled her shoes from her feet, and tossed everything away for worry she'd only try to retrieve them.

"Come," Rune whispered, rising to his feet, taking her hand and leading her toward the water. He pulled her in after him when she seemed hesitant to do more than merely wade in the shallows.

He swam them out from the shore to where the water was far

deeper, so deep she couldn't touch the bottom. The water rose high on his chest. He laughed deeply when she clung to him, with a slightly frightened look in her eyes. "You cannot swim?"

"No." Serena shook her head, worried that he would see fit to drop her. She clung to him closer than she felt she had right to, considering the lack of anything between them.

"Then I shall have to teach you," Rune told her reassuringly, nudging her to lie back in his arms and soothing her until she seemed relaxed enough to do as he asked. "Just lie there, keep your arms at your sides, and float. I will not let you fall."

Serena tried her best to do as he asked, and it seemed to be working for a time. She was startled at first when he leaned down to kiss her, but his arms held her up instead of letting her sink. It took a moment for her to notice that he had begun walking them toward the shore. She was unaware until her body left the water, but she was still cradled carefully in his arms.

Rune carried her lovingly and tenderly, not breaking his kiss until he knelt in order to lie her down on the blanket.. Serena offered no more resistance than a soft whimper when he resumed the kiss, lying down next to her. He rolled until his body half covered her own. Her cries were soft until his hands slid slowly downward. Her legs shivered as his hand slid between them. His lips parted from hers so he could study her expression.

"Be brave," Rune told her, leaning down to kiss her gently again. "I will not hurt you, but I do wish to touch you."

Serena lay there shivering under his touch. Rune's hand stroked her gently in places she'd never dared to let anyone touch her before. The things he was doing to her were not painful, or rough as she'd long feared they would be. The more time passed, the more her fear began to fade away, and soon she was surprised in herself to find that she was not only kissing him back, but moving back against his fingers, guiding him.

Her sighs only seemed to encourage him. Rune rolled the rest of the way atop her, easing his weight gently onto her. Serena seemed mildly nervous, and her body tensed briefly and then relaxed again under him. Rune raised his head to look into her eyes. He was relieved when she didn't protest, her eyes closed, and her fingers gently dug into his skin.

Serena whimpered when his fingers went back to stroking her. Rune whispered into her ear as she started to tremble, though; she could not make out the words, his touch made her go weak each time a wave of pleasure washed over her.

Her breath caught in her throat when he pushed into her. She dug her nails hard into his back, gasping as her body gave into him. It hurt, though; she could tell he was trying to be gentle. The heat of him inside her was overwhelming, and mercifully brief. Rune moaned, shivered, and then was spent. He was still buried inside her when he went weak. He panted, his breath warm against her neck.

"Did I hurt you?" he whispered when he felt a tear run down her cheek. He kissed it away as she lay there, still shivering. "I am sorry, my love. I did not wish to frighten you by telling you it might hurt. I did not want fear to be the thing that stood between us any longer."

Serena could only gaze up at him, scarcely able to see his face beyond the glow of the moon that shone so brightly in the sky behind him.

Rune was silent afterward. He rose and pulled her after him, leading her back into the water. He kissed her as he washed them both, at least as well as he could manage with only water.

He gathered their clothes and led her through the woods toward home again, holding her close to his side, both of them wrapped in the blanket as they walked together. They breathed a sigh of relief to find the house quiet and empty, except for Lucy still sleeping.

When he lifted her against him again and nudged her toward the bed, she went willingly. She let the damp blanket fall to the floor as he reached to quietly close the bedroom door behind them.

"I will stay with you," Rune whispered. He drew the covers back for her and lay down next to Serena, wrapping her in his arms, and sighing contentedly.

She lay there, long after he'd gone to sleep, so many thoughts and conflicted feelings running through her mind. She did not hate him, and she was no longer afraid to have him close, but she still could not say she loved him. Things just weren't that simple anymore.

CHAPTER ELEVEN

SERENA WONDERED, if only for a moment, if what occurred the night before was nothing more than a dream she remembered far too vividly. But Rune was lying next to her, sleepily pulling her back against him the moment she stirred.

She scarcely opened her eyes when his hands began to explore her body. The boldness of his touch removed all doubt that what happened had been no mere illusion. She gasped into his kiss, her legs shaking as his fingers teased her gently at first, and the sensation only intensified, the more she responded to his touch. By the time he entered her, she had long lost the will to stop him. She cried out softly as he moved within her, unable to do more than cling to him.

"It has been so long since I have felt this," Rune whispered afterward, looking into her eyes as Serena still lay beneath him. He was content for the first time in what seemed a lifetime to him. He would have been happy to lie there for some time had he not heard soft footfalls in the hallway outside the bedroom door.

"Who could be there?" Serena said with a start, knowing she had not heard the door of Lucy's room open. She nudged Rune off her, making a desperate attempt to reach for the blankets to pull them back up before the door swung open.

Jane stepped through the door before they had time to completely cover themselves. Averting her eyes, Jane looked away and waited until they were both decently covered.

Serena blushed furiously, embarrassed, and more than a little ashamed at the expression on Jane's face as she looked the both of them over with a stern and disapproving glance, her face it's own deep shade of crimson.

"This is an interesting development," Jane said, crossing her arms before she turned toward the door. "I will speak with you both in a few moments. I will be waiting in the kitchen, come to me when you are both decently clothed." Without another word Jane walked out and closed the door.

Serena heard her footsteps stop briefly at the door to Lucy's room, and then two sets of footsteps disappeared down the stairs.

They sat in silence while trying to compose themselves before Rune threw the blankets off again.

"Have I offended her?"

"I don't know," Serena replied, shrugging and waiting for the heat to drain out of her cheeks. She tried hard to look at his face and not his body. "It's her own fault for not knocking first. I think she was expecting to find me, but not, us."

Rune nodded, that much at least made sense to him.

"Stay here," she told him. "Your clothes are filthy, let me find you something clean to wear."

She left him sitting there while she tossed a nightgown over her head and left the room. She crossed the hall into what had once been her grandparent's bedroom. It held the old familiar scent of cedar and mothballs when she opened her grandfather's closet. She remembered his work clothes well, and the clothes he wore on Sundays. They were still right where they should have been.

She checked the sizes on the old pairs of jeans, unsure at which to choose, although no one pair looked smaller or bigger than any other. Her grandfather had not been a thin man, and his body had once been thick and muscular like Rune's was, at least at a time before illness had taken its toll on him.

She decided on a well-faded pair of jeans, soft and broken in with age. She easily found one her grandfather's white undershirts in the top drawer of his chest next to the door. It was the same drawer where he kept his handkerchiefs, and to her surprise, an old collection of pinup trading cards that seemed to have once come from cigarette packets. It was likely something he'd brought home from the war. Her grandmother would have had a fit if she'd found them.

Serena didn't know whether to be happy or sad at the memories, so she tried not to dwell on them. She didn't want Rune to be sitting in her room naked half the day waiting for nostalgia to loosen its hold on her. She made her way back into her room to find him sitting on the side of her bed with an old scrapbook open in his hands. He closely studied the photographs within.

"How did they make these paintings? Here in your home, they are everywhere," he asked her, seeming to be absorbed most of all by the photographs that were in color. "These people, who are they?"

"My family," she answered, a little sad as she sat down next to him. She leaned her head on his shoulder and pointed as he turned to the next page. "The little girl in the red dress, that was me, a very long time ago."

It was one of many family photos that found her dressed in a homespun velvet dress with a hand-embroidered lace trimmed collar. She remembered just how embarrassed she had been wearing all those homemade holiday dresses when her friends were wearing clothes that were modern and store-bought. She had not thought before of how old her grandparents had been then.

Her mother had been the youngest. Her grandparents were already well past middle age long before Serena had been born. Her upbringing had been very old fashioned for the early part of her childhood. When she left home at twelve, Serena had been woefully unprepared for the world she found out there.

"This is how our child may look someday," Rune whispered, touching the photograph fondly. He closed the book with a sigh and set it gently back on the nightstand while noting the look in Serena's eyes. "I did not mean to make you sad."

"You haven't, Rune, it's nothing but an old memory," Serena told
him, laying the pile of clothing on his lap. Inside she was still feeling
confused and conflicted. Everything between them had changed so
quickly. She had been afraid of him before, but even though that fear
of him had passed, she was still afraid of just how quickly things were
unfolding between them.

Rune stood and dressed, having figured out the undershirt easily
enough, but he stood fumbling for how to fasten the jeans. Serena
helped him, trying her best not to injure him with the zipper. Rune
grinned as she went about her work almost unthinking. It was the
closest he had come to getting her to touch him. Once fed through the
belt loops, he fastened his belt quickly enough on his own.

He followed her down the hall and into the bathroom after she
dressed herself. She was soon trying to give him a crash course on
indoor plumbing. He understood the concept of the toilet well
enough once she had, much to her embarrassment, demonstrated the
process. Rune seemed startled at the noise when she pulled the flush
handle, canting his head as he watched the water drain away and then
refill again.

"It's nothing that will hurt you," Serena told him, raising the seat
for him, not wanting to find it wet later. "When you press on the lever,
it sends the dirty water away underground." Serena had never in all
her days thought she would ever have to explain that to anyone, at
least not anyone older than a small child. It never occurred to her
before that moment that there were so many things about her life and
her world that she took for granted, that Rune would have no way to
understand.

Serena gave him the privacy to do, as he needed. She made her way
down the stairs and found Jane waiting for her in the living room, not
the kitchen as she had said. She was alone, although Lucy or one of
the others was in the kitchen rattling dishes around.

"This is an interesting turn of events, Serena," Jane said, her face
still wearing that expression of stern disappointment that many
others were known to wither under. "Wasn't it only yesterday, you
told me that you did not want him?"

"I did not think that this would happen," Serena answered, feeling as though she were being scolded like a small child. Her face once again flushed with shame and embarrassment.

"You do not think, and that is your trouble, child," Jane stated harshly, not caring if she sounded unkind. "That man's heart is not a game. You shouldn't lead him on if you don't mean to stay with him. He shouldn't have to wait for you to make up your mind, whether or not you can give him that."

"Things have changed, and I don't know how to feel now. After yesterday, he seemed so different somehow. I don't know if I can explain," Serena said, hugging herself. She tried hard not to cry at the sting of Jane's words that maybe, deep inside, she knew she deserved.

"My dear, it's you that's changed, not him. That's all I can say. You need to think this through carefully, and soon," Jane said, walking past her and toward the kitchen without another word.

The bathroom door opened upstairs, and Rune's heavy footfalls started down the stairs.

Looking in Rune's eyes as he came closer, Serena knew that Jane's words were true. She had to sort out what had happened between them, and why. When she figured out her feelings, he deserved the truth about them, even if the truth hurt. The last thing she wanted to do now was hurt him.

CHAPTER TWELVE

THE GATHERING at the summerhouse that evening was a somber one. Jane waited for all to assemble before speaking, even more cautious to keep count of those gathered than before. The children old enough to listen were given a place in the front. Little ones that were small enough to need holding were not the ones that night's lecture was intended for, but Jane felt it important that they be included anyway.

"I'm sure you are all aware of the situation yesterday. One of our children went missing," Jane stated plainly, making sure she spoke loud enough for all those gathered to hear her. "I will not tell the name of this child. She has already been spoken to, and the situation dealt with. There is no reason to speak of it further to her. However, I will take this moment to remind each one of you to be mindful of the boundaries we have set in place at the edge of our border. They are there for a reason and are there for your protection. No one is permitted past the stone wall at the western edge of the woods under any circumstances. I cannot state this strongly enough. There are dangers that we simply cannot protect you from if you choose to go there."

"That being said," Jane continued. "The council has come to a consensus about a new rule that we feel simply must be implemented.

I know that some of you will not be fond of this change, but we feel it necessary to protect the most vulnerable among us. As of this evening, no child, or old one under the age of seven years old will be permitted to travel through the woods alone. Even those capable of remaining in their homes, will be assigned a caretaker who lives close to them to look after them."

Lucy blushed furiously from where she sat on the bench a few feet away. Serena watched her, seeing her so uncomfortable made her displeased at Jane's direct manner and lack of tact. Serena wondered if it really had been the decision of a council, and not just the council of Jane that had made that decision.

"Thankfully, there are not many among us that this rule applies to that are not already directly under someone's care," Jane added. "Those people already caring for a child in their home will not be given additional responsibility to care for more. But in the meantime, a choice has been made on who will be assigned to the four small ones who fit this designation. Agnes will look after Tara, and Joe is to care for Orville. Daniel will be cared for by Naomi, and since they are new to us, but live closest to her, Serena and Rune are to care for Lucy together."

By the time Jane's speech was over, Serena could tell Lucy was seething, a scowl that would have been humorous on any other child's face accompanied the deep shade of crimson her cheeks had turned in the last few minutes.

Jane scarcely had time to stop speaking when Lucy bolted for the door. She screamed with frustration as soon as she was outside and a distance down the beach from the others that had begun to spill out of the building after her.

Lucy ran as fast as she could to the end of the jetty some distance away down the shore, sank to her knees, and cried uncontrollably. She howled and hurled all the small stones she could gather around her knees into the water. When she'd run out of stones, she only knelt there with her face in her hands sobbing.

"Give her a few minutes, walk slowly," Jane said when she saw Serena start to run after her with Rune following in her footsteps. She hadn't said another word before she'd sent them down the beach to look after her.

"Go away, Jane, damn you," Lucy growled when she heard footsteps coming up behind her. She'd turned and hurled a rock in the direction of the sound before looking up.

Rune's eyes narrowed when the small stone bounced off his chest, having stepped in the way to keep it from hitting Serena instead.

Lucy's eyes widened to see the expression of anger on his face, even if she was still fighting back sobs. Dirt smeared across her tear-stained face from where she had tried to dry her eyes.

Rune didn't say another word before lifting Lucy from the ground as if she were no heavier than a rag doll. He raised her until she was face to face with him. The girl froze with fear and ceased her struggling when Rune growled, "I am your guardian now, little one. You will never strike me in anger again. Do you understand?"

Lucy nodded, but it was clear Rune was far from finished with his lecture.

It was all Serena could do to not intervene on Lucy's behalf, even as much as she was afraid not to. Rune's wrath was nothing to be trifled with. She believed, or at the least very much hoped, that he would not harm the child and only meant to frighten her.

"Little one, you would still be lost had I not come for you," he told Lucy sternly, his nose scarcely an inch from her own to ensure that she could not look away from him. "You will respect me, and you will obey. Do you understand?"

"I hate this," Lucy sobbed back at him, looking as miserable as if her world had been taken from under her. It likely had been.

"Your consent is not required, your compliance is."

"I'm a hundred and eighty-one years old. I am not a baby."

"Then stop acting as if you are. Calm yourself, and accept that others must now care for you. You have brought this on yourself."

Those last words stung Lucy to the bone, hurting all the more to know they were true. Her control of her emotions and mind were already fading, especially since her return from the lighthouse garden.

The time she'd spent there was still a huge gaping hole inside her memory.

She fell, yet again, into child-like sobs. Rune could not comfort her even as he cradled her against him.

Tears welled in Serena's eyes as Rune turned to look at her. Lucy's cries awakening her own fears about her future if she remained in this place.

"Is this what we have to look forward to?" Serena asked, tears running down her cheeks. She shivered, trying hard not to fall apart inside. "She's scared, Rune, we're all scared. Please don't be hard on her. This is enough."

"Enough, we will go home," Rune replied taking a deep breath to calm himself. He turned and began the walk without a word, his pace only slowed to ensure that Serena could walk with him.

Not much was said as Rune took the trail along the river. It was a less direct way back to where they were going, but it happened to be the way that he knew best. This way he didn't need anyone to guide him.

Lucy protested part of the way and asked to be put down and not carried like a baby. Rune still would not let her walk, he worried that she was upset enough to run off again. In the end, Lucy agreed to be carried piggyback along the trail instead of continuing to be cradled in Rune's arms. It was an alternative that was not quite as humiliating as the other. She didn't put up another word of protest until she noticed that Rune was returning her to Serena's house and not her own.

"I don't want to stay here. I want to go home, my home," Lucy protested loudly when Rune sat her down on the steps of Serena's front porch. "If you won't take me there, I'll go the rest of the way home alone."

"If I take you there, will you stay and not wander off again?" Rune asked her seriously. He leaned down until he was almost nose-to-nose with her, making her look him in the eye. "I will take you, if you will swear it. If you break your promise, I will not trust you to make one again."

"Yes."

"Yes, you what?"

"Yes I promise, okay?" Lucy said, once again becoming visibly upset. She looked as though she were ready to pull out her hair. "I just want to be by myself right now, am I allowed?"

"Since you have promised, as you wish," Rune said stooping down to let her climb back onto him. He was already weary of it, and would do as the child asked if it meant a more peaceful evening afterward.

"This evening, when a little time has passed, come to me," Rune told Serena. He kissed her briefly before leaving her standing on the front steps with a befuddled expression.

Rune carried Lucy off toward her home. When they reached the tree line, he turned back to see Serena closing the door. The soft glow of candles came to light inside. He wished to be there with her alone, but duty often came first when it came to so many things.

They were halfway to Lucy's house when the ground started to shake. The air filled with the deafening bellow of the foghorn. The mist crept in, almost seeming to rise from the ground itself.

Lucy screamed in his ear, begging him to hurry faster. There were few things in this world Lucy feared more than the fog.

The lighthouse in the distance began to sweep the night, and the ground shook with so much force, Rune feared it would crumble under him. He stopped under a large sycamore tree to brace himself against it.

"We have to get inside," Lucy screamed almost unable to hear her own voice over the deafening sound that echoed through the night.

The fog was thick, leaving them scarcely able to see anything in front of themselves. It wasn't until Rune glanced up that he noticed a ladder leading to a small building in the branches of the tree. He lifted Lucy onto it and yelled for her to start climbing.

Lucy didn't remember where she was until she reached the top of the ladder. She froze as she pushed the trap door open and crawled out onto the tree house floor.

Rune was hesitant to go inside, his broad shoulders barely narrower than the opening. He fit through but barely, closing the trap door behind him. He turned to see Lucy crawling over to sit in an old threadbare chair with all the legs broken off. Rune watched as she reached for a box of matches that were inside an old tin. She lit one and used it to light an old stump of a candle that sat in a dish on top of a small wooden crate. It seemed she knew the place well.

"I have not been here in long time," Lucy told him. The horn had faded, but the fog pushed through the cracks and a mist hung in the air inside the tree house.

"What is this place?" Rune asked. It was obvious to him that the objects scattered around the room had been salvaged by children.

"Our tree house," Lucy said sadly, drawing her knees up to her chest in the chair. "He built it for me, well, Charlie and some of the others did. This was our special place once we became children again."

"Where is he now?" Rune asked, not knowing the name as someone among those that he had met thus far. It genuinely saddened him to see tears come to Lucy's eyes.

"He is gone," she whispered, fighting back sobs, though her eyes also shone with mild anger as she tried to fight the emotion welling in her chest. "He went away just before you came, you took his place."

"The last night of the fog?" he asked her, remembering that much of when he had first found himself in this place. "Does this fog mean that someone else has come?"

He watched Lucy nod, a look of fear in her eyes as she looked toward the small window that was only covered with a wooden shutter. "Someday I will go as well, but by the time it happens, I won't know myself. It happens to all of us in time. As we grow younger, we forget who we once were and all we knew, then we are gone."

"Are you afraid?" Rune asked her, sadness washing over him as Lucy seemed to only be able to nod in answer, and then once again began sobbing. She bit at her lip as she tried to fight the tears away.

"Do you love her?" Lucy asked plainly once she'd been able to stop her crying.

Rune nodded, reaching out to take Lucy's hand and tried to wipe the tears from her still-dirty face. With the dirt on his hands from the climb, it made little difference. "I am hers, and she is mine."

"One day it will tear your heart to pieces to lose her," Lucy told him, her bottom lip still quivering. "One day you will be lovers, and years later, there will be a child before you who sees only their best friend that cares for them. That is unless the two of you are so mercifully close in age that you will grow young together without missing the other, until you are too young to know the other is gone. I wish that happened for Charlie and I, but I still have five years to be alone, and I don't have all that long until I will forget myself, everything and everyone. It's already happening, more every day."

"I have given my promise, and I will keep it, as you did," Rune told her quietly, longing for all he had lost as well sweeping over him. "You will not be alone, we will be your guardians, and we will be by your side and care for you, always. I too had my love stolen from me, but here is a chance, when I expected nothing but sadness and anger. In the end anger destroyed me, do not give in to it."

He sat with her until the last of the fog rolled away. Then he helped her climb down from the treehouse and, holding her hand, they walked the rest of the way to the old unpainted, clapboard farmhouse that had long been her home. She said nothing, but hugged him tightly before making her way inside and closing the door.

Once inside, Lucy sank to her knees on the floor trembling. She fought off the tears until she heard Rune start to walk away. Finally, she allowed herself to fall apart as she looked around the room filled with mementos of a life that was already beginning to fade from her memory. She already remembered much more of that world than the last, and what she did remember was slowly and surely slipping right through her fingers.

CHAPTER THIRTEEN

SERENA HAD GONE to her room as soon as Rune and Lucy departed, peeling off her clothes and lying on the unmade bed with her knees drawn up to her chest. The pillows and sheets still smelled of him, and she lay there unable to put a name to what she was feeling.

Everything was changing fast. Attachment and affection were distant memories to her; another lifetime. She feared it, but all the same, could not deny how much she longed for it. Had her craving for affection caused her to fall too soon and naively into Rune's arms? She truly had no basis for comparison to judge it by.

She got up and walked to the bathroom to draw a bath only to have the foghorn begin to sound moments after she turned off the water and sank into the tub. The blaring noise shook the house, leaving her holding onto the sides, screaming.

She wished Rune were there so she could cling to him, wanting him to protect her from whatever nameless thing could be coming out of that fog.

Serena remembered what had come out of it the time before, both him and someone far more sinister and terrifying, someone she was praying with all her being would not return. The fear of it was overwhelming. She rinsed off and climbed from the tub. When the trembling subsided, she rushed to her room and locked the door behind her.

Serena dressed quickly, almost unthinking, in what had once been her most comfortable clothes: her wide-legged black lounge pants, a tank top, and her old black zipper hoodie.

She had little time to do more than towel dry her hair. Her clothes were already damp around her shoulders as she made her way downstairs to lock the doors, watching the fog as she peeked through semi-closed curtains.

Looking out into the night she saw nothing, the sky's perpetual twilight was grey and darkened by the fog. Even the moon couldn't penetrate it. Her eyes strained to make out the tree line where she'd last seen Rune, but he did not come. Fortunately nothing else moved in the darkness that she could find, not that it was something she hoped to see.

She was still sitting there, just inside the window a short time later when the fog cleared. The night became quiet and eerily still.

Light flickered in the distance as others began to search for the newcomer. The lighthouse faded to a soft glow, its beam no longer turning to and fro.

It was only then that Serena gathered the courage to step outside. She wasn't going out empty handed, so retrieved the old wooden baseball bat her grandparents had kept just inside the door for protection. She took it with her as she stepped out into the night, not wanting to break her promise to Rune. She carried the bat in one hand, and her grandfather's old lantern in the other. She made her way to the path, walking cautiously.

She remembered the way well enough, though she tried hard not to think of the last time she passed this way. Her memory was still a little fuzzy and she struggled to recall the last part of the journey she'd experienced in the fog.

Serena took a couple of wrong turns and had to double back again. Finally, she saw a glow in the distance and followed that path, careful to stay hidden among the trees until she saw where that firelight was leading her. She remembered Rune's bonfire and shivered with the memory of all that had happened the last time she was drawn to it.

She didn't step closer until she was sure she had found her way correctly. Giving the fire a wide berth, she tried to stick to the shadows while moving toward the house. She was shivering so badly, she could scarcely hold the lantern steady. Her grip tightened on the bat with a sweaty and trembling hand as she neared his doorway.

Serena screamed in fear when someone came up behind her, grabbing her by the wrist of the arm that held the bat. She swung the lantern around and sobbed with relief that it was only Rune standing there.

"You scared me half to death. I was so frightened of the fog," Serena cried, letting him take the bat from her.

"But you came," he answered, pulling her toward the house and lifting her into his arms to carry her inside. Once he put her down he bolted the door and took the lantern from her hand, dousing the flame and hanging it from a hook overhead.

Rune hadn't had much time to clean up the house, but he'd made a sizable dent in the chaos Ardal left in his wake. Serena's heart still pounded when she thought of the last time she was inside these walls.

She knew by his expression that he could sense her fear. He pulled her hood down and away from her eyes, taking her hands in his and drawing her closer to him. Her heart was still thumping wildly when he leaned down to kiss her. This time, she surprised herself with how tightly she clung to him.

She made no move to resist him when he pulled at her clothing. He unzipped the hoodie, letting it fall the floor at her feet. The thin straps of her top broke under the weight of being pulled down and off her, leaving her bare chest pressed against his. Rune slid his hands under the waistband of her pants, slipping them off her hips to let them pool at her feet.

Once he undid his belt, the baggy jeans that she had loaned to him slid off easily. She'd no sooner kicked free of her own shoes and clothing than his hands were on her again, pulling her to him, her body pressed tightly to his. Serena tried to calm herself and allowed

Rune to touch her. Behind closed doors, his touch had ceased to be gentle. His grip was firm and insistent as he pushed her backward away from the threshold and lifted her by her hips when she struggled to go quickly enough to please his impatience.

Serena soon found herself placed in a pile of furs close to the hearth and pinned under him. Rune did nothing to muffle her cries this time as she lay beneath him shivering while he touched her as he wished.

"Fight your fear," Rune whispered to her, still able to see it in her eyes as she looked up at him. She made no plea for him to stop, but only cried out to him as he took her, somewhat less gently than he had before. Her back arched into him, and the fear in her gave way to pleasure, but never completely faded away.

"What must I do to take this fear from you?" Rune asked her afterwards, Serena still beneath him and clinging to his muscular form.

"It's not you," Serena answered, her voice still quivering. Then, for the first time, she hesitantly leaned up to kiss him. She softly curled her hands into his hair. "I am the cause of this. It's just old memories haunting me. I've waited half my life for them to fade away."

"Will you conquer them, or continue to let them make you a prisoner? I will do no worse to you, woman of mine, than I have already done. I fear, the night I forget myself, you will shatter beneath me." Rune's voice was calm but serious. His face showed a vague expression of worry.

"Please be patient. I just need time," Serena told him, trying to reassure him as much as herself. "Yesterday I would not have believed this could happen between us, or that I would be able to let any man touch me as you have. So much has already changed."

"Days ago you cowered to have me near, and tonight you came into my arms on your own, I am not blind to it," he answered, kissing her forehead tenderly and noticing, for the first time since she'd come to him, she'd stopped trembling.

"Tonight, when the fog came, I was terrified. I wished you were with me so badly. I've never felt that before, not for anyone. I have no idea what that means."

"That your heart is mine, you need only make the choice to give yourself to me. I have already given myself to you. All I have is yours, but you must learn to trust in me. For all the fear that I have caused, never once have I meant to hurt you. There is never honor in causing a woman harm."

Rune kissed her before rising to his feet, leaving Serena shivering from the cold as he walked away. Confused, she sat up, wrapping herself in one of the furs. Deep in the shadows of the loft above, Rune moved about purposefully, coming back down the ladder with something in his hand that made the faintest jingling.

Serena was confused when Rune knelt before her, a chain in his hand. He pulled her close to him, and slipped the chain around her neck. She looked down to find it held a small ring full of what looked to be old-fashioned keys. "These are the keys to all I possess, which are now rightfully yours for keeping, keep them well, wife of mine."

CHAPTER FOURTEEN

Serena lay awake, staring into the flames while Rune slept, his body curled around hers. She was unprepared for what had taken place. Rune had assumed, that their spending the night together meant that they had consummated their marriage. She did not want to leave him, but things had gone much too far, and too quickly than she'd bargained for. She did not know what she feared more, displeasing him, or remaining silent until she could seek the advice of the others. She counted on little help from Jane, feeling her counsel as of yet had been only self-righteous and cold. She would receive no pity, let alone consolation from her.

She had almost managed to find slumber, before a loud pounding at the door broke the silence. Rune awoke and leapt to his feet before she'd even had time to roll over.

"Cover yourself," he told her, tossing her the pile of her clothing that he'd left near the door.

She had little choice but to pull the pants on and zip the hoodie with nothing under it in the short time in which she had to dress herself.

Rune took little time to pull on his own clothes. He unbolted the door while she still sat there pulling on her shoes. Outside, in the night air, Jane, Robert, and some of the others waited.

"Serena has not been located. Is she here with you?" Jane asked sternly, peering over his shoulder only to have him open the door wider to let her see for herself.

"Yes, she is here, you speak as if she should not be."

"When there has been a fog, all those who are not small children are to now meet and become searchers," Jane told them, expecting to be followed, "Tonight, you both will come with us. Whoever has come must be found by morning. When they awaken, someone must be there to help them. Occasionally, but not often, that person is a child unable to care for themselves who must be found and cared for. We take no chances."

"Must the whole realm be searched?" Rune asked, turning to help Serena to her feet.

"We have an idea of where to begin looking," Jane answered him plainly. "There are two sorts of people in this world when it comes to the fog, those who cower inside and fear it, and those who watch carefully to see what is taking place. I am one of the latter. Considering what happened the night you came, no one is to undertake the search alone from now on. We will go when we have gathered together."

Serena watched them silently, believing it better to say nothing at all. The last thing she wanted was another lecture so soon after the last. It was not the time, and she would speak of her troubles later.

Serena followed without question as she was led out into the night. She stayed close to Rune's side, only mildly less fearful than she had been before, if only for the numbers of those walking with her, a dozen or so of the strongest and most reliable men and women.

They walked in silence for a while, unless Jane gave the occasional order, and eventually split into two groups at a crossroad. The newer searchers were paired with those that had been there longer and knew the woods and the paths.

Robert led the group they followed, also joined by two other young women whose names Serena did not know, though she had seen them at the gathering hours before.

Each searcher, or pair, carried with them a lantern and some means of signaling the others, be it a whistle, or even a string of firecrackers.

Between the two of them, Rune only had his sword and a small coil of rope. Serena carried the lantern, as Rune followed her, never removing his hand from the hilt of his sword. He searched the darkness for any sign of trouble, but he did not ease even when he found none.

Robert joined them as they split paths yet again, down a road where beech trees formed an arch across the path overhead. The ground became rocky and uneven where there had once been a meadow.

"This is it," Robert told them, nodding them onward and into the clearing. "We normally would not come with weapons, but after last time, we prefer not to take chances."

"Caution is often the wisest of choices when you are unsure if you seek an enemy or ally," Rune said, letting Serena walk in front of them with the lantern though she went otherwise empty handed, which was not to her liking. She was to run and fetch the others if there was even a hint of a problem, leaving the men to fight whatever came out of the darkness.

A search of the field ahead revealed nothing but a tumbled down shack, perched among a grove of various nut trees. Walnut, chestnut, and other nutshells littered the warped wooden steps that were next to a rock used to crack them open. The once-white shack had faded to grey as most of the paint had cracked and peeled away. Broken windowpanes were covered with plywood, the sagging roof patched here and there with mismatched shingles and sheets of scrap metal. A single well-worn wooden rocking chair swayed on the weathered floor of the front porch as Serena brushed by it.

Robert went first through the door, and they crept into the small, two room shack as quietly as the creaking floorboards would let them.

Serena was shocked and dismayed by what she saw there. The room was clean, but only paths led between the furniture and stacks of crates and boxes filled with what she could only guess were treasures gleaned from the things others had thrown away.

She nearly screamed when she, by chance, happened across a mirror and saw the horrible sight displayed within it. Rune stepped in front of her to silence her cries. The room they stood in was a charred and burnt shell, with crime scene tape across the windows.

"How horrible," she whispered when Rune released her, but still held her against him. She was already in tears for whoever must have dwelled here. After a life lived in poverty, they met their end rather violently.

She turned her head toward the doorway of the second room, aware before the others that she was not the only one weeping. She waved them to keep their weapons down, and then opened the door only a crack, searching for the source of what she thought at first was a young child crying.

Serena pushed through the doorway, more sad than terrified. She saw what looked to be a waif-thin teenage boy curled into a ball in the corner shivering and crying on top of a single filthy mattress that lay on the floor. His clothes were in rags and his long hair was matted. There were no shoes on his feet, the soles of which were filthy and calloused.

"Who are you? How did you put out the fire?" The boy asked her, raising his arms to shield his head when Robert and Rune came into the room behind her. "Go away please, stop hurting me."

"We won't hurt you," Serena told him, wanting to break down and cry with him, even as she tried to hold herself together. "We came to chase the others away, they won't hurt you anymore. What's your name?"

"Alec Olney," he replied, only daring to peer at her from behind his arms as he cowered.

"I'm Serena, this is Rune, and that is Robert," she informed him, nodding to the others. "We wanted to make sure you are safe, are you hurt?"

"It doesn't hurt now. They hit me, they threw rocks at my window," Alec said, pointing to where the small window in the room had shattered in one small pane, and he'd only been able to cover it with the little cardboard and duct tape he had available to him. "Are you here to take me away?"

"Only if you want to come, you don't have to stay here if you don't want to, we will help you," Serena told him, turning and noticing that the other group had caught up to them. Thankfully, Jane's group had not come in yet. Serena could only imagine how badly Jane would frighten him if she'd found him first.

"There is a house not far away," Robert added, "every night everyone gathers there, we eat together, and we tell stories. The children play together outside. You can come, you are welcome."

It was obvious to Serena that Alec seemed to have only child-like understanding of the world around him. It was likely he'd been raised all his life in this isolated place, sadly surrounded with others who had meant him harm. He'd likely never known anything else. He reminded her of a child or two she'd met in the system that had grown up severely neglected. She had no idea what she could do to make him trust her.

"No one will make you stay Alec, you can come home whenever you wish," Serena tried to assure him. "You will have fun there, they will be kind to you."

It had taken some doing and assurance before he'd left his crouch in the corner and followed them outside into the night air. Alec blinked at the small crowd gathered on the front lawn, sitting together in the long grass, except for Jane, who had perched herself in the old rocking chair.

Alec seemed awestruck at the size of the moon overhead, seemingly unable to decide if it was the moon, or the others around him he was more concerned with. "Will they come and take me to the children's home now?" he asked, not seeing a police car, even though he eyed the distance as if expecting to see the flash of lights any moment.

"No," Jane spoke up, shaking her head, summarizing from the

words Robert had whispered in her ear just what the situation was. "Your house has moved to where the bad men cannot find you, Alec. There's no reason to be afraid now."

"I can't go to church with you. I don't have any clean clothes," Alec stammered, hanging his head in shame at his tattered clothes and bare feet.

"We aren't going to church, but someplace like it, Alec. We can always find you some new clothes, and we will share with you," Jane said, standing from the chair and holding her hand out to him. "Would you like to come with us now, Alec? We will bring you home if you don't want to stay."

Alec was silent as he walked with the others down the paths towards the summerhouse, nervous and shivering as he looked around him. His eyes glanced up occasionally to the moon when the view was not obscured by the trees overhead. He seemed to hesitate and stop when Rune tugged at Serena to take her down another path towards home instead of continuing onward.

"Serena," Alec said, glancing back at her, his eyes filled with worry, hesitant to go forward.

"It's okay, Alec, they'll take care of you," she said, trying to reassure him. "Rune and I will come to see you in the morning, I promise."

She watched the others lead Alec away before turning back to Rune. He pulled her close to him, his arm encircling her waist as they walked silently, even as her tears were once again falling. She saw in Alec a life that could have easily been her own had hers taken a different turn. She understood all too well what it was like to be afraid and alone.

Rune didn't argue when she asked him to take her home. He climbed the stairs with her in silence until they were in her room with their clothes falling softly to the floor. Once under the covers, she pulled him to her, crawling into his arms. For the first time, and much to her surprise, she wanted his touch, wanted to feel him inside her. As badly as it frightened her, she truly wanted him.

CHAPTER FIFTEEN

SERENA AWOKE LATE the next morning, leaving Rune to sleep as she dug through her closet looking for something to wear. She pulled on an old tunic dress over a pair of faded and torn boot cut jeans. She jumped when she heard the door open behind her, and turned to see Lucy peering in the doorway. Serena struggled to do her hair reasonably well without being able to see herself in a mirror.

Turning to see Rune nearly stirring, she shooed Lucy back into the hallway, following her out and trying to close the door as quietly as she could.

"How did you get here? Don't get yourself in trouble," Serena whispered to her, knowing she'd likely be in for it along with her, if word were to get back to Jane about Lucy already flaunting the rules.

"Don't worry I ran straight here. Besides I was getting bored waiting for one of you to wake up and come to get me," Lucy said, rolling her eyes as if she really were a child. "Sit down on the steps, let me help you with your hair, maybe you can fix mine, I think it's crooked today."

Serena sat down on the steps and handed Lucy the brush. She winced as she brushed the rest of the tangles away, her attempt at braiding giving her more tangles than she had to begin with. Serena had been used to braiding her own hair, but wasn't accustomed to having to do it without being able to see herself.

"I used to do this every morning, with my mother and my sister." Lucy said as her hands worked skillfully, making quick work of the wreath braid Serena had been attempting.

Lucy carefully pinned it into place before bringing the ends of both sides together to braid them at the nape of Serena's neck. She tied them off tightly and carefully with elastic and a piece of ribbon she'd taken from the basket of hair things Serena had been working from.

"That must have been fun. I never had any sisters, or a mom, just my grandma and grandpa," Serena told her, waiting patiently until she finished. She thanked her and waited for Lucy to pass to sit on the step below.

"We can do this together now every morning if you want, just you and me," Serena offered, taking Lucy's long, chestnut-colored hair out of her braids to brush it. It fell down her back in soft waves.

"That would be nice," Lucy answered, sighing and trying to stay still enough for Serena to finish the French braids she'd replaced the pigtails on each side of her head with. "It's getting a little harder to do it myself as time goes on."

"It's always easier to do someone else's hair." Serena smiled. As she finished tying off the ends, pleased to see that, for the moment, Lucy was happier than when she came in.

"If it gets too hard, you can always use the water," Lucy told her as she gathered the brush, ties, and ribbons they had not used and put them back into the basket.

"What do you mean?" Serena asked her, confused. She set the basket to the side.

"The mirrors, as you know, need to be avoided, but for some reason the water only shows this world as it is," Lucy said turning to her. "I didn't discover that for a very long time. I'd almost forgotten what I looked like by then."

Serena remembered the other evening and how the moon had reflected off the water. She'd been so distracted that she hadn't even realized what it was about that sight that was so important, and now she knew. She felt as if she may as well have been blind not to see it.

"I only found out because I fell face first into the water once at a pond pretty close to here." Lucy laughed as she stood and made her way down the stairs, smoothing the wrinkles out of the skirt of her dress as she waited for Serena to follow her.

Once downstairs they made their way into the kitchen, Lucy taking a seat at the table after she put the kettle on the stove. Serena dug through the cupboards to find them something to eat, not much of a challenge, since her grandparent's pantry had always been no less than stuffed full. Easily enough, she found the oatmeal and a homemade jar of peaches. She dished out what they needed into a bowl, and placed the jar back on the shelf in the pantry, leaving a small amount of juice and peaches in the bottom so the jar would be replenished at moonrise. Their food supplies always replenished if a small amount was left inside.

Breakfast was almost finished when she heard Rune moving around upstairs.

Rune pulled on the same clothes as the day before, calling Serena's name as he walked through the house in search of her. Lucy called up to him to tell them where they were.

They were quiet as they sat at the table eating breakfast together. Rune finished his large bowl of oatmeal and what was left of the peaches in the bottom of the bowl, eating them as if he had never tasted one before.

"Don't eat them all at once Rune. There are plenty for later," she teased him, watching him drink the juice that still remained in the bowl.

It pleased him to look over her hair, his fingers reaching to examine the braids.

Lucy seemed less surprised than Serena expected when he leaned close to kiss her. The girl feigned embarrassment, looking away until they finished.

Rune laughed softly as he leaned away from Serena, his hand reaching to rest on Lucy's head affectionately.

They left for the summerhouse as soon as Serena and Lucy had finished washing the dishes.

Serena reminded Rune they had a promise to keep. Serena still worried about how Alec was handling the change as they walked. Rune held the lantern and Lucy walked between them.

The lighthouse, thankfully, remained dark and quiet in the distance, even as they reached the path that took them along the river to the shore. The summerhouse was already aglow, the fire lit much earlier than usual.

The children ran back and forth along the beach, and for the first time in the days that Serena could remember, Lucy let go of their hand to run swiftly down to the beach to chase after them.

Lucy laughed as she joined them splashing in the waves. Serena wondered if she would ever find that sort of joy again, to push away her troubles, smile, and play. Childhood's end had come for her all too soon, many years before it should have. She wondered if the emptiness it left in its place would ever be filled. There were so many things she had hoped and planned for that could now never be.

Serena was so caught up in her thoughts, she barely noticed Rune taking her hand as they walked, her mind instead turning to a sight that drew her in. It seemed to be the same owl as before, perched upon a low branch of a river birch watching her, and for a moment, it held her gaze. Its head bobbed to and fro as it trilled, not moving away until she stepped away from Rune to approach it. Only then did it spread its wings, swooping silently overhead before disappearing over the water and down the shore toward the lighthouse.

"Are you all right?" Rune asked her, concerned to find her distant as she stood to watch it go. He pulled her to him to get her attention.

"Did you see the owl?" Serena asked, unable to fathom how he could not have.

Rune shook his head with a confused expression.

She could not have imagined it. "I was so sure I saw one just now."

"In the days I have been here I have seen nothing," Rune answered as he tugged at her to continue their walk ahead. "Not a bird has sung in the trees, and not a creature, save us, has crawled across the earth. This realm is a most peculiar place."

"It seems so," Serena whispered, almost doubting herself, had she not seen it so clearly. She was quiet again until they reached the pier. She looked up when she heard the distress in a boy's voice, coming from the end of the pier.

Alec sat perched on a small wooden crate, his head in his hands. A girl stood behind him, a hairbrush in her hands, doing her best not to hurt him as she tried to brush the tangles away.

Quite a bit of hair, too matted to be tamed littered the floor of the pier at his feet. Alec cried and begged for them not to cut it, but sat still, relenting once they'd agreed to only trim it to his shoulders. Jane stood watching the proceedings, with a tired look in her eyes, making Serena wonder if she had ever gone to sleep since they'd last spoken to her hours before.

Alec had been bathed, and was dressed in clean clothes, but was still barefoot. He had an old beach towel wrapped around his shoulders as they worked on his haircut.

The girl did her best to try to get the sides even, despite Alec having great difficulty sitting still. He fidgeted in his seat, wincing each time the scissors came close to his ears.

Serena could only imagine how he must be feeling.

Rune led her into the summerhouse, finding them a comfortable seat near the fire and pulled her against him. She rested her head against his chest as she stared into the flames, jumping with a start when a bright light flooded through the room, disappearing and then returning. She didn't realize at first that it was the lighthouse until Rune stood, pulling her after him back outside.

There was a chill of tension in the air as those in the summerhouse ran to gather together. The children screamed as they left the water, and ran as fast as their feet could carry them for the summerhouse doorway. For only that moment, the light swept the night air with no mist to be seen.

"What is it waiting for?" Jane murmured, where she now stood only feet away.

It seemed, briefly, that all would be well, until the foghorn sounded softly at first, then bellowed. The shockwave knocked Serena from her feet and onto her knees. She buried her head against Rune's chest and screamed as he curled around her protectively. The waves burst towards the shore, drenching them as they crashed into them.

Jane and Rune tried to pull her to her feet again and toward the summerhouse doorway. The fog began to roll in, the thickest yet that they had seen.

Rune carried her over the threshold, sinking to the floor with her by the fire. By then the roaring had subsided. Only Jane stood in the doorway, wedging her arms against it to hold steady as she watched the night, waiting to see what was taking place. For the first time that Lucy could remember, even unflappable Jane was afraid.

CHAPTER SIXTEEN

"So many so soon, this doesn't make sense." Jane hadn't realized she'd spoken the words aloud until she felt Rune behind her peering over her shoulder. He'd somehow crossed the room without her noticing, leaving Serena huddled in front of the fire with Lucy.

Jane's eyes studied the direction that the beam seemed to be traveling, searching the darkness before coming to rest more than once in an area not terribly far from her home. Jane could not fathom why this fog unnerved her more than the others, but soon found her answer when she heard a sound that she not heard in years. Gunfire and the deafening roar of artillery shells echoed in the distance, though she could not find the source, or even judge their distance with the fog hanging between them.

Jane turned, pushing Rune away from the doorway, the shots echoing around them meaning few of them did not know what they were hearing.

"The storage cellar, get the children down there now. Go!" Jane shouted, no question that she expected to be obeyed.

"You, go with them," she told Rune, not overlooking that he was the only one among them who was armed. "Rune, I want you to guard the children from the cellar doorway, no one passes until I give word this is over."

Rune nodded, helping to carry the little ones that were too small to walk on their own to safety. He passed the last child down the stairs before he stood, hand on the hilt of his sword readying himself for combat, should the need arise. In the darkness that was only lit by a single dim lantern the children cried, despite the soft murmurs of their caretakers trying to comfort them.

Jane peered through the glass of the now locked doorway, standing silently after having doused the lights. The summerhouse had no blackout curtains, and she could do little more to conceal their location. Even the fire in the hearth could not be doused without doing more to draw unwanted attention.

The minutes seemed like an eternity. The gunfire and shelling ended as quickly as they began. The fog cleared and the lighthouse faded to a soft glow, ceasing its turning.

There in the darkness, Jane waited and listened. The woods beyond the door were silent and still. She had no more to arm herself with than the heavy iron poker from the fireplace, which she gripped in her hands tightly. At that moment, she gave less than a damn what anyone thought. No one was going into the woods until they'd been searched, the children would have to bed down here for the night as best they could. Until she could be assured the danger had passed, she was taking no chances.

When a time had passed in silence, she allowed the children to leave the cellar. She covered the windows that faced the beach in sackcloth as best as she could, with the help of some of the others. As the fog cleared, she saw no evidence of damage; no flames lit the night from the trees in the distance. Indeed, the night was now eerily silent.

"I need a small group of men to be volunteers, no women," Jane asked, unsurprised to see Rune raise his hand, followed by Robert. Soon, she had a small group, but not quite half a dozen. It was the majority of her usual searchers.

"The ladies will stay here and arm themselves with whatever they can find. The men will come with me into the woods. No one is to come after us unless we do not return by morning. Am I understood?"

Jane said not another word until she'd led the group outside, waiting to hear the sound of the door being bolted. Afterward, she led the others down the beach, toward the correct road into the woods. They walked in darkness with no lanterns.

Jane's steps were unsurprisingly sure. The beam had shone unnervingly close to her home, leaving little doubt just where they would be searching; somewhere close to the north or east of her own home.

"You should go back, stay with the others," Rune said as they walked, the axe he'd retrieved from the chopping block firmly gripped in his hand as he walked next to Jane.

"I will send no one to a place I will not go," Jane answered, trying somewhat too much to seem as though she were made of steel as she walked.

Rune, however, could not be fooled, easily sensing the fear Jane held underneath the surface, even though she walked determinedly.

"Battles are not a woman's place, you should leave," Rune said stubbornly, reaching to pull Jane back to look at him. Jane glared at him as if her sheer will would move her through him.

"It is not a battle I seek, but to avoid one," Jane growled at him, struggling to keep her tone low while making it clear to Rune that if she had to, she would push past him. "We do not know what may be waiting for us, but we will not cause them harm, unless they intend to harm us. You are to disarm, and capture, but not kill. Am I understood?"

They had no time to finish their disagreement. Robert signaled them from ahead, waving for them to join him where he crouched behind a large patch of rhododendron plants. Close in the distance, a meadow of wildflowers gave way to a lawn surrounded by a well-tended garden. A small country cottage nestled in it; the roof styled to resemble a thatched roof that it had likely replaced from an earlier time. The windows were dark, and nothing moved that they could see in the garden. No evidence of the shelling, or damage to any building or trees had been seen for the entirety of their short journey, nor was there any now. It was as though the sound itself had been all but a phantom.

"Remember what I have said, you are not to cause harm, unless harmed. Am I understood?" Jane asked, turning to look at the others, and most pointedly, Rune. She stepped from the darkness and walked forward quietly, winding her way across the lawn while staying close to the shrubbery and making her way toward the house indirectly.

The house remained dark and quiet as Jane crept closer, dropping lower to creep by under the windows. Carefully, she inched her way upward to peek inside. She gasped to see a man sprawled face down on the floor inside, his clothing torn and riddled with what appeared to be shrapnel and bullet holes. She almost screamed as she flew to the doorway unthinking, throwing open the door to run inward and kneel at the man's side. He wore a soldier's uniform.

She scarcely heard the others as she pulled to roll the man over, unable to manage until Robert pulled with her. Rune took watch in the doorway as Jane tore off what remained of the man's shirt to tend to his wounds. There were none, even though blood clearly stained the cracked slate floor where he lay, though it was quickly fading. He was breathing and alive, his chest rising and falling, though he was drenched in blood. He was in shock and on the verge of unconsciousness.

"Help me get him to the bed, hurry," Jane cried, letting Robert and the others, all except Rune, lift and move him the short distance. She tore the blankets off the bed, rolling the thickest to prop under his feet as soon as he had been laid into place. She covered him with another to keep him warm.

"Run back and get Martha. She's the closest thing we have to a healer among us," Jane shouted at Rune, confident that he would be able to handle anything that waited in the darkness, even though she feared sending the younger men into it. She breathed a sigh of relief to see him go, watching Robert take Rune's place as watcher in the cottage doorway. She soaked a rag in water from a pitcher and bowl nearby, using it to clean the blood away from the soldier's face.

There was nothing for her to do but wait as Rune disappeared into the darkness. She feared the return of whoever had done this, but less than she feared leaving the soldier alone in this state, should that person return for him. It would be a first to have something of this sort happen, but she no longer took for granted their safety or peace. She would not rest easy until the soldier awakened and was able to tell her just what had become of him and how. Until then, Jane could only assume the worst.

CHAPTER SEVENTEEN

THE WAIT SEEMED to take half an eternity. Jane sat in the darkness of the cottage, perched in an old rocking chair that she'd dragged over to the soldier's bedside. The woods remained quiet, however, it did nothing to dispel her unease that whoever had caused his condition could still be out there.

Rune remained on watch outside with the others as Martha entered, leaving Jane to close the curtains on the cottage windows in a bid to hide the light from the oil lamp.

Jane tried to avert her eyes as Martha cut away what remained of the soldier's torn clothing. Martha bathed him with the rags that had been soaked in only tepid water. Much to her amazement, he showed no sign of outward injury, despite shrapnel and bullets having ripped his clothing to tatters.

All it seemed that could be done was to treat him for the deep state of shock that had overcome him. They bundled him under his blanket again to keep him warm, adding yet another when his body resumed shivering. He did not awaken, though his head tossed fitfully.

All through the night, Jane and Martha took turns watching over him. Rune and Robert stood guard over them from the cottage doorway.

The others had been sent back to the summerhouse to watch over the rest as they slept, although not many besides the children were sleeping, having stayed up in turns to mind the others.

Rune longed for the softness of his bed and to have his wife next to him. He sat on the dusty ground, his back propped against the wall next to the cottage doorway in the shadows. His axe rested between his knees, its handle propped against his shoulder.

For the rest of the night, the lighthouse remained silent and dark. The air carried a mild chill and the sky was so clear, every star could be seen, though Rune could find none of the constellations he'd been taught in his youth. Those strange stars, offered him no guidance, nor would they show him the way home. They shone brightly even in that eternal twilight. He had found no purpose in this strange realm, save protector of his wife and the child entrusted to their care. When needed he was not by their side, but instead sitting in darkness far from them. He awaited a nameless enemy that had yet to come, one he had begun to doubt the existence of.

Serena slept no better; lying on the floor of the summerhouse, using an old flour sack stuffed with rags for a pillow. She stared at the pumpkin moon through the window, which had been uncovered so those inside could keep watch. Lucy slept next to her, her head resting in her lap, tossing fitfully, muttering to herself as she slept about hard tack and where to graze the horses until morning.

The sound that had accompanied the fog was a roar like nothing Serena had ever heard before, but Lucy and the others among them that had lived through war in their lifetime, could only hope to forget it. Those still able to remember, used their words to bring hope to the others that, in time, their fear would pass. That morning would find the peace they had known, restored. No amount of gunfire or bombs could steal that hope away, as long as it continued to live within their hearts. Fear would pass, but hope and love would live on.

As the hours passed, many slept but just as many remained as sleepless as Jane, still perched in that ancient rocking chair. She more than once dozed when she had rested her eyes for what she intended to be moments.

It was Martha who had shaken her completely awake again. The soldier had finally, after many hours, begun to stir and asked to be given water. Martha poured a little in a glass. She and Jane struggled between them to help him sit up enough to manage to sip at it. They rolled up the pillows and propped them up behind him, trying to keep the blankets tucked around him in the process.

The soldier said nothing as he took the glass and tried to drink the rest of the water with trembling hands. The glass nearly rolled from his lap when he finished, had Martha not reached to catch hold of it.

"Am I in the hospital?" he asked weakly, his voice scarcely above a whisper. Confusion etched his face seeing two women fussing over him instead of a medic.

"No," whispered Jane, thinking it kinder to be reassuring until he recovered. "You have been taken home to recover. How did you come to be in the place that we found you? What happened? Do you remember?"

"No, no more than the sound of bombs and gunfire, but you get used to that after a while, until you nearly sleep through it once your watch is over," he answered, leaving Jane wondering if he were being truthful or evasive in his answer, not that she expected him to trust her.

"What is your name, soldier?" Jane asked him, taking the glass from Martha and sitting it on the nightstand next to the bed, making no move at first to refill it, even as he requested it.

"Luke Fernsby, may I ask yours, madam?" he replied impatiently as he waited for Jane to refill the water. His head turned to watch her pour, looking ravenous as it was brought back to him.

"This is Martha Weaver. She is your nurse, and my name is Jane Boyd. You could say that I am, well, next best thing to the Mayor here at this time."

If Luke suspected that anything was amiss, he gave no hint.

"Are you hungry? Do you think you could manage a small meal?" Jane asked him, noting the hungry look in his eyes once she had mentioned food.

"I could do more than manage. I've not eaten in days thanks to being pinned down by gunfire." Luke answered quietly. More strength came back to his voice now that his thirst had been tended to.

"A light meal then. I'll have it brought to you when it's ready," Jane said, turning away from him and opening the door to find Rune still awake, but Robert nodding next to him just outside the doorway.

"Go back to the summer house, fetch one of the others to bring food for him. Go quickly," she told Rune, watching him climb to his feet before he shook Robert awake and thrust the handle of the axe into his hands.

Rune did not object. The summerhouse was very much where he wished to be; if only to see with his own eyes that all was well. The woods were silent as he walked. Nothing moved within the trees, each window he passed was unnervingly dark. It seemed to him that they only sought to frighten themselves; instead of facing this enemy they feared straight-away as he would have. He understood not, why they had cowered underground, and seemed to be terrified of only thunder. He knew nothing of guns or bombs, only the blade and hammer.

The summerhouse was as dark and silent as when he left it, the door open and ready for him before his feet crossed the porch. He was unsurprised to find Serena and Lucy asleep near the fire, curled up together. He knelt next to Serena, waking her carefully.

"Come, you are needed, let the child sleep," Rune told Serena, helping her to her feet, and taking her toward where the kettle over the fire was waiting. "Gather a meal together and follow me. Jane has requested it for the newcomer."

Serena nodded and went to work with some of the others, collecting what was needed. They ladled soup from the kettle into a thermos and gathered it into a basket with a small parcel of bread left over from their evening meal. Rune took a piece for himself to sate his own hunger.

"What frightens you?" Rune asked, as he saw the fear in her eyes once they began to walk together. Serena stayed close to his side. She did little to hide her fear from him, though he wished she would do more to hide it from others.

"There is much that has changed since your time that you don't understand," Serena told him as she strode next to him, much more careful with her footsteps in the darkness. "There is no longer honor in war, only destruction. The rulers hide safely away, while they send men and women to die by the thousands in battles they refuse to fight."

"There will come a day when some men will no longer care about honor. They will kill even women and children, without mercy. Instead of armies, they prefer to attack those who are unarmed and unable to defend themselves. That is the time that I grew up in. The horrible stories you hear about those things that are happening, are always in the back of your mind. You can't stop them. All you can do, is keep living in spite of them; hoping and praying there won't be a next time, even when it feels as though the world is coming apart."

Rune did not know what to say. He watched Serena continue on walking. Tears fell from her eyes, but this time, she did not even attempt to wipe them away. All he could do was take her hand and continue to listen and try to understand what she was telling him.

"There was a warm day in the autumn, a few months after I went to live in the foster home. I'd already lost my family, and after I heard the news of an attack on the capital city of my country, and another that was one of the largest cities, I thought the world was ending. They showed horrible images of what had happened over and over again. I don't even think you could imagine those things." Serena didn't even know how to begin describing skyscrapers or airplanes to him, let alone buildings burning and collapsing into ruin the way they had that day from the impact. "The world did not end; the buildings burned, thousands of people died, and the rest of us all kept on living, but everything changed. Our lives were never quite the same as before. I was twelve then. It was the worst year of my life."

"But you survived and grew strong," Rune said, unsure of what else to say.

"Sometimes I don't feel nearly as strong as I seem," Serena replied, finally dabbing at her eyes, not wanting Jane to see her crying. Serena had, at that moment, felt more alone than she ever had in the time she'd come to be there. There was much she knew that none of the others shared in common. It seemed a blessing to her that they'd known a more innocent time, even if each would beg to differ that no time was innocent, and each came with the troubles of its day.

They walked the rest of the way in silence. Rune remained quiet even after they reached the clearing. He led her to the cottage, rapping softly on the door.

Jane showed them inside, giving Serena a soft nod in appreciation before she took the basket from her hands. Jane set it on the table nearby, uncapping the thermos before she poured a serving into the lid that served as a cup. She placed it on a tray with a spoon, and what was left of the bread.

Serena watched him silently, turning to let herself be wrapped in Rune's arms.

Jane placed the tray into the lap of the man who rested there. He looked gaunt, unshaven, and weak.

Luke's hands trembled but he did his best to eat carefully. He eventually gave up on the spoon, and chose to lift the cup to his lips, dipping his bread in what remained of the broth, but he ate hurriedly.

Jane wasted no time refilling the cup, reminding Luke to finish it more slowly. He complied, if only begrudgingly, letting her take the tray away as soon as he'd finished the second helping. He lay back against the pillows after thanking them. His eyes closed and, within what seemed like seconds, he was asleep.

Jane gestured for Rune and Serena to follow her outside. She closed the door behind her and waited for Robert to join them. "I think the danger has all but passed. If trouble were coming, I believe it would have already come. Robert, go and tell the others that they may go home once they awaken," she told them.

Robert nodded, a sleepy look of relief in his eyes. He turned and made his way across the meadow. It was obvious he would be happy to have sleep find him as soon as the news had been delivered.

"I will see you both tomorrow," Jane told them.

Serena and Rune watched her make her way back inside the cottage.

Serena's eyes were already heavy as they doubled back to find the last familiar path that they knew toward home, hers being the closer of the two.

Rune carried her up the stairs. She was already half dreaming as he tugged her clothes off her. He fell into bed next to her, far too tired to do anything more.

CHAPTER EIGHTEEN

THEY PAID no mind to how much time passed. Morning came and went. There was nothing but the hands of an old clock to show the passage of time. Several times Serena had awakened to find Rune still sleeping deeply next to her.

She almost let herself drift off again until she heard the clock chime five times, meaning they'd nearly slept through the evening gathering. She shook Rune awake and went to draw them a bath. Serena let the water run while she went to gather a change of clothes for him. She half dragged him out of the bed and toward the bathroom after her.

Steam rose from the old claw foot bathtub as she leaned over to turn off the water. She tested the temperature with her foot before she slowly sank into the bath. Rune lowered himself into the water behind her.

"The hot springs brought into our home, how clever," Rune remarked as he rested his back against the back of the tub behind her. He sighed contentedly, pulling her back to lie against him and held her tightly as his lips found her neck.

Serena could do little more than whimper, though she found it did little to dissuade him. His long legs curled around her own to keep her still. His touch was far from innocent as he bathed her and became even less so, the lower his hands traveled. Her legs trembled with anticipation when his hand slid between them. She lost all thought of watching the time. The next few moments lost in a blur of heated bliss. Afterward, he turned her until her belly rested against his, a satisfied gleam in his eyes as he watched her pant.

"You need to learn to behave," she whispered to him half out of breath before kissing him.

"I do not know the meaning of that word," he teased her, giving her bottom lip a gentle nip before he finally let go of her.

Rune sat back contentedly watching her finish her bath as she sat astride his lap. He gave no objection as she pulled him to sit up so she could assist him. She'd resigned herself to the fact that he would do as he pleased, purposefully pushing her buttons and making her push through what fear still remained in her.

It was all but gone as they climbed from the tub and lost themselves in each other, rolling around on their towels on the bathroom floor. The minutes ticked away, leaving them dashing for their clothes in order to get to the gathering on time.

Serena managed to pull her hair into a messy braid in the time that remained. Her hair was still quite damp as she dressed herself in comfortable jeans and her favorite sweater, finally sliding her feet into a pair of walking shoes.

Rune bypassed the clothes he'd been offered to climb back into his own, seemingly more comfortable dressed in what truly belonged to him. She did not want to admit it bothered her that he wore them for days at a time.

"Tomorrow you should bring me your washing, I will clean it for you," she said as she waited for him to pull on his boots. She wanted to be helpful and not nag him about it. "Lucy and I will need to do our washing as well, we may as well wash everything all at once."

"I will bring what little I have if you wish, but I do not have as many clothes as you would assume," he said, nodding to her dresser and closet.

"All the more reason I should wash them more often," she said, offering him a smile. She looked sheepishly at the shirt she had half-torn off him nights before and held it up. "Besides, I really should see about getting this mended."

Rune shook his head at her with half a smile, taking the torn shirt and tossing it back onto the chair with a laugh.

He took Serena's hand in his as he led her toward the stairs. They went through the kitchen instead of out the front door as usual, so Serena could gather the food she had planned to bring as her contribution to the evening meal.

Serena stopped in her tracks. A chair was pulled out from the kitchen table, dirty dishes and what remained of a meal sat on top. She doubted it would have been Lucy, who was always so careful to clean up after herself.

"Someone's been here," Serena said, trying not to look as afraid as she felt. Her eyes tried to take stock of what had been disturbed.

"They must have been hungry," Rune remarked, letting go of her hand to let her tend to the mess. He watched Serena carry the dishes to the sink, and then mill around the room, checking the cupboards and pantry.

"Yes, they must have been," Serena muttered to herself, sighing as she noticed a few empty spaces in the pantry that had not been there before. "Whoever it was has taken a little of the food with them, we'll just have to start keeping the doors locked."

"We should at least ask who it was that came, and why it was needed before we assume the worst," Rune added, seeming much more a voice of reason for that moment than Serena had expected.

"You're right, we should be going," Serena said, trying for the moment to let it go. She took Rune's hand again as they stepped off the back porch and into the cool darkness of the woods.

Rune carried the lantern as they walked; taking the trail he knew the best that led past his own home. He took a short moment to check all was well before he led her onward, toward the trail along the river. It was a winding way to go when time was short, but he cared not. Nor did he believe anyone else would if they were only a few minutes delayed.

The beach was silent and empty as they walked down the shore, but the windows within the summerhouse were brightly lit. They arrived to find the others waiting for them.

Jane had already come and gone, coming only long enough to gather food before taking a meal for herself and the others, and making her way back toward the cottage. She'd come herself to give Martha a much needed chance to catch up on some sleep, but did not want to stay any longer than necessary; at least until she knew for certain that the newcomer was recovering.

Alec was, for the moment, asleep in the corner, inside a sleeping bag that one of the others had found for him. Serena studied him as she and Rune sat down to eat their meal together.

"He's good with the children, but he's still pretty scared," Lucy said as she joined them at their table, easily following the subject of Serena's gaze, knowing she'd been worried about how Alec had been adjusting.

"The people who have been through the most are usually the kindest," Serena remarked, knowing it to be as sure a truth as she had ever known. Those who had not suffered often lacked the empathy to understand the suffering of others.

She was not surprised to see Rune nod in agreement. He was far too busy eating his dinner to remark, famished as he was from having missed the previous night's meal. Once he'd been sure the others had been well fed, he showed no shame in going back for a large serving of seconds that disappeared nearly as quickly as the first.

Serena finished most of her dinner, giving the rest to Rune. Her body was still stiff from having spent most of the night on the floor.

Even Lucy seemed eager to depart. They stayed no longer than was polite to talk with some of the others. They made their way back out into the night. Lucy walked quietly in between them until they were far down the beach and out of sight.

"Jane seemed scared tonight when she came back from wherever she's been," Lucy told them, keeping her voice low so she wouldn't be overheard, by those passing on the trail. She didn't stop walking, knowing her small steps were slowing the others. "I haven't seen Jane this unsure of herself since she first came here years ago. I wonder what it is about this man that has her feathers so ruffled?"

"Figure of speech," Serena remarked, seeing the confused look in Rune's eyes at Lucy's words. They would have to remind themselves to make their meaning more clear and not speak in metaphors as much as they were used to.

"What is he like? I assume you have met him," Lucy asked, curious to know just who it was they were dealing with and why Jane was letting this man get to her.

"I only met him for a moment, but from what I gather, he's a soldier. He didn't look well when I saw him last," Serena replied.

Rune nodded, seeming to agree with her answer.

"That explains it then," Lucy said, laughing to herself. Not surprised now that she'd heard Serena's description of the newcomer. "Jane is a hard one to understand, but she has her reasons. Jane was married to a soldier once. Apparently a great war began only a handful of years after they married, and her husband went off to fight in it. From what I've heard her tell, he came home quite a different sort of man than before. He was unfaithful, drank heavily, and began beating her and their children. Within months of his coming home, Jane was expecting the birth of a set of twins, but she lost them one night after he beat her. Afterward, when she came home from being in the hospital, she asked her husband Frank for a divorce, but he refused her. He had her locked away in an asylum, telling everyone she'd gone mad from her grief."

"Jane said they did horrible things to her in there, and it was a very long time before she could convince the doctors to let her leave. Her family was catholic and threatened to disown her if she dared to ask for a divorce again, so she had no choice but to go back home to her husband and stay with him."

"How horrible," Serena said, cringing and finding it no wonder that Jane seemed so guarded.

"It would never have happened with my people," Rune told them, a tone of displeasure in his voice obvious to hear. "Where I am from, any woman has the right to divorce a man that abuses, or even displeases her. Everything she owned, and even the children would be hers to take with her and do with as she pleased."

"And yet, they try to claim that the world has only gotten more civilized since those days. They must be joking," Serena replied, shaking her head, feeling quite sorrier for Jane than she ever believed she could after the insight Lucy had given them.

Lucy didn't comment on it when they returned to Serena's house and not hers. She even helped clean up what mess had been left in the kitchen before they settled in the living room to listen to her grandparent's old phonograph.

Serena was taken aback to see Rune's amazement at the sound, but she could not help but smile at his curiosity as Lucy demonstrated how to change and play the records. Her grandparents hadn't played them often, but she remembered several of the songs that Lucy had chosen. *When It's Lamp Lighting Time In The Valley* seemed to be one of her favorites. It got several plays, unlike many of the others. It was possibly a song Lucy had known from late in her life before, seeing as she had hummed it easily enough.

Eventually, Lucy fell asleep curled up on the sofa, fussing only a little when Rune lifted her in his arms and carried her to bed. Serena removed her shoes before she tucked her in. That same sadness that had no name that had lead her into Rune's arms nights ago, now welled in her again as she watched the child sleeping. She had no idea why it almost always nearly moved her to tears.

She was nowhere near sleep, so they returned to the living room below, and she lay on the sofa, watching Rune go through the old cabinet of records. Rune understood nothing of the writing, or the titles, but relied on Serena to tell him what she knew. She did not know many of the records, but could easily tell him which ones had been her favorites. As a child, she hadn't remembered the words to some of the songs being so shockingly inappropriate. She marveled at how the times had changed. Some things men would not have thought to say in those days would have been shocking if they'd been sung in her lifetime.

"I'll have to teach you to read someday," she whispered, her hand reaching to touch his shoulder where he sat on the floor in front of the sofa. She watched him change yet another record as if he couldn't get enough of them.

"You understand the writing?" he asked, turning to look at her, surprised to see her nodding.

"Where I am from, Rune, almost everyone who wants to learn can read," Serena said reassuringly. "If you teach me to swim, I will teach you to read," she told him, offering him a warm smile. "It seems both of us have a lot to learn. There's still so much I don't know about you, and so much you don't know about me."

"There is time, wife of mine, we will learn that, and so many other things, together," he said, turning his body to lean down and kiss her softly as the next song began to play. *Ain't Misbehavin'* almost seemed ironic, considering Rune's usual brand of mischief, when he crawled up onto the sofa to lie atop her. Who did she think she was fooling? Behaving was the last thing she wanted him to do.

CHAPTER NINETEEN

JANE TRIED to open the door quietly when she reached the cottage. She brought dinner in the same basket as the night before. This time it consisted of something a little more substantial than soup, though a thermos of that was there as well.

When Jane entered the room, she was not surprised to find Martha asleep in the rocking chair, but she was shocked to see the soldier out of bed. He gripped the bottom of the window frame with both hands to stay upright as he looked out of the window with a clearly confused look on his face.

"Mr. Fernsby, you shouldn't be out of bed quite yet." Jane sighed, hurrying to set the basket on the table and make her way across the room to steady him. She grabbed a bathrobe she found hanging in the wardrobe to wrap around him as she did her best to avert her eyes, seeing as he was still completely naked.

"Something's not right here," Luke said, putting up a fuss, but still allowing her to bring him back to the edge of the bed. "What happened to the Manor house? It should be right through those trees, just over there; you can see the top of the tower for miles around."

"Relax, Mr. Fernsby," Jane said, trying to reassure him. She sighed with frustration when Luke only wanted to sit down and wouldn't allow himself to be tucked into bed again. "I'm sure the trees have just grown taller since you were here last." It was a lie, she knew it was, but she wasn't sure that he was in any condition to hear the truth, not yet at least.

"I can't help but notice you're American, has England run out of its own nurses? What's an American woman doing over here in England when there's a war on?" Luke asked her, showing himself to be slightly the cantankerous sort. "Shouldn't you be back home where it's safer for you? Where you don't have bombs raining down on your head?"

"If I were, then I wouldn't be where I'm needed," Jane stated plainly. She turned away from him, making her way to the table to portion out their dinner. "Will you be wanting your dinner in bed, or would you like some help making your way to the table?" she asked him as she finished filling their water glasses.

"I'd rather try eating at the table if I can," Luke answered her; still not quite sure of her and just what she was doing here. Being sent home to recover from wounds, it was the first he'd ever heard of this sort of nonsense.

Jane gently woke Martha from her nap in the chair. They both helped to steady him as he stood from the bed. He was far better than the previous evening, but they still worried he would hurt himself if he fell.

Luke put up minimal fuss, but he seemed relieved to settle into the dining chair. He was glad they'd chosen to sit him in the one at the head of the table, which had arms that he could use to brace himself if needed.

He was already hungrily eating the second bowl of soup that had been set before him. He managed the spoon well enough on his own this time, his hands not shaking nearly as badly as they had the previous evening. He seemed to be getting his strength back, slowly but surely. He finished his soup far more quickly than either of the women, and sat patiently waiting for them to finish. Luke munched on one of the dinner rolls he'd taken from the basket on the table.

"How long will I be staying then?" Luke asked Jane, not even taking the time to butter the second roll as it seemed to be disappearing just as fast as the first. He was curious to know.

"Only for a little while, Mr. Fernsby, you'll know all there is to know soon enough," Jane replied, trying to offer him a reassuring smile that she hoped looked at least somewhat genuine. "For now, all you have to do is rest, and let your strength return. You are already doing remarkably well."

It was true. Luke was, much to her relief, past the point of danger and only needed time to recover. She could scarcely imagine how he was going to deal with what he'd need to be told once he did.

"I expect I'll need to be getting back soon as I can," Luke said, digging into his plate of beef and noodles over mashed potatoes, as soon as Jane had time to set it in front of him. Even being made out of tinned beef, to him it tasted like heaven. He didn't remember his manners until halfway through the plate. "This is the first real hot meal I've eaten in months, I thank you both for the trouble you've gone to."

"We are happy to help, Mr. Fernsby," Jane answered with Martha nodding in agreement.

"Please, call me Luke. Mr. Fernsby sounds so horribly formal. I've got too many people already calling me that. Fernsby, over here! Fernsby, mind your head. I'm so tired of hearing it; after the war, I just might change it."

Jane, for the moment, was genuinely amused as she listened to him ramble on. His color was looking a lot better than it had moments ago. She ate slowly from her own plate, trying to overlook his lapse of table manners, but couldn't help but smile at his animated demeanor.

"Tomorrow, I think I should send a letter to my father." Luke sighed contentedly when his plate was finished. He sat back in the chair, his arms against the armrest. "He'll be wanting to know where I am, and how I happened to make my way here instead of back to my flat in London; if the flat's still there that is."

"It's hard to say," Jane answered, feeling sad for him. "You won't know until you try, it couldn't hurt to write your letter, but I very much doubt that much in the post is making it through these days."

Jane hated this charade, the elaborate deception she'd convinced herself at first she was only carrying on for his sake. She still had no idea why she felt compelled to soften the blow for him, and not the others, including the boy back at the summerhouse, whose care she was currently neglecting.

"Martha, when dinner is finished, go back to the summerhouse and make sure that young Alec is well, then go home and sleep if you wish," Jane told her, unsurprised to see the look of relief in her tired eyes, knowing she'd slept little more than she had these last couple of nights.

"Who is Alec? Your son?" Luke asked, curious to know more about Jane. Seeing as she was the woman in charge, it piqued his interest; he wanted to know more about just whom it was he was dealing with.

"No, Mr. Fernsby, I mean, Luke," Jane replied, catching herself as soon as she slipped on his name. "Alec is a young orphan we discovered living alone in an abandoned house a couple of nights ago, a short distance from here. He's being looked after now by some of the other villagers, but I really should check up on him as soon as you're strong enough to be left on your own."

"Don't allow me to stop you, I'll be all right on my own for a while," he replied, pushing his chair back from the table. "I'd just like to kindly request that you help me back to bed first, but before you do, I'll be needing to answer the call of nature."

Jane tried her best not to be embarrassed as she helped him, to what she at first assumed to be a closet, only to find that a small bathroom had been built inside. It featured a toilet and small stand up shower, with little room to stand between them. She stood outside the door facing outward as she left him to go about his business, not opening it again until he assured her he was finished and covered again.

It was hard for Luke not to poke fun at her embarrassment, but he managed. He let her help him back to bed.

Jane turned her back toward him until he'd settled in and covered himself with the blankets, his robe draped across the foot of the bed. The sigh of relief she breathed afterward more than obvious.

"You could always check the top drawer of the dresser, there may be some undergarments or pajamas there, couldn't hurt to look," Luke teased her, trying to ease her embarrassment. He didn't want her to think he meant to offend her on purpose, if offensive was how she depicted his behavior. The sooner the situation was remedied the sooner they'd both be more comfortable.

Jane nodded; going to the dresser and looking through the drawers he indicated for the clothing he wanted. She found both the undergarments and pajamas with no trouble. She stood with her back turned again as he sat back up on the side of the bed to dress.

The pajamas fit well enough, but obviously were not his own. The monogram on the pocket carried a similar, but different set of initials, likely those of his father.

"You can look now, is this better?" Luke said before Jane turned to look at him again. He didn't argue when she shooed him under the covers and tucked him in tightly. "You'd be a lot lovelier if you smiled, Miss Boyd," Luke told her, noticing the flush return to her cheeks as she looked away from him.

"Mrs. Boyd," Jane answered, making what may have been a too obviously hasty retreat to the rocking chair, trying not to look him in the eye.

"Ah, I should have known. Your husband is a lucky man."

"He was, I'm a widow, Mr. Fernsby. I'd really prefer not to speak of him right now," Jane stated. That much was honest; she didn't want to speak of Frank, let alone think of him anymore. Their marriage hadn't exactly been the happiest. Good memories of him for her were a little hard to come by. He'd returned home a changed man after the war, nothing like the young man that she had fallen in love with.

"I'm sorry."

"It's all right, you had no way of knowing," she answered, feeling bad for having been so short with him. Being defensive was almost like second nature to Jane, a habit she'd have to be careful not to quickly slip back into. Luke's familiarity was skirting the edge of comfort.

Another night, and she owed him the truth, she told herself while watching him settle under the covers. His amber-colored eyes studied her silently before he closed them.

Too dark by the candlelight to read, she instead turned to the knitting she'd brought with her from the summerhouse, using it to distract her mind from the rush of thoughts passing through it. She wanted to forget those thoughts of the past, but Luke seemed to be awakening them.

Apart from being without any of her children, her life had been a far happier one here than the one she left behind, all bar one regret. Her sons had not waited for her there. They'd likely come and gone long before she'd come to that realm. She would not allow herself the hope of reconciliation with them in whatever came after this new life. She believed in that once, and had been gravely disappointed.

CHAPTER TWENTY

LUCY WAS the first to notice something amiss when she and Serena returned to the summerhouse the next morning. They opened the door to find it quiet and empty, nothing out of place but a rumpled sleeping bag and pillow in the corner.

"Oh no, Alec's flown the coop!" Lucy yelled, though there was no one but Serena to hear her. She didn't know who was supposed to have been watching him, but she was beginning to panic. Obviously, whoever it was hadn't been doing their job.

"Go get Jane!" she yelled to Martha when she saw her sleepily stumbling from the nearest trail that led to the woods.

Alec had no idea where he was, or even what may be out there. Even their island was not without its dangers.

By the time Martha was running to fetch Jane, Lucy and Serena were on their way to the beach, running as fast as they could to find Rune, he'd returned to his own home to tend to things there.

Lucy knew the trails far better than Serena, leaving her little to do but follow her. Serena was badly out of breath by the time they reached the clearing, and Lucy only slightly less so. There had been no fire to guide them this time but Lucy could not help but remember the way, even if Serena could have not so easily found it on her own.

The heavy door of the house stood open, but Serena did not find Rune when she peered inside. The house was silent, even when she called for him, but could barely do so. She trembled when she crossed the threshold, still trying to shake the feeling that she should not be here on her own, though she knew Rune would assure her otherwise.

It took her a moment to acclimate her eyes to the darkness within. The fire and candles were unlit, and the only light came from the doorway behind her. Lucy followed her inside with the lantern. She checked the loft above, and found nothing but darkness.

The home itself was once again in a state of disarray, much like her home the night before. The larder had been ransacked, and used dishes with a few scraps from a meal had been left on the table. Nothing else in the home, as far as Serena's sense of limited recollection could see, had been taken or disturbed, except for one of the fur blankets that no longer lay atop the pile near the hearth.

"This is very strange, where could he be?" Serena asked, turning to look at Lucy to see an equally perplexed expression.

"I don't know, but I don't like this," Lucy had replied fidgeting where she stood, appearing equally as frightened.

"Maybe you should go and tell Jane we can't find Rune either. I think the new cottage is pretty close to where she lives," Serena told her.

Lucy ran out the door, leaving her in darkness to kneel on the furs next to the cold, dark hearth.

Serena fumbled about in the dark to find the flint and a piece of steel next to the hearth. Managing to light the pile of small twigs already inside was proving harder than it had seemed. She blew at the sparks to encourage them to take light, but it only made them go out instead. She really hadn't the first clue how to light a fire that way, and she was starting to think it would be better to sit outside and wait for Rune to return.

A shadow flickered on the wall and a soft scuffle on the floor alerted her, too late, that someone was behind her. They seized her roughly from behind and dragged her kicking and screaming backwards away from the hearth. She was thrown onto the pile of furs, hard enough to knock the wind from her.

She froze. He raised his weapon over his head, and then stopped when she screamed his name. A look of horror and recognition registered in Rune's eyes when he realized who lay beneath him.

The knife rattled to the floor. Rune drew her close to him with trembling hands. He hadn't harmed her, but he'd come so close. He never thought that she would be the figure he'd come home to find crouched in the darkness. He had returned earlier to find his home had been taken from, the same as Serena's.

Rune had searched the woods surrounding him, but the trail had gone cold, this person was skilled at covering their tracks. He returned empty handed from his search, striking out with blind anger when he came across someone kneeling in the darkness by the hearth. His wife had nearly paid dearly for it.

He was unsurprised when she pushed back against him, too frightened to listen to his apology. He did little but hold onto her tightly when Serena struck out at him in fear with her fists.

"Rune let go of me!" Serena screamed, doing her best to slip out of his grasp. Tears blinded her, but his arms released her. She half crawled, half ran out the doorway, only to stumble to her knees when she tripped over the threshold.

"Please do not go. I am sorry. I did not know it was you," Rune whispered, having come after her. He wrapped his arms around her waist before she could clamor to her feet.

He was terrified when he turned her toward him to see that same fear she'd had of him before returning. His heart sank at the tears and terror in her eyes. "I am deserving of your anger, but please do not leave."

"Who else did you think it was? It is insane to attack without knowing," Serena yelled, her hands slamming into his chest, although it was little more than a glancing blow, and not nearly hard enough to phase him. He was damned right she was angry, and was only growing angrier now that the adrenaline was starting to wear off.

"I expected the thief still here or returned, or did you not notice what was done?" Rune asked her, his tone still apologetic but serious. "I do not know of your home, love of mine, but where I come from, anyone who would come into your home to steal, would sooner cut your throat than face you with honor. If you are wise, you do not give them the chance."

"If I had been the thief, would you have killed me?" Serena asked, her body trembling. She wasn't sure she truly wanted to know the answer, but she felt she needed to hear it...she needed to know.

"Were the thief a woman, and unarmed, no. It is forbidden," Rune answered, feeling shame that she would have doubt of the answer. "She would have been bound, and brought to the elders to be punished, nothing more."

Serena still did not know whether to let him pull her close or run away as she whispered, "If it should ever happen again, I will go and not return. You hurt me." She meant it, more than anything she had ever said to him.

"And I am sorry. I can only swear that I would never knowingly strike you in anger. If I ever do, that will be the day I no longer deserve to be yours. I will not be unworthy of your forgiveness, or I will deserve to live with that shame," Rune told her, his head bowed, eyes downcast, and not caring if she saw fit to strike him again.

He raised his head again when he heard footfalls coming toward them through the trees. He glanced up to see the confused look in Lucy's eyes when she'd caught sight of them kneeling there. She was out of breath and nervous when she came to a stop in front of them.

"Jane needs you to come, she says to hurry. Lock your doors," Lucy said, gasping in between words and trying to catch her breath as she waited for Serena and Rune to scramble to their feet.

Rune was happy to lock the door. He pulled Serena after him, following Lucy as quickly as Serena could go. He lifted Serena onto his back so they could go faster, when she had trouble keeping pace.

Rune could not have found the trails they travelled down without Lucy's help, some of the paths she led him down not any he had traveled in the times they had walked together.

Serena somewhat understood the direction they were going, her suspicions were confirmed when she saw the familiar Spanish moss covered trees. Her nose detected the scent of lilacs long before they came into view.

The gate of Jane's white picket fence stood ajar, and parts of her victory garden looked picked through and trampled. Jane stood nervously in the doorway, having come home to check her own home when Lucy had alerted her to the trouble. She paced, waiting for Serena and Lucy to come closer. She'd been lucky, her doors had not been locked, but only old bread and some homemade jam had been taken.

"It appears we have a thief among us," Jane told them.

"Why would anyone steal here? Everyone knows we all share?" Lucy asked, puzzled to consider that any of them would even think of it.

"Food was taken from my home also and a blanket," Rune answered quietly, trying to stick to the subject at hand. He wanted to confess to what he'd done to accept his punishment. There would be time to do that later.

"It also seems that young Alec is missing, last seen early this morning sleeping before Robert went to wake Martha. He was gone only a short time, so I do not believe Alec is the source of this. There has to be another, and we should find him."

"I will do what I can to help with this," Rune told her as he waited. Robert had gone to gather searchers once Martha had told him of the trouble. It was the same half dozen men who'd searched for Luke two nights ago.

"I do not think I need to remind you, this person is to be captured, but not harmed," Jane said, most pointedly at Rune. She drew Serena and Lucy close to her, waving the men away to start their search.

Jane led Lucy and Serena into the house without another word. Serena lingered in the doorway, turning back to watch Rune and the others disappear into the shadows. Only after he was gone did she step inside and close the door.

She did not know what to say, so she said nothing as Jane put the both of them to work helping her clean. The busier Serena stayed, the less she would have to think, much less feel. Talking would come at a time when she had a more logical mind, and not when she still felt as if she were screaming inside. At this moment, she felt anything but rational.

CHAPTER TWENTY-ONE

RUNE and the other searchers walked in pairs, paying close attention to the areas near the homes things had been taken from. All were close to a certain part of the woods, not horribly far from where the new cottage appeared, though the locations formed an arc around the area that Rune felt they should be searching. He saw no sign of anything new when they tried to search the area around both his home and Serena's. He was ashamed of himself for shrugging off her unease so easily the evening before. If he'd listened to her, the situation may have been dealt with sooner and with a lot less trauma.

As the newest of the searchers, he'd once again been paired with Robert. While Robert looked not much older than a teenage boy, he was far older and wiser than he appeared.

With Lucy growing younger these last few years; Jane had come to rely on Robert heavily to care for the others, knowing even she could not hope to do it alone.

Robert had proven himself to be committed and capable, but he certainly was not the fighter or tracker that Rune had proven to be. He was glad to have Rune on their patrol; he certainly never wanted to be facing against him.

The thief was spotted fleeing into the trees from a low cape cod styled house belonging to one of Martha's helpers a short time ago. Carol had gone home that afternoon, to put one of the children in her care down for a nap, only to find her door ajar and someone ransacking the kitchen. Terrified to confront the intruder alone, she had run to the closest neighbor, who sent word to Jane before returning with a small group to make a confrontation. However, by the time they'd returned, they'd only caught a fleeting glimpse of the thief disappearing into the trees with a bundle made of dishtowels in her hands. Her bright red hair flying behind her as she ran on bare feet, wearing little more than a threadbare patchwork dress made of old rags.

Having an idea of the sort of person they were seeking did not help their search, but maybe discovering where her abode was located may help.

Jane's only idea was that she had arrived the same night as Luke and had been overlooked. If that were the case though, it would be the first time that she could recall that two newcomers had ever arrived on the same night.

They now concentrated in the area slightly to the north of the cottage, where the ground seemed somewhat rockier than it had before. The meadows gave way to gently rolling hills.

Rune pointed out to Robert what, at first, only appeared to be a wall face of rocks set into a hillside. Upon further inspection, there was a small opening that served as a doorway. The dug out home was carved into the hill itself, its front was made of the native stone and covered in moss. It blended almost seamlessly into the hillside. It would have easily been overlooked were it not for Rune's trained eye.

"I think we have found the home of our thief," Rune said, staying among the trees as he watched and waited to see if there was any movement nearby. No light shone within the darkness of the doorway, and no smoke rose from the chimney hole.

"What do you think we should do?" Robert asked him, studying the surroundings carefully and taking note of where they were in a small notebook he carried with him in his breast pocket.

"One of us should go back and tell the others, the other should wait here to keep watch in case the thief returns before the others can be brought back to help confront this person. If it is a woman, perhaps a woman should be among us then," Rune replied, settling himself against a tree well off the path but within view of the doorway. "I think it best that you be the one to return, and I will wait."

Robert nodded in agreement and whispered, "Will you be all right here alone? It may take some time for us to return." It seemed a silly question almost a soon as he'd asked it. Of course, Rune was the last person among them that would need someone to protect him.

Rune settled into the brush, his back against the tree as soon as Robert turned to leave. From were he sat, he had a clear view of the doorway, but could not easily be seen himself. He drew the hood of his cloak up and over his eyes to shade his face and better conceal him in the shadows.

There was little to help Rune judge the passing of time as he sat there. The brightness of the moon cast shadows behind him, though they only changed little throughout the night. The woods were silent once Robert's footsteps faded in the distance. Rune stayed quiet and still, his eyes carefully studying the darkness around him, slightly more than angry that this thief, whoever they happened to be, was the cause for his present state of misery. That anger only brewed the longer he waited.

He almost didn't hear her quiet approach. She moved through the brush barefoot avoiding the trail. There was a sizable parcel tied up in her hands as she crept along. Once she reached the clearing, she stopped and looked around while perched at its edge, a short distance away from him.

Rune waited until she turned her back in his direction before rising to his feet. He stepped silently from his hiding place to follow her into the clearing, careful not to make a sound until his long strides carried him within almost arms reach of her.

She was a mere slip of a girl, wearing a badly torn dress and his rabbit skin blanket thrown around her shoulders as a cloak, though she had nothing with which to pin it together. Her ginger-red hair fell in badly tangled ringlets that had been crudely cut slightly longer than shoulder-length.

The girl was unaware of his approach until he was merely inches behind her. She screamed loudly as she tried to run, the parcel bursting open as it dropped from her hands. He wrestled her to the ground without more than a futile struggle on her part. She was no match for his strength. Thick scars covered her body where the torn collar of her dress draped off her shoulders. She cried loudly, screaming to have him smitten by strange gods when he used the rope he carried to bind her. He left her lying there to inspect what she carried.

There was nothing in the parcel but food, except for a few pieces of clothing that she had taken and the towel she had wrapped it in. He felt no less angry inside; the girl was not a common thief, she was stealing food out of hunger. He left everything where it lay, and rolled the girl over to face him, dragging her by her hair when she fought him. He pinned her to the ground by her throat, even though his hand did not tighten.

"You will listen to me, and listen to me well, little thief, if you do not wish for me to harm you. My patience has already been worn thin." He growled, glaring down at her, only to see fear and defiance in her pale green eyes. "You have already nearly cost me something I hold dear. Had I harmed her because of you, rest assured, you would die very painfully at my hand. Make no mistake of it."

"What are you going to do with me now, Northman?" Iona replied, struggling, though she had no hope to wrestle free of him. "Will you take me home, and make me a whore? What can you do to me that has not already been done?"

"Forget your stories of my kind, you know me not," Rune shouted, drawing back his hand to strike her, but caught himself before he threw the blow when he saw the girl cower. "You will be punished, but not at my hand. I would not take you to my bed. No thief is worthy to bear my sons."

He almost lost patience with her, and was already on edge when he felt a hand on his shoulder. He swung around to find Robert and the others. Rune grumbled, as he rose to his feet, and walked a short distance away. Once there, he leaned against a tree to calm himself as he waited for them to deal with the girl.

Iona complained loudly when she was dragged to her feet and carried in between two of the strongest searchers down the path. Robert gathered her ill-gotten gains and retied the towel into a parcel, handing it to the woman that had come with them to help secure her. He sent her down the path after the others before turning back to check on Rune and joining him with a heavy sigh.

"You did well holding back, I think I'd have clocked her," Robert said, trying to be reassuring, though it did little to lighten Rune's spirits. "Unfortunately, only half our job is over. We still have Alec to find, my own fault really for not taking him with me when I went to wake Martha up this morning."

"We will go," Rune said. He turned to follow him, even if the last thing he wanted to do was any more searching. The boy surely wasn't in the area of the woods they'd already covered, but that left quite a large area left. The others had already been told to look out for him if he came past their homes. The other team that had been sent out to look for him had still not reported back.

The boy was apparently trying to find his own way home, but he could have easily gotten lost on the winding roads that led through the forest. His home had been one of the first places searched, but word had been sent back almost immediately that he had not turned up there. One of the older children had been placed there on watch in case he did turn up.

They were halfway down the ridge when Rune heard a noise from below and over the side of a steep ravine. He peered over the edge, moving until he found a better vantage point. Rune heard something crush under his boot, the remnants of a handful of broken sugar cookies lay just where something had, a short time ago, gone over the side of the ravine. Weeds and small branches were trampled down and snapped off.

"Over here," he yelled to bring Robert back from where he'd gone ahead of him.

Robert gripped Rune's hand as he leaned over the edge. Alec lay on the ground a good distance down the steep embankment, his arm twisted at a painful angle, and he was bleeding from a sizable gash on his head.

"Go, get the others, and bring more rope. I will climb down to him," Rune said calmly, not wanting to alarm the boy and have him fall further down. He dropped to a crawl, and he began to inch his way down the slope before Robert could object.

Robert waited to ensure Rune made the descent safely before he turned and fled down the trail.

Alec was barely conscious when Rune crawled to his side; his arms and bare feet were covered with cuts and scratches.

Rune did the best that he could to stop the bleeding, taking the boy's handkerchief and pressing it tightly against the deep cut on his forehead.

"She stole my cookies. I told her I would share, but she pushed me and I fell," Alec muttered, trying hard to stay awake and let Rune know what had happened to him, though he was fading in and out badly.

Rune did not need to be told. He could already guess just who had done this to him. It made him want to rip that little red haired hellion apart. He tried to choke down the rage inside him. He had promised he would not let his anger get the better of him. *She will pay*, he told himself.

Knocked out cold awhile, and with his arm broken; Alec couldn't climb up the ravine on his own. The others built a makeshift stretcher to pull him up.

Rune climbed up easily enough on his own, walking at the boy's head as they carried him back to the summerhouse where Martha waited to treat him.

Once carried inside, Alec was lowered onto a table to be tended to by Martha and those she'd gathered to assist her. By then Jane, Serena, and Lucy had been summoned and met Rune on the beach outside before he'd had a chance to go looking for them.

A short distance away, Iona screamed from where she'd been tied to a tree with Rune's coil of rope. She cursed at them loudly to set her free.

Rune managed not to go over and shove something in the girl's mouth to shut her up. He was much too tired to put up with any more from her.

"That is the one, she has done this, all of it," Rune told Jane nodding his head toward Iona. "I will tell you of my own transgressions later, should you see fit to punish me as well."

Rune said not another word before he turned away, leaving Serena and Lucy standing there looking stunned. His feet carried him down the beach and to the end of the pier where he sat cross-legged as he stared off into what looked to be an endless ocean. He wondered, for the first time since he'd been there, if there were distant lands or just a limitless sea that stretched on forever? Would he be able to sail his way home?

He had not stirred from that thought until he felt gentle hands on his shoulders. He turned to find Serena kneeling behind him, her face wet with tears as she let him pull her to him. She wrapped around him tightly.

"There's nothing to talk about, lets just put this behind us, please?" Serena whispered, curling into his lap and reaching up to kiss him gently.

Rune sighed heavily in agreement, wanting no more than to have that himself.

"May we go home, please?" Was all he asked of her, helping her to her feet after she crawled from his lap. He took her hand and they turned their backs on the chaos down the beach. He cared not if they called after him, he would not have gone back, and his patience was worn thin. All they wanted was to be alone.

They walked together in silence, Serena clinging to his side tightly, even with the filthiness of his clothes. His body still trembled with the anger that he was now doing his best to walk away from.

The door of his home would stay bolted that night as she led him to her own. The house was empty and still as they stepped inside. She locked the door and ushered him upstairs after her. She only left his side to draw him a warm bath, lighting the candles gathered around the room, bathing them in a soft glow.

When he undressed to climb into the water, he pulled her after him, gently tugging at her clothes until they fell to the floor. She eased into the water with him, letting him draw her close and straddling his lap as he held her tightly against him. Serena sighed as they kissed deeply, her body moving in time against his, this time though, she did not shy away to feel him harden against her.

Before he knew it they'd climbed from the tub, and she lay still soaking wet under him in the middle of her bed. Serena no longer cared that he was anything but gentle as he took her.

Rune lost himself in her, hearing only cries of pleasure, and when he looked into her eyes, for the first time, he saw no hint of fear.

CHAPTER TWENTY-TWO

LUCY STOOD HORRIFIED in the doorway as she watched Alec's wounds be tended to. His arm wasn't severely broken, but the shoulder was badly dislocated. He had to be held down while it was put back into place, and again while they stitched closed the wound on his forehead. They had nothing to give him, except some weakened ether on a rag over his face to numb the pain, though they could tell it did little to relieve it. They could only hope it might make it mercifully more difficult for him to remember afterward if he were only partially conscious.

His arm was wrapped in plaster. They were careful to hold him still as they waited for it to dry. They positioned it close to his body, using bandages to hold his arm in place across his chest. The bib of the fresh overalls he'd been brought helped to reinforce the sling as they fastened the straps over it.

The other scratches and cuts were easily tended to once the rest was finished. Alec was left to sleep off the effects of the ether before they lowered him back onto his sleeping bag in a warm corner of the room where he could be looked after easily.

Outside, tied to the tree, Iona struggled until her wrists were bloody. She screamed until her voice went hoarse but her complaints only fell on deaf ears. Lucy, Jane, and the rest of those gathered there, had more important matters to attend to with Alec's safety to be concerned with first.

Her cries caught the attention of more than one of the small children who had felt compelled to stand and stare at her. Their guardians covered their ears, and led them out of earshot when they caught wind of what she'd been uttering in their direction.

Jane had no patience for dealing with the girl until they figured out what to do with her. She couldn't very well be released to go about her own devices, especially if she'd harmed Alec, which had already been more than implied, though he was in no shape as of yet to confirm it.

They'd been left with little choice but to find a place to confine her, the root cellar of the summerhouse would have to do temporarily until other accommodations could be made long term for her, were they deemed necessary.

Robert had installed a sturdy lock on the door, to be reinforced by a wooden beam in case the lock failed, or she managed to kick through it, which he doubted.

Iona's rage seemed to turn to fear when she was finally untied from the tree. Her hands remained bound as she was dragged toward the summerhouse and into the darkness of the cellar. No windows to speak of, there was only the light of the lantern Jane carried with her as she followed them below.

"It seems we have more than a thief among us, but someone truly evil enough to push a young man over the edge of a cliff and leave him to die," Jane stated plainly, her eyes boring holes into Iona as she was held up in front of Jane to face her.

Before she caught hold of her temper, Jane struck Iona hard across her face, unconcerned when she left her mouth and nose bleeding. Jane would not have stopped, were it not for Robert pulling her away, holding onto her until she calmed herself and regained her usual composure.

Iona said not a word, shivering in fear, seeing no mercy in the eyes of those that stood around her, not even the eyes of the child called Lucy who glared at her from the staircase.

"You will stay here for now until other arrangements can be made, but mark my words, you will not see light of day until I can be assured you are no longer a threat to us. If you ever wish freedom, it will have to be earned with your actions, not your words. Cut her free," Jane grumbled letting the men holding her cut the ropes.

They left Iona kneeling there in the darkness, the door closed and bolted behind them, not even so much as a lantern or a single candle left for her to see by.

Lucy spent the rest of the day before the gathering sitting at Alec's side, and keeping careful watch over him. Jane returned to the cabin to take food to Luke, and to see how he was faring, hoping that by some prayer he'd slept most if not all of the time away.

Luke was out of bed again when she let herself inside, using the keys she'd found on a hook next to the door.

"You didn't have to lock me in," Luke said, turning to look at her from the same windowsill he'd been looking out of the last time she'd come, though this time he was much steadier on his feet.

"I'm afraid there was a bit of a crisis to attend to. I wanted to be sure you were safe until it was over," Jane answered matter-of-factly, knowing he had to have noticed her less than polished appearance, and the blood splatter that stained her dark blue gingham dress. She had not bothered to go home and change before going to see him, though she now wondered if she should have, only to chastise herself for caring how she looked.

"Would you mind at least telling me what's going on, and just when I'm going to be leaving?" Luke asked her, unbuttoning the shirt of the pajamas to let her see his chest and stomach. "I can't help but notice, there's only the same old scars I've had for years now. You said I was sent home to recover, only I don't appear to be wounded."

"I knew you'd be asking as soon as you were feeling better," Jane said, sighing and sitting the basket with their dinner down on the table, not that she really wanted hers the way she was feeling. "When we first found you, Mr. Fernsby, you were lying face down on the floor of this cottage in a pool of blood. Your uniform was torn to pieces, and you were suffering from shock and hypothermia." Jane noticed the look of confusion and disbelief in his eyes when she turned back to look at him.

"That's impossible. I wasn't here. Last I remember I was in a foxhole somewhere in France. We'd been pinned down for days," Luke said, a look of silent alarm spreading across his face as he considered just what was happening to him and where he might be.

"You are not in France, Mr. Fernsby, nor England, or if you may be wondering, certainly not Germany. You are not a prisoner here any more than I am," Jane replied, crossing the room to open the door of the cottage, leaving it ajar for him and then handing him the keys to it. "Once you leave this cottage, you may find a far different world than you remember outside that door."

"What is this place?" Luke asked, wondering how the cottage itself could have been an illusion, if it were one, it had been faithfully recreated. He was no one important enough for anyone to go to such an elaborate rouse for. He was not an officer, and he had no information that could be any use to anyone.

"This is your cottage, your home, though it is no longer in the place you remember," She told him nervously, trying to straighten the rumples out of her dress. "None of us know how we came to this place, but myself and many others live here together, each in his or her own place. There is no going back to that world, Mr. Fernsby. Over the years though, many of us have tried."

"Do you mean I've died?" he asked, erupting into nervous laughter. He struck his chest to show her he was good and solid. "That's ridiculous, we both stand here living and breathing. Don't be mad, woman."

"Oh, I am quite serious, and quite sane," Jane replied maybe a little too bluntly. He did have reason to question her honesty, but she would not abide by being accused of insanity. If anything, she was all but too grounded in reality. "Are you feeling up to a walk then, Mr. Fernsby?" she asked, feeling much more comfortable being formal. She pushed him back to arms length, at least in a metaphorical sense.

"I think I could manage, if it will explain what in hell's name is going on here, Mrs. Boyd," Luke said, feeling it only right to toss the formality back at her. He was still wobbly but, not wanting to be helped, he brushed past her and out of the door with nothing on his feet but an old pair of slippers he'd found under the bed. "A quick trip up to the Manor House should clear everything up," he muttered, starting his way toward the path in the proper direction, his dinner ignored and long since forgotten about. Jane followed, wondering how long it would take him to find out for himself things were not what they seemed.

Jane closed the door behind them. There was no reason to lock it now that their little thief had been apprehended. She had already grown weary of the day's events, and she wasn't sure she had the patience to deal with explanations properly.

"It should be just around the bend in the road here, just behind those trees! Why isn't it there?" Luke shouted, running his hands frantically through his hair. He reached the next clearing only to find empty stony ground and no sign of the Manor House, or that any home had once stood there.

"I told you, Mr. Fernsby, that this place is not what it at first may seem to be. This is not your England any more than this is the America that I knew," she told him, arms curled across her body, standing unfazed and detached. She'd given the same news to others many times. "You found your cottage here, because it is the place your heart considers home, just as we have all found our own home here. There is no president, no king, and no country here, only the people who share this island together. There is only one way to leave it, and that is for our time to come, as it has already come for us before."

"This is insanity, send me home!" Luke yelled, drawing close to her. Jane stood firm and did not back away, or even cringe when he closed the distance between them. He stared down at her as he growled. "You end this game now, or I will be the one to end it." It was only a very thinly veiled threat.

Jane's only response was to turn her back on him defiantly and walk away, having no care if he chose to follow. She didn't stop, or even look back as he shouted after her to come back. She kept a pace that was steady and slow, giving him ample chance to catch up with her once he realized threats would not get him the reaction he hoped for.

She said not a word as she led him toward the summerhouse at a leisurely pace, pointedly leading him in a way that would carry him in easy view of as many of the other homes as she could manage without making the trip far too long and overwhelming for him. She tried to remain expressionless as he gaped, and then stared dismayed at all that he was seeing. She refused to answer another solitary question until they were together with the others, lest she lose her patience and her temper for the second time today.

Jane sent Luke ahead with Robert when she found him in the clearing at the end of the trail. She sat by herself on a downed tree, looking over the others milling about in the distance on the beach and outside the summerhouse.

Crazy, insane, mad, they were words Jane had never wanted to hear again after she'd come home from her time in the hospital, expected to put the loss of her twin sons behind her with no time to mourn them. She'd been forced to suffer in silence, ridiculed and punished for weakening under her grief. Jane would never allow herself to feel that helpless again, even if it took pushing the whole world away.

CHAPTER TWENTY-THREE

WHEN SERENA AWOKE, she found that she had been dozing to the sound of her grandparent's old phonograph playing in the living room downstairs. She rolled over to find the other side of the bed empty, though the blankets were still damp. Distressingly enough the hands on the clock showed they'd slept completely through the evening gathering, however, they'd left such a short time before it that she doubted anyone would complain.

It was now well past midnight. She slipped a nightgown over her head and crept downstairs in her bare feet. Rune sat there still naked, hovering over the box of records, examining them carefully. He'd grouped them together in piles by the picture on the labels. It took him a moment to notice her approach. The volume of the music had concealed the sound of her footsteps.

"Which one was about the moon? I want to hear that song again," Rune said, only remembering the color of the label but unable to read a single word. He thrust a good pile with the right color in her direction and waited impatiently for her to dig through them. The only song of that nature she could find in her stack was called *Talking to the Moon*, though Rune shook his head when she put it on the turntable, certain it was not the one that he remembered.

"Maybe it just talked about the moon in the song, and it's not in the title." Serena shrugged, trying to remember which records they'd played. Discouraged, she passed the stack of records back; content to let him play his way through them if he wished.

She felt the chill of the evening on her skin and rose from the floor to walk into the kitchen, digging through the laundry to find herself a pair of warm socks to put on her feet. She was shivering as she put them on, the old clay tiles of the kitchen floor felt like ice. Before making her way back from the laundry room, she picked up an old pair of pajama bottoms that had been her grandfather's for Rune. She offered them to him, only to see a confused look in his eyes, though she did not understand how he could not be cold sitting there naked. She felt chilled even while wearing a nightgown and socks.

Rune only relented to put the pants on when Serena reminded him that Lucy had not yet come home, and that he may wish to be decently clothed if she happened to walk in. Serena was almost worried that someone else hadn't brought her home by then, even if she chastised herself for worrying that much over someone who wasn't actually a real child at all.

A short while later, she looked at Rune in between records and asked, "Do you think we should find where Lucy is and bring her home? I'm a little worried she hasn't come or sent word by now. Sometimes I feel like we aren't doing a very good job of looking after her like we are supposed to."

"If you wish to find her, we will go," Rune answered. He turned off the turntable, closed the lid, and sat the records aside in a neat pile on the end table for later.

Rune didn't complain until Serena returned downstairs from getting dressed with more clothes for him. She rolled her eyes when she saw him trying to tuck the legs of his pajama pants into his boots.

"Here, put these on, you can't go out like that," she muttered, at least trying to offer him some jogging pants that would be easy for him to pull up on his own.

"They are trousers, why not?" Rune asked, looking at her strangely, still wondering what the deal was with all the different sorts of clothes, it made no sense to him.

"They're only made for sleeping in."

"Clothes for wearing only while sleeping, strangest thing I have ever heard."

Rune laughed audibly, set the clothes aside, and turned to go out the door not even bothering to put on a shirt, even though Serena was bundled up in her hoodie and jeans.

"Aren't you cold?" she asked him, trying to keep up with him until he'd slowed his pace.

"This is nowhere near cold for me. You would not be fond of my home in winter if you believe it is cold now." Rune chuckled to himself, his mood lightening for what seemed to be the first time that day. He was almost on his way to having a good sense of humor for once.

Serena was the one that carried the lantern as they walked, she being the one that needed it far more than him.

Rune easily could have found his way in the dark under the trees, but she was far more prone to stumbling in places where the path became dark than he would ever be.

By now, they both knew the path to the summerhouse well enough that one could have made the journey alone, even if they preferred to go together. Serena still found it unnerving how the woods were so silent, no sound of crickets or birds or any of the sounds of dusk that she remembered from her childhood on the farm. Nothing alive ever moved through the trees, except for the owl that the others swore to her could not exist, though she was certain of what she'd seen.

She didn't hear anything until they neared the end of the trail to find only the glow of the fire and one dim light inside the windows of the summerhouse. There was no one on the beach outside. The waves rumbled softly, crashing onto the shore, and voices came from inside the open summerhouse door.

They found Lucy curled up asleep inside Jane's old rocking chair near the fire. Alec also slept soundly a short distance away. Having already slept, Robert was relieving Martha to take the night watch over him. They spoke to themselves in the corner and only nodded when Rune and Serena came indoors.

An intermittent banging and soft wails rang out on the other side of the cellar door coming from inside.

Serena could only imagine how Lucy and Alec were managing to sleep through it, though she soon discovered that Lucy was not nearly as asleep as she seemed.

Lucy sat up as she heard them approaching, looking up at them with tired eyes. She seemed weary from more than exhaustion. She turned her attention back to Alec who groaned softly in his sleep.

"I wondered if or when you were coming back for me," Lucy said as she stood slowly and stiffly from the chair to cross the room and tuck the blankets around Alec again where he'd half thrown them off. "He's hurt pretty bad, but I think he'll be okay. It's hard to believe someone would be this cruel for no reason."

"Some men truly do not need a reason," Rune said, helping the girl back to her feet. He lifted her up in his arms, fighting the urge to smile when she tried to wiggle away from him. She flailed as her feet left the floor, and she found herself bear hugged against him. "Listen to me little one, and understand me. For many people this is their way, they know nothing else. They will not learn easily to live another way, as I also must. Were you to ever see me angry, I would shudder to imagine what you would think of me. Anger makes monsters of all of us if we allow it control. I am learning this."

Rune noticed the thoughtful look in Serena's eyes at his words.

Serena could still see his shame for what happened hours before reflected in his eyes. She could almost forget in that moment that Rune was capable of the degree of rage she'd seen as he held Lucy in his arms. She knew he had not meant her harm, but the fear she'd felt wouldn't fade from her memory easily. Forgiveness was simple; forgetting was often a much harder feat to accomplish, especially when trying to forget things you truly wanted to forget.

"Do you think he will be all right if I go home and sleep?" Lucy asked Rune, peering over her shoulder to look at Alec. He groaned, shrugging off the blanket she'd only just covered him with. "Jane found him something for pain. I think he'll be out cold the rest of the night, but I'm still worried."

"He will be all right. Robert will be here to look after him if he wakes up," Serena tried to reassure her as they all watched a very tired Martha make her way out the door. Robert settled into Jane's rocking chair, opening a book to read once he'd turned up the wick of the oil lamp on the table next to him, prepared it seemed for a long, un-eventful night, though they all tried to ignore the wailing again on the other side of the cellar doorway.

"It's nothing, just the thief locked in the cellar, we couldn't very well leave her tied to the tree all night." Robert said, noticing the look of mild alarm in Serena's eyes as she listened to the girl cry and pound at the door. "Jane's going to find a better place to keep her come morning, don't worry. We just can't have the girl running amok until we've figured out what to do with her, not with the trouble she's caused already. I'll watch over Alec, don't worry, just go."

Lucy was too exhausted to complain when Rune carried her the whole way back to Serena's house. She was sound asleep by the time they arrived with her head resting heavily against Rune's shoulder.

They tried to take her in quietly, carrying her upstairs, and putting her to bed without waking her. She fussed when Serena took off her shoes, and stirred long enough to change into a nightgown after Rune left the room, but quickly snuggled under the covers, and was asleep before Serena had time to close the bedroom door.

As she stepped into the hallway, Serena could already hear the sounds of the phonograph again. Rune was back where he had been before they left. *When Your Hair Has Turned To Silver* was the first song he played, soon followed by *Whispering Hope*. It became obvious to Serena that he vastly preferred the ballads and songs with simple arrangements in comparison to the big band records with faster tempos made for dancing. At least they both agreed on something. Teaching Rune to operate the phonograph by himself had, it seemed, opened up a world of wonders for him.

After watching him play his way through the records without finding the one he'd wanted for a while, she went to her grandmother's desk. She took a felt tipped marker from the drawer and one of the index cards her grandmother had once written recipes on. On it, she neatly wrote the word moon in large carefully formed letters. She could have easily helped Rune find the record he was looking for, but more importantly, she wanted to teach him how to find it himself.

"Rune, this is the word you are looking for, moon," she said quietly, kneeling down next to him, and placing the index card in his hand. She spelled out the word for him carefully. "Now you can find it yourself, and when you are ready, I'll teach you more words."

"This is moon." Rune smiled as he took the card from her, renewing his search with more enthusiasm now that she'd shown him what to look for. He smiled broadly when he found *Blue Moon* in another pile of records. It had a different picture than he had remembered, but the same color of label as the one's he'd been examining.

"This is the one." He sighed with a satisfied expression when he heard the opening notes. "I think I like this song best of all, but I have many yet to hear."

"And now you know how to find it again." Serena smiled warmly back at him. "Soon, you'll be able to read all of them on your own, but one word at a time for now. Everyone has to start somewhere."

CHAPTER TWENTY-FOUR

Jane was finishing washing her morning dishes when Robert came in the door, looking tired, unkempt, and a little winded. Deep scratches ran down his face and neck.

"What's happened to you?" she asked him, turning with alarm to wet a clean dishtowel and ushering him into a chair to have the scratches tended to.

"More like who." Robert winced as Jane washed the scratches. She grabbed her first aid kit from the cupboard and doused the wounds with some antiseptic that burned like fire.

"Mind telling me how she got the chance?" she asked, dabbing the dried blood away with cotton.

"I figured I'd be nice and bring her down some food before the others showed up for the morning. Let's just say, we aren't on the best of terms now," Robert answered, not saying more about it.

Jane wasn't sure if that was all there was to tell, or if for the first time since she'd known him, Robert was actually being evasive.

"You should have known better," she told him, for once not liking the feeling in the pit of her stomach. She thought it was as likely to be her, and not him causing it.

All she could think about was how badly she wanted to slap Luke and make him eat his words; even if she knew it would make her seem the lunatic he accused her of being. She still wasn't sure why she was letting his words get to her, or why she even gave a second thought to the fact that he had an opinion of her.

She shooed Robert out the door to go home and sleep so she could think about her options. She could continue to ignore Luke blatantly. The longer she thought about it, the more it seemed preposterous. Her only other option seemed to be to confront him, but she didn't know if she could keep her temper in check. However, it was morning, and she had more important things to do than to deal with him that day.

There was the not so small matter of what to do with the girl presently locked in the cellar. Jane finally realized she didn't even know her name yet.

Jane wondered if they were partially at fault for her predicament for not finding her sooner, but that didn't absolve the girl of her behavior completely. Instead of making herself known and asking for help, she'd instead chosen to steal, and it seemed, even attack the first person she'd come into contact with. It didn't bode well for convincing Jane, that she didn't deserve to be locked away.

Jane considered some of the options as she made her way toward the summerhouse. She waited for a meeting with some of the builders and craftsman among them to talk about accommodations for the girl, long term. Now that they knew the location of her home, and they felt it best to find a way to confine her to it.

They discussed it as they made the long walk from the summerhouse to the dugout. Jane couldn't believe the girl's home seemed to be little more than a hole in the ground. To her, it explained why the girl behaved as if she were almost feral.

In the end, it was surmised that since the door on the hovel swung inward, it would be covered with a second barred gate that swung outward. Bolted securely, deep into the rocks that surrounded the doorway, the iron gate would not easily break and could be salvaged from someone's broken fence.

Jane left the workmen to the job, satisfied that it would take them merely a couple of days to accomplish the work, the hardest part of which would be drilling into the rock with only hand tools to aid them, but they were skilled, and she had no doubt they would manage.

She purposefully tried to skirt her way around the location of Luke's cottage on her way back to the summerhouse. Her steps were rapid and deliberate as she made her way down the roads, noticing the change in nearby scenery. She almost didn't notice Luke standing with his back to her at the crossroad. He turned in circles, cursing to himself, and obviously lost.

Jane stepped off the path, watching him from behind the trunk of an elm tree. She was amused to see his frustration, looking over the marks he'd already made with a stick in the dirt, only to find that he'd been traveling in circles and unable to find his way either to the summerhouse, or even back to his own home again. The paths did have a way of turning back on one another if you didn't know which way you were going.

"I just keep going in blasted circles," Luke shouted, stamping the dirt and tossing the stick. He was red faced and panting from the frustration and exertion of having been going nowhere for nearly half an hour, in the dark, with no light to help find his route. He kept finding the same scratches he'd left in the dirt when the trails had looped back around on him yet again.

"Who is raving like a lunatic now, Mr. Fernsby?" Jane asked coldly as she finally stepped around the tree to see Luke spin around to face her. "Are you finally ready to admit that what I told you last evening is true? You can keep denying it and walking in circles if you wish, but I believe we both know that wouldn't be the wisest course of action."

Luke looked every bit the every-man of his time. He wore an earth-toned sweater vest, and a cream-colored, button down shirt that he had smartly tucked into his dark brown trousers. His tie was neat, a tidy knot holding it firmly in place, and his shoes were well polished, albeit they'd picked up some dust from the trail from all his walking. The look on his face was one of exasperation and annoyance. He had been hoping to run across someone while trying to find his

way back to the summerhouse, but had sort of hoped it wouldn't
be her.

"It'd help if someone would put up some signs here. The blasted
trails all look the bloody same," Luke grumbled, annoyed that she only
seemed to find his frustration amusing.

"There's no need to curse or be angry, Mr. Fernsby." Jane said,
unable to keep a straight face to see him losing his cool.

"You're damned right I'm angry. I've been going in circles trying to
find some answers, and not one person can tell me how to get back to
where I've come from. I don't know how you feel about there being a
war on, but I have a duty to the others to get back to it. I can't jolly
well be sitting here doing nothing when every man we have is needed
out there," Luke shouted, his eyes wild, his frustration growing the
longer he spoke of it.

"The war is over, Mr. Fernsby, it has been for years now," Jane told
him, unsurprised to see the disbelief in his eyes. She crossed her arms
and waited for her words to sink in. "The war was won, but it seems
you did not live to see the end as I did. The boys came home, but none
of them were the same. We went back to our lives, and we carried on,
no different than all those who went before us."

"Impossible," he blurted out, angrily scraping his hands through his
hair. "If this is to be believed; where and when are we now, Mrs.
Boyd? This place sure as hell isn't heaven."

"It seems, Mr. Fernsby, that this place exists outside of time. Some
others here are from a time before our own, but others have lived and
died in a time that came after. There is a girl that came to us a short
while ago, who seems to be the youngest yet, so I can only imagine she
is of the time that should be."

"If there is a way to come here, there must be a way to leave."

"Not that any of us have found in many years, Mr. Fernsby, though
many have tried. Several who crossed our borders have vanished and
have never returned."

"Is that a threat, Mrs. Boyd?" Luke asked her as she brushed past
him, waiting for him to follow her or be left behind if he didn't catch
up to her.

"Only if you wish to take it as such, Mr. Fernsby."

Luke could follow her or not, sink or swim if he must, but Jane was in no mood to coddle him. He could go where she was going, or find his own way back home. She didn't slow for him to catch up to her side, but somehow he managed. He was stubborn, but she was sure she could outmatch him. Handsome devil that he was, she pushed that thought to the back of her mind. Until he accepted reality, and what was, she'd only be his worst nightmare.

CHAPTER TWENTY-FIVE

Lucy was awake, but had yet to leave the pastel yellow-colored room. For the moment, she was content to explore through the drawers and the closets, even if she had a nagging feeling that she shouldn't be. There were so many dolls, toys, stuffed bears, strange automobiles, and a curious black ball with liquid inside that seemed to only give answers to questions. There were books, and pictures colored in with odd smelling sticks of colored wax. The closet was filled with beautiful dresses. After ruining the last one, she was almost afraid to borrow another.

After a while of sitting in her nightgown coloring, she chose a pretty yellow sundress that came with its own set of matching bloomers. It was shorter than she liked, but seemed modest enough with the bloomers.

She heard Serena moving around downstairs in the kitchen, so she brought the brush and hair ribbons she wanted with her when she came downstairs.

That morning, Serena had found a large can of corned beef hash, frying it up with the eggs that seemed to replenish themselves in her grandmother's egg basket on the counter each morning, as long as she left one inside and buried under the cloth in the bottom to keep Rune from finding it. The smell was almost more than she could bear. Her grandfather had always joked that this particular dish resembled dog food, but it had nonetheless been one of his favorites.

Serena knew there was no sense in waking Rune; the smell of the food cooking would wake him. All she would have to do was wait for him to wander downstairs. Things were becoming almost predictable, even if that was still not quite a comfortable feeling. It was too much like she'd always dreamt of, but not quite who she imagined finding in her life.

Sometimes if she closed her eyes and tried to forget for a moment about where they were, and who they were, Serena could almost imagine Rune and Lucy as the family she'd always longed for. They'd live together on her grandparent's farm and spend time with their friends on the beach. In a perfect world, Lucy would have a handful of siblings with spun gold hair, and their sister's penchant for mischief. Sometimes, it felt like just another hopeless and painful fantasy that she knew could never be, but knowing the truth couldn't keep her from dreaming it.

She'd been careful to put the not quite empty hash-can back on the shelf where she found it when she heard Rune coming down the stairs. She tried not to smile, watching him stumble in, still half asleep, to sit at the table. She almost had to stifle a laugh as she watched him wait with Lucy, with not quite complete patience, as Serena finished serving their breakfast. She served Lucy first, and then dished up as much as she thought she would eat onto her plate. The rest of the hash, and the most sizable quantity, she pointedly emptied onto Rune's plate, setting it down in front of him with a soft thud just to hear him laugh. If he left the table still hungry today, it was no one's fault but his own.

Breakfast finished, dishes washed, and their hair done, Serena and Lucy left the house while Rune enjoyed a hot bath. They were going toward Jane's instead of the summerhouse when they heard a commotion in the distance.

Jane and the soldier Serena had met nights before were having words. Jane walked away from him, and he'd run to catch up.

Serena and Lucy hung back, following at a distance but not quite out of earshot. They were curious as to where they were going, and what the man had said that seemed to have Jane so upset with him. He was certainly feeling better than he had the last time Serena had seen him.

"What do you think he did?" Serena asked, actually sort of glad it was not she on the receiving end of Jane's ire. It was almost satisfying watching her be upset with someone else.

"I don't know, but he's sure got her knickers in a bunch," Lucy quipped, making Serena cant her head at what, for Lucy, was a very odd analogy. Lucy's humor was usually squeaky clean. She really hoped she hadn't been rubbing off on her that badly.

"Do you think he made a pass at her?" Serena asked, laughing at Lucy's remark.

"Nah, he's still got kneecaps." Lucy laughed, covering her mouth as she almost snorted loud enough to be heard down the road. "Jane doesn't do affection, she used to go on and on to Charlie and me about how romance was nonsense, not that I believe her. They're calling each other by their last names, this is just too much."

Serena felt as if her stomach was going to burst if they laughed any harder. It was the first time she had truly laughed in the entire time she had been there. There were moments when she feared she would never laugh or smile again, but surprisingly, it was passing. She couldn't say she was truly happy, but small moments of joy were finally shining through.

Instead of following Jane and the soldier all the way to the summerhouse, they took another path that let out down the beach.

The waves became bigger and the shoreline rockier the closer they came toward the lighthouse.

For reasons neither of them could explain, Serena and Lucy felt only dread being so close to the lighthouse. They both remembered the events a few nights ago. Neither wished to be even as close as they had been on the beach if the lighthouse were to come to life, though for that moment, it remained still with a soft glow within.

That soft glow at the top was enough to send Serena and Lucy fleeing as fast as their feet could carry them back into the woods. Serena's hair stood on end as she ran, expecting that at any moment the shockwave from the fog horn would sweep her off her feet and carry her out to sea by the waves without Rune there to hold onto her. That terror was one of many that plagued her mind as she ran, careful to ensure that Lucy was not too far behind.

They didn't stop to breathe a sigh of relief until they were back among the trees and off the beach. They dropped to their knees in the first small clearing they came to. They could hear the sounds of children running happily down a path that passed nearby as if they hadn't a care in the world, but it still took what seemed far too long to calm the pounding of their hearts.

"I was afraid. I don't know why," Lucy said, her eyes filled with fear as she looked up at Serena. She nervously pulled at the buttercups in the grass that were already staining her knees.

"It's not just you, I was too. It just felt as if something horrible would happen if we didn't run away," Serena answered, her voice shaking, not sure she really had words to explain all that had passed through her mind as they fled the beach.

"I don't think we should walk that way again," Lucy said, shivering, but fighting her way to her feet. She stood there until Serena caught her breath enough to join her.

"I don't think so either, but I'm not sure the others would understand," Serena said, hugging herself as she and Lucy resumed walking.

She saw the owl again. It sat perched on a high rock a short distance ahead, in clear view, though Lucy had not seen it that time either, nor mentioned it. She hadn't been afraid until she noticed it watching her, remembering what had come shortly thereafter last time she had seen it. Serena was afraid that if she told anyone again, they'd only think she was starting to lose her mind.

CHAPTER TWENTY-SIX

SERENA DIDN'T WANT to go back toward the beach, let alone the summerhouse, but against her own sense of comfort, she had to at least accompany Lucy there. She made it clear that she had no intention of staying, at least no longer than was necessary to be polite to the others. The gathering was not for many hours, and she wished to spend the day in a quiet place, far from that damned lighthouse.

A part of her wished to go home and forget about gatherings or responsibilities. She wanted to lie on the sofa, listen to those old records and lose herself in a book. She'd never had time to do those things before she'd come there. Her life before had always been spent working, giving her no time to do more than sleep at her own apartment. She was grateful to find herself in that old farmhouse, and not the shabby apartment she'd only been miserable in.

Lucy ran ahead of her once they reached the clearing where the summerhouse sat, no doubt in a hurry to get inside to check on Alec.

He was awake and sitting up in a comfortable chair, with an ottoman under his feet when she joined them. She was unsurprised to find Lucy hovering around him, plying him with sweets and cookies. Alec seemed to look at her no differently than any other child among them, even though she seemed determined to mother him as she had Serena in the first few days after she'd arrived.

None of them were quite certain just how much of their predicament Alec truly understood, but he was sweet natured, even when in pain and frightened. He still did not seem to understand why Iona had pushed him, but he was reassured when Lucy had told him that they wouldn't let Iona harm him again.

"Is she here?" Alec asked, looking nervous and using his good arm to pull the blankets up to his chin.

"Yes, but she is in the cellar, and she is not allowed to come out until it is time for her to go home. No one is going to let her come near you," Lucy replied.

Serena watched everything from the summerhouse doorway. The unease inside her had not subsided, nor was her desire to leave lessening as time passed. If anything, seeing Alec's fear was only worsening her own.

She slipped away without a word, walking without breaking into a run, back toward the closest path into the trees. She felt as if she could barely catch her breath, her heart pounded in her ears until she traveled far back into the woods. She stopped to kneel at the foot of an ancient oak. It was the worst anxiety attack she'd had in years.

Frightened tears started falling as she knelt there, hugging herself and shivering as she fought to catch her breath. She feared she would lose her grasp on her sanity and start to see those damned owls again, but none came and the woods remained silent around her.

She screamed in fright when hands landed softly on her shoulders. Her voice failed her as she spun around to see Rune standing over her in the darkness.

"Are you hurt?" Rune asked, concern in his eyes as he knelt to scoop her up.

"No, but I'm afraid," Serena answered as she held onto him, shaking like a leaf, and unable to stop the tears from falling.

"All will be well, we will go and find the others," Rune whispered, rising to his feet while still cradling her against him.

Serena shook her head.

"I don't want to be near the others. I just want to find a quiet place far from here," Serena said softly, her voice still quivering. "I don't want to think about what's happened these last few days, the fog, or that damned lighthouse. I understand now why even Lucy is so afraid."

"Did something happen?" Rune asked her, turning to walk back the way he had come, still carrying her in his arms. He was not surprised when she squirmed to be let down to walk beside him.

"Lucy and I were walking on the beach, far down the shore, and then suddenly I looked up toward the lighthouse, and it was so clear in my mind. I could just picture it, the lighthouse, the fog, and being swept out to sea. I think Lucy did too because we both ran back toward the woods as fast as we could. I was so frightened that at any moment I'd be swept away if you weren't there to hold onto me."

"But you were not, and I am here now. I cannot always be near, so you must be brave. If I am not there to hold you in my arms when fear or danger comes, I will be there for you to run to once it has passed." Rune kept his arm around Serena all the way back to his home. He held the lantern for her as he let her unlock the door.

Serena sat by the light of the lantern quietly, as he lit the fire within the hearth as easily as if he'd been given matches. If only he'd known of her foolish attempts to light it, she was sure he'd be ashamed of her incompetence. She tried to study the things he did differently.

"What is it you wish, love of mine?" Rune asked her, when he turned to notice the way she was watching him.

With the fire lit and crackling to life, he crawled the short distance to where she knelt atop the furs, looking sad and weary. The lantern was put out and set aside carefully before she climbed into his arms with an eagerness he didn't think possible from her mere days before.

"Make me forget," Serena whispered, reaching up to cup his face before she kissed him softly.

"Are you wanting me, or merely a distraction?" Rune asked her pointedly. He had no preference to her answer, but he wanted her to believe that he did.

"Am I allowed to want both?" she asked with a sheepish expression, worried for a moment that he would push her away, but she sighed contentedly when he pulled her closer.

"Yes, wife of mine, you are more than allowed. You want me; I have very much wished to hear those words from you."

Serena sighed as Rune's lips found her neck, his whiskers rough against her collarbone. She did not wait for him to tug at her dress; she was already pulling it up. He helped her lift it over her head, leaving her all but bare straddling his lap.

He growled low in his throat and tore her panties in his impatience to remove them. His mouth sucked down on her neck harder, determined to renew the mark that had until then been fading. This time she did not fight him or try to pull away.

Her sighs became whimpers when she felt his hands slowly sliding downward, not the slightest hesitation in his touch as he pulled her tighter against him. She moaned into his mouth when he raised his head to kiss her deeply, letting herself be rocked against him in his lap. She was lifted upward into his arms only to be laid back down on the furs again.

Rune did not bother to undress in his impatience, taking her as soon as his trousers were undone. He smiled at her gasp, enjoying the feel of her hands gripping the sides of his tunic. "If you ask, I will give," he told her, not expecting more than her cries in response. All he wanted was to do his best to please her, in however long a time he was capable of holding off what always seemed inevitable.

He did not lie naked at her side until afterward. They lay facing each other holding the other tightly. She could feel the warmth of the fire on her back as his fingers gently raked across her skin.

"You make me forget," she told him, her fingers curling into his hair as her thumb traced his jawline. She had never noticed how blue his eyes were until she saw them in the brightness of the firelight as he gazed down at her.

"Forget what, love?" Rune asked her, placing a soft kiss on her forehead.

"How afraid I am."

"Of what, love?"

"Of this place, and what will happen to us if we stay," she said softly, her voice once again trembling.

"There is nothing to fear, we will face it all together," Rune told her, concerned to see the sadness in her eyes when he spoke those words.

"If we can never have a child, will I be enough for you?" Serena asked him, almost unable to look at him when she asked him that question, knowing just how badly he wanted a son.

"You fear that I will leave as all others have done?" Rune asked her, she seemed unable to answer, but he saw her tears and pulled her closer to him, trying to dry her tears with kisses. "You are my wife. I have given you my word; have no doubt in it. When one of us parts; it will be to the next world, and if you go first, I will quickly follow."

CHAPTER TWENTY-SEVEN

LUKE LOOKED Alec over with a concerned expression on his face. He examined the crude stitches Martha had done. They were not as neat as would have been the standard, but adequate unless he wished to reopen the wound. "This is going to scar, no way around it."

"You didn't actually go inside the summerhouse yesterday, did you, Mr. Fernsby?" Jane asked, rather annoyed with him. First he questioned her sanity, and now it seemed even the best care they'd been able to give the boy. "You never once mentioned that you had medical training, Mr. Fernsby, and when we found you, as I recall, you were the one in need of a doctor."

"I'm no doctor, Mrs. Boyd, just an Army Medic," Luke said, turning to Jane. Her arms were crossed and defensive. "I'm not a miracle worker, but I can usually handle minor injuries and keep the boys stable until more help arrives."

"There is no more help, Mr. Fernsby, only us. We do what we can with what we have," Jane answered, maybe just a little too angrily for even her own liking. Something about this man was pushing all the wrong buttons. "I assure you, this is not the sort of injury that we see here often. Young Alec was attacked; he did not injure himself on his own."

"Where is the man responsible for this?" Luke asked, rising to his feet and coming closer, making Jane want to take a step back, though; she would not back down from him so easily.

"She is, at the present time, locked in the cellar until we can prepare a better place to confine her. The men are working on it now," Jane answered matter-of-factly, making it a point to keep her gaze direct. "As soon as they have finished installing the bars across her doorway, the young woman will be confined in her home until she proves herself no longer a threat. She not only injured the boy, but she stole from several homes, though it seems she did that to feed herself. Most of what we recovered once she was captured was either food, or things she could use to keep herself warm. Her home contained little, not much more than a pile of thatched straw for a bed, and some beaten up pots and pans for cooking."

"Sounds like someone hungry and desperate to me, Mrs. Boyd. You see a lot of that with a war on," Luke answered her, "I don't mean to sound like I am trying to make any excuses for her actions, I'm just trying to make sense of it all."

"I told you, Mr. Fernsby, there is no sense to be made here."

"It sounds to me, from what you've told me, and what Alec has said happened, that the girl was either desperate or frightened, probably both. There'll be no way of telling until you're able to ask her questions in a way that won't scare her out of her mind. I've been hearing the crying coming out of that cellar since I stepped inside. Is this how you treat everyone who misbehaves here? Lock them in the dark by themselves?"

"It isn't often we have to deal with this sort of misbehavior, Mr. Fernsby," Jane answered him, furious. He was practically a stranger and knew almost nothing of this world, and their predicament. How dare he question her motives? "It is only rarely we see violence of any sort here, but rest assured, we intend to see that it is dealt with and that this young lady's transgressions do not repeat themselves."

"And if they do, Mrs. Boyd, how would you be prepared to deal with it?" Luke asked, stepping almost toe to toe with her, wanting to get a good feel for the honesty of her answer, but more so, to see if she really would turn tail and run when confronted.

"We'd have no choice but to banish her beyond our borders, Mr. Fernsby," Jane answered firmly, more than ready to let her hand fly at his face if he came even an inch closer. "There are borders here, that even we do not cross, barring danger to one of our own. She would be shown past the gate, and it would be sealed behind her."

"You would consider that a humane solution?"

"It's more humane than other alternatives I could think of, Mr. Fernsby. Would you prefer we go all 'eye for an eye' and push her off a higher cliff?"

"You are maddening, do you know that, Mrs. Boyd?" Luke said, losing his patience with her, almost certain she was driving him there on purpose.

"Will you guys stop fighting?" Alec shouted, looking distressed and trying to lift himself up out of his chair.

His concern shook them for a moment long enough to distract them from their disagreement. Jane rushed to try to settle Alec back into the chair again. She could only leave it up to the others to try to soothe him when Alec did not respond well to having her or Luke close to him until they calmed down.

Jane was tired of arguing. She stormed off outside, walking away without looking back until she was a good distance down the beach. She perched herself on the rocks, with her back toward the summerhouse, staring out at the ocean. She was no fonder of it than she had been in all the time she had spent in this place. Nothing about it, or the sky, ever changed, except the size of the waves.

Only that oversized moon that moved within the sky told of the passage of time, crossing the sky each day, only to arise on the other side as soon as it had finished setting. The moonrise was the beginning of their day, as the midnight hour would have been in the life they had left behind. Their nights were the hours the moon hung low and crept slowly toward the horizon, only to rise again. There had to be some way to mark the passage of the hours, or time would once again start running together; she feared the very thought of it.

"I don't know what I've done to upset you, Jane Boyd, but I have not meant to cause offense," Luke said, standing a few steps behind her.

Jane turned around, surprised to see Luke standing there. She took a deep breath, fighting the urge to be angry at him for following, even if she could not help but give him a piece of her mind. "You questioned my sanity, you called me a liar, and now you've cast doubt on my ability to lead the people I've been helping to care for, for almost twenty years, Luke Fernsby. What is a lady supposed to think of your words?"

"I was upset when I said those things before, and I'm sorry, but I was quite serious about what I asked moments ago. Leading is not easy Jane. I want you to be sure that the decisions you make are ones you can live with. You have no idea of the bad choices I have made that I must live with."

"You don't think I know how that feels, Mr. Fernsby? I care for these people, day in, day out; if they need me, I am there for them. You don't think it kills me to know that there are things that even I cannot save them from? Until this happened, the worst enemy known to us has been time, watching my friends, people I care for, growing younger before my very eyes, until there's nothing left of them but a helpless babe, that one day fades away and is gone. That is the hell we are up against, knowing that someday, no matter what you do, that's going to be your fate as well."

"I know you care for the others, but you can't take care of them by pushing everyone away from you," Luke said thoughtfully. "You have to let someone else take care of you too. I don't care who that happens to be, but you can't shut the whole world out, or pretend you're the only one trying to hold the sky up over our heads. It's nonsense like that that really will drive someone mad. Whether you believe me or not, I have been there."

"You don't know a thing about my life, or what I've been through."

"And you don't know mine, Jane, and you never will unless you stop throwing a wall up between us. I want to be your friend, and I want to help you; that's all I'm asking. Let me at least try to be a voice of reason, even when you're thinking I'm only trying to be the devil's advocate."

"Do you still think I'm insane?" she asked him, trying to get to the bottom of what had been his most painful remark.

"No, and I'm sorry to have said it, but my goodness woman, you're ridiculously headstrong, and you're not easy to win over," Luke replied, not even trying to hide his frustration as he paced. He kicked at a loose pebble with his shoe. "Do you really want us to keep going around like this? I'm exhausted, and I'd much rather go back to us just being Jane and Luke if you don't mind? Please?"

Jane turned from him, having been distracted by a flash of light. Horror filled her as the beam of the lighthouse started to sweep the night. She shot up from the rock to her feet, grabbing Luke's hand and pulling him quickly toward the safety of the tree line and off the beach.

"Jane, what's gotten into you? Where in the bloody hell are we going?" Luke shouted at her, letting himself be pulled along, only to have his voice drowned out by the billowing of the foghorn. Terror filled him.

The ground shook violently under their feet. He and Jane stopped under a large and sturdy oak tree, using the trunk to steady themselves as the beam of the light swept over their heads and came to rest a short distance to the Northwest.

There were no sounds of bombs and gunfire. The horn and the fog faded away as quickly as it had begun, the lighthouse returning once again to its pale, steady glow.

"What the hell was that?" Luke asked her as they stood there in the quickly fading mist.

"The lighthouse and the fog announce the presence of a new arrival," Jane told him, beginning to hurry her way back toward the summerhouse where she knew the others would be waiting. "Last time we saw the light, it was you that came, and now it seems there has been another. I have never seen so many come so quickly in all my years here."

The first of the searchers were already pouring onto the beach, coming as soon as the fog had cleared enough for them to do so safely.

Jane had been sure enough of the direction of the beam that they'd gone ahead in a team of half a dozen, leaving Luke standing next to Lucy.

Jane wished to waste no time in her searching. When the light and the fog were brief, it usually foretold the coming of a child who must, above all else, be found quickly. No more than twenty minutes had passed when someone on the second team blew a whistle as a signal that something had been located. The new house was a short distance to the North of where Jane and her team had been looking.

It did not take long for them to hurry to catch up with the others, the clearing containing only a shabby looking tract house with broken shutters and a badly cracked sidewalk. The yard was unkempt and littered with badly sun-faded lawn toys.

The house was filthy and cluttered inside, the floor covered with discarded clothes, papers, and scattered toys for both older and younger children.

Jane paid no mind to the kitchen or the laundry beyond the living room through an archway. She made her way straight through to the hallway toward the bedrooms.

She could hear him already crying before she found him. It was a little boy with dark hair and a dusky complexion who wore shabby footy pajamas with holes in the toes. Jane figured he could be no more than two years old. He stood in the crib with only a stained sheet and no blankets. Jane rushed over to him, lifted him from the crib, and tried to soothe him.

"I'll take him back with me to the summer house," Jane told Robert. "Stay here awhile and look through things. See if you can find something, anything, to tell us what his name might be."

Jane turned back when the child started to cry. She reached for a threadbare stuffed dog, which seemed to have been his only companion as he slept. The child seemed less afraid once it was handed to him, holding onto it tightly for the rest of the walk back to the summerhouse.

Jane left the boy to Martha's care, until a long-term caregiver among them could be decided upon. Though well practiced as a mother, Jane was all but certain that she was not the caregiver he needed.

As much as Jane loved small children, it sometimes broke her heart to pieces to be near them; especially this beautiful little dark haired, dark eyed boy. He bore more than a passing resemblance to how her children had looked at a similar age. No, she could not be the right one to care for him, but it did not keep her from wishing he were her own just a little too badly.

CHAPTER TWENTY-EIGHT

Serena had been content to lie there, letting the glow of the fire warm her skin. Her fingers gripped the softness of the furs when Rune lay over her once again. Her soft cries became frightened ones when she heard the low roar of the foghorn and the earth began to move beneath them.

"Do not be afraid. I am here," Rune tried to reassure her as he held onto her more firmly, pinning her harder into the furs, and thrusting his hips in time with the shaking. He wished to make her forget her fear, and to pleasure her until the trembling passed, though that had not come until well after the sound had faded away.

"All has passed, and you lie safe in my arms," Rune told her, lying his head on her breast afterward.

Serena's hand stroked his hair as she thought of how badly she wished they could lie there and forget the world outside the door. They both knew, however, the coming of the fog would mean yet another knock at the door if they did not rise to make their way to the summerhouse on their own.

It was only with disappointed sighs that they rose from the floor, pulling their clothes back on. Serena did not care to know what was out there. All she wanted was to stay with Rune and go back to lying by the fire next to him.

"We need to go to my home on the way," Serena told him, trying to keep the skirt of her dress tugged as low as it would go, blushing and self-conscious as they made their way down the path for her lack of underwear beneath her clothes. "I need to get better clothes on for the search, you've torn them."

Rune chuckled low in his throat. The arm that had been wrapped around her waist slid under the back of her skirt to caress her bottom. "Next time you would do well to take them off on your own."

Rune's soft laugh turned into a roaring one when she reached to swat his hand away before holding onto it tightly for the rest of the short walk in a bid to keep him from trying it again. He waited on the porch, rather amused with himself as Serena went inside to get dressed in more appropriate clothes and shoes. She was still zipping her hoodie when she came outside. Rune reached to close the door behind her.

"You need to learn to behave." She could only shake her head and giggle at him when he swatted her behind as she made her way down the steps and toward the trail.

"I have told you, I do not know the meaning of that word." He smirked, taking her hand and holding it tightly as they hurried down the trail. Jane would already not be happy about the amount of time that had elapsed between when they'd heard the foghorn and when they'd manage to arrive.

The woods were quiet again as they walked, and only the very last lingering bit of the mist clung faintly in the low-lying areas. When she only seemed to be slowing them down trying to be careful of her footing, Rune had seen fit to do what he often did to Lucy. He lifted her onto his back to carry her as if she weighed almost nothing.

Serena decided to take her revenge by biting at his ear playfully and laughing at his warnings to her about what would happen later if she didn't stop. At least she had been laughing too hard to be quite as afraid as she had been before they left.

They were confused to find many of the searchers standing

around in the clearing outside the summerhouse waiting with Jane nowhere in sight. Luke and Lucy were among them.

Lucy explained that Jane had already left with the first handful of searchers that had made it there the quickest. It was unusual for her to run off so quickly and not wait for the others.

Serena stood by Rune's side as the small crowd debated and wondered if they should go searching after the first group. They had no idea where to even begin looking for them. They were becoming very worried when Jane emerged a few moments later carrying a tiny boy with shaggy dark hair in her arms.

The tears had still not dried on his cheeks when Jane came close enough for Serena to study the little boy's face. The child's knuckles were almost white from hanging onto a filthy, well-loved, brown and white stuffed dog with grubby hands. He buried his face against Jane's chest when he saw Rune drawing near, letting out a plaintive wail.

Serena felt as if her heart would crack into pieces to hear his cries, and she was relieved when Martha rushed out from the summerhouse to take the child inside, but she feared he would not be easily consoled.

"What could he be doing here? He's just a baby," Serena asked Jane, ready to cry herself for reasons she couldn't explain.

"Those that come here can be of any age," Jane said quietly. For a moment, she seemed sad and visibly weary. "I cannot fathom what could have happened to him that sent him here. I'm not sure I want to try."

Jane stepped away, going off to sit by herself further down the beach. Serena watched her go, and was slightly surprised to see Luke and not Lucy, following slowly after her.

Lucy came closer to them, poking Rune in the ribs to break their embrace. She stood, arms raised, asking to be picked up. It was the only way, short of making them kneel down to her level, that she could look them both in the eye as they talked.

"He'll be all right. They're usually just sad and scared for the first few days. Don't cry," Lucy said, reaching to poke Serena on the nose in an attempt to make her laugh. "Believe me, the children always handle the change far better than the rest of us. We'll just have to see whom he bonds with. That person will be the one to take care of him, or at least help the person who does, if there's a reason they can't."

"You know, sometimes, until something like this happens, I almost forget how old you really are," Serena told her, her arms reaching to hug Lucy in between her and Rune.

"Someday soon, I'll forget that myself," Lucy said, almost looking a little sad, though that look in her eyes passed fleetingly.

"When that time comes, we will care for you," Rune said, trying to reassure her. He tickled her cheek with the roughness of his whiskers, worried that Lucy would cry if he did not make her laugh.

Lucy squirmed and squealed to get away from him, but Rune held onto her tightly. "I know, stop it, stop it!" she screeched, but Rune did not cease until she went limp as a noodle and stopped pummeling his back with her tiny fists.

Lucy was in no shape to cry, let alone draw in a steady breath. She nearly wet herself, and would have if it had gone on much longer. "That's not fair."

"You both keep telling me to behave. I do not know the meaning of that word." Rune laughed heartily, finally standing Lucy back up onto her feet.

"Not funny," Lucy said, shaking her head before taking each of them by a hand and pulling them toward the summerhouse.

Inside, some of the children rested on the floor near the fireplace, staring with dismay at the tears of the newcomer. Some of the smaller ones joined him in wailing as Martha changed his diaper and gave him a sponge bath. She dressed the boy in clean pajamas once he smelled of the sweet perfume of the soap, but he could not be consoled until he'd been given a bottle full of milk.

Alec looked alarmed when the boy toddled over to him, climbed up onto his lap, and leaned back to rest against his belly as he drank his milk. Surprisingly, he wouldn't let the boy be moved away when someone had come to retrieve him. The child was asleep within minutes, clinging onto that stuffed dog that he dragged over there with him.

"Looks like you're going to be stuck with him for a while Alec. Is that all right?" Lucy asked him, stepping away from Rune and Serena to let them settle themselves at a table with the food they'd brought with them.

"We can both sleep here; it's a comfortable chair," was all Alec had to say about it. He closed his own eyes, apparently just fine with letting the child stay right where he was for the time being.

It was some time later before the rest of the search party returned. Robert and a couple of the others appeared disturbed. Robert could barely look at Lucy when she came closer, especially when she noticed that his knuckles were bleeding.

"How did it happen?" Lucy said alarmed. She tried to keep her voice low enough not to wake the little boy or alarm the others. She dragged him over to Martha to have the cuts tended to at the sink.

"Relax, old woman, I just punched the mirror," Robert told Lucy, trying to calm the anger that was still just below the surface. "I couldn't help it after what I'd seen on the other side. I should have known better than to look."

"Someone killed him, didn't they?" Lucy asked him, tears welling up when Robert nodded. "What's his name?" she asked him, wondering if he'd at least been able to find out that much. Far too often that wasn't the case, and they had to choose a new name for a child too young to tell their own.

"Andrew," Robert told her after taking a minute to calm himself. "Though, it seems they may have called him Drew."

"Drew it is then, we'll let the others know when they ask." Lucy nodded, walking away from him and making her way to the table where Rune and Serena waited for her.

Lucy picked at the meal that was set in front of her as she tried to find the words to explain. She watched the changing expressions on their faces as she told them what she now knew. In all the years she had lived there, the sad stories had never become any easier. If anything, Lucy was feeling them more deeply than before, now that she was a child again herself.

"We will go home," Rune said. He rose and picked Lucy up out of her chair, letting her climb onto his back as he and Serena started to make their way toward her home. "We can listen to the pretty music and tell stories, but for tonight, little one, no more sad ones."

They spent the rest of that evening sitting around the coffee table in Serena's living room, accompanied only by candlelight. Rune told stories as the music played softly in the background. He told of the northern gods, brave warriors, and beautiful women, but even he looked slightly sad when he spoke of his home, and his family from before.

"Children; I'd almost forgotten how much I missed them," Rune said quietly. He sat on the front steps with Serena staring up at the moon, after Lucy had gone to bed.

"Did you have any before?" Serena asked him quietly. Rune had never hidden his life with Kitta from her, though it was not often he spoke of it. She assumed the memory was a painful one.

"One daughter, two winters old when last I saw her. Kitta hid her to keep Ardal from finding her. I left my daughter to my mother's care when I went to go in search of her."

"What was her name?"

"Her name is Liv," Rune said, turning his gaze from the moon to look at Serena's face. "I have missed my daughter greatly in the time I have been away. She would almost be as Lucy is now if I had stayed, she reminds me so very much of her."

"Did you ever find out what happened to her mother?" Serena asked, needing to know more than wanting to, if Rune was willing to speak of it.

"I searched for many months following Ardal's footsteps. At first, I found some of his companions, but not him. I tortured the truth from the first before I killed him, and again from a second man before I believed it. Once out of sight of land, Kitta threw herself into the sea, rather than let herself be taken. She did not believe herself worthy to return to my arms after what Ardal and his men had done to her. I would never have turned her away."

Rune was trembling with anger as Serena tried to console him. Tears fell from her eyes, though he only stared blankly, unable to let his own fall. "From then on, all I could think of was hunting him. Every day only brought me closer to revenge. When that moment came; I gave my own life to take him to Hel with me. The rest you know, as you were there."

"Yes," Serena said, trying to dry her eyes as she came to kneel facing him on the ground between his knees. She wrapped her arms around him tightly. "I understand, so much more now about what happened between us then. I'm sorry that I did not understand, but I was so frightened."

"I would never have harmed you," Rune said, pulling her to him and resting his head atop of hers.

"Now I know, but you were quite a scary sight to behold when your hammer smashed the ground next to my head." She laughed, and so did he, looking back on it.

"I was a beast, but you have never backed down from me," Rune said, finally raising his head to look into her eyes. "Trust me when I say, I would have you no other way than that, wife of mine."

Serena followed quietly when he rose to his feet, holding out his hand to her. She rode on his back again through the darkness, clinging to him as they took a now familiar trail to where the moon again shone brightly off that shimmering pool she remembered well. They kissed deeply, their clothes scattering across the ground before she followed him into the water. She floated in his arms peacefully, staring up at the stars. She trusted he would not let her fall.

CHAPTER TWENTY-NINE

"I JUST WANT to be alone for a while, old woman, stop trying to mother me," Jane said, hearing footsteps coming up behind her, assuming they belonged to Lucy.

"You must be expecting someone else, Jane. I'm not mothering anyone," Luke said, still keeping a careful distance between them.

Jane spun around surprised, but not as much as she should have been. He was close to becoming a thorn in her side. "What is it you want?" she asked him, sick and tired of the arguing. All she wanted was some time to be alone.

"Just to talk, and to ask how you're feeling," Luke said, trying to keep the tone of his voice quiet and steady, and not give her any reason to feel provoked.

"I'm fine, there's no need to worry over me," Jane said. She turned to stare out at the water, hoping that he would take her answer as truth and leave, though she doubted it.

"You're not fine, Jane. I saw the look in your eyes when you came back from the forest tonight. You're anything but all right, and you're not fooling anyone," Luke said, closing the distance between them. He watched Jane shiver when she felt him standing behind her, even though he made no move to reach out to touch her.

"I will be once I've had time alone to think," Jane told him, trying a little too hard to hold her head high and straighten her back. Jane cried in front of no one, and if she chose someone to witness her tears, it wouldn't be him.

"See there you go, throwing that wall up again. I wish that you would stop. Lie to yourself all you want, I can see right through it though," Luke replied, bending down until his lips were almost pressing against her ear.

She shivered. He was far too close for comfort. She looked into his dark brown eyes as he invited himself to sit down next to her. "And just what would you have me do, stay and let it eat me alive? I know when I've reached my limitations."

"No," he answered, still leaning close. "That's when you need to talk to someone and let them share the burden before it tears you up inside. No one can do that for you, Jane, unless you allow it."

Without warning, Luke leaned in to kiss her. Though, she struggled at first. When his hand curled into the hair at the nape of her neck, her resistance faded. He didn't let her go until he was sure she wouldn't backhand him where he sat. She stared at him, utterly stunned, when he released her and rose to his feet.

"You are a devil, Luke Fernsby," Jane said only to hear him laugh softly at her words.

"And you, Jane Boyd, need to learn to do more of what you'd like to, and a little less of what you should," Luke said, holding his hand out to her. It didn't surprise him when she would not take it.

"We all do what we must."

"And I just have. Should you wish to discuss it, you know where to find me. Until then," Luke said, with a slight bow. He turned without another word, making his way back toward the summerhouse.

Luke figured it was high time he found someone to help him back to his own home before he was stranded there for the night. He was already far beyond tired and his strength, while returning, was still not quite what he'd have liked it to be.

Jane watched him go, trying to fight back the tears that were threatening to fall now that she was alone. The dam opened and she lost the battle. She allowed it to break only as briefly as she could manage, taking out her handkerchief to dab at her eyes to keep her makeup from running. She allowed no one to see her in that sort of state.

She almost called after him, her footsteps already having carried her halfway back to the summerhouse when she saw him leaving with some of the others who lived near him. She only stopped and stood to watch him go. Besides, Jane knew she had duties to attend to and her new charges to look after. She wanted to find Luke and give him a piece of her mind. She wouldn't until she was more clear headed, and had time to gather her thoughts about what she was actually thinking, much less feeling.

"Such a devil, just wait until I see you again!"

CHAPTER THIRTY

SERENA WAS ALARMED to hear screams coming out of the summerhouse when she arrived the next afternoon with Lucy. For the first time in days the cellar door was ajar. Jane stopped her from going inside, putting her arm across where she stood in the doorway. Serena looked at her; confused and frightened by the sounds, especially as she heard voices. She recognized only Rune's among them.

Rune had left the house after Robert had come to fetch him at Jane's request, though he wasn't able to tell her why. He'd left just after they'd eaten their breakfast, leaving her and Lucy behind to finish cleaning up and hang their washing in the back yard. They hadn't left to find him until she and Lucy had done their chores, they'd put on nicer clothes, and done each other's hair.

It was not the sort of spectacle Serena had expected to come upon. The only words she could make out of the conversation below were rope and stretcher. All the screaming drowned out the rest.

In the cellar, Robert and a few others had all but given up on subduing Iona enough to get her to cooperatively travel the distance to her home. That was when they'd called on Rune to assist them, which had made the girl even less cooperative than before.

Iona had already hit, scratched, or bitten nearly everyone in the room. One unlucky person had already found his hand sliced open with a sharp piece of metal she'd happened to find in the time she'd been below.

None of the others were skilled fighters, at least not in unarmed combat. It took only seconds for Rune to do what three or four others could not. He wrestled her to the floor, pried her improvised weapon from her hand, and pinned her face down in the dirt.

Rune dragged her over, letting the others hold her face down so he could bind her arms and feet to the stretcher as tightly as he could manage before securing her body. The last thing they needed was for her to be thrashing around as they carried her.

"For heaven's sake, someone put a towel or a blanket over her, no one wants to see that," Jane blurted out as she watched them carrying the girl up the steps on the stretcher.

Rune was at her head, and Robert was holding onto the other end at her feet. The way the rope had been wound through her legs and around her hips had caused Iona's dress to ride up, leaving her bottom quite noticeably exposed.

Serena turned a deep shade of red and turned away when she saw, making Rune wonder if she was upset with him since she couldn't quite bring herself to look in that direction.

An awkward moment or two passed before someone found an old sheet to drape over her. It would cover the girl from her shoulders to her ankles and leave Robert in a much less awkward predicament.

The stretcher was set on the floor as the sheet was being tied into place, leaving Rune a brief moment to pull Serena away from the others. He'd have to be blind not to notice her discomfort. It had taken several seconds for her to look up at him, and only after he'd turned her another direction.

"Are you displeased with me?" Rune asked her pointedly, the expression on his face one of concern. He had only been doing as he was asked. Considering the situation at hand, none of what had been asked of him seemed unreasonable.

"I'm not angry, Rune. I'm just not quite comfortable with this." She sighed, trying to keep her answer quiet, not wanting to stir up Jane's ire unless she had to. "I really wish they'd stop using you as their ball bat."

"Ball bat?" Rune canted his head, looking at her confused, making Serena want to smack herself for not remembering Rune would not have the first idea what she meant.

"I'm sorry. I forgot you don't know what that is. It's kind of like a big stick that you hit things with." Serena shook her head, frustrated. "What I meant is, I wish they'd stop using you as a weapon when they have a situation they don't know how to handle. They need to learn to fight their own battles, especially when it involves tying up a girl who really isn't wearing much."

Was Serena starting to feel slightly possessive? Rune couldn't tell for sure, but it was starting to seem so. It was the first time he'd noticed her setting any sort of claim to him, and telling him where she stood and what she expected as a wife would have done.

"You needn't worry, wife of mine, I am yours, not hers," Rune told her, reaching out to caress her cheek. He was happy when she curled her face into his hand instead of moving away.

"I know. I believe you," Serena answered, closing her eyes and letting Rune draw her close to him. "But, I don't think it's quite fair for them to put you in a situation where anything can be put into doubt. Jane should have been down there herself helping, not leaving it all to you if she wanted this done."

"Agreed, I will ask it to be so if this happens again," Rune said, kissing her softly on her forehead with a deep sigh. He did not think it an unreasonable thing for her to ask of him.

"I don't want this to take all day, let's get going," Jane said sternly to Rune from across the room where Robert stood waiting.

"Where are you going?" Serena asked, looking back and forth between Jane and Rune, her arms crossed defensively.

"Jane has requested that I assist with taking the thief back to her home. We should not be long," Rune answered, noticing a look from Serena that was half a glare more focused on Jane than him.

"Well then, it seems I'm coming too," was all that Serena had actually said. She had not raised her voice, or lost her temper, but

Rune could tell she was drawing a line in the sand. It was a statement of fact, not a request.

Jane wasn't pleased with the delay to her plans, or Serena's stubbornness for that matter, but she wanted to get the matter over and done with. Further argument could do no more than stoke her aggravation, and she was already far beyond stressed. "Follow me." Without another word, Jane led them out the door, not breaking her stride even for Robert and Rune to each pick up the stretcher.

Serena walked at Rune's side. They followed Jane as she walked at a determined pace several steps ahead of them on the trail. Serena was not sure what had happened the last few days, but Jane had gone from cold to gratingly bitchy.

The girl on the stretcher was doing no more to calm Serena's nerves or her temper, especially when she heard the names and curses she was throwing, most of them directed at Rune when she realized he was carrying her. Rune didn't pause or say a word to her in retaliation. He was exhibiting far more patience than Serena had once believed him capable of possessing. She likely would have believed the horrible deeds the girl implied he was capable of only a short time before, had she not come to know him better since.

They'd been halfway to their destination when first Jane, and then Serena, noticed something odd along the trail. Small arrows and rings made of medical tape were plastered to some of the trees at different crossroads throughout the woods. Once or twice Jane muttered to herself before stopping to rip the tape off the tree and let it fall to the ground.

"Would you mind not doing that, madam? I worked hard last night to put those up!" Luke said, stepping around the corner of another trail, where he'd just seen Jane taking down his marks.

"You'd do well not to waste precious supplies littering the woods, Luke Fernsby," Jane said, staring at him, annoyed both at the tape and the man's disheveled appearance. "Would you mind stepping aside? We have business to attend to."

The delay gave the rest of the group time to catch up to Jane, who caught the look in Luke's eyes when he realized just what was going on.

He took in the sight of Iona tied to the stretcher.

"Jane, would you mind telling me just what in the hell you think you're doing carting the girl off through the woods like this? You couldn't have just let her walk?" Luke asked, crossing his arms and not budging an inch to get a rise out of Jane; it was working.

"Well, next time we need to move her, we'll let you get to be the one she bites and stabs then," Jane replied, ready to skin him alive if he didn't move out of the way. "The preparations have already been made to put her under house arrest. All we're doing is taking her home, or would you rather we tossed her back into the cellar?"

"I'd rather you started treating the girl like a human being."

"I'll start doing that when she starts acting like one and stops attacking anyone who comes near her."

"What do you expect after the way she's been dealt with until now?"

"Do you think you could have done better? You're more than welcome to come with us if you'd like to be the one to untie her when we get there," Jane said, laughing manically at him. "I really don't think you'll make it away from her unscathed, but if you don't believe me, please, by all means; feel free to try."

Jane pushed past him and kept walking. Luke turned to follow her with the rest of the group fast on his heels.

There seemed to be fireworks between them, but not necessarily the good sort. Serena already thought that Jane and Luke were fighting far too much like an old married couple that was completely miserable together.

Once they reached the part of the trail where the ground started to get hilly, they had to watch their footing. By then, Rune was fairly sure of where he was going. The heavy, improvised iron gate was already securely in place, and Jane had already obtained a lock and a short piece of logging chain with which to secure it. She withdrew them from her bag as they carried the girl inside.

Jane and Serena were at least sensible enough to watch from

outside the doorway as they laid the stretcher down on the floor of the dugout. Rune sat astride the girl's waist to pin her down. Luke and Robert worked at the ropes to untie her.

The girl began thrashing as soon as her hands and feet were free, her feet more than once caught Robert in his stomach and chest before he could roll away from her. It caused Rune to utter a not-so-empty threat to snap her neck. He yanked the girl's head backward as she was in the process of trying to go for Luke's eyes with her nails. Luke's eyes escaped unscathed, but he still received angry jagged scratches to his right cheek.

Luke backed away, leaving only Rune there, with his hands both wrapped firmly across her mouth and nose, smothering her. The girl scratched at the leather gauntlets that covered his arms unable to claw her way through them.

Iona's face turned from red to almost blue, as she flailed, unable to breathe. Rune didn't break his hold on her until he felt her start to go limp.

Jane screamed at him to release her when she and Luke noticed what Rune had done. Luke shoved him away from the girl after he'd released her. He rolled the girl over onto her back to make sure that she was breathing. She was out cold but alive.

"How in the hell was that necessary?" Luke yelled in Rune's direction as Rune rose and moved toward the door, leaving Luke to tend to the girl.

Robert pulled the stretcher away.

"If you don't believe it was, next time I'll let her take your eyes," Rune answered bluntly, sliding past Jane to find Serena. Much to his relief, she didn't seem to have noticed what he'd done from where she'd been standing. "I'd suggest everyone get out and lock the door, she won't sleep long. You can be sure when she does awaken, she will be very unhappy with whoever is fool enough to still be inside her door," he told Jane before taking Serena by the hand and walking away, taking her with him.

"What did you do?" Serena asked, noting the glare that Jane had given him before they'd left.

"Nothing that will cause her permanent harm," Rune stated, trying to be truthful with as little detail as he could get by with. "I kept her from breathing to make her fall asleep. I assure you, she will awaken soon, frightened but otherwise well."

"I don't understand, why?" Serena told him honestly, confused and a little frightened by his confession as they walked together, even if she could tell Rune had taken no pleasure in doing it.

"To keep her from causing further harm to others. She already injured several of those who were supposed to have brought her home. One of them badly with a piece of metal she somehow fashioned into a weapon," Rune answered, feeling she really did deserve an explanation, not that he believed it would absolve him in her eyes, or in the eyes of the others. "That was when Jane sent for me, when the others proved incapable of subduing her. If she did not wish me to do what I felt needed to be done, perhaps I was not the one she should have called on."

"That's why I said the things I said before," Serena answered, the look in her eyes one of concern, and unease. "Jane needs to stop using you as a weapon. You never should have been put in that position, just because she didn't want to get her own hands dirty."

"The other men here do not seem to be fighters," Rune said matter-of-factly as they turned the corner of another trail. He drew her with him into a thick grove of live oak trees hung heavy with Spanish moss, the glow from Serena's lantern the solitary thing to break through the darkness.

"Perhaps they need to learn," she told him as she followed, careful to stay close to him and skirt around some of the low-lying branches. "They can't always rely on you, Rune, they need to learn to stand up for themselves."

Serena did not know what to think when Rune only nodded in agreement. He pulled her along until they were out of sight of the trail and into the darkness where not even the moon was able to penetrate the canopy overhead. She let out a soft cry when he took hold of her firmly, pushed her back against one of the ancient trees, and took the lantern from her hand. He dimmed the light and hooked it onto a small branch overhead.

"Do I have your trust, wife of mine?" Rune asked her pointedly, pinning her harder between himself and the tree. Serena quickly nodded her answer, but he could still clearly see just a hint of fear in her eyes. "Then do not cower, touch what is yours."

Serena's face flushed as he took her hand firmly and guided it to him, wanting her to feel, that which for that once, was neither hardened, nor growing. She looked up at him confused and unsure of the reason for his insistence.

"As you can see, I do not desire her, nor did I take pleasure in doing what I have done," Rune told her, letting go of her hand once he was sure she was certain of what he was telling her. He was rather surprised when she did not pull away from him.

"I had no doubt," she whispered, her face still flushed, her hand only falling to her side again now that he'd released it. "Rune, it's not your faithfulness I'm worried about. I don't want Jane to make you feel as if you have to obey her orders, especially when they might cause harm to someone."

"What would you have me do?" Rune asked her, his tone serious. His body relaxed, no longer leaning heavily against hers as his tension faded.

"Teach some of the others to fight if you must. I will never fault you for defending yourself or others. Rune, you shouldn't allow yourself to be used to exert control just because it's what Jane wants you to do for her," Serena told him, her voice just above a whisper. "I'm starting to see why Lucy is so upset with her. Jane is growing a little too fond of pushing her weight around."

"So it seems, but what has Jane done to her besides give the girl to us to care for?" Rune asked her, skeptical that things were quite as bad as Serena took them for.

"You don't know? Lucy's never told you?" Serena asked, canting her head at him, a little confused.

"Told me what, love?"

"That until only a short time ago it was Lucy and not Jane who was leader here. She went behind Lucy's back to gain control by making the others believe Lucy was no longer capable of leading," Serena answered. "Even now I've noticed Jane seems determined to treat her as if she really is a child, and not as the old woman she actually is. I realize that looking at Lucy it is easy to see a little girl and forget she is so much more than that, but Jane has known her long enough to have no excuse to forget."

"Jane is strong willed, but she will only have control if the others allow it," Rune answered, considering what Serena had told him.

"Before you do what she says, I want you to ask yourself if it's something that should be done, or something she just wants you to do for her own reasons. Don't be afraid to tell her no. There's way too much of that going on around here. Promise me, please?" Serena asked him with a sigh, reaching up to touch his cheek while running the back of her fingers along the roughness of his beard.

"All right, I will consider this. Let us speak of this no more and go home."

Serena was all too happy to oblige, relieved when he took her hand and led them back to the path toward home. She tensed as she heard the cries fading away behind them indicating that the girl had awakened to find herself caged, just as Rune said she would. Neither of them turned or even looked back. They quickened their steps, Serena yet again climbing onto his back to make the journey faster.

So many thoughts ran through her mind as she leaned her head against his. Of all the things Jane said, there was one thing Serena had to admit to. It was not only Rune, but also she that had changed. Through all that had happened, she'd finally chosen him.

Serena's arms wrapped around his shoulders tighter, and she curled her head down to brush her lips against his cheek. Her voice almost trembled as she at last found the courage to say the words, "I think I love you, husband of mine."

CHAPTER THIRTY-ONE

JANE, much to Luke's frustration, had no interest in waiting to make sure the girl awakened, before they dragged Luke out the door and chained the gate shut. They didn't bother to shut the flimsy wooden door behind it.

Luke, predictably, was anything but amused with the behavior he'd seen, least of all Jane's. The others only seemed to be perhaps too blindly following her.

"So, I take it you intend to keep the girl in there indefinitely?" Luke growled at her, relieved that the girl seemed to be moving. She groaned as she slowly crept toward consciousness. "Who died and made you god, madam? If she can't get out, how is she going to feed herself? You've already seen the girl has nothing. You could at least provide her with food and some comforts if you're determined to keep her a prisoner here."

"That's where you're wrong, Mr. Fernsby," Jane told him stubbornly, standing with her arms crossed defiantly after she'd finished securing the lock. She tucked the key into her bra under her bosom, where he didn't dare try to reach for it. "I refuse to reward her for bad behavior; if the girl wishes freedoms and comforts, she will have to earn them."

"So, you intend to starve her into submission?" Luke asked her, eyes narrowing with anger. He did not at all like the sound of what he'd heard coming from her mouth of all people. "Honestly madam, it makes you sound no better than the Nazi devils we've all been fighting against, or have you forgotten?"

"You take that back now!" Jane screamed at him, letting her hand fly in a fit of rage and backhanding him hard across the cheek Iona already had bleeding. Luke's blood spattered across her knuckles.

The blow rocked Luke, but he stood his ground, wincing as he rubbed his cheek and saw the blood, as Robert only watched and said nothing. "Does the truth hurt? At the very least tell me you have the heart to make sure she's clothed and fed well. You can't keep her caged like an animal and expect her to behave like anything less. Have some sense…and some morals whilst you're at it."

Jane rolled her eyes at him, fuming inside that he refused to recant the insult. Instead, she added, "Well then, perhaps since you are so concerned for her well-being, you should be the one to look after her. We'll see just how soon you tire of it."

"Delegating the things you don't want to do yourself to others doesn't absolve you of responsibility, Jane. It sure as hell doesn't make you a leader, only someone effective at barking orders," Luke told her, his anger growing the longer she refused to hear reason. "Did these people elect you to make choices for them, or did you just appoint yourself? Judging by your attitude, I'm going to assume it's the latter."

"You're being awfully presumptuous for someone who's been here not quite the length of a week, Mr. Fernsby," Jane told him, moving to step away and quite unpleased when Luke seemed determined to not let her pass. "Arriving in a uniform does not mean you get to be the one in charge here, any more than your being a man does, at least not in my eyes. I refuse to spend another lifetime taking orders from the likes of you, just because I'm a woman."

"You really think that's what this is all about?" Luke scoffed. "For Christ's sake, this has absolutely nothing to do with what you've got inside your blasted knickers, madam! What it does have to do with is your stubbornness, and your refusal to listen to anyone's opinion but your own. You'd do better to stop assuming the worst and let others make their own choices. I sincerely doubt today's events would have come to this, if you'd have just dealt with the girl calmly in the beginning when you'd had the chance, and could've given her time to explain herself. Now she's probably striking out blind at everyone 'cause you've got her scared half to death, thinking you're all out to harm her. You've given her no reason to think otherwise."

"Have you so easily forgotten what she's done, Mr. Fernsby?" Jane growled. "She shoved Alec over the edge of a cliff, and she easily could have killed him. At no time has she appeared to be the slightest bit remorseful."

"Have you given her a chance to be?" Luke yelled back at her. "No, you just locked her in a dark hole in the ground without giving her the slightest chance to explain herself. And if you should know, from what I learned by talking to the boy myself, it's bloody likely the girl was scared out of her mind and thought she was defending herself. He chased her, he caught her, and she pushed him away. That was how he fell. Have you even bothered to ask Alec how it happened, or were you still so angry she'd stolen food from your house that you didn't want to know? There's a big difference between someone who steals out of greed, and a frightened girl dressed in rags who steals for survival."

"You're being ridiculous now, Mr. Fernsby."

"No, if anything, I'm being quite serious. I just think you can't stand to admit you may be wrong. Life isn't black and white, Jane. When it comes to good and bad, no one person is all one or the other; some of us need more reminding of that than others."

The silence around them was interrupted by frightened sobs. The girl knelt in the doorway, her hands wrapped around the bars of her makeshift cell door.

Iona's cries devolved to wails of dismay, finding the door securely chained, only able to push her body against it before she collapsed into sobs.

Luke noticed the gauntness of the girl's face, and how her bones protruded when the collar of her dress slumped off her shoulder.

"She's starving to death, Jane, and if what you said of the means of our arrival is accurate, starvation is likely how she came to be here."

"I already told you, Mr. Fernsby, you're in charge of making sure that she's provided for now. If she's hungry, you'd better get to finding her something to eat," Jane said, brushing past him in his distraction and taking Robert with her. "I'll leave you to it, I have other things to tend to."

"Fine, Jane, run away, you know bloody well what I'm saying is the truth!" Luke called after her as he stood and watched her walk away, torn between chasing after her and making sure the girl in the hovel was provided for. In the end his conscience won out.

"I heard what you said," Iona told him with reddened eyes when he walked back over to stand just out of her reach near the doorway. Her voice was cracked, and her throat was dry and hoarse from all her screaming.

"You were starving?" he asked her, already certain he knew the girl's answer before he saw the nod she gave.

The hollowness of her cheeks looked even more prominent now that he'd come close enough to study her face.

"Yes, I was so hungry I felt I would die if I could not eat, so I stole it. They have so much more than they could need," Iona said weakly, looking up at him with pleading eyes. "Do they want me to die here? I have nothing. I thought the Northman would kill me. If you will not help me, why did you stop him? It would have been kinder to let me go quickly."

"I will do what I can for you," Luke told her, trying to fight down the awful feeling in the pit of his gut that made him want to hunt down Jane and give her a taste of her own medicine. "I cannot free you, because I do not have the keys, but I can bring you food if you can be patient while I gather it. Until then, this is all I have to offer you." Luke reached into his pocket and held out his hand to offer her a single gala apple that he'd plucked from a tree in the garden surrounding his home.

Iona cowered as she reached out with shaking hands to take the apple from Luke's grasp, half expecting him to snatch it away. No sooner was it in her hands, she'd devoured it ravenously, moments passing before she noticed the saddened look in his eyes as he watched her.

"I will bring you more to eat, but you must be patient and wait for me to return," Luke told her, noticing the frightened look in Iona's eyes when she asked him not to leave her there alone. "I swear to you; I will return as soon as I can. Until then, sleep and save your strength. I will see if I can find you a blanket before I return, and one of my mum's dresses for you."

Luke had to force himself to turn and walk away. He listened to her at first call after him, and then scream as she struggled to shake at the bars trying to free herself when he didn't return. He walked as quickly as he could toward home, holding his hands over his ears as he went, trying to block out the sound.

Honor and duty were all that would keep him moving toward home and not the summerhouse to make Jane regret the day she'd met him. He had a promise to keep, revenge could wait until he'd fulfilled it. Once he had, Jane had it coming. Luke was going to knock her down off her high horse once and for all.

CHAPTER THIRTY-TWO

ALEC HAD BEGUN GETTING antsy almost as soon as he was fully awake and unhappy that the others kept shooing him back into the chair. All he wanted to do was get up and look around. He'd been chased back several times, but when no one was looking, he kept making his way over to the window to watch the kids running back and forth on the beach.

That second night, Drew was not among them, perched instead on the steps outside on Carol's lap, no happier than he had been the previous evening. Lucy was trying her best to cheer him. She and a couple of older children were entertaining him with songs and simple games, though they did little to assuage his tears more than temporarily.

Lucy could not help but notice Alec's distress at being kept penned in, or his concern at listening to Drew's cries. It was obvious to her, if not many of the others, that Alec, while slow and child-like, meant no harm to anyone. He showed what only seemed to be genuine concern for the boy's distress.

"He lost his mama, didn't he?" Alec asked Lucy when she'd finally left the others to return inside the summerhouse to gather a fresh handkerchief to clean the tiny boy's face.

"Yes, Alec, he has, all of us have. None of the little children have parents here, at least not their real ones. That's why everyone will help take care of him."

"But what's going to happen to Drew if his mama doesn't come back?" Alec asked her, his uninjured arm tugging nervously at the straps of his overalls and the sling that held his other arm.

"If she doesn't, then soon we'll all help choose a new mama or papa for him that lives here, and he will stay with us," Lucy answered him calmly. It was more complicated than that, but Lucy was trying to give him simple answers she thought he would understand.

"You have a new mama and papa now, don't you?" Alec asked her, remembering a little of what he'd seen over the last few days. "Serena is your new mama, and the big man is your papa. He scares me."

"Rune won't hurt you, Alec, you don't have to be afraid," Lucy told him, trying to lead him back over to his chair. She got him to sit at least, but she only shrugged when he wouldn't allow himself to be tucked back under his blanket. She was sure his bare feet had to be freezing cold. "Rune won't hurt anyone unless they are trying to hurt him, or somebody else, well at least, not unless they did something really bad. He just looks scary, but he's really not, I promise."

Alec didn't relent about being covered up until he saw Jane come through the door. Lucy could tell that Jane frightened him, most likely due to her sternness. Her foul mood radiated off her as soon as she came in the door, making Lucy only want to stay clear of her.

Lucy was relieved that, for the moment, Jane only seemed interested in the coffee. She poured herself a large mug before skulking off into a quiet corner near the window to drink it. Jane perched on the window seat that Alec had vacated only a moment or two before.

Jane's eyes stayed peeled to the path she'd come from not long before as if she expected to have been followed. Lucy could not decide whether it would be better if the person she was expecting were to come or not. Jane seemed to be all but itching for a fight.

"I'm taking Alec out to the pier with me. I think he could use some fresh air," Lucy said, tugging at Alec's hand and helping him to toss the covers aside again. She really didn't want to give Jane much chance to object, nor did she want Jane to take her foul mood out on him if she walked out and left him there alone.

Within seconds, they were out the door. Lucy handed Carol the handkerchief for Drew before she tugged Alec further down the beach.

The pier was a short distance away and not so far that they couldn't be seen, so she didn't think it would give Jane much leg to stand on that they shouldn't be there.

On the way there, Alec kept stooping to pick up leaves, much to her annoyance, but she didn't say anything to him about it. She just encouraged him to keep walking before Jane got the notion to come after them, or give them a reason they couldn't go.

The pier was mostly empty when they settled in at the end. Alec did his best to sit down without having to rely on his hands. He let his feet dangle into the water as if he didn't have a care in the world. Lucy sat cross-legged, glad of the bloomers under the sundress.

Alec sat quietly, doing his best to fold the leaf in half with only his good hand until he had poked the stem through the bottom to make a loop. He gently placed his leaf boat onto the water at his feet. Within minutes, three or four others joined the first. Alec settled back, satisfied with his handiwork.

Lucy was unsure what to do until Serena or Rune came back to get her. She'd stay clear of Jane and hope someone was traveling the way she needed to go back toward Serena's home. Given that chance, she'd be far more comfortable with the thought of spending the rest of the day there, even if it were alone. She'd be fine with the room full of toys or the old phonograph to keep her company.

For that moment, Alec was all that seemed to keep Lucy there, her wanting to help him winning out over her desire to leave. She was determined to linger until Alec's leaf boats held no more appeal for him, and even more so, until Jane appeared calmer. Until then, Jane was unpredictable at best, and she would take it out on anyone who annoyed her. Alec...poor Alec, with his strange child-like ways, would have been all but a sitting duck waiting for her to go off on him.

CHAPTER THIRTY-THREE

LUKE'S HEART was still pounding when he finally reached the cottage. Fortunately for him, Jane had not managed to remove all his trail marks. Once he found his way back to where he'd met up with her, it had been fairly easy going. He just had to be sure along the way to make new ones to help him find his way back again. Thankfully, he didn't have very far to travel.

The cottage was predictably quiet when he made his way indoors. He scavenged his way through the larder, looking for food that he could put together quickly. He wasn't much of a cook. He came across some tinned beef stew, but couldn't think of a quick way to heat it. He still possessed the old thermos that Jane had left behind, so he decided to do his best to create a half decent meal.

It was a large family-sized can, so he dished out half of it into a saucepan, sitting the rest on the shelf for later. He sat it on the old pot-bellied stove, the only way he could figure to warm it. He gathered up half of the leftover bread from his meal the day before while he waited for it to warm. He added a few crackers out of a box he found in the cupboard and tied it all up into a parcel inside a clean handkerchief, along with a sizable piece of cheese and some smoked sausage he got out of the larder. He placed it all into the basket that Jane had also left behind.

It seemed to take forever for the stew to heat, but not as long as it would have if he hadn't stayed busy. He set the thermos into the sink and poured the stew into it, doing his best not to spill a drop. He filled the thermos to the brim, but ended up with a little still left in the saucepan. Grabbing a spoon from the table, he ate the rest straight out of the pot, sopping up the last of the juice with the hardened crust of the day old bread. That finished, he filled an old glass milk bottle with water from the sink, capping it, and then testing the seal to make sure it wouldn't leak.

The thermos capped, and the outside cleaned from where he'd spilled only a little bit down the side, Luke placed the thermos and bottle into the basket. He set an old spoon inside before he remembered his promise of a dress and a blanket.

Luke threw open the doors of the old wardrobe, nearly overcome with the smell of mothballs and old wool. His mother was a tiny woman, but Luke knew that his mother's few simple dresses would most likely be quite big for her seeing as the girl was frighteningly thin.

He finally settled on the long sleeved work dress his mum had once worn when working around the cottage, or tending to her garden. It seemed to be the most rugged thing the wardrobe held. He doubted it would be worse for the wear, or ruined if it became dirty, and it would hold up much better than her nicer Sunday dress. The only thing he'd been able to find the girl for her feet were an old pair of heavy winter stockings, and his mother's only well worn pair of slippers. Even if he couldn't be sure of her size, he took them anyway, knowing they would keep the girl's feet warmer than wearing nothing at all.

The blanket itself had been easy to find; he took a heavy, dark grey wool one out of one of the chests. The blanket smelled heavily of cedar, and he had fond memories of having used either it, or the handful they had like it, on winter nights when he'd been young.

He gathered the dress up along with the blanket and basket again before leaving. He stopped in the garden along the way to pick another handful of apples and pears from the trees, placing them in the basket for the girl to have to snack on until he had time to bring another meal.

Though it had been less than an hour by the time he returned to her clearing, he already feared he'd been gone far too long. The girl lay asleep across the doorway, her head still resting on the cold iron bars. She'd further bruised her hands and wrists in a fruitless struggle to free herself, but the door had held fast. It was almost more than he felt he could bear to look at her lying there that way, trapped and helpless.

Iona startled awake just as she heard him draw close, retreating further into the darkness beyond the doorway before she remembered the things Luke had done for her only a short time ago. She lingered there, crouching just out of reach as she watched him set the basket and the bundles he'd brought with him down at his feet, kneeling down to peer in at her.

"I promised you that I'd return, and I have," Luke told her, trying to keep his voice quiet and soothing. The look he saw in Iona's eyes was still far from one of trust.

"Now what must I do to have what you have brought here? I have nothing to offer but myself," Iona said with a trembling voice, turning until her back was toward him. She pressed her rear against the cold bars and began to raise the skirt of her threadbare dress. Scars crisscrossed her back from a whip and extended all the way down to the tops of her thighs.

"Please don't. I won't have it. Not like this," Luke told her, averting his eyes as he reached to take her by her wrists. He gently pushed down on her hands until she'd covered herself.

When Iona turned to look at him once he'd set her hands free, she looked frightened and confused; afraid she'd displeased him.

"I don't have anything else to give," Iona whispered, her voice still shaking when she turned back to look toward him. Her eyes never once met his, but they did look all too longingly at what he'd brought with him.

"You needn't give me anything, especially not while you're locked in that cage feeling like you owe me a blasted thing." Luke said firmly, trying not to sound as angry as it made him feel, not at her, but at the circumstance they found themselves in.

Luke watched her eyes as he began to take her dinner from the basket, first handing her the lid of the thermos filled with the still steaming hot stew and the spoon he'd brought for her. Once she was busy eating, he opened the parcel, setting the handkerchief on the ground in front of her and placing the bread and the slices of cheese on it for her. He had to remind her more than once to slow down, lest she make herself ill from eating too quickly. The thermos would only hold a couple of lid-fulls, plenty he thought for now, until she became more used to solid food again.

"I just realized that I forgot to ask your name. I'm sorry for that," Luke told her in a somber voice as he watched her finish eating. "My name is Luke."

"Iona." Was her only reply, as she looked up at him; barely able to clear her mouth in between bites of bread she was using to soak up every last drop of the stew.

"It's good to finally know your name, Iona." He sighed as he took the handkerchief back before starting to wrap up the sausages, crackers and fruit inside of it for her to keep for later. "I do wish we had met under better circumstances than this."

Iona watched him closely as he took yet more items from the basket, wrapping them carefully in the still mostly clean square of cloth, handing it through the bars to her.

"I will need to go for a little while until this evening. These things are in case you get hungry before I can come back. Please do try to make them last," he told her as he let her take the parcel from him before also giving her the bottle full of water and a cup he'd brought from the cupboard. After she'd taken those things, and carefully set them aside, he reached for the other bundle, unfurling the clothes and blanket for her to see. "These might not be the finest, Iona, but they should keep you warm. I do wish that I could do better for you, but this is all I can do for now, other than promise I will return again to you soon."

Iona looked up at him, still almost terrified of being left there alone. The prison that had been made of her home was almost every bit the darkness in which she'd been kept in before, save for being able to see the sky through the doorway.

"I wish you wouldn't go," she whispered, taking the rest of what he gave her when it was offered, and wrapping her body at once in the blanket. She rubbed the roughness of the wool against her cheek.

"I know," Luke answered, almost unable to stand the sight of the sadness and frailty in the girl's eyes. "There are things I must do before I can return, so it may take some time, but I will return when evening has come. I think you should try to sleep again. It will make the time I am gone pass quickly."

That time as Luke walked away, Iona did not scream and flail against the bars, but it broke his heart just as badly to hear her sobbing as she sat in the doorway until he was out of sight.

It had to end, Luke thought to himself. If Jane refused to see sense, then he'd have to go around her and make the others see it for her. The sadness never faded, but the anger built and only burned hotter with each step he took toward the summerhouse where he was sure she'd returned to. Even if others surrounded her, it would not deter him from saying the things he was certain needed said. If she struck him again, he wasn't sure he could remain a gentleman.

The clearing was quiet when Luke left the woods, only a couple of people lingering on the pier further down the beach. He recognized Alec and Lucy, having met them both before. He passed a few women and children on the last bit of road, Martha and the others taking sleepy little ones home to their beds for their naps. Luke offered them a quiet nod as he passed. He was almost to the porch when he spied Jane watching him from the window as he approached.

Jane rose to her feet as Luke came in the door, looking mildly concerned that for the moment, they seemed to be alone. She could easily see the anger in his eyes as he came close to her with swift and deliberate steps.

"The key Jane, give it to me now," he growled at her brushing her chest with his outstretched hand and glaring at her with a rage he could scarcely contain.

"I do not take orders from you, Mr. Fernsby," Jane said defiantly, all but laughing to see him so emotional over nothing more than a common thief. "I'll let the girl out when I'm damned good and ready to. Until then, I told you, she's your problem, not mine."

"You will give me the keys, or there will be consequences, Jane," Luke answered sternly, pushing closer until Jane was forced backward, tumbling off balance back into the window seat.

"Don't touch me, Mr. Fernsby, you would not dare," Jane snarled at him, shoving him away and trying quite blatantly to aim a kick to his crotch.

Expecting as such, Luke deflected it. "I would have before, but now that I see who you really are, there is no way I would have you. There is a big difference between a strong woman and a shrew, and you, Mrs. Boyd, are definitely the latter."

Luke said not another word before he seized hold of Jane roughly, tossing her over his shoulder. She screamed and pounded her fists against his back, as he carried her toward the still open cellar doorway and into the darkness below. He sat her down on the dirt of the cellar floor against one of the support beams using his weight to keep her pinned as he took a couple of scraps of the rope that had been used to bind Iona. Luke used it to tie her wrists to the beam before he used another piece to bind her ankles together. Her wrists were only bound with slipknots; he knew she could easily escape from them once she calmed down. The harder Jane screamed, flailed, and pulled against them, the harder they would bite into her skin.

"Whatever you intend to do, you will pay for this," Jane growled as he stepped away from her, leaving her to struggle against the ropes.

"So you dish out punishments, but you cannot take them?" Luke laughed when he stood and walked away, pausing at the bottom of the stairs, if nothing else but to gloat. "I told you, Jane, I will not touch you, only give you a taste of what you've done to that girl. If you ever want to leave this cellar, you'll give me the key to free her."

"Never."

"Never is a very long time, Jane. I suggest you make yourself at home," Luke said calmly as he climbed the stairs. He shut the door with a resounding thud. He used Jane's padlock that was still sitting open in the hasp and locked the door.

Looking up as he moved toward the door, he saw Lucy's frightened expression as she ran inside the summerhouse, dragging Alec behind her. The fog rolled in the door behind them as she slammed it shut, and the foghorn roared to life, shaking the ground and rocking them where they stood; the sound conveniently covering Jane's screams from within the cellar.

There was no mistaking the fear in Lucy's eyes, even if Alec and Luke did not share her dread. Alec knelt next to her, trying to comfort her as she covered her ears and screamed. Being in the summerhouse or near the beach was not the same as being further away. With no trees to muffle the sound or block the shockwave, the roar of the horn was deafening, and strong enough to be felt clear to the bone.

Luke lifted the girl into his arms as soon as the shaking subsided enough to let him cross the room without stumbling. "It's done, it's over, and you will be all right, little one." He carried her outside, and onto the porch, beckoning for Alec to follow him before Alec closed the door.

"I'm older than a rock, and I still don't like the fog," Lucy complained at being carted off outdoors, not ceasing her squirming until Luke set her back on her feet.

"I know, but the others will be coming soon, and based on last time, this seems to be where we need to wait," Luke told her, kneeling until he was almost eye to eye with her.

"And what about Jane?" she asked him, remembering that Jane had been inside, and she surely had not seen her leave.

"Let's just say that Jane is indisposed for now and won't be joining us."

"Where is she? What did you do?"

"Plausible deniability, little one, but I promise you, she is safe. When this is finished, it's only her pride that will be wounded, I assure you."

CHAPTER THIRTY-FOUR

SERENA COULD FEEL the mild chill in the air as they neared home. Rune did not take the path she had expected. The unease in her did not rise again until his feet left the path, carrying them into the darkness of the forest in between his home and her own. She heard the sound of dead leaves crunching beneath his heavy footfalls as he walked. All Serena could see was darkness beyond the halo of light the lantern shone.

"Rune, where are you taking me?" Serena asked him, knowing he had to hear the unease in her voice. Serena knew only the carefully memorized paths that led from her home to his, and back again, but Rune walked seemingly undeterred, and the path was now far beyond sight.

"Where we are going, wife of mine, is only a short distance more," Rune told her, for that moment purposefully vague in his intentions and their eventual destination. He could feel Serena's fear not only returning but also growing, with each new step he took further into the darkness, a darkness he did not fear.

It was not long before he reached the small clearing where the earth grew soft beneath his feet. Serena shivered as he stopped there, letting her slip off his back. She hugged her arms around herself as she studied what surrounded them that she could see.

"Do you trust in me, wife of mine?" he asked her as he took the lantern from her hand and doused the flame. He set the still hot lantern aside before moving toward her again.

"Rune, don't, please. I can't see!" Serena cried, her arms flailing around her as she searched the darkness for him, beginning to cry out in fear when she could not reach him.

Rune gave his own eyes a moment to adjust to the darkness before he circled behind her, stifling her frightened cries as he sidled up behind her, whispering, "Trust in me, close your eyes, keep them closed. There is nothing to fear."

Serena was still shivering when Rune withdrew his hand from across her mouth. His arm settled to curl across her chest, and the other wrapped around her waist, pulling her tightly against him. He kissed the back of her neck softly before he turned her to face him to be sure she'd done as he asked.

Undeterred, Rune still reached for the soft cloth belt that tied at the waist of her dress. He untied it and pulled it free before he slipped it over her eyes. Satisfied that it would make more than an effective blindfold, he tied it securely into place.

Serena stood trembling as her dress slid off her shoulders and pooled on the ground around her feet, before Rune whisked it away. He did not stand satisfied watching her until he'd stripped her bare, leaving her standing there, three short paces away, as he stepped backward away from her.

"Stay calm and listen to the sound of my voice. I am here. I will not leave you," Rune told her. Her hands reached out, searching for him as he stayed just out of her reach.

"I'm afraid," Serena whispered with a shaking voice, listening carefully and trying to follow the sound of his voice. She was not fond of this game, or the darkness, but Rune seemed determined as always to make her face her fears.

"There is nothing in the darkness that is not there in the light,"

Rune answered, trying to reassure her. He undressed himself, piling his clothing on the soft ground along with hers.

Rune's bare feet made not a sound as he circled behind her, kissing her shoulder before he untied the belt from across her eyes. This time he did not stop her from crying out as he unbound her hair as well, working it loose to fall in soft waves down her back. He whispered for her not to open her eyes until he'd finished and turned her toward him.

When Serena opened her eyes; she saw not the blackness she remembered, but Rune staring back at her in the dim light. There was not enough light to see details, but enough to easily make out his form and find her way through the trees without stumbling. She let Rune pull her to him and lift her from the ground and into his arms as he sighed deeply.

"The darkness and the night are nothing to fear, my love," Rune said softly as he sank to his knees, cradling her across his lap. "In times of trouble, it is the darkness and the hidden places that will protect you and keep you safe. If I am not near to you, remember this. You must seek them on your own."

"How can I find my way on my own?" she asked him, knowing she was as good as wandering blind were he not with her. "I'm not like you, I don't know how."

"You will learn, but first, you must leave your light behind. It not only blinds you to what is just out of its reach, but it allows others to find you easily. Once you learn to make your way in the darkness without it, there is nowhere in this forest you cannot travel if need be."

"How will I find my way home without the path?" she asked him, confused when Rune only laughed to himself softly. He shifted his weight, and she found herself lying on top of their carefully piled clothing.

"Look to the sky," Rune told her, still kneeling at her side as he lifted her chin and directed her gaze heavenward at the stars. "Take note of the stars, look for formations and where they are known to travel. They have guided ships since time unknown."

"But they've all changed," she answered, confused for that moment when Rune lay down beside her. He reached to take her hand in his, his own gaze trained on the sky.

"We need only find the lode star, and where it rests in this strange sky. The new constellations will be ours to find and name." Rune sighed, his tone distant, almost melancholy. "I've spent many nights lying in a field or on a ship, studying the stars overhead. I have dearly missed watching the lights dance across the sky, they are lost to me here."

"If you could go back, would you go?" Serena asked him, confused at the sadness in his voice.

"Only if you could accompany me, wife of mine," Rune replied with another deep sigh as he rolled over until his body was half covering hers. "There is nothing left for me in that world that is not already lost to me without you," he whispered before kissing her softly.

"And your daughter?" Serena asked him, her own voice picking up a tone of sadness also.

"Liv would no longer know me. I would be only a stranger to her now if I returned to her. I cannot teach her the things she must know, not without a mother to guide her."

"I believe she would have been glad of your return, even if you had come home alone, until you found a new wife to help care for her. I never knew my father, and even now, I still wonder what he must have been like and if I look like him. I must, because I don't look much like the pictures I've seen of my mother. I never knew her either. I grew up as Liv will, with a grandmother. At least she will know your name, and hear stories of you. I've never known my father's name, if my mother even knew herself who he was, she never told. That secret died with her when I was no older than Liv."

"You would have much to learn to live where I come from, but I know you would have made a fine new mother for her, as you will for our children," Rune whispered as he rolled the rest of the way to lie over her, kissing her softly. He felt her body yield to him as he settled between her thighs, no longer able to resist the temptation to touch her. He pinned her beneath him, uncaring if half the woods heard her cries as her legs trembled.

Now that Rune knew how her body reacted to his strong and steady rhythm, his touch was overwhelming. The shivering soon spread throughout her body. Eyes closed, she almost had not noticed the mist gathering around them until she felt the chill of it curling across her skin. It enveloped them almost as soon as she felt Rune begin to enter her. Blinded, she could see no more than his face, hovering just above hers.

"Close your eyes. I am here," Rune tried to reassure her, able to see the fear in her eyes even through the fog as the ground began to shake beneath them. The foghorn bellowed, though not nearly as loudly at this distance as it would have if they were they closer. "There is nothing in this fog that will harm you. Don't be frightened. Feel me. I could be no closer than within you." Rune held onto her tightly, until, lost in the moment, the fear faded from her.

When Serena opened her eyes again, the sky was filled with stars, even as the mist that surrounded them still clung to the ground. She was exhausted and shivering, despite Rune's warmth as he lay recovering his breath, his head resting at her breast. A cold chill and shudder ran through her bones as she looked up to see the barn owl staring back at her, perched on a low branch in the nearest tree. Its feathers looked white as snow by the starlight as it peered down at her, curiously. As if it knew she was watching, the owl swooped low overhead, flying across where she and Rune lay; out of reach, but close enough that she felt the breeze of its passing. Serena heard the ruffle of the owl's wings when it ceased its dive, vanishing too quickly into the trees for her to turn her head to see which way it had gone.

Rune quite predictably never noticed, except for hearing Serena gasp as her body tensed beneath him. He assumed it was from the way he was absent-mindedly suckling at her breasts, as he sometimes did when he was content after lying with her.

"When our first son is born, I wish to name him Soren to honor my father," Rune told her, as he moved back up her body to place a soft kiss on her lips. He wrapped her in his arms feeling her shiver.

Serena nodded; afraid to say more for fear that she would not be able to say the words, at least not without the trembling of her voice giving her away.

"We should go," he whispered before he rose to his feet, helping her to rise after him. He smiled when he watched her shivering, only half from the cold.

Dressed once again in their clothes, Rune wrapped her in his cloak before leading her through what was now to her only grayness, and not the blackness she had once perceived. The closer they neared to the edge of the woods, the more the color of the sky and the world returned as the fog began to fade. The road to the summerhouse no longer seemed dark as she and Rune walked hand in hand through the last traces of the mist.

Even if she no longer needed him to guide her on the way, there was no denying how much she wanted him near. Some things about him still frightened her to her core. He had never once promised her that loving him would be easy.

CHAPTER THIRTY-FIVE

THAT NIGHT CARRIED a coldness that could not be explained, one that did not seem to bother any of the searchers, except for Serena. She stayed close to Rune and was still wrapped in his cloak. The air carried more of a breeze than was usual, and the lighthouse glowed in the distance as they searched the area somewhere near the southwestern shore.

Luke joined in their search that evening, along with Robert, who comprised the last member of their team of four. Jane, for all her usual insistence at being at the forefront of everything, had been conspicuously absent when they'd gathered together.

Serena could not understand the nervousness on Lucy's face when she'd seen her standing on the porch of the summerhouse with Alec, almost as if guarding the doorway and hesitant to let anyone go in. What was going on that she didn't know about?

No one carried a lantern this time, Rune having left it behind at the summerhouse to be retrieved when they returned. Some time had passed since Serena had come to that place, but the fog and the lighthouse brought the same dread it had that first evening.

It had brought her Rune as well, but she was still trying to banish the rest of that evening's events from her memory.

The place they all now called home was far from the idyllic paradise many of them had been promised, except for Rune, who had never been raised to expect such a thing.

He'd adapted to the change far better than most, and made every new thing he learned a part of himself. He was far from the stubborn ox he first seemed, even if he was still just as determined and steadfast as he had always been.

She was the one who struggled to accept change, and craved stability where there was none, except for being close to him. He'd gone from being her nightmare, to the only safe refuge she had in the world.

Serena had no idea why tonight should be different than any other search. Her teeth chattered from the cold, a chill that seemed to leave the others unaffected, much to her confusion.

The air carried a sense of unease she could not explain until she noticed the change. The paths were suddenly different and she realized, much to her dismay, that she recognized the place they'd stumbled into. She had seen this dilapidated converted garage before. It sat tucked back into the trees in an overgrown field piled full of junk cars and broken discarded machinery. She froze, barely able to draw in a breath from the sheer panic she felt before Rune had taken notice of her expression and turned back to her. He looked at Serena, concerned and perplexed when he saw the color drain from her face and her tears start to fall.

"I know this place. I know who lives here. This is Kendall's home," Serena said before she fell apart. Rune stopped the others and pulled her against him to comfort her before they could go further.

"It will be all right, my love. She may be happy to find a friend awaiting her here," Rune said, stroking her hair as he held her. He was both confused and even more worried when his words caused Serena to cry harder. Her fingers dug into his sides as she held onto him tightly for comfort.

"You don't understand, Rune, I don't think she will be happy to see me. I may be the reason she's here. We were together in the same accident, the one I died in that brought me here. What if she's here because of me?" Serena could barely get the words out. She was relieved, happy even, when she'd discovered Kendall was not here, in this place. It meant that she'd lived. It was killing her inside, even after all this time to see her home suddenly appear.

"You do not know when or how her days may have ended," Rune tried to reassure her, cupping her face in his hands to make her look up at him. "If what happened to you both is what brought her here, then as you said, it was an accident. You did not mean to cause her harm. You have told me how this came to pass. You were in fear for your life. You were running away and your wagon crashed. It could have happened to anyone. If you had not run away, you both would have perished in the flames anyway. It is better to be brave. Greet her as a friend and help her into this new world, do not turn away from her."

Serena nodded, even while the tears still fell. Robert looked uncomfortable as he eyed the building in the distance. Luke placed a hand on her shoulder, trying to be comforting when Rune kissed her forehead and stepped away. Even if she could tell he didn't mean to be unkind, the expression Luke wore was one of impatience, that of a man that obviously had much more important places that he would rather be. Serena had no idea what else could be so important in this world, but she had no intention of asking him.

It didn't take long for Rune to nudge Serena forward. Serena went in alone, figuring Kendall was far less likely to be frightened if she went alone than if the entire group were to enter.

Serena walked, head down, across the litter-strewn, badly cracked concrete floor covered in throw rugs, making an obvious effort not to look into places where she knew there would be mirrors. She found Kendall asleep where she often had been as a child, on a pile of old discarded mattresses that were stacked in a corner, covered with several threadbare blankets. Her few clothes and other possessions were strung among a stack of old laundry baskets and stolen milk crates against a nearby wall. Another overturned milk crate, next to her makeshift bed held: an oil lamp, a box of wooden matches, and an old battery powered solid-state radio.

"Kendall, are you all right? Wake up," Serena called to her, kneeling next to the bed, but not trying to touch her.

Serena knew better than to do that. Kendall was well known for lashing out in her sleep, or at anyone who laid a hand on her to wake her.

It didn't take Kendall long to stir. She sat up, looking around the room quite confused to find herself there with Serena sitting next to her.

"What am I doing here? How did you get here? You died, they told me you died," Kendall said, looking at her, eyes wide and in a state of panic. Frightened tears poured down her face. She looked older than Serena remembered by several years. Her eyes were sunken, and she was nearly bone thin, but Kendall had struggled since adolescence with an eating disorder, so Serena found it not much of a surprise to see her so thin again.

"I did die. It was some time ago for you, but not long ago for me. Wherever we are isn't heaven, but we're sure as hell not burning here either," Serena told her, not really sure how to begin to explain. "If you're here with me, Kendall, you just died too."

"Liar!" Kendall screamed reaching down to shove her backwards away from the bed with a surprising amount of strength for the shape she was in.

Kendall dove after her onto the floor, leaving Serena no choice but to block the blows as Kendall attacked her in a fit of rage. When she wouldn't stop or listen to reason, Serena had no choice but to hit her back and wrestle with her until she had her pinned to the floor. Luke and Rune finally entered the house to break up their catfight.

"You left me, and this is all your fault. You promised me you'd never leave me!" Kendall screamed at her as Luke dragged her away, restraining her until she calmed down.

Serena got the same treatment from Rune. He pinned her arms against her as he wrapped her in a bear hug and refused to let her loose. Serena struggled against him, growling with frustration as she glared at Kendall, "I'm not lying, you stubborn assed bitch, listen to me!"

"You are fighting like children, calm yourselves, both of you," Rune told them, definitely something odd to hear coming from him. Rune normally would have been the most likely one to start a fight among all of them. "I thought the both of you were friends, this does not seem the way to greet an old friend."

"I was trying to be polite and explain until she attacked me," Serena said struggling only to find Rune hugging her tighter. He kissed her cheek and whispered to her, trying to calm her. Usually she would have been the first trying to calm him down, and it was odd to find that shoe suddenly on the other foot, so to speak. "I don't care how upset she is, she threw the first punch. I'm not going to let her scratch my eyes out just to make her feel better. If she hits me, she's getting it right back. She ought to know that by now."

Rune kept hold of her until she wasn't struggling anymore, and seemed to be calming before he turned her toward him and kissed her. "I am sorry, my love. We should not have sent you to do this alone, and listened to your concerns. You know this woman better than any of us. It may be best we leave any further explaining to another she is not as likely to be angered by."

Serena looked up at Rune and nodded, and then hugged the breath from him before turning back to look at Kendall, who Luke had also released. If looks could kill, she probably would have dropped dead where she stood. Robert had been doing nothing but observing from the doorway, a little confused by it all.

"I think perhaps this is enough of you trying to explain for now, Serena. You should probably be going, give yourselves both some time to calm down and talk again in the morning," Luke said to Serena before looking back and forth between the both of them. "I think young Robert here can maybe stay around and answer her questions for now. Rune can take you home, and I've got other business that requires my attention."

Luke wasn't about to tell anyone that he had reasons of his own for wanting Robert busy and away from the summerhouse. Robert was the one who seemed closest to Jane, and Luke worried he would let her loose, given the chance.

Lucy was keeping watch over the summerhouse for the time being, keeping away anyone that would have a chance of hearing her until he had a chance to get back and make his case for those keys again. He didn't mean to be impatient, but he was in a hurry to get back to it. Even if he had no luck with the keys tonight, there was always the next morning, bright and early, but even if that was the case, he'd still made a promise to Iona that he needed to keep. Luke wasn't big on being forced to break his promises.

Serena held back her tears until Rune led her outside and started to walk with her toward home. The bruises and scratches on her cheek were burning, but that had nothing to do with her tears. She'd been hoping for a friend, but she'd been met with nothing but seething anger, much as she feared she would be. Kendall's angry words still rang in her head most of the way home. She climbed onto Rune's back so he could carry her the rest of the way. His shirt was soaked with her tears long before they made it home. She clung to his shoulder, shivering and teeth chattering from the cold, even with his cloak still wrapped around her.

She hadn't started to warm until they made it home and he'd drawn a hot bath for her. Much as he usually did, he climbed into the water with her, letting her rest against him as he held her.

"Do you fear your friendship is no longer?" Rune asked her after a few moments, noticing her tears had finally stopped flowing.

"It's hard to say, Rune. I'm not sure. It's always been complicated. Sometimes Kendall would love me, and sometimes she would treat me like the enemy. We met as children a year after I became an orphan; the same foster family took us both in. She's cruel sometimes, but she's the closest thing to family I have left. Even if she hates me, I don't want to give up on her."

"Then do not give up; be her friend, even if she will not be yours." Rune sighed, not sure what other advice to give. "Eventually, she may realize that your affection for her is genuine, and you both can make amends."

Serena nodded, finding it ironic that Rune was now the one giving her sensible advice. He was definitely no longer the man he once appeared to be. She had fallen in love with him, and once she'd stopped fighting it, she'd fallen hard.

They said nothing more as they finished the bath and went downstairs. She made them dinner, and then curled up on the sofa wrapped in one of her grandmother's old handmade quilts, watching Rune play with the phonograph. His favorite records and hers now lay in their own neat pile. They listened to them before Rune began exploring the other stacks that remained untouched. He smiled whenever he found a song he liked the sound of, and added it to the pile of records he wanted to hear again.

When he smiled, it was the most beautiful thing she'd seen in that world. On evenings like tonight, where they lost themselves in making out on the sofa before finally going up to bed hand in hand together, she could almost forget how afraid she'd once been of him. She'd never in her life been so happy to be proven wrong.

CHAPTER THIRTY-SIX

LUCY WAS STILL SITTING on the porch of the summerhouse when Luke arrived. By then she'd caught on to what the situation was with Jane, not to say she wasn't amused by it. She kept Alec outside with her as she waited for people to start filtering back from the search, but as of yet, not many had come, those that had she waved away. She told herself that she shouldn't be so eager to revel in Jane's indignity, but part of her almost wanted to rub the present turn of events in Jane's face, despite knowing that Jane would make her pay dearly for it later somehow.

She knew Jane had heard the foghorn, and she'd listened to Jane pound on the inside of the cellar door, yelling for Alec to take the key she'd slid under it to unlock it.

Lucy hushed Alec to keep quiet and pretend she wasn't there when she picked the key up herself and slid it into the pocket of her apron. When it hadn't worked, none of the words Jane spouted off had been kind. She reminded Alec that Jane was just upset and not to take the names she called him personally.

Lucy managed to put together some dinner by the time Luke arrived; she and Alec were finishing up eating on the steps. The search had fallen during a normal mealtime, but no food had been prepared until she'd done it. She stood on a chair at her short height, but had managed it well enough herself.

"We're still the only ones here don't worry," Lucy told Luke when he walked up to the steps. "She's been pounding on the inside of the door for almost the whole time you've been gone. She even tried to slip Alec the key under the door and get him to unlock it, and she called him terrible names when I wouldn't let him."

"Ah, it just figures that she loses her temper when she doesn't get her way, and she turns on anyone who doesn't jump right to what she says," Luke said scratching his chin and looking at Alec apologetically for having dragged him into the middle of this mess. "Her problem is with me. She shouldn't be taking it out on the both of you. I'm sorry for that."

"Don't worry about it. Here, you'll probably want this," Lucy said, holding the key out to him in the palm of her outstretched hand. She'd fought the urge to take the damned thing and bury it and make them search the entire realm for something to cut or smash the lock open with. She wasn't quite that cruel.

Luke tried not to laugh, but he couldn't fight down the small chuckle that had broken through. "It seems Jane's surely not liking a taste of her own medicine, then again, not many do when confronted with it. I suppose I should go and give her a chance to give in, but I'm doubtful she's going to have changed her mind quite this quickly. She seems far too much of the stubborn sort for that."

Luke was already steeling himself while Lucy and Alec went indoors.

Alec went to his sleeping bag in the corner and curled up there. Lucy took their dishes to the sink, and Luke followed her inside and asked quietly if she wouldn't mind putting aside a bit of the leftovers for him to take to Iona.

Lucy, thankfully, seemed willing to do as he asked. She agreed that Iona had needed to be punished, but had never quite expected or been comfortable with Jane taking it to quite the extreme she had.

The sound of Luke's heavy footfalls brought Jane to the door to pound at it again, yelling for someone to fetch the key from the floor and unlock it.

Luke stood with his hands in his pockets for a moment, before he made his way to the door, finally saying more sarcastically than he should have, "Yes, Jane, that key is most helpful if you want this door unlocked, but see, in order to do that, I'm going to require both of them."

"You, bastard, unlock this door now! This isn't funny. You just wait until I get out of here and get my hands on you," Jane growled, screaming through the door and pounding her hands against it so hard it rattled. The door was far too good and solid to give that easily.

"Oh, that's right, Jane, it's not funny, is it? It wasn't funny when you did it to her either. You've only been down there a couple of hours at best. How do you think it felt for her being trapped down there for days without a kind word, or a real chance to explain herself?" Luke said, trying to keep his volume under a yell and keep himself calm even though he felt anything but. "A leader that isn't willing to listen to both sides of a matter and be fair is nothing but a tyrant. You should never, ever, mete out punishments you would not accept for yourself, or someone you cared about if the situation were reversed. Otherwise, you're nothing but a blowhard that's good at getting other people to do your bidding. One set of rules for them and another for you doesn't work, Jane."

"She needed to be punished for what she'd done. What she did was inexcusable."

"And so was what you did to her, Jane, did you stop and think about that? You, by yourself, acted as judge and jury. Did you bother to hear her side, or even give her a chance to explain herself? No, you locked her in the dark like an animal in a cage, treated her like she wasn't even human, and you expect her not to strike back at all? This isn't the way to gain her trust, or mine. She's nothing but a frightened girl that was on the brink of starvation, and instead of helping her, you punished her for stealing food. The only reason she pushed away from Alec was that he frightened her, by trying to touch her when she pulled away from him. He doesn't understand that not everyone is his friend, and that some women who have been hurt aren't fond of strangers."

"I don't care what you say. I'm not giving you the key to just let her waltz out of there and get away with it," Jane yelled, pounding on the door again. She was clearly more infuriated than before, and not in the mood to listen to what he was trying to tell her.

"Well, then, it looks like you may be in there quite a long time. You'll either give me the key to her lock, or I'll never unlock yours, and yes I've got the key now. It's nice and safe in my pocket, but until you give me hers, no deal. Have a nice night in the cellar, Jane. I'll be back to see if you've changed your mind in the morning."

"You open this door now!" Jane screamed, "You just wait until I get out of here, you are going to pay for this."

"And who's going to make me pay, Jane? You?" Luke was to the point he was almost finding it sadly amusing. Listening to her was like listening to a small child throwing a tantrum. "Come to think of it, no you wouldn't be capable of doing that by yourself, would you? You use other people to push your weight around. They're going to grow tired of that. I already have, and if I've tired of it this quickly, I'm sure I'm not the only one that's already had it up to here with you trying to be the boss of everyone. You're not the bloody Queen, Jane, so stop acting as if you are. I'm tired of talking. You're going to have a long night in there, screaming at no one. Goodbye."

Lucy sat in the rocking chair, trying to laugh quietly enough that Jane wouldn't hear her. Jane's anger may not frighten Luke, but it did frighten Lucy, considering she was smaller and a lot less able to fight back if Jane set her mind to exacting revenge.

The meal he'd asked Lucy for was already packed up and loaded into a basket along with some other supplies and another jug of water.

Luke nodded a quiet thank you to her before gathering the basket and heading back out the door. He had a promise to keep, and if he didn't manage to find a way to out-stubborn Jane, he'd find another way to free Iona from her cage. A plan like that would take time, though, something far less pressing than making sure she was fed and clothed in better than rags.

He didn't pass anyone on the walk back through the woods. The trail marks he left made it simpler to find his way, but he doubted he would need them for long. His compass didn't work; however, there seemed to be no North for it to point to, leaving the needle spinning endlessly in circles. Maybe this realm was the mythical North, and the needle could not point to where it already was?

Luke found Iona as she had been before, curled up asleep in the doorway with her head resting against the bars. This time, however, she was dressed in his mother's dress and slippers and wrapped in the warm wool blanket. She didn't raise her head until he came near and called to her. She looked up at him sleepy-eyed and mildly frightened before she remembered who he was and the promise he'd made to her.

"I was almost afraid you wouldn't come," Iona said, her voice and her appearance still frail. Her eyes never left the basket as Luke set it down in front of her and began taking out her meal. "You look angry, did you get into trouble for helping me?"

"I'm not angry with you, Iona. I'm angry with them, or more so, the woman that leads them. The others just follow her orders, and most of them don't question why, but they jolly well should," Luke answered, trying not to sound as cross as he felt.

It wasn't until he sat down that he noticed Lucy packed two meals and not one. He set the first in front of Iona, and he took the second plate for himself.

"The people with the coldest hearts always do seem to be the ones who seek power, good men would never want it," Iona muttered, doing her best to eat carefully. It was hard to work around the bars, she had to thread her arms between them and keep her face pressed against her prison so she could lift the spoon to her mouth.

"I can imagine it's difficult to eat, when you can't even fit the dish through the bars" Luke said, shaking his head. There wasn't much else for him to do than to make sure she ate her dinner and had enough water and supplies until morning. It hurt him to hear her crying when he left her sitting in the doorway.

That night, he couldn't sleep. He tossed and stared at the ceiling.

They hadn't come for him yet with torches and pitchforks, so he could only assume Jane was still where he'd left her.

The guilt that gnawed at him had nothing to do with Jane, but everything to do with leaving Iona alone in the dark. It wouldn't leave him be until he gathered his bedroll, another wool blanket, and a couple of old pillows. He made his way back through the woods.

He didn't sleep peacefully until they were both camped out together, each on their own side of the doorway, Iona's head perched on the second pillow he brought with him. She seemed so different than she had hours before. She reached for his hand gently instead of trying to harm him, her hand in his when they fell asleep.

CHAPTER THIRTY-SEVEN

LUKE SLEPT LIGHTLY, as he'd been accustomed to doing so for some time. Trying not to get shot at or blown up didn't make it easy to sleep, not that it really worked out that well for him in the end. His foxhole had been hit with a shell during one of his brief periods of sleep. At least he hadn't been awake for the end and hadn't known what hit him until it was over; silver linings and all that.

It wasn't the sound of approaching footsteps or the rain that awakened him this time. It was a soft touch against his cheek, and Iona whispering to him.

"You've been asleep for hours. You did tell me not to let you sleep after the little arrow was pointed at that thing that looks like what you drew in the dirt," Iona told him with a nervous expression. "I think that's now."

Luke raised his watch, checking the hour hand to find she wasn't horribly far off. He sat up, folding his bedroll and using it to sit on. He used the matches he brought with him to light the lantern before he'd dug into the basket, looking for the breakfast he'd brought; crackers, fruit, cheese, and smoked sausages.

Iona looked at him bashfully as they ate facing one another

through the bars. Luke reminded her not to eat so quickly or she'd make herself ill.

By the light of the lantern he could see the girl more clearly. Iona's skin was pale and covered in freckles, much as one might expect from someone with her shade of ginger-colored hair. Her pale green eyes spoke of someone who had seen far too much for one short life. She looked hardly older than a girl, late teens or early twenties at most in age. Yet, her body was covered in scars that told of just how hellish her short existence must have truly been.

It was hard for Luke not to feel guilty as he looked at her. His attempts to free her were feeble, but he was doing more than most. After what he'd done, he might find himself on the other side of the door locked inside with her, once Jane had been freed and decided to hand out his punishment.

It perhaps wasn't the brightest idea, but even if it went wrong for him in the end, it would be worth it as far as he was concerned. The only thing he regretted if they did lock him up, was he wouldn't be able to help Iona. If that happened, they'd hopefully be in it together, and the girl wouldn't be left to cry in the dark alone.

Their meal finished, Luke took the key from his pocket and turned it over in his hand. He thought about the ramifications of the situation. Iona's own eyes watched the glint of light the key gave off from the lantern each time it turned in Luke's hand. He read the brand name on the key under his breath, wondering where he'd seen it before. He looked over the lock that was holding the logging chain that kept the gate closed, only to find that they matched.

Luke's eyes widened. His hands shook, trying to get the key into the lock, as he stammered, "I wonder. Could it be?" Luke screamed, bursting into what must have sounded like half crazed laughter. He sprung to his knees when the lock popped open in his hands, and he started unwinding that chain. "Unbelievable, in the dark she gave me the wrong bloody key, I've had it all this time! Come on, hurry, and get up."

Iona started shaking and looked like she was about ready to cry. She scampered into a standing crouch in the doorway as Luke finished unwinding the chain. He folded up the blanket and bedroll before crouching and ducking inside with her.

Once indoors, Luke stashed their pillows and blankets in the corner, leaving them near the other supplies he'd brought Iona that she hadn't used yet. "Keep these here, just in case they do bring you back here. I'm afraid I've made them angry enough that I'll probably end up locked up myself. I'm going to try to keep you with me, but I can't promise that will work, so at least if these things stay here, you won't be without them," Luke told her, tugging at her hand and leading her out into the open. He held the lantern firmly in his other hand as he tried to hurry her down what he knew was the path toward his home.

Luke was afraid he was only going to run into trouble on the way, but the path remained quiet and empty for the length of that short journey.

Iona looked frightened, and stuck close to his side as they walked. She was glad for the slippers he'd found her to keep her feet from hurting quite so much on the stones.

Luke stopped along the way to pick more apples off the tree, just in case he didn't get the chance to go back out for more.

He knew it would do no good to run. There wasn't really anywhere on an island to go. Luke bolted the door, and he prepared a better meal for Iona to eat. Then he went about getting the bed in the loft ready for her to sleep in, knowing she likely would want to sleep more before morning came.

Once she finished eating, he explained the concept of the shower for her, helping her to adjust the temperature of the water, and then leaving her to it, thinking she'd feel better once she was all cleaned up. He gathered one of his mother's good warm nightgowns for her to dress herself in once she was finished.

Luke knew Iona had been glad for his mother's hairbrush, even if he had to help work out some of the worst of the tangles from her hair. He helped her to gather it back into a simple plait and fasten it at the end.

She looked completely different staring at Luke in the light than she had in that darkened doorway. She still looked somewhat gaunt, but with a few good meals in her, some of the color had come back to her cheeks and she didn't seem nearly as weak as before.

It hadn't taken long for her eyes to start getting heavy once she was done with the hot shower, had a full stomach, and was dressed warmly. Luke led her upstairs, where he'd already turned the covers down for her on the bed.

He left her to drift off to sleep after helping her tuck herself in. He heard her marvel, muttering about the softness of the lumpy old mattress, but he imagined, it was probably the softest thing she'd ever slept on.

Once she was settled, he went back downstairs, climbing into the larger, more comfortable bed that had belonged to his parents. He figured he may as well get a few more hours sleep if he could, because he knew what was likely going to happen once Jane was freed, and he wanted to be wide awake to deal with it when the time came.

Once again when Luke awakened, it was to a touch on his cheek and a kiss to his forehead. He muttered and shifted still half asleep until he realized he felt the warmth of a body pressed against his. Groaning softly, he opened his eyes to find Iona had climbed into his bed. She was under the covers, lying next to him.

"I told you before, you don't have to do that," Luke whispered, looking up at her. It was more difficult to resist the urge to touch her than he ever thought it could be. He had to know she wasn't offering herself only for his sake, or he knew too well the guilt would eat him alive afterward. "We should sleep, we are bound to have a long day ahead of us once the others awaken, Iona."

It was a clumsy attempt; but Luke appreciated the sentiment behind it, when she leaned down to kiss him. He had a feeling Iona, sadly, had only experienced being taken by force, not that he had any intention of harming her that way.

Things had taken quite a turn in only a few hours, and not in a way he expected. A short time before she'd gone for his eyes and clawed up his face with scratch marks. Now she kissed them apologetically as if trying to heal them, before she'd snuggled down tighter against him and closed her eyes. Iona was anything but what he'd first expected. Even if he barely knew her, he couldn't help but care for her and want to help her. He had to find a way to protect her from Jane. He had to find a way to make sure Jane's wrath fell on him, and not her.

CHAPTER THIRTY-EIGHT

JANE FUMED and pounded on the door long after Luke left. Her hands were bruised and stinging from her efforts as she sat down on the steps in the dark so she'd be less likely to fall. She knew Alec was upstairs, but she suspected he wasn't alone there.

How dare Luke? The man waltzed in and had the nerve after only days to consider himself an authority when Jane had spent years helping to look after everyone. With Lucy no longer fit to lead, she was the most qualified, at least in her mind. Hard choices had to be made for the good of all of them, and most of the others were far more emotional and less detached than Jane was when making those decisions. She resented the fact that Luke questioned her authority when he was nothing but a near stranger to all of them and their way of life.

She was locked up in the dark, and Luke had the only key. He'd all but shoved it in her face. It was exactly what she'd done to the girl for a handful of days. Jane didn't understand Luke's gall at insisting his actions were justified. The girl was a thief, and she'd tried to kill someone, from what Alec had said. Why was Luke so determined to give the little red haired heathen the benefit of doubt? Was her comfort and freedom more important than the safety of the rest of the group? Jane didn't think it was.

Luke thought she lacked compassion, but she hadn't ordered the girl killed, and she hadn't banished her to the west beyond the wall.

All Jane had done was have the girl confined until they were sure she wasn't a threat to the safety of others. If he didn't agree with her methods, she hadn't exactly seen him offering better solutions. The girl had gotten violent, and Jane had dealt with the situation as best she could.

The foghorn had long since faded. Jane had hoped it would have brought rescue with it, but it had only brought that smug and stubborn ass of a man back to taunt her. She had no idea how much time had passed since the sound of the horn had faded.

Time was blurring together in the dark, but Jane wasn't one to fall apart at a temporary setback. If Luke didn't return and let her out in the morning, she had no doubt that all she'd have to do was get Robert, or whoever else heard her cries through the door first, to take the door off its hinges and free her. Once that happened, Luke was going to pay dearly, and he'd be damned lucky if she didn't just lock him in the girl's cage with her since he liked her so much.

Jane couldn't even think of Luke without becoming angry inside. Jane was convinced his neutrality made him more of a liability than fit to lead anyone. She'd dealt with the threat. Luke would have been content to coddle the girl, and let her get away with it completely as far as she could tell.

Jane's eyes were growing heavy when she heard another set of footsteps overhead. It was a woman's footsteps. She could tell from the way the heels clicked against the floor. She jumped to her feet and started pounding on the door, screaming, "I'm locked inside. Let me out!"

"Do you know where the key is?" Martha asked. She recognized Jane's voice and began fighting with the lock.

"Luke has the key, he's the one who locked me in here. It'll do no good trying to get it from him. Go get Robert, or one of the other men, they'll just have to take the door off," Jane told her sternly.

"I'll go wake Robert, he was up most of the night with the new girl, but I'm sure he'll know what to do. I'll be back as fast as I can," Martha replied before turning and hurrying herself out the door in search of Robert or any of the others.

Lucy sensibly had let herself out once it was late enough for most of the others to be asleep. She'd taken Alec to Serena's house with her to keep him out of the crossfire.

She tucked him into the other bed in the room she slept in so that when that door did open, Jane wouldn't take her anger out on Alec.

By the time Martha returned, Jane was impatiently pounding against the door again. Robert had brought both tools and Paul with him. Jane sat on the steps and covered her ears as they removed the pins holding the door hinges in place. The door opened enough for her to squeeze out, and she impatiently shoved by Robert in her eagerness to get out of the cellar.

It was all Jane could do to keep decorum and not cuss like a sailor. She told Robert and Martha how she wound up in the cellar. "It was Luke Fernsby who locked me inside. It was a little while after we came back from locking the thief away, just after Martha took the children for their naps. I was sitting here having coffee; he came inside, demanded the key to free the girl, and attacked me when I wouldn't give it to him."

"Why in the world would he do something like this? It doesn't make sense," Martha said, not understanding the situation, at least not much more than the bit she'd been told second hand.

"He seemed plenty angry enough in the woods yesterday, he and Jane had quite a fight over the thief," Robert told Martha, not horribly surprised that Luke was capable of what Jane had described. "Apparently, he disagrees with the punishment that was decided, and he has his own ideas on how he feels we should have done things differently."

"Just wait until I get my hands on him. I am going to find him and make him pay for this," Jane growled, impatient and much more in the mood for action than conversation. She'd done far more than enough stewing already, sitting in the dark.

Robert stopped Jane from tearing out of there to go straight after Luke. "Don't go alone, Jane. At least wait and gather a few people to go with you. If he did this, he might do something far worse if you confront him alone again."

Luke had to be punished. Jane wasn't about to let the humiliation she suffered go unanswered. Jane had a lot of good qualities, but forgiveness wasn't known to be one of them once you got on her bad side. Jane knew nothing if not how to hold a grudge, and once you were on her hit list, you rarely, if ever, left it until she was damned good and ready to make peace with you. Luke had angered her before, but now she was furious, so furious that even Robert risked her wrath to remind her it was best to go after Luke when she calmed down and had a more level head.

The council had only consisted of she, Robert, and Martha since Lucy had been ousted. Jane had seen to it that Lucy had been shown to be sufficiently incompetent, even though Jane had set her up for her downfall and she wasn't nearly as mentally incompetent as Jane's manipulation had made her seem. The girl only had a year or so at most of her rational mind left before she became completely child-like anyway. Jane hadn't wanted to wait that long to take control.

Lucy had seen right through Jane, and she had interfered far too often against Jane's scheming as she'd ousted the other child members of the council one by one, until she was all that remained in Jane's way. Jane made sure that the council members she'd gotten rid of were never replaced with new members.

Decisions were supposed to be agreed upon by all three remaining council members, but Jane did more than her fair share of pushing her weight around. She at least seemed to have Robert sufficiently intimidated on most occasions; he went along with whatever her decisions were. Martha, however, was harder to win over, making Jane on more than one occasion overrule her with Robert's help in order to do as she pleased anyway. It was a rarity for Robert to show any sign of dissent; it took Jane aback.

If Robert was showing signs of dissent, and Martha balked as well, Jane couldn't put them back into line, and there were few people capable of helping her get her point across. Rune was the exception to that rule, but his relationship with Serena was making that more difficult than Jane had anticipated. She had plans for him, but the girl seemed determined to interfere as well, which Jane could only assume was Lucy's doing.

Robert reminded her about the newcomer the night before. Jane wasn't interested until he mentioned that she and Serena had once been friends, but that the girl had attacked Serena shortly after her arrival. Robert, for the most part, could do little beyond that than explain Kendall's side of things. Words spoken in anger often were not the most flattering account of anyone's personality, but Jane wasn't exactly worried about niceties. She wanted more information that she could possibly hold against Serena later, if she kept interfering in her plans for Rune.

Rune was strong, and more intelligent than he at first appeared to be, but his loyalty to his new wife was complicating Jane's plans to turn him into her strong right hand, so to speak. Having someone else in Rune's ear giving contrary advice, especially the wife he adored, was not making it easy to bring those plans to fruition. If the new girl, Kendall, was that determined to exact revenge on Serena, she just might prove useful in driving a wedge between her and Rune.

Jane knew if she could keep the others angry, she could stoke it as she'd done in the past to get obstacles, like Lucy, out of her way. If they were fighting each other, they couldn't turn on her. Jane had no problem keeping up that game until everyone fell back into line, knew their place and stayed there. Until then, she'd only make everyone's lives as miserable as her own.

CHAPTER THIRTY-NINE

SERENA AWOKE with her face still burning, and her cheek sore to the touch. She knew it was a little swollen and bruised even without a mirror. Rune's arms, as usual, were curled tightly around her. He always clung to her as he slept. Moving only caused him to tighten his hold, or in some cases, awakened him if she resisted his grasp enough.

Serena had given up trying to wear a nightgown to bed, it never lasted more than a few moments before Rune was tugging it off. Extra blankets and staying curled tightly against him made up for what would have been that additional layer of warmth. Stirring Rune and trying to escape his grasp in the morning usually only resulted in one outcome. Serena was far less inclined to complain than she once would have been.

This morning's attempt to pull away caused him to mutter. She tugged a second time, and then he'd rolled half on top of her and pinned her, kissing her neck as his hand wandered, almost aimlessly at first and then a lot more pointedly. Serena lost all will to protest long before he lay over her. Mornings as of late had almost always begun this way. Rune was not content to leave their bed until they made love at least once, if not a second time.

Serena almost went back to sleep afterward, with Rune still lying halfway on top of her, when she heard an unexpected voice out in the hallway. She tried to sit up, but by the time she had, Rune had heard it as well and was already standing from the bed. He reached for his sword, always left within easy reach, before he crept toward the door, inching it open.

Rune hadn't bothered with dressing, so it was a good thing he found Lucy and Alec talking with their backs turned in the hallway outside the bathroom door. Assured of no danger, Rune closed the door to find Serena climbing out of the bed as well. He laid his sword on the cedar chest at the foot of her bed and dressed himself in the clothing she'd washed for him, even though it was the last thing he had wanted to do.

The morning had been quiet as of yet, but Lucy knew that would only last until Jane was free, and then all hell would likely break loose. Once that happened, Lucy was afraid of the revenge Jane would seek, not only for Luke, but Alec and anyone else she suspected of conspiring with him. It wouldn't be the first time Jane had turned vicious, although she tended to do it in not so obvious ways. After all, the last thing Jane wanted was for anyone that wasn't her target to see her bad side. Jane had to maintain the illusion that she was nothing but a stern, benevolent leader. It wouldn't do at all to have anyone find out how manipulative and spiteful she could be when she wanted her own way badly enough.

Lucy wasn't surprised at the knock on the door when she and Serena had finished making breakfast.

Jane didn't wait for anyone to answer the back door before she opened it and walked inside.

The look on Jane's face couldn't be described when she stepped inside, bringing Robert with her. Lucy knew that look; the one that meant Jane was out for blood, and she knew only one person in that place could have made her angry enough to be in that sort of mood.

Serena and Rune had no knowledge of the previous evening's events, but Lucy wasn't convinced that was a good thing. Lucy had planned to discuss it with them once they were all gathered around the breakfast table, but Jane's arrival had unfortunately cut her off at the pass. It had meant that it would be far more likely they'd hear Jane's side of what happened before Lucy had the chance to explain otherwise.

Jane played the victim, recounting her ordeal of being tied up and locked in the cellar, giving Alec a death glare as she told the story. She conveniently forgot to mention the events that occurred after Rune and Serena left that had led up to the conversation with Luke. She definitely left out anything about her assaulting Luke in a fit of anger. To hear Jane tell it, Luke had attacked her out of the blue without any provocation whatsoever. Lucy knew a complete line of bullshit when she heard one, but she was afraid that Serena and Rune wouldn't.

Lucy explained that Alec had walked her home last night, seeing as she wasn't allowed to travel through the woods alone anymore, and that he'd been with her in Serena's guest room. That was only partly a lie, but nowhere near the line of total crap that Jane had been spinning, so Lucy felt no guilt whatsoever in telling it.

Of course, Jane told Serena and Rune she feared for her safety. She wanted Rune to go with her when she, Robert, and some of the others went to confront Luke about what he'd done.

Lucy could not help but see the look of annoyance on Serena's face when she realized Jane would be dragging Rune into the middle of things to do her bidding. Serena wasn't hiding her distaste of the situation from Rune at all. Knowing Jane, she'd try to twist it to make it look like jealous immaturity in the eyes of the others if Serena put up too much of a fight about it.

A young girl, who had been sent to check on Iona, pounded on the door. The girl was out of breath when she recounted to Jane that the gate keeping Iona confined was open and that the girl was gone. She swore the lock had been open and discarded on the ground when she found it and not broken open.

The fury in Jane's eyes was visible; her hands trembled with rage when she realized her mistake. Cracks were showing in her usually calm demeanor, and Lucy hoped that everyone gathered there was seeing them as clearly as she was.

Jane's strained voice thanked the girl for that bit of news, and she sent her out the door to go about her business, closing the door behind her just a little too hard.

Lucy could tell Jane was ready to hurt someone, if not several people, and that logic and reason weren't ruling her mind at that moment. Jane was completely blinded by anger, and anyone who got in her way was going to get hurt, and hurt badly.

Lucy recognized the look on Serena's face as fear when she shook her head at Rune while Jane's back was turned, silently begging him not to involve himself.

Serena knew why Jane was here, to get Rune to be the one to enforce her edicts again. She despised the fact that Jane expected Rune to do her bidding without question.

Rune wasn't inclined to let Jane sway him, especially when he noticed how angry she was. As Serena had told him the day before, she only seemed to want to use him to make others obey her. He didn't stop eating. He watched and observed the situation around him, and he wasn't going to let Jane's tirade interrupt his meal.

"Rune, I would like you to come with me now. I'll be leading a small group to find Luke and confront him about what has happened," Jane said, her tone still one of impatience, and her temper obviously having only cooled to a simmer.

"Do you want me to subdue him for you, or do you only wish for me to protect you if he tries to cause you harm?" Rune asked, waiting to hear the answer to his question before he made his decision.

"Both. Something must be done. This cannot go unpunished," Jane snapped back at him, frustrated that she even had to explain herself.

"I believe that if Luke truly wished to harm you, he would have done so instead of only locking you behind a door. Confront him if you must, but I do not wish to involve myself unless other means to resolve your disagreement have been tried and failed," Rune told her.

Her demeanor was doing nothing to sway him to her side. If anything, it was only making his wife's words ring even truer in his mind.

Jane's eyes narrowed, and she looked on the edge of losing her temper when she told Rune, "So be it. I'll be back, but remember, if anyone gets hurt, it's because you would not help. It's on your head, not mine."

The air chilled visibly as Jane stormed out, dragging Robert after her when she hadn't gotten what she'd come there for.

"I don't think we should go the summerhouse today." Lucy said, picking over what was left of her breakfast.

"I don't either. I don't think any of us should go anywhere near Jane until she calms down," Serena answered, eating even though her appetite had all but left when Jane had come in.

"If you're waiting for Jane to stop being angry and holding a grudge, you'll be waiting a really long time," Lucy muttered, stuffing another bite of toast into her mouth.

"Is what Serena said true?" Rune asked, turning to look at Lucy, with a serious expression. "You were the one who once ruled here, were you not? Did Jane obtain power in an honorable manner, or did she obtain it by deception as Serena has told me?" The question might have seemed a little moot, but to Rune the answer truly was important.

"Ruler is a strong word for what I was. I once led the council, when it actually was a council, not the way Jane runs it today," Lucy replied, once she'd finished her bite of toast and taken a drink to clear her throat. "In the old days, there were five of us, not just three; Charlie, Daniel, Orville, Tara, and myself. When our decisions were not unanimous, mine was the deciding vote. Jane gained power by making the others believe I was growing too young to make good decisions anymore. She set me up by doing things on purpose to make it look like my mind was slipping, and that I was weak and unfit to lead. Of course, she wasn't honorable. By then, Charlie and the rest were too young to speak on my behalf. The council was eliminated one by one, except the ones on her side, in the same manner. Now it's just Robert and Martha, and Robert is far too afraid of Jane to ever stand up to her. He knows he'll just end up like the rest if he ever angers her."

"So, she obtained her place by treachery and not by honorable means?" Rune asked again, as if wanting to clarify what he was all but certain Lucy had told him.

"Yes, that's exactly what happened, but there isn't much we can do if the others won't stand up to her. I'm far too small now to even have hope of fighting her. I've been hoping that someone would come along that was strong enough and smart enough to see the truth about how Jane really is, and put her back in her place. She's turning into a tyrant. Luke was telling the truth, about the girl. Jane never once gave her a chance to explain what happened, and Alec admitted to me that the girl only pushed him because she was afraid. She stole food because she was starving and had nothing. Instead of helping her, all Jane could think to do was beat her and then lock her away with no chance to speak her side."

"Had it been your choice what would you have done?" Rune asked Lucy, wanting to judge her wisdom for himself.

"I would have had her confined as well, just in a kinder manner, and not locked in a pitch black cellar by herself. I would have made sure she was cleaned up, clothed, and fed at least. I would have listened to her side of the story, and talked with Alec as well once he had recovered enough to tell me his side. Jane was so blinded by anger that the girl stole from her that she never bothered to do any of those things. She just beat her and then locked her away. It's no wonder the girl lashed out the way she did when Jane tried to have her moved back to her home. She probably thinks that, because of what Jane did, all of us only want to harm her."

"My actions so far will have done nothing but convince her of precisely that," Rune answered Lucy truthfully, though it rarely, if ever, occurred to him to speak anything but truth. "It was me that caught her, and it was me that helped Jane subdue and confine her again when she was moved. Hearing your words does make me question if my actions were honorable and justified, but at the time, I had no reason not to take Jane's words as fact. It was only after Serena told me what you confided in her that I began to question it."

"Jane's not going to be happy that you are questioning her, I'm sure. Jane doesn't forgive, and she definitely holds grudges," Lucy told him with a worried expression. "If she doesn't get her way and gets angry enough, she'll do everything she can to get back at you. She won't do it outwardly for everyone to see. It will be in subtle ways, like she did to me, but rest assured; she will hit you exactly where it hurts when you least expect it."

CHAPTER FORTY

JANE FUMED on the way to the summerhouse. Her plans had been thwarted. Her level of control seemed to be slipping, and the one small seed of dissent that Luke had sown had started a cascade of others, shattering her carefully crafted routine to pieces. It wouldn't do. She had to find some way of gaining control again before everything went to shambles.

The searchers had come back carrying news that Iona and Luke had been located at Luke's cottage, not exactly a completely illogical place to look for them.

Jane set a plan into place to have the girl confined and Luke restrained as well for his trouble for the foreseeable future.

It took a while for enough workmen to gather with the necessary materials. Jane had the lock taken off the cellar door of the summerhouse now that she knew she'd had the correct key in her pocket, and they re-hung the door. The hasp and padlock were taken with them, along with hammers, nails, screws, and several good strong panels of wood.

Jane scarcely said a word on the walk through the woods to the cottage. Robert gave her a wide berth knowing she was in that sort of mood. Her plan, until she'd gotten there, was to enter the house, by force if necessary, and have the girl taken back to her own home and locked in again. Luke was to be trapped in his own home by sealing the doors and windows shut.

That plan went out the window in a fit of rage when she arrived at the cottage and peered into the window to see Luke and Iona sleeping together, curled tightly against one another.

Jane saw red, just seeing the two of them lying there together. She'd been right about Luke, Jane told herself. Men who went off to war like him and Frank really were all the same. She turned away from the window unable to hide her rage, her cheeks burning furiously. She gave orders that the door was to be sealed without delay, setting one crew to work on it immediately. Another pair started working on each of the windows.

Luke awakened with a start to hear what he at first thought to be furious pounding on the door, but it wasn't the knocking he assumed. It was the sound of several long, sturdy nails being driven through the door and into the doorframe, nailing it shut long enough for a padlock to be installed without interference.

Luke pulled on his trousers as fast as he could, as he walked toward the window, only to find it being covered along with the others on the first floor. Darkness overtook the room as they were nailed closed with he and Iona still inside.

"Jane, what in hell are you doing?" Luke yelled, yanking at the doorknob, only to find it was useless to try opening it, even when he'd undone the lock. He had no choice but to go up to the loft and try to get his head out of the window up there. He reached the top to see that someone was putting a board over it as well.

"You know damned well what I'm doing and why, Mr. Fernsby," Jane yelled from outside as Luke neared the door again. He found Iona frightened and sitting on her knees, crying almost hysterically. "If you're concerned about your little whore, more than the safety of the people on this island, then she can just stay in there with you for all I care. Neither of you are leaving that cottage until we can be sure that the both of you are no longer a threat."

Luke yelled and pounded against the door, but the nails held. Jane didn't say another word. She and the others had walked away, and the garden outside had gone quiet and still.

Iona was still whimpering when Luke turned back to her to help her up from the floor, pulling her into his arms to comfort her.

"All will be well, Iona, we're together. You're not alone," he whispered to her, trying to be reassuring. "We have plenty to eat for a good long while, and all the water we could need, a good bed to sleep in, and a fire to stay warm. We're in no danger here, I promise."

"Are they ever going to let us out? Why won't they listen?" Iona asked, her voice still trembling. Luke tried to dry her tears, but he couldn't stop them falling. The only light in the place was from the fire. He drew her over to the table, taking a match and lighting one of the oil lamps his mother had always kept to read by on stormy nights.

Iona calmed a little once it was no longer as dark. She still looked barely more than a frightened girl, standing there barefoot in his mother's old nightgown.

Luke stoked the fire; glad he'd seen fit to keep a good supply of wood indoors. He'd been instructed of the way items replenished themselves, and he had started being mindful. He would make sure Iona was as well, so that it continued to happen and their supplies wouldn't dwindle.

Iona helped herself to a handful of grapes and raspberries, and had needed not much more than a gentle reminder to leave some for later so they wouldn't run out. Luke set about making them a more substantial breakfast of scrambled eggs, toast, and a bowl of porridge.

Iona always looked suspicious and guarded while she ate, but by then, she at least seemed to be trusting that Luke wasn't going to take the food he'd given her away. He offered her a cup of tea to wash it down with, now that it had cooled enough that she wouldn't scald herself if she drank it too quickly.

Luke didn't know what to think when Iona gathered the dishes as soon as he'd finished eating. She took the rest of the water in the teakettle and mixed it with water from the sink before she began to wash them.

"You needn't do that by yourself. I don't mind helping," Luke told her. She shooed him away and took the dishtowel out of his hands when he tried to help her do the cleaning.

"I'm not going to be staying here without earning my keep," Iona told him, blushing as she got back to work, wiping down the table once she was done scrubbing and drying the dishes. She wouldn't hear of him lifting a finger to help her, and gave him a long-suffering look until he settled into the rocking chair to watch her.

Iona didn't come closer until the work was finished. Luke's breath caught in his throat when she knelt at his feet in front of him, laying her head into his lap. He hadn't been prepared for what came next. He took a staggered breath as his hands took hold of hers to stop her, his voice trembling as he whispered, "Iona, you don't have to do this."

He was not exactly sure what to think when Iona genuinely laughed. He tugged her gently upward as he stood from the chair until she was standing in front of him.

It did Luke's heart good to see Iona looking at him with a genuine smile on her face. It was hard to say no when she was looking at him that way. Obviously, in the past earning her keep had meant more than keeping the house clean. Iona was clearly confused by his reluctance. She'd only done what would have been expected of her before, in any experience she'd had thus far.

Luke had no idea how he was going to impress upon her, that she wasn't obligated to offer herself to him in that way. Figuring that out seemed as if it would make however long they were going to be confined together even more an exercise in self-control than he'd bargained for.

CHAPTER FORTY-ONE

JANE'S TEMPER was still boiling as she made her way back to the summerhouse to get ready for the evening gathering. The workmen had, for the most part, headed home to put their tools away, leaving her to take the last part of the path alone.

If she'd been angry with Luke before, now she was more furious than ever for reasons she couldn't even explain. He'd not only defied her at every turn, he'd freed the thief without a second thought, and even taken her to bed like a common whore. Jane didn't understand why that bothered her as much, if not worse, than anything else Luke had done. He was just like the rest of them, led around by his hormones with no regard for right and wrong.

Martha stayed clear of Jane; she had come in and gone straight for the coffee pot. She sank into the window seat as she settled in to drink it. At least Martha had the sense to keep the small children quiet and out of Jane's hair.

The summerhouse was starting to fill up as people began to gather. Lucy, Alec, Rune, and Serena were conspicuously absent, which was doing nothing to make Jane's boiling temper lower to a simmer.

A few moments before the gathering began, Robert came in, bringing Kendall with him.

The wheels in Jane's head were already turning as she watched Kendall sit down to eat with Robert. The girl looked older than Serena, and she was likely to have lived some time longer than Serena had. Based on what Robert had told her earlier, she was still holding quite a grudge for some perceived slight she believed Serena had committed toward her.

With little to be done after the meal was finished, people sat and talked quietly amongst themselves. Jane let it be known that she wished to speak with Kendall alone before she went home. She wanted to get a feel for what the girl knew about Serena, and just what sort of information she might be able to use against Serena if it became necessary to knock her down a peg or two.

Rune was far too inclined to listen to his wife. Anything that could sway him to Jane's favor and make Serena look unreasonable, incompetent, or unreliable, was exactly the sort of thing she needed to hold over Serena's head. She was willing to do anything to put the odds of Rune's cooperation back in her favor. Without him, she had very little chance of squelching dissent if someone like Luke, or one of the others stronger than her, became determined enough to oppose her.

Jane didn't say much until she and Kendall had walked down the beach to sit on the rocks. She didn't want anyone to overhear the sort of things she had to say, or the questions she planned to ask.

"You're Kendall Bolton I presume? My name is Jane Boyd," she'd told her, settling into the rocks and trying to let her anger simmer so she wouldn't appear anything else other than maybe a little stern and matronly.

"Yes, I just got here last night. I'm still trying to figure out how. I guess Serena must be telling the truth, because when I woke up this wasn't just another messed up dream. My eye hurts, but when I looked in the mirror..." Kendall shuddered not finishing the thought.

"You saw your home as it is now, not as it was when it was your home. It happens to us all. It's best to cover the mirrors up or put them away where they cannot bother you," Jane answered, trying to do her best to appear warm and sympathetic to her situation.

"My eye still hurts. I can't even see how bad my face looks, but I'm sure I got her back just as good." Kendall groaned, gingerly prodding at what she was sure was a black eye and swollen cheek. She winced from the pain.

"You have a good black eye going there, and some bruises, but nothing that won't heal with a little time. We'll find you some ice to put on it when we go back in a few moments, and I can get you something to help with the pain. Why did she strike you?"

"I hit her first. I was so angry when she told me what had happened. I'm still angry. It never would have happened if she hadn't left me. Serena promised me she'd never leave me. We were both in the wreck, and then they took us to different hospitals. She was hurt a lot worse than I was. They wouldn't let me see her. The doctors said only family was allowed in, but she was my family. Then one day, a while later, Mom came and told me that she'd died."

"It appears a good deal of time had passed for you between when she left and when you arrived here. For Serena it's only been a short while. That explains why she looks just as she did when you last saw her, while you've aged. She's made a home here, even fallen in love and married."

"You mean the tall, long haired man who was with her, the one who pulled her off me?"

"Yes, that would be the one. His name is Rune. They both arrived here days apart." Jane conveniently left out the circumstances of how they met, figuring it was best to let Kendall believe it had been purely a romantic attraction that had brought them together and not quite the still enigmatic chain of events that had transpired.

"It does make me wonder what he sees in her. I've never known Serena to go anywhere near a man before. She's always been afraid of them. I guess frigid wouldn't be all that inaccurate of a description. I'm shocked that she'd let a man anywhere close to her, let alone have sex with one."

"It's probably best left unknown, but she wasn't the only woman here that had her eye on him. Your guess is as good as mine why he chose her, and not one of the rest of us. I would suffer to guess, that if she really is as frigid you've implied, that Serena probably won't have his eye forever. It will only be her own fault for not keeping him satisfied if that happens."

Kendall was a bit surprised at how bluntly and candidly Jane was speaking about the situation. She didn't tone down any of her thoughts on the situation when she asked, "So, I take it from the way you're talking, you're one of those other women that had your eye on him?"

"Oh no, dear, Rune is far too young for me, but I can think of a couple of young ladies I think would have been a far more suitable companion for him. Their relationship has proven to be quite a distraction for him when it comes to keeping him on task in the role I wish for him to take on here. I'm afraid Serena's insecurity is interfering with him being able to perform his duties quite often as of late."

"She can be just a little clingy sometimes, then again, she doesn't really have much of anyone else. Most of her family died, and the aunts and uncles that were left hated her mom so much they wouldn't take her in. She doesn't even have a dad, because from what I heard, her mom slept with so many different men for drugs that no one knows which one it could have been. A social worker gave Serena to her grandparents, but they both died, and she wound up in a foster home. I met her there when we were thirteen."

"You were living with the same family, so you know her quite well then?"

"I'd say I know her really well. Eventually I got to go home with my mom. I was only there because we didn't have a place to live at the time, but Serena got stuck there until she was old enough to get a job and move out on her own. We worked at a lot of the same places, including the diner we were working at when the wreck happened. I told her not to drive so fast, but she was worried we wouldn't get away from the fire fast enough. The smoke was just too bad. I know she tried to stop, but we just couldn't in time. It's her own stupid fault she's here."

"And you're angry at her for getting you both into that situation? I would be also," Jane replied, amused the girl had already given her far much more information than she had hoped for. Kendall was angry, rash, and far too eager to vent her anger to anyone who would listen.

"You're damned right I'm angry," Kendall told her, tears welling in her eyes. "It was all her fault. If that wreck hadn't happened, I wouldn't have been hurt. If I hadn't been hurt, I wouldn't have had to take those pain pills. I couldn't stop taking them. I tried, but I'd get so sick if I didn't have them. Eventually I started looking for cheaper ways to take the pain away. It was all I could think about every day. I must have taken too much. If I really have died, it's her fault I'm here. Serena ruined my life."

CHAPTER FORTY-TWO

THE END OF PEACE, as Serena had started to know it, hadn't begun with more flying fists but with whispers. She could not help but notice the sideways glances she was being given, or the hushed whispers that stopped when she came into the room. Kendall, and those she'd enmeshed herself with, seemed to always be at the center.

Jane, quite pointedly, had done nothing to stop what was happening. If anything, she was fanning the flames. Jane loved gossip, especially the more twisted the story became as it went from person to person.

Kendall knew far too much about Serena's life. She was eager, in her spite, to tell every dirty little secret she knew about Serena's past to Jane and anyone else who would lend her an ear to listen.

It took Rune some time to catch on to what was happening. Lucy noticed immediately, but the rumors and gossip hushed for the most part when Rune came near.

Lucy had told him that it was very likely Jane wanted him to believe that what was being done was only in Serena's head. Gaslighting was one of Jane's favorite weapons when she was targeting someone for exclusion. Lucy couldn't begin to imagine why

Jane was targeting Serena, who had done nothing to deserve
her wrath.

It was fortunate, Serena surmised, that she'd been so honest with
Rune about her past from the beginning. Few of the things Kendall let
slip were of any surprise to him. He asked a few questions, usually
only when he caught wind of something that had been twisted, mostly
the rumors about her being of unknown parentage.

Rune knew she was an illegitimate child, and that her mother had
slept with men to support her drug habit, but Serena preferred that
not everyone know. A lot of people looked at her far differently than
before, especially those from a time before it became so normal and
accepted to have children out of wedlock.

Luke and Iona had also not been freed, nor had Jane given hint of
any inclination to free them from their makeshift prison. It hadn't
taken long for Lucy to figure out what had become of them with Rune
and Serena's help. Little could be done for them without rousing
suspicion and sending Jane on even more of a tirade. There was a
small window in the bath that wasn't large enough to crawl through,
but it was large enough for some supplies to be passed in, and to hold
a conversation clearly once the screen had been removed.

Their society was quickly forming into two camps, those that
sided with Jane, and those who saw through what she was doing and
were starting to realize that she needed to be stopped. Those in the
second camp, once they were recognized for what they were, quickly
became targets, either for rumors, or covert hostility.

Jane, up until recently, had not resorted to violence but her
manner of handling Iona had proven she was capable. They could
only assume that had been her plan all along for Rune. She wanted to
use him to do her dirty work so she could keep her own hands clean
and seemingly blameless. Rune was strong, and a force to be reckoned
with when angered, something Jane had wanted to take full advantage
of.

When rumors and subtle tactics no longer sufficed, Serena knew it
was almost certain that Kendall would only get more vicious. Kendall
hadn't attacked her again physically, something Serena could have

easily guarded herself against. Kendall would start going after things and people that she loved as she had in the past when she'd been angry enough. Kendall had more than once stolen and destroyed her belongings, even sabotaged her friendships and relationships with other people out of anger and jealousy.

Serena had more than once wondered why she'd even kept her as a friend, and the only reason she could think of, was that she had no one else. Even if Kendall was more like an enemy half of the time than an actual friend in her previous life, she was all she'd had short of being completely alone.

This time, however, Serena wasn't alone. She had Rune and Lucy, and it seemed now, Alec. He was becoming a permanent fixture glued to Lucy's side, avoiding Jane as much as he could. Once Alec had stopped fearing Rune, they had seemed to have finally become friends. Rune had taken the boy under his wing, so to speak, and taken on a more fatherly role as he had with Lucy, even though he was only twelve years older.

Serena was trying to find what happiness she could in what she did have, even if it was difficult. Lucy had tried to assure her it would blow over and things could not keep going this way forever. Eventually Jane would slip up and people would start to see what was happening for the ridiculous lot of utter nonsense it actually was. All any of them could do was hang in there together until it happened.

Something, however, was still nagging in the back of Serena's mind. Lucy's words were only empty assurances in an attempt to keep her spirits up. She especially felt that way every time she saw that accursed barn owl that she was seeing too much for her comfort as of late. It did nothing to placate her already spinning mind, or her anxiety. If anything, it only gave her the gnawing suspicion that the worst was yet to come.

CHAPTER FORTY-THREE

THE DARK CORNERS Serena's mind had gone to since Kendall's arrival had not done them any favors. If anything, the longer things went on, the more depressed she became and the further she retreated into her shell when she wasn't home with Rune or Lucy.

Kendall picked up on her reaction like a shark would sense blood, and figuratively twisted the knife in her back deeper.

It couldn't go on this way, not without it driving Serena insane. She was already throwing up a wall to block the pain away, one that it was getting harder and harder for anyone to penetrate. They'd found her weakness, and that happened to be her love for Rune. When rumors had not swayed him to abandon her; Serena began to fear they'd not hesitate to stoop even lower.

Rune had taken it upon himself to check on Luke and Iona at least once a day. He figured it was the least he could do, even if apologies given through the tiny window for his past behavior felt far little too late. By then, it had been agreed upon that something had to be done about Jane, but until Rune had a more accurate assessment of who could be relied upon to be on their side, he had no intention of acting. Luke had charged him with finding out who else was open to the idea of a rebellion. As impatient as he was to be free, he was willing to put aside his own comfort to lull Jane into a false sense of security, at least temporarily.

Many quiet talks had taken place between he and Luke at the window, usually during the hours most of the others would have been at gatherings or sleeping.

Rune never lingered more than several minutes, careful to be sure they weren't overheard. The things they spoke of tonight weren't much different than most, except for the concerns Rune had for his wife. He wasn't fond of speaking of his troubles to just anyone, but he hadn't wanted to burden Lucy with his concerns more than she was already burdened with the same ones herself.

"What's on your mind, Rune? You seem troubled," Luke asked with a worried expression on his face. Iona was sleeping, so they were alone at the window for once. He and Iona had no routine. They had simply taken to doing the things they could to pass the time, mostly sleeping, and puttering around the house.

"Now that she has you and the girl trapped, Jane and Kendall have made Serena the new victim of their scheming. I cannot understand what she could have done to deserve this," Rune told him sighing heavily. He crossed his arms as he leaned against the side of the cottage. "I am the one that Jane should be angry with. I am the one who will no longer obey her, but each time I refuse, it is Serena they punish and not me. Serena has nothing to do with my choices in that matter. She and Lucy made me aware of Jane's treachery, but the choices I have made are mine, and I would much prefer she take her anger out on me."

"Oh eventually she will, once she figures out your weakness, but until then, I think she's gone after your missus because she's easier to hurt. That girl, Kendall, is so blinded by her anger, it sounds as if she's feeding Jane all the ammunition she could possibly hope for," Luke replied with a somber tone to his voice. He was sympathetic, but there was only so much he could do, being still locked inside. "I don't think the girl realizes Jane's only using her, she probably thinks she's found a friend who dislikes Serena as much as she does. The woman can be bloody convincing."

"What would you have me do?" Rune asked, lost for once, trying to think of a solution short of turning back into the brute that most of those there assumed him to be. "I cannot just sit idly by and let my wife's good name and heart be destroyed. I want them to leave her in peace and take their anger in her place."

"Mark my words, your turn is coming, but not until they've all but destroyed her. If Jane thinks Serena is the reason you're not listening anymore, she'll do anything in the world to tear the both of you apart. You're too strong together. Soon they'll do whatever they can to plant the seed of doubt in that girl's mind about how much you love her and what she means to you. Divide and conquer is the oldest trick in the book and that woman knows it, Rune."

"What can I do? I could lock her up again as you did, but Serena and I would only find ourselves in much the same situation that you and the girl are in now. There are too many people willing to come blindly to her aid. Until I am sure we have allies, I don't believe that course of action is possible. I am worried what would become of my wife and the children if I were unable to watch over them."

"I can't say I blame you. Keeping people turned against one another is how people like Jane stay in power, especially if they can use angry and frustrated people who only want someone to take their pain and troubles out on. She'll take you all apart one at a time, unless you can find a way to get the others to band together and put a stop to it. It's not something you can do alone, sometimes it takes an army, even if it's a peaceful one."

CHAPTER FORTY-FOUR

THE DAY BEGAN like any other; with work to be done. There was cooking and baking to do, and laundry to hang out on the line. Rune left once their meal was finished, taking a warm portion to Luke and Iona along with a tin full of scones that Lucy had helped Serena bake for them. He hadn't been gone quite twenty minutes when the fog rolled in and the horn started to blare, just as he'd arrived at Luke's cottage and handed the parcels inside.

Unlike many of the others, Rune wasn't afraid of the fog. He stood by the cottage watching with interest and telling Luke what he could see and where the beam of light had fallen when it stilled.

The fog meant a search party had to be formed, so Rune couldn't linger. He made his apologies and began making his way, the fastest way he knew, to the summerhouse.

He didn't bother going to Serena's home on his way, knowing she would meet him there once the fog had cleared. It wasn't often they were separated during a fog, but he had confidence that she could make her way on her own as she often did. He had a good chance of meeting up with her along the end of the trail if he walked slowly enough.

He was most of the way to the summerhouse when he heard a

scream. It didn't sound like Serena, thankfully, but it did sound like the cry of a young woman in distress.

The path through the woods was tricky in places in this part, and it was unwise to stray from it to try to take shortcuts due to the deep ravines that were hard to see. He wasn't horribly far from the place Alec had taken his tumble, in similar terrain along another trail.

Hearing the fear in those cries, Rune broke into a run. He was careful to stay on the trail and watch his footing. It didn't take him long to find the source of the cries. A woman's hands clung to a tree sapling at the edge of a ravine, trying to pull herself up, likely having lost her way in the fog and fallen off the trail.

"I am here, I will help you, hold on," Rune called out, kneeling down and doing his best to get his arms up underneath hers so he could wrap them around her. He had to pull her up by her body, and not her hands or wrists which would slip too easily, especially if she'd already been struggling to hang on far too long.

The girl screamed and cried until he pulled her up and got her away from the edge and out into the middle of the trail again. It wasn't until her long dark curls had been pushed back from her eyes that he realized the girl he'd just rescued was Kendall. He couldn't lie to himself, even if he'd known, Rune still wouldn't have just left her to fall, much as he'd have entertained the thought.

"Soon as you have caught your breath, hurry yourself along, carefully next time," Rune told Kendall, figuring it wasn't going to do much more harm to leave her there to cry. He had no more sympathy for her now that she was out of danger.

Kendall started after him down the trail, feigning that Rune was walking too fast, and she couldn't keep up with him. "You're not going to help me find my way?" Kendall called after him until he came to a stop and turned back to look at her. She took a step in front of him to keep him from leaving and did her best to try to seem more helpless than she was. "How do you think I got into this mess? I got lost in the fog, and I don't even know which way to go." The part about the fog was true at least, even though now that it had cleared she knew very well where she was, and that the trail that led to Serena's house wasn't all that far behind them.

"If you want to follow, you will just have to keep up on your own," Rune told her trying to brush past again only to have Kendall stubbornly stand her ground with an enigmatic expression.

"I haven't even thanked you properly yet, or are you that afraid I'll bite? I can only imagine the line of bullshit Serena's got you believing about what really happened," Kendall told him, stepping closer when she saw Serena and Lucy coming into view, but he wouldn't have noticed with his back turned to them. Her expression turned to a smirk and she waited until he tried to sidestep around her to grab hold and lean up to kiss him. It didn't get the reaction she'd hoped for.

Rune was quick to push her away, letting her fall to the ground. Serena had seen, something he'd become aware of when he heard Lucy let out a string of curses. Kendall laughed from her spot on the ground.

Serena didn't say a word; she stood frozen, seemingly not even hearing Lucy's words when she began to cuss at Kendall. Rune stammered his apology walking toward her. Instead of coming close to him, for the first time he could remember since she'd chosen him, he saw tears start to fall and she turned and ran away from him.

Enraged, Lucy leapt on Kendall. Kendall had no trouble blocking her blows and tossed her aside before walking away toward the summerhouse, still laughing.

Lucy seethed as Rune pulled her up from the ground and lifted her onto his back. He started after Serena who, unfortunately, by then was well out of sight.

Serena hadn't gotten far on the trail before she broke into a faster run. It was all she could do to keep from screaming. She ran, blinded by tears and not really caring where she was going other than away from there. It wasn't the first time Kendall had done this sort of thing.

Kendall had seduced almost every boy Serena had shown even the slightest interest in when they were in high school, and even since. What frightened her most of all is when Kendall set her mind to do it, she'd always won.

Serena was scared to death that if Kendall now had her sights set on Rune, she didn't stand a chance of stopping her from taking him.

Her mind played every trick it could on her as she ran, especially those doubts Jane and Kendall had been so carefully picking apart. She thought of what she knew Rune wanted more than anything that she couldn't give to him. Those things had gnawed at her from the beginning, but now those festering doubts were threatening to tear the confidence she once had in his love for her to pieces.

Her teeth chattered even with the exertion of the run. She finally looked around and realized she had no idea where she was or how far she'd gone.

The path she was on didn't become familiar until she noticed branches that had been cut through with an axe. A few steps more and she saw the wall looming overhead with the barn owl perched atop of it staring down at her.

The gate had been padlocked at Jane's order, not that Serena cherished the idea of passing that way again. The owl flew North away from the shore, so she followed the wall that direction, figuring it had to eventually lead somewhere. She pushed through the undergrowth. Rune was right about learning to walk in the darkness. She wasn't nearly as afraid of facing what was ahead of her as she was behind her if she turned back.

Some distance away, there was a section of the wall that had crumbled and collapsed. Serena climbed onto it. It wasn't all that had been left in ruins. Whether it had been a fortress or some sort of temple, Serena had no way of knowing, but the arches and pillars that still stood towered far overhead. She made it to the other side of the wall and made her way inside, winding her way in between the well overgrown parts and all the trees and vines that had grown up inside, covering the ruin.

Somehow, she became too fascinated and sad to be afraid. The shivering stopped when she came to a dais where a silver haired old man waited for her. He was tall, and his hair fell in almost wild curls around his head. His clothing was strange, though inexplicably she felt at ease with him. The air he projected was of someone wise and almost grandfatherly. The barn owl swooped down and landed on one of his broad shoulders.

"Why is it you've come here, child? What has you in so much pain that you cannot let go of that world?" Sulwyn asked her with a sad expression.

"Something I want very badly that I cannot ever have if I stay. I never knew just how badly I wanted it, until I could never have it," Serena told him giving him an honest answer.

"I do have the power to send you back for a time. The wish that is written on your heart will be granted, but you will suffer greatly to have it. In one year's time, you will have to return and leave it behind in that world, and you cannot return again until your appointed time has come. Are you prepared?"

"To have that part of him, I would do anything," Serena replied, her voice not much over a whisper.

Sulwyn held out his hand to her, and she took it as he led her to what looked like a featherbed covered with silken blankets that had been made up on another smaller platform in the center of the dais.

"If you are certain, lie down and sleep, child. When you open your eyes, you will awaken back in that world," Sulwyn answered softly as he helped her to lie down. He covered her with the softest blanket Serena could ever recall feeling against her skin. "The owls will be there, to remind you that what I have said is no dream. You will return in exactly one year. Be prepared to say your goodbyes and know that you may not interfere with the destiny of another. Everything comes, as it should, in its own time. Do not trouble yourself, but have faith in it, all is well."

He'd no sooner spoken the words than Serena's eyes grew heavy. The weight spread from her eyes to the rest of her tired body and soul. She felt as if she were sinking not only into sleep, but like the weight of the world was pressing down on her. Even if she wanted to turn back, she was too far-gone with sleep. There was nothing but silence.

CHAPTER FORTY-FIVE

RUNE RAN with Lucy on his back toward Serena's house. He couldn't run the risk of leaving the child behind to potentially face Jane's wrath if she were found wandering alone. He took her into the house, listening to the small child curse under her breath. Wet, angry tears streamed down her face. It was the only place he figured Serena would have gone. When they arrived, however, the house was empty. He and Lucy had searched every room. Rune could scarcely breathe for the feeling that clawed at him, threatening to turn him back into the very beast of a man Serena once feared.

He had no choice but to leave Lucy with Alec. He took off at a run to where it had all begun, cursing himself for his sense of honor instead of leaving Kendall to fall when he had the chance.

The footprints he found in the soft earth told him everything he needed to know. Serena had not taken the path home, but fled down another to the west. If he had been looking before, he would have seen. He couldn't undertake the search alone, but he no longer trusted Jane or most of the others to help him. In his heart, he knew they'd only hinder him out of spite. Luke had been right, it had been coming and, like a fool, he'd let his guard down.

Without even stopping, he was soon on the trail at a full run toward Luke's cottage, going towards the only help he believed he could rely upon. He arrived out of breath. Rune pounded on the window and waited for Luke to answer him, his heart still thumping in his chest. He had to find her, but he needed help and if he ran into danger, it was best he wasn't on the journey alone. Luke came to the window blurry eyed.

"Rune, what's happened now?" Luke asked, noticing the stricken look on Rune's face, even through the tiny window. He wasn't prepared to see fear on the face of a man he knew to be far braver than most, and it shook him.

"It's happened, you were right. They found a way to make her doubt. Serena ran away, and I know where she's gone. I need your help," Rune told him, still winded as he fought to keep himself calm enough to stay on task. "Tell me what I must do to free you."

"One moment," Luke told him before leaving the bathroom. He woke Iona, telling her to dress herself. He pulled the rest of his own clothing and shoes on, digging through a box of his father's tools. He took out the claw hammer and handed it to Rune out the window. "Take this, and pry off the board that's on the kitchen window, the one that faces away from the path. I'll go and knock against the board so you'll know it's the correct one. While you work on it, I'll finish gathering the other things we'll need. Let's get moving."

Luke stepped away from the window and ran to the kitchen, opening the window itself and tapping firmly against the board that covered it until he heard Rune beginning to pry the board away. Luke went to gather the things they needed, finding his field pack and tossing the supplies inside, rope, his knife, and an axe that he could have easily cut through the boards himself with. He put new batteries inside his torch, and also tossed an extra set into his pack, just in case they were gone longer than one set would allow for.

Iona was dressed by the time Rune had the board off. Luke knew she couldn't help but be a little afraid when she saw who was outside the window, even if she'd accepted his apology days before and was accustomed to his conversing with Luke. Hesitantly, Iona let Rune lift her to the ground before Luke passed his pack out the window and scrambled out behind her. He brought with him another handful of nails, much to Rune's confusion.

"Before we go, we need to nail the board across the window again to make it look like all is as it should be," Luke stated, lifting the board back up and handing Rune the nails so he could begin hammering them back into place. "Hopefully this will fool Jane into thinking we are still inside for a time, and she won't be out looking for us before we can find Serena."

It didn't take Rune much time to see his logic. He got the work done quickly before they gathered their things. He handed Luke the hammer and took the axe, holding it firmly in his hand as he followed Luke, going as quickly and stealthily as they could back toward his home.

Once inside, Rune lit the fire, finding it difficult not to remember things that had taken place there, both good things and things that made him feel ashamed. Once he had the fire going well, he gathered the rest of the things they needed. It was time to depart. Iona didn't hide the fear in her eyes when she knew Luke was leaving her behind. They reminded her to bolt the door with the heavy beam from inside, and to stay there until they returned for her.

There was plenty of food and clean water for her for several days, if they had to be gone that long. Rune hoped they would be gone a far shorter time than that.

It didn't take long for Rune to take Luke back toward where he'd last seen Serena. Rune knew the search parties would be busy in another part of the woods, so they worked quickly enough to follow her trail, hopefully before the others had time to trample it over.

Luke, thankfully, much like Rune was used to hiking long distances. He stayed behind Rune as he looked for signs of her trail, watching him become more crestfallen the closer the wall loomed. The trail didn't lie about her passing this way. He found scraps of fabric from her clothes, and a few strands of her hair where she had to push past branches.

Rune used the axe to cut his way through parts of the trail that had regrown, making his passage much slower than hers. The fear of being discovered didn't bother him as much as the fear that Serena could be lost, or lying hurt somewhere in the dark. It would take far longer than he feared to find his way to her.

An hour or more of walking passed before he and Luke reached the gate through the wall. Rune found the chain and lock right where he wound them securely and fastened it the last time he'd stood at that gate. Serena could not have passed this way. It didn't take him long to find where she'd begun following the wall to the North, not down another trail, but blazing a new one through the brush. It would be much harder for him to make his way through.

Once they caught their breath and took a drink of water, there wasn't much to do but get to work making themselves a wider path following the one she'd taken. Luke used his torch to light the way briefly when it became difficult to tell which way she passed. There was no sound to be heard but their own heavy breathing as they worked at the places where the brush became too thick and had to be cut back.

Hours passed and the moon had gone down by the time they found the toppled section of wall. Rune and Luke allowed themselves to sit down on it and rest. Without enough light to work by except torchlight, they'd given up following the trail any further until the moon came back up to light their way.

By then Rune was sick with worry, refusing the small bit of food Luke offered him but gladly accepting the cup of water. He hadn't meant to rest more than a few moments, but as soon as he laid his head down, he fell asleep from sheer exhaustion. He wouldn't go back, couldn't, until he found her. The thing Rune feared most of all was losing his new wife, just as he'd lost the first. If losing Kitta had nearly destroyed him, he had no doubt losing Serena would lay waste to all the good she'd found in him. He'd turn back into the monster the anger made of him, before she gave that hope back to him.

It wasn't until several hours later that Rune awoke to Luke shaking him. The moon had finally risen high enough that they had hope of following the trail again, which seemed to grow cold at the toppled section of wall that Luke and Rune slept upon. To Rune, that had meant she'd not gone anywhere from there but over it. Once he and Luke finished the climb, he picked up the trail again. The going was not quite as difficult as it had been on the other side.

Both were as taken aback to see the ruin as Serena had been. Following her path here was much simpler than it had been before, now being mostly tall grass and ferns, though occasionally overgrown with vines that were far simpler to cut away than branches.

It didn't take them long to find their way to the dais. Rune broke into a run when he noticed Serena sleeping. He wanted nothing more than to wake her and pull her into his arms.

"Stop. Do not touch her," A voice called to him from behind. He turned to see an old man standing there just as Luke hurried to his side.

"She is my wife. I have come to take her home," Rune told the old man defiantly.

"Until the time has run its course, she must not be moved if you wish for her to return unharmed. Her body sleeps, but she is not here. She has returned to the life she once knew for a time, eleven more days she will sleep. When she returns, she will tell you why she has gone herself. That is not mine to say," Sulwyn told Rune quite firmly, though it was not meant as a threat, only a mere statement of fact. "Until then, she must be watched over, and guarded, but never moved from where she sleeps. If you speak to her, she will hear you as she dreams, and it will help her find her way back to you when the time comes for her to return."

CHAPTER FORTY-SIX

PAIN. It was the first thing Serena felt when she awoke. It was almost blinding. The heaviness she felt as she'd fallen asleep hadn't faded. Machines beeped and she heard voices in the room, even if what they were saying made no sense. She tried to claw her way toward consciousness, lapsing a couple of times before she finally managed to open her eyes. She took in the room with blurred vision. She was unable to do more than cry out with a raspy voice. Her mouth and her throat were dry, and her lips felt cracked. She could only wiggle her fingers.

Monitors beeped, and then a signal wailed when she wiggled enough to slip a sensor that had been clipped to her finger off. The nurse looked at her in a panic when she saw Serena awake and looking back at her. She disappeared into the hallway before she returned to the room with some other nurses that were soon joined by a doctor.

Serena couldn't do much more than cry and protest as she was poked and prodded. Needles were jabbed into her skin like she was some sort of pincushion.

It was several moments before the doctors seemed satisfied that her reactions were voluntary, and she genuinely was awake. It had taken a while, but the more she tried to move her stiff arms, the stronger they got. Her legs stubbornly proved useless and numb.

The first few days were a blur of being wheeled about in her bed for tests of every known description. How long she slept, no one would tell her. She knew the words she wanted to say in her mind, but it was difficult to speak them. A man had been sent to her room to begin working with her, helping her to exercise her arms to get them stronger. A woman had also been sent to aid her in beginning to speak again.

There was nothing wrong with her mind. Serena knew what it meant when the doctors used the word paraplegic. She'd never walk again, nor could she feel her legs, even if she still had sensation above her waist. The clearer she could communicate, the more her circumstances were explained to her. She hadn't been asleep, days, or even weeks, but over a year. She was breathing on her own, and had shown signs of active brain activity, so she'd been kept comfortable in hopes she'd eventually awaken. No one had expected it to take quite as long as it had.

Once she was staying awake for hours at a stretch, and she'd been weaned onto more solid foods again, Serena had been released from the hospital and into the care of a therapy center attached to one of the local rest homes. She recognized it as the same place her grandfather had been sent to after her grandmother had passed away.

Life settled into a routine there rather quickly. She watched far too much television in between rounds of therapy. Her life in that other realm almost felt like a dream she remembered far too vividly. When she slept, she almost always dreamt of Rune, or sometimes when not him, she dreamt of Lucy. More than once at night, she opened her eyes to see the barn owl perched outside her window watching her.

The morning began like any other, having been told she was being assigned a new physical therapist that was going to be working with her on getting her strong enough to get out of bed and move around with a manual wheelchair.

Owen was softly spoken, but he reminded Serena vaguely of Rune when he knocked before coming into the room. It was mostly because of his coloring, his eyes, and the way he carried himself.

Owen spent an hour with her after breakfast every morning, and sometimes even came again in late afternoon before dinner for a shorter time. Like Rune, he had a kind heart, but he could be quite a tyrant when it came to pushing her buttons and making her work harder than she sometimes wished to. He stubbornly refused to let her give up, and especially so when she became frustrated with her limitations. If she cried, he'd sit and comfort her, but as soon as her tears were dried, he'd go right back to pushing her forward again.

He was the first to notice something was amiss weeks later when Serena started getting ill after breakfast. She had to stop exercising a couple of times to fight off the nausea that was overwhelming her. They lightened the nature of her exercises to ones she could do from her bed in the morning, and moved the heavier ones to the evening session while the doctors ran tests.

Serena was the only one not confused when it was discovered that she was three months pregnant. There had of course been a lot of questions, none of which Serena could give answers to. The police understandably began an investigation of the men who could have come into contact with her while she was in the hospital. Serena knew it would prove fruitless.

Serena was surprisingly calm, considering what was implied had been done to her, and she didn't become agitated until the possibility of an abortion was suggested. She wasted no time making it quite clear she had no intention of terminating the pregnancy. If she decided she could not raise the child with her disabilities, she intended to give birth to it and place it up for adoption.

Her exercises had been modified in light of her condition, but Owen still spent an hour or more a day being a harsh taskmaster, telling her that if she did have any hope of getting strong enough to take care of the baby, she'd had to work a lot harder than she had been. The baby wasn't going to accept stopping because it hurt, or because she was tired, which was an excuse she gave to him quite often.

"Come on, you've only done two sets, not three, get the lead out," Owen teased her as she looked up at him panting from the bench she'd been strapped to where he had her doing rowing motions to build up some strength in her arms and back.

"If you think it's so easy to do, being wrapped up like a mummy just using your arms, you do it," Serena grumped at him, sweat already dampening her forehead and her flushed cheeks. She begrudgingly went back to doing another set.

"Could do it with my eyes closed." Owen chuckled, ticking her off even more when he tucked his feet under the bench and did a sit up for every rep she counted.

"You don't have to be so chipper in the morning, or such a damned show off," Serena muttered, pushing her way through the last few she had left to do, knowing it was the only way to get him to shut up about it. Owen had discovered, much to her annoyance, that when she was wimping out, getting her mad at him enough to just do what he asked was the best way to get her to push her way through it. The longer she'd come to know him, the more he'd become like Rune in ways that were almost infuriating.

Serena didn't talk to anyone about the things that happened to her when she was sleeping, or the place she'd gone and the things she'd seen. She was convinced they'd only tell her she needed therapy of an entirely different sort. It only added to the loneliness she felt, especially when she lay in bed at night, thinking of Rune. She never realized that she'd miss him this badly. She was frightened that if what Sulwyn had told her proved true, she'd only go back again to find Kendall had taken her place. The thought of that had more than once brought tears to her eyes.

She hadn't had a single visitor since she'd awakened, and there was no one she wanted them to call. The aunts, uncles, and distant cousins of hers that still lived couldn't have cared less if she lived or died. As much as he angered her, Owen had become the closest thing she had to a friend. Sometimes before the evening session, his wife Hanna, who worked there as a dietician, was the one who brought her meals in. Hanna was supposed to be helping her to eat. Fine motor skills were another thing Owen was working with her on, and Owen refused to let Hanna feed her. He made Serena do it herself with Hanna guiding her.

The two of them seemed to have an interesting relationship. Hanna and Owen had known one another since they were children, growing up in the same small isolated farming town. They'd fallen in love in high school and gotten married just after graduation. A few years after they'd married, Hanna had been diagnosed with cancer, and she'd spent a handful of years battling it before finally beating it.

They'd put off starting a family while Owen was working his way through college, but the cancer was what dashed their hopes of the big family they'd once planned. Hanna was healthy, and that was all that mattered, or so Owen kept reminding her whenever she found herself in tears over the matter.

As the months passed, and she got to know them better, Serena thought of their story more and more. Especially as she came to grips with knowing she'd have to find a home for the child inside her. She'd get to hold it, but would not live to see it grow up. She knew how badly Hanna wanted children, but no adoption agency they'd spoken to would consider accepting someone in remission from cancer for so short a time, if at all.

By the time she'd made her decision, Serena was far enough along that she knew that she was having a son. The ultrasound picture she'd been given was always kept in a photo frame on the nightstand next to her bed. She marveled, watching her stomach as the child rolled and kicked inside her. All she wanted was to know that he'd be loved and cared for once she was gone, and when she looked at Owen and Hanna, she saw more than enough love to move mountains. She just had to find the courage to ask them if they'd even consider what she had in mind for both her son, and for them.

CHAPTER FORTY-SEVEN

DAYS PASSED and Rune didn't leave Serena's side. Luke and Lucy often made the journey between Serena's home and where Rune sat next to her in the silence of the ruin. There was nothing to keep him company in the moments he was left alone with her there but the owls that he swore, until then, must have been only her imagination. He regretted not believing her, more than he ever thought that he would, even for something so small and seemingly unimportant.

He wished more than anything that he could close his eyes and join her in sleep until she awakened, but that wish was not granted. There was nothing he could do but watch over her. He slept by her side with his arm curled around her protectively as he always had. He would allow no one else, except Lucy, to touch her.

The fear in Lucy's eyes had been plain to see the first time Luke had brought her to that place. She'd stared ghostly pale at Serena's face, touching her to be sure she was breathing and looking more child-like than anyone had ever seen her. She came often to help him watch over her after that, though they were careful to leave and make sure that Luke had gone back into hiding before the moon got too high in the sky.

Luke was growing impatient to leave his hiding place and have the situation with Jane be over and dealt with. He worried that his staunchest allies were both presently lost to him until Serena awakened. That too had been Jane's doing, as far as Luke was concerned. Jane had fanned the flames and not reigned in the hellion of a girl when she'd had the chance to, out of nothing but sheer spite and hatefulness.

Lucy noticed Luke shivering that morning, as they walked back toward Serena's home. Iona waited there with Alec for them to return. She and Alec had become friends now that they'd made their apologies to one another. They realized the other wasn't as frightening as they once seemed.

"What's bothering you, Luke? Don't tell me it's nothing," Lucy asked him, noticing the way he seemed to be so deep in thought. He wasn't frightened, but Lucy could tell when someone was trembling with anger when she saw it.

"It has to end. Something has to be done about her." Luke answered quietly, his voice far calmer and controlled than the rest of him. "The things she is doing, and the things she has done are doing nothing but tearing what you've all worked so hard to build here apart. Why won't more people stand up to her? She's only one blasted woman. She's not a leader; she's just the one who shouts the loudest. The rest of us are only pawns to her, and I wish others would open their eyes and see it."

"To oust Jane you'd have to get Martha and Robert to both be willing to stand up to her," Lucy told him, not slowing their walk, even if her voice took on a much more serious tone about the matter. "When I led the council, there were five of us to prevent this sort of matter, now there are only two others. Robert is rather fearful of Jane after seeing what she's done to others that have opposed her. It won't be easy to gain his trust and make him take a stand. Martha may be easier to persuade; she does stand up to Jane occasionally. She is far more likely than Robert to listen and see your side, if you can convince her that Jane has her own interests that don't share those of us all at heart."

"Will they still listen to you if you talk to them?" Luke asked, curious at just how much influence Lucy still had among the others.

He'd gathered she'd once been a well-respected leader, who had done much to make their society what it was. He had faith some of the others would be inclined to at least hear her out about the matter at hand.

"Those who have been here the longest, the ones that know me best, are the ones that may," Lucy told him, sighing deeply. "They knew me before I became a child again, and see me for all I was. I often play the childish fool for Jane far more often than I should, if nothing but for my safety. I am far too small now to defend myself anymore. It won't be long, a year or so at most, and I truly will be the child that Jane and a lot of the others take me for. I don't wish to leave this place still in her hands when that happens. The thought of that frightens me just as badly as what is coming. What is going to happen to all these people I have come to love and care for once I am gone? A new council must be chosen, a council capable of standing up and doing what is right. I could easily see both you and Rune taking the lead, but there must be more than three or four that sit upon it. All sides must be heard, and choices must be made with people's heads and hearts for the good of all. They've lost sight of that. Decisions that affect so many cannot be left in the hands of so few, or worse yet, only one."

"You sound like a wise woman to me. If I'd have been here sooner, I would have taken your side, for the lot of good it does me to say that now. You do realize that the only way out of this mess we're all in is together?"

"I know that, Luke. But who's strong enough or brave enough to stand up to her? We'll need more than just the two of us."

"I realize that, Lucy. That's why I want you to talk to the others. I want you to tell them the truth about what's being done and what's happened, especially the last few days, and make them understand. All that's gone wrong has been enough to drive Serena to near madness, and brought one of the strongest men I've ever met to his knees. It has to end now, or only God knows which one of them is next, make them see it."

"It won't be easy."

"Nothing good ever is. Every good deed I've ever done my whole life has been an uphill battle, and I've sat in plenty of trenches saving men's lives with bombs raining down on my head. Nothing is more deadly than the enemy that hides among you and pretends to be your friend, and that's exactly what Jane's become. I have faith in you, Lucy. Please help me. I cannot do this alone, but together we stand at least a fighting chance of taking control of our lives again. If we don't at least try now, while we have the chance, we'll be wishing until the end of time that we had."

CHAPTER FORTY-EIGHT

SUMMER WAS MOSTLY GONE and autumn was quickly approaching. There wasn't much for Serena to do every day besides write in her journal, now that her hands were somewhat working well again. Owen told her it was excellent practice for fine motor skills, so he brought her the journals and all the pens she could ask for, adding thick rubber grips to them to make them easier for her to hold on to.

Unable to think of anything else to write about, she wrote to her unborn son, writing in her journal a series of letters, calling him by the name his father had already chosen for him. Rune believed, as his ancestors did, that the dead returned to their loved ones through their names. Since the moment she'd been told she was having a son, he'd become Soren to her. She stubbornly refused to consider calling him any other name.

The police's witch-hunt for Soren's father had come up empty, just as Serena knew that it would. Serena knew they'd never find him, because Soren's father was not of this world any longer, and hadn't been for a long time. They could not find what was not there to be found.

True to what Sulwyn foretold, the pregnancy was not an easy one. The closer to term she neared, the more difficult it became. In her condition, complications were a given, and she'd known it from the beginning. As summer stretched on toward autumn and the birth grew closer, her blood pressure and the risk of clots from her being chair bound grew higher. Owen's visits with her became shorter, but much more frequent throughout the day.

By then Serena had made up her mind about what she wanted. More than one adoption agency had been there to speak with her, leaving notebooks full of names and photographs of couples on their waiting lists for her to choose between. Serena wasn't sure she liked the idea of any of them. She doubted the agencies would be as benevolent if there weren't profit to be made for them for finding a home for her child.

When Owen and Hanna came in around dinnertime, Serena was particularly discouraged. She noticed more than once how sad Hanna became when she talked about her baby, and when she had looked over brochures from those agencies that wouldn't even consider a couple like them as candidates.

The time when Hanna was helping her with dinner was usually the quiet few minutes of the day she got to spend with her husband. He took his break during that time and spent it with Hanna in Serena's room, working with Serena directly after when Hanna left. That day, however, Serena had more to say during the end of dinner than idle chatter, something she'd been meaning to ask for weeks, but hadn't worked up the courage until then.

"There's something I've been wanting to ask you both," Serena spoke up quietly, once Owen had come in and pulled up a chair close to them. "I'm sorry in advance if it might be a little out of line, but please just hear me out, okay?"

Serena noticed the skeptical look on Owen's face when she approached the beginning of the conversation that way, but he took a deep breath noticing how nervous she was, and asked her, "What's on your mind, hun? I'm almost afraid to ask."

"I know that you're both aware, I've been trying to decide what to do about my son. I think we all know that I'm not going to be able to take care of him on my own without help." Serena took a staggered breath, almost ready to cry over it again, but she breathed deeply and stopped herself long enough to finish asking what she had to. "I know Hanna's told me that you've both wanted a baby for a long time, and that she can't have one now, and I was wondering if the two of you would consider adopting my son."

Hanna dropped the silverware that had been in her hand. It fell onto the tray and clattered before she managed to catch hold of it, sending it noisily to the floor. Serena had been prepared for their stunned expressions, she only hoped she hadn't upset them.

"Why us?" Owen asked after a moment, knowing Serena had days to pour over all of those binders which were filled with couples who had much more money, and almost anything someone could dream of wanting their child to have.

"Because I'm scared to give him away to a stranger," Serena answered, tears starting to fall, even as she tried to hold it together enough to answer him. "You both take such good care of me, and you love each other so much, that I think you'd love him just as much as I do. I wouldn't have to wonder where he is, how he is, or if he's loved, and that's all I care about."

"And you wouldn't want anything in return?" Owen asked, knowing things like this usually came with a catch, not that he'd known Serena to be that sort of person.

"There are only a couple of things I'd ask, but it's not money if that's what you're assuming. All I want is for you not to change his name, only his last name to yours. The only other thing I would want is for you to bring me pictures, and if you would please, bring him to see me as often as you can. That's all I'd ask of either of you."

"We'd need time to talk about it and think it over," Owen told her, even though Serena could tell just how badly Hanna wanted to say yes right then.

Owen was overwhelmed enough they had to drop the subject for then before any of them got so emotional that work wouldn't be done.

They went through the motions of getting her exercises finished once Hanna left the room. Owen was quiet for the rest of the time he was there, but she'd have been blind not to see how deep in thought he was over her proposition. Serena didn't allow herself to finally break down and cry until after he left and there was no one else but the old woman across the room who was snoring peacefully, and far too hard of hearing to be woken by her heart shattering sobs.

The closer the birth loomed, the more frightened she became, but not of the birth. She was afraid for her son. Unable to raise him herself, she could only hope Hanna and Owen would accept what she had offered to them. Serena was all too aware that the clock was counting down to the day she'd have to return to Rune and that other life. If her son was born on schedule, she would not live to see him turn four months of age before she'd have to leave him behind.

Serena wasn't afraid to go back, even knowing what was facing her once she returned. The how, and how painful it might be, was the only part she wasn't looking forward to. Their son would be alive, and a part of her and Rune would continue on in this world. It was all she could have dreamed for. She'd be able to see Rune again with a smile on her face, instead of tears in her eyes. She'd tell him about their son, and how she'd faced the end a second time, just to give that gift to him.

CHAPTER FORTY-NINE

LUCY HAD NEVER BEEN FRIGHTENED about who she could trust until then. With Luke still in hiding, it was up to her to seek out the others and get them to listen. She feared it would be far more difficult a task than she had bargained for, and she had no illusions that things were going to go swimmingly.

Lucy first approached those she'd known the longest, even though many of them were now children not much older than her. Many of them knew the truth about Jane, but like Lucy, feared they had no hope of standing against her.

Martha had proven easier to sway than Lucy feared, especially when she'd told her the truth about why Serena and Rune had been absent.

"Martha, you've known me longer than almost anyone who isn't smaller than me now. Have you ever known me to lie about something this important?" Lucy asked her, trying to stay calm and make her case, but worried it wouldn't be possible.

"You do realize what you're implying, Lucy? Do you really think even Jane is capable of hurting someone like that on purpose?" Martha asked her. She did not want to believe it until Lucy reminded her of the past.

"You mean like she did to Charlie, the others, and me? Jane lied, Martha. She went behind our backs, and she set us up for our downfall for no other reason than to get us out of her way. Rune wouldn't do as she said, so Jane's gone after Serena, because she thinks Serena is the reason Rune won't obey her."

"Why would she do that? I've noticed that Jane, Kendall, and some of the others have been giving Serena a rough time, but I had no idea that was the reason. What is she hoping to accomplish?"

"Exactly what she's already accomplished. Or haven't you noticed that Serena is gone?" Lucy told her. Her eyes burned with angry tears she couldn't contain anymore. "Serena ran away, well past our border, after what Kendall did the other night. It was the last straw, Martha. Rune has gone in search of her, and I don't know if, or when, they'll be coming back. Don't you see what she's done now?"

Lucy refused to divulge Serena's location, for fear Jane would catch wind of it and find some way to bring harm to her while she lay helpless.

Lucy herself had witnessed Kendall's treachery first hand, so the things she told Martha, about what had driven Serena away, were far from hearsay.

Martha admitted Jane was still putting on a good face, but even she had noticed she was fanning the flames the moment she was sure no one was watching, with the help of a few others.

Jane's closest circle, if they could be called as such, consisted of only a handful of people, with Robert kept fearfully on the fringes of it, afraid of Jane's wrath. Jane pretended to be a caring matriarch, but she was a true friend to no one but herself. She did not lead to serve the others, but to have them serve her. Kendall was her most recent favored pawn. She'd successfully removed opposition from Rune and Serena from the equation for the time being.

Lucy feared what would happen if Serena did not return, she worried what would happen not only to her, but to Rune, who she feared would be all but broken by it. He already blamed himself far more than he should for what had happened. He hadn't invited Kendall to do what she'd done, and he surely had not encouraged it. It was hard for Lucy not to remember the things Serena had told her about Kendall when they were growing up.

Serena had only just found the beginnings of security with her new family, when Kendall had returned and pulled the rug out from beneath her all over again. No one had to explain to Lucy what Serena had been feeling, that had driven her to that state of desperation. It was the fear of Kendall either driving Rune away, or her taking him from her.

In the days that Lucy talked to the others, she discovered that, of those old enough to fight, roughly a third were on Jane's side or still sitting on the fence undecided. The question was, were their allies willing to organize and take the power back for themselves? They agreed something needed to be done, but almost all of them, except for Luke, seemed afraid to lead and stick their neck out first.

Once they knew their numbers, a meeting was arranged for Luke to speak to them. It was hard not to pick up on the stench of fear, even with their numbers being far greater than those backing Jane. Most hadn't been swayed to action until Luke told them he wished for there to be minimal violence involved in the matter. He wanted Jane and those closest to her confined, as she'd done to him, but not harmed until the community as a whole had decided what was to be done about both her and the others. Those that had been following her out of fear would be given a chance to redeem themselves and make amends, but those who could not be reasoned with would likely receive the same punishment that Jane received.

The time for action was quickly approaching, the longer they delayed, the more chance Jane would learn of their plans and take steps to thwart them. They would gather together and carry out their plans as soon as the moon set that night, leaving only a few hours in which to prepare. The logging chain, lock, and key were recovered where they'd lain discarded, and were ready. That left enough time for Luke to make his way to talk to Rune about their mission.

Luke knew even as he left that Rune would not be persuaded to come. He meant only to be sure he brought him more supplies than normal, in case it was a while before he could return to bring more.

One had to admire the man's love for his wife and his persistence. Nine days had passed, and he'd never once left her side. Three more, and were the old man to be believed, Serena would awaken and return to Rune. He would not leave her to wake without him.

Luke found Rune lying next to Serena with his eyes closed, and his arm curled around her.

Rune opened his eyes and sat up the moment he heard Luke approaching, even as hesitant as he was to let go of her.

"Do you bring news?" Rune asked as Luke sat the heavily weighted pack at his feet, having filled it as full as he dared to, without encumbering himself too badly to make the walk.

"Yes, but whether it is good news, or cause to worry, remains yet to be seen," Luke answered, his unease about the matter plain to see. "Lucy has helped to gather many of the others together, and tonight, soon as the moon goes down, we are taking the reins of power back from Jane and those close to her. We will take them while they sleep, one at a time if we must. Jane has already built her own prison; she just doesn't know it yet." Luke meant of course, the hovel that had been Iona's home where Jane had once confined her. There was no way out, but the doorway that Jane herself had ordered barred and chained closed.

"Does it worry you that you will not have my help?" Rune asked, considering Luke's expression as he talked. There was a heaviness that hung in the air. Times were uncertain for all of them.

"We each will do as we must. I cannot say I do not understand why you must stay by her side, especially now. She is defenseless without you to watch over her. You aren't the only one worried what would happen if the wrong person found her sleeping and helpless. If they've done this much to harm her, I have no doubt they'd go even further, given the chance to do so."

"Nine days she has been sleeping now, and three yet to come, if the old man is to be believed. I do not know what I will do if she does not awaken and return to me."

"I hope, for both your sakes, that is not what happens. Whatever she has returned to that world for, must be something that she wanted very badly, and I can't even begin to guess what that must have been."

"Nor can I. I wish she would have waited and given me a chance to explain."

"Your heart was in the right place, and you aren't to blame, Rune, someone took advantage of your kindness to wound her. If she wanted to use you to hurt Serena that badly, and had failed that time, she'd have only found another way. I have no doubt the girl only wishes to make Serena as much, if not more miserable than she feels. What happened to them both was an accident, and if what Lucy heard holds true, the girl spent years blaming Serena instead of seeking help for her addiction. That is what killed her, not your wife. The girl has no one to blame but herself for her own choices."

"Then what is to be done?"

"For starters, when we go after Jane and the others tonight, she is going to be going with them as well. She's been far too eager to do Jane's bidding and used her favor to do nothing but hurt others. I don't believe Kendall deserves the benefit of doubt any longer, regardless of how much Serena may still care for her. I won't allow her to continue doing as she's done, count on that."

"So you will be going soon?"

"Yes, I will be. I hadn't meant to linger even half this long, but I wanted to make sure you had provisions to last you a while, in case this takes longer than planned. If you are careful with what I brought you and ration it, it should last you until she awakens if we are not able to return before then. Look after yourselves. I'll return as soon as I can."

There was nothing but silence once Luke's footfalls faded into the distance. Rune had a drink of the water Luke had brought him. He lay back down where he'd been before, closed his eyes and talked to Serena as he drifted off toward sleep again.

Luke was nowhere close to sleep, having slept the better portion of the day away before Lucy had come to awaken him for the meeting. Anger had a way of keeping him well alert as he carefully made his way back toward what was to be the staging ground, the grove of oak trees between Iona's home and Jane's.

They didn't need much in the way of weapons, just a few small coils of good, heavy rope, and skill with the knots they chose.

Jane would get a taste of being carted along on that stretcher she'd had Iona tied to, as would anyone else who insisted on putting up too much of a struggle. Lucy waited with both he and Iona as the rest began to gather. Luke would have preferred that the ladies not be involved, but he'd been unable to convince either of them to sit it out.

If anything, Iona and Lucy both wanted to be there to see the smug look wiped off Jane's face once she realized what was going to happen to her. Luke would of course have the only key, which would not be on his person, but hidden in a location of his choosing to keep anyone else from knowing where to look for it once Jane and the rest were secured inside their makeshift prison.

By morning they'd have accomplished their goal, or failed miserably, either way it didn't matter. If Luke failed, at least he wanted to know that, like in his last life, he'd gone out fighting among friends. The time had come, and there was no turning back as that ragtag group set off into the darkness together, to do what they all knew had to be done.

CHAPTER FIFTY

As THE LAST month of her pregnancy loomed, the suffering that Sulwyn had warned her of truly came to light. It began subtly enough not to be noticed, or to be mistaken for normal complications of her pregnancy. It started with swollen feet and hands, and her becoming fatigued during therapy with Owen faster than normal. It wasn't until the shortness of breath started to become worse, and she began to cough that it had been diagnosed as symptoms of early heart failure.

Four weeks before the baby was supposed to be due, and two weeks ahead of schedule, Serena had been rushed to the hospital for an emergency caesarean. The baby's heartbeat was healthy and strong, but it was Serena's heart that was in distress. Her blood pressure had fallen dangerously as she lay on the table during the delivery. She faded in and out of consciousness and was barely able to keep her eyes open until she heard her son's first cries. Someone brought him over to her so she could see him, if only briefly.

His lungs were strong, and the boy cried loudly. The nurses remarked over his headful of snow-white blond hair, and his sky blue eyes so much like Rune's, it nearly brought tears to her eyes. When she looked at the boy, she clearly saw his father's face, and almost none of her own.

"Does your son have a name?" The nurse asked her before taking him away, so his crib card could be made out.

"His name is Soren Rune," Serena replied before she drifted off again, surprisingly unafraid.

She swore she heard Rune talking to her in her dreams, so many times the last few months, and this time was no different. It wasn't time to go to him yet; she still had a little time to wait.

She woke a couple of hours later to find Owen keeping watch over her with a grave expression on his face as he sat in the chair next to her bed. He and Hanna had been at the hospital the entire time since they'd gotten the call that she was being admitted. Hanna was in the nursery spending time with Soren until Serena awakened and was strong enough to hold him herself.

"Have you seen Soren? Is he doing well?" Serena asked Owen, her voice not much over a whisper. Her first thoughts on awakening were of her son, even as she still trembled from the medicine that was being dripped into her veins to prevent hemorrhaging.

"Hanna is looking after him now. I've been in to see him, he's beautiful, Serena. He's healthy and strong, and quite a big boy for being a little early."

"I wish I'd gotten to see him for more than just a moment." Serena sighed, turning her head to look at the nurse across the room that had been keeping an eye on her recovery. As soon as she'd noticed her awake and responsive, she'd come over to collect another set of vital signs, and she still wasn't completely pleased with the results. Serena was thankfully showing signs of improvement.

Serena wasn't able to see Soren until the next morning when the doctors felt safe about moving her into a regular hospital room. With Owen's help lifting him from the bassinet, she was able to hold him. The doctors carried out more tests before it was decided what medicines she needed to take, for the troubles her heart had been having.

Serena couldn't get enough of holding him and letting him lie in her lap when her arms grew tired. She sang to him softly and told him stories about his father during the times she'd been left alone in the room with him, knowing no one was around to hear. She knew they would have called her insane, if she told them where she believed in her heart Soren had really come from. When she saw Rune again, she wanted to be able to tell him every last detail of those first few days before she had to say goodbye to him.

It was harder than she thought it would be when the time finally came, and Soren went home with Hanna and Owen instead of with her as Soren Rune Wagner. The crying had not helped her shortness of breath the first night, even as she looked over all the photographs they'd taken, what must have been a hundred times.

She would see Soren every Saturday on their day off from work, and knowing that didn't make saying goodbye to him any easier. There was so little time left, just under four months before she had to return, and she had a lifetime's worth of love to give to her son before she left him behind. It made her happy to know that he'd be loved and cared for by people that she'd chosen. It was the one thing that brought her peace of mind when worry for him crept to the surface.

She had little worry for herself, knowing to who and what she was returning to, it was only the worry of *how* that frightened her as the time grew closer, and it was just when she'd finally found something that was very much worth living for.

CHAPTER FIFTY-ONE

ONE HOUSE AT A TIME, the group moved throughout the night with only coils of rope and stealth to aid them. Those on the list had been as quietly as possible taken from their beds and bound and gagged before they were taken to the cell Jane had so carefully built to hold someone else, soon to become her own prison.

They understandably left Jane for last, seeing as she was the most likely to put up a fight and raise a ruckus when taken. Except for those guarding the hovel and keeping watch over those already inside, the entirety of the group had gone to confront Jane together. Individually, they'd have each been too terrified of Jane to say a word, but together, they were finally brave enough to stand against her.

Jane was sleeping soundly in her bed when they slipped silently into her house. Luke smiled at the terror in Jane's eyes when she awoke to see him standing over her. He covered her mouth as he and a couple of helpers gagged her and tied her up. They dragged her to the floor and secured her to the same stretcher that she'd had Iona carted away on. Jane was still in her nightgown with her hair up in curlers, making her look quite the sight.

For the first several hours, none of them were untied in order to keep them quiet and not give them any chance to alert the rest with their screaming, but once Jane was inside with them, they'd been cut loose one at a time through the bars. They hadn't gone after the people who had taken a neutral position, only those who had proven themselves to be on Jane's side, or in her pocket, so to speak. Sharing in her punishment were a half dozen others that, unfortunately for him, had included Robert when he couldn't be reasoned with.

Jane shouted and cursed the loudest. One of the women cried, unable to understand why she'd been tossed inside, even if the rest of them knew damned well why they were there. Kendall screeched that her being in the predicament had to be Serena's doing, swearing she'd done nothing wrong.

"Liar!" Lucy screamed at her, seething, knowing she wouldn't be able to get out and cause Serena any further harm. "Serena has been gone for days, and you know damned well you're the reason she ran away. You went after Rune for no other reason than to hurt her, right when you knew that she'd see everything. I'm not blind, Kendall, I was there. I saw you do it with my own eyes. Don't you dare call me a liar."

Kendall sulked, having been pushed further back from the doorway by Jane. Kendall knew it was the truth, Lucy could tell by the look on her face that she hated being called out on it.

If Lucy hadn't been there and seen it all herself, she could scarcely imagine that Kendall would have admitted to what she'd done. She'd have likely made Serena out to be as jealous and controlling as she was by projection, or at the very least, made it seem like she'd blown something she'd swear was completely innocent out of proportion.

Door secured, there wasn't much reason to post a watch, but Luke had it done anyway. He assigned pairs of volunteers, to assure they were still there at certain intervals throughout the day.

Key in his pocket, Luke made his way back to the ruins after he'd gone back to his home and spent time ripping the boards from his windows and removing the padlock and nails from his door. Iona had been content to settle herself in once that work had been done, promising him she'd have a meal ready when he returned.

Rune was where Luke left him the night before, still sitting there watching over Serena, having long since grown weary as a tenth day crept near to the time he'd last seen her. Rune changed when Lucy brought him fresh laundry, but he hadn't left to bathe, or so much as lie in his own bed the entire time he'd been waiting.

"It's finished, Rune. I came because I thought you'd want to know," Luke told him, a little worried over the defeated look on the man's face as he sat there, unable to do more than he'd already done.

"Two more days." Rune sighed, feeling as if the days had been crawling far too slowly for him. "Last night, she almost seemed to be stirring, but she didn't wake, only drifted off again. Sometimes, for a moment, she talks in her sleep but I can no longer understand the things she says, her words come out in a tongue that is strange to me."

"Language is no barrier here, Rune, we all understand one another, but Serena is not from your home. She grew up in what would have been known in your time as Vinland. She lived far across the ocean, in a time that was hundreds of years after you lived and died, and decades after even I lived and died. If I were still living in her time, she'd be young enough to be my great-grandchild. Time doesn't hold quite the same sway here, other than to pull us backward again toward the beginning."

"The longer I sit here waiting, the more I ask myself what could she have wanted so badly that I was unable to give to her. Was she truly afraid that I would abandon her and take someone else over nothing more than the words of gossiping women? I refuse to let myself be a pawn in the games they play. Look what they've done, and what they've made of us. She's done nothing to deserve their wrath, but I have done things to deserve yours, and here you stand as my friend. Sometimes this world makes no sense to me."

"The world rarely makes sense, that world or this one. You would have thought they'd have learned enough from the last life not to bring their troubles and pettiness to the next, but it seems like some of us really have learned nothing. I was studying to be a doctor, what you'd likely think of as a healer, when the war began. I got called away from my studies and into service. I went to war to save men's lives, not to take them. It was against the oath that I took as a healer to do no harm, but I must admit, I more than once had to break that vow to defend myself. Being a peaceful man doesn't mean you are weak, it just means having the wisdom to know the difference between when it's the time to negotiate, and when it's time to stand your ground. The time for negotiating with Jane and the rest has long passed."

"What will we do with them when this is over?" Rune asked, wondering himself what the solution to that particular dilemma was going to be. Their realm did have its limitations, and they couldn't very well leave Jane and the rest confined to that small hovel forever.

"First things first, a new council will be formed, it's been decided there will be seven that sit on it, no longer just three. I will lead in the interim until another leader can be elected, with Lucy as my advisor for the time being. I have come to ask you to take a place on the new council and entrust something to you."

"And what would that be?" Rune asked him, even more intrigued as he stood up and stepped toward him, having a good long stretch after sitting and lying still for far too long.

"This." Luke held the key to the lock confining Jane and the others in his outstretched hand for him to take. "Anyone who might be quietly plotting to free her would be searching for it on me, or hidden away in my home, and that's exactly why I shouldn't have it. I know darn well there's no other man in this realm strong enough, or tough enough, to take it away from you."

The last remark almost got Luke a smile and the threat of a laugh from Rune as he took the key out of Luke's hand. He tucked it securely away with the other keys he carried with him.

"Now, there is nothing to do but wait and discuss the solution to this matter. If they cannot live among us, then we must find a way to live apart from them in safety. I have to stay for now. When I return, I would be glad to serve on this council and help however I can with bringing this matter to a close. From what I gathered from Lucy's words, this has been let go far too long."

"It's going to be important that the solution be agreed upon by at least the majority among us. At least that way it cannot be implied that we just came in, took over, and did what we wanted. There will be a meeting tomorrow, the usual time, and it will be discussed when we've all gathered. Lucy or I will come afterward, to give you the highlights and let you know what solutions have been suggested. By then we should also have a good idea of who else this council will be consisting of. That will be voted on as well, or at least a temporary council, until we've all had time to choose a more proper one."

"Two more days. When she awakens, we will come home, and I hope we can move on from this to what future is ahead of us here. I hope it is a good one afterward."

"Just keep faith in that, Rune. Believe she will return to you, and she will. I am sure that when she does come back, she will have a good story to tell you about where she's been and what has happened. I can feel it in my bones."

CHAPTER FIFTY-TWO

LIFE FOR SERENA had become irony at its worst. She lived for Saturday, and the few hours she got to spend with Soren. Each passing week meant the clock was winding down, and she was growing weaker each day. There'd been tests and medications, but none had seemed to stop, or slow the progress of the disease. Serena's heart was failing, and short of a transplant, she didn't have much in the way of hope for recovery.

Her time with Owen no longer consisted of exercises to strengthen her, but to keep her limber and cut down the risk of blood clots forming from her being unable to move.

She was quickly growing too weak to be kept on the transplant list, even on an emergency basis, and once it was known, her visits with Soren became shorter, but much more frequent. Hanna took to working shorter hours to be home with Soren more. Serena frequently saw Soren during the last hour of Owen's workday when Hanna came to pick him up from work.

Soren was growing into a bright and beautiful child. Even at such a young age, he was inquisitive and curious about the world around him. He rarely cried during the time she saw him, and he seemed content to lie in her arms or lap as she told him stories and sang to him, even as the breath to do so was growing harder to come by.

The photographs were what got her through the dark hours spent alone. She slept longer each day as she grew weaker, but those photographs stayed clutched in her hand, or under her pillow in a small photo album. They were the first things she wanted to see when she awoke, and they were the last things she saw when she closed her eyes.

She spent the last few days she was awake, writing letters to Soren in her journal. She wanted to tell him about his father, and she no longer cared that anyone would tell her that it was only a fairy tale, or a trick her mind played on her as she lay there dreaming all those months.

As time drew close, those dreams drew her back into them. She crossed into that world for the second time in her sleep on a Saturday morning, just as Owen and Hanna had come into the room with Soren to ask after her. She'd only been waiting to tell him goodbye.

She'd asked long before not to be brought back, and she'd told them she wouldn't come even if they tried. She'd no sooner let go of that world, than she'd awoken in the featherbed on the dais. She turned her head to see Rune lying by her side, his head resting on her shoulder.

As soon as she stirred and began to cry, his eyes opened, and he pulled her against him. She was only strong enough to curl her arms around his neck when he sat up, pulling her into his lap. Rune didn't care if Serena saw she was not the only one in tears.

"Quickly, give her something to drink and something simple to eat. She will need it, after having been asleep for so long," a soft but rumbling voice that belonged to the old man said from behind them.

Rune lifted his head and did as he was told, helping to lift a cup full of water to her lips. Serena drained it quickly and asked for more. He had little to give her to eat other than the last half of a sandwich Lucy had brought to him. He fed it to her slowly with a second cup that was the last of the water Luke had brought.

"Now that she has awakened, you must carry her home, and place her into your bed," Sulwyn told him quietly as he gently touched the top of her head, causing Serena to drift back off to sleep in Rune's arms. "She will sleep again until moonrise, and when she awakens, she will have quite a story to tell you."

The path cut wider by then and the weeds well trampled down, the walk back through the woods to their home was not nearly the ordeal it would have once been. Rune walked slowly, mindful of his footing as he cradled Serena in his arms. The woods were quiet, and the wind was still as it was on most nights as he walked. He passed no one. The hour had come when most would have been creeping home toward their own beds. Moonrise was only a few short hours away.

Lucy opened the door for him when she saw him coming, and she helped him tuck Serena into bed before she brought him a bowl full of hot soup. As soon as he'd finished it, his eyes began to grow heavy. Lying down next to Serena, he curled his arm around her again before Lucy slipped out of the room and closed the door.

CHAPTER FIFTY-THREE

SULWYN WATCHED in silence from a corner of the room as they slept. It wasn't often he left his lighthouse, but he felt the need to come, and for the first time in many, many years to explain. The place had fallen into shambles, and a part of him had begun to wonder, if uncertainty was part of what had driven so many of them into acts of desperation such as this over the years.

He couldn't, of course, tell the child everything. There were things about this realm and all the others beyond it that were not his to tell. He hoped to at least give her, and through her the others, maybe some small peace of mind.

"Wake up, child, wake and forget that you were ever broken," Sulwyn called softly to her, placing his hand gently on the top of Serena's head and stroking at her hair with father-like fondness.

Serena looked up at him with quiet confusion until she remembered him from their talk within the ruin. She wondered if she was dreaming, until she noticed that she could move not just her arms, but everything. For the first time in months she was free of pain and not struggling to breathe.

"How?" she asked, wanting to cry again as Sulwyn helped her to at first sit up, and then stand, holding onto her for her first few shaky steps before she remembered how to walk again.

"Your body was only broken in that world, it never needed to be here. Once you let go of it, the pain let go of you as well. People here only carry the scars they choose to bring with them. They could banish them with simply a thought if they only released them. Now that you have done it yourself, you can help others to do it."

"Will I ever see my son again?" Serena asked him sadly, it being the first question on her mind, though from the look in Sulwyn's eyes she knew the answer before he even spoke the words.

"Not in this lifetime as you know him now, but when you grow young again, and return to that world, you will cross paths in the next life. Souls that bond together pass together, into the next life. Think of life as a circle, when it comes full again, it doesn't end; it only begins again, but in the balance of before. You go forward to grow old in that world, and go backward to grow young and move on to the next life in this one, just as innocent as you began your last. I could tell you what will happen, if it will ease your heart, but when you fall asleep again and awaken you will not remember. No one should know too much of these things, which have already been written in their stars."

"Tell me, even if I will forget," Serena asked pleadingly, wanting to hear his answer, even if she'd have no memory of it later. She wanted more than anything to know her son would do well, and that they really would cross paths again someday, even in another lifetime.

"You and Rune are not only bonded together in this world, you will also love one another again in the next and possibly even longer. When he is reborn, he will be Soren's son, as he was in his last life. When you return, Lucy will be your mother. Charlie, the man that she loved so much in this realm will be your father. I will not tell you who Rune's mother may be as she is someone you have not yet met, but she will be coming to this realm soon and will be a friend to you all."

"So, we will be together as a family again?" Serena asked, tears starting to fall from her eyes only to have Sulwyn reach to dry them as they stood at the window. She turned to gaze at the woods outside and the ever-present twilight.

"You had only one child in that life, but in the next, you and Rune will have many, just as he wished. The years for both of you will be as long as they were short this time. You will both grow quite old together, though precisely how old is not mine to say." Sulwyn smiled, helping to dry her tears again as he walked her back toward the bed, this time only holding her hand as she made her way there on her own power.

Serena had scarcely returned to the bed but her eyes were already growing heavy. Sulwyn tucked the covers around her gently, just as he had done before, the last time she'd seen him.

"Sleep, child, and when the moon rises, tell him everything."

CHAPTER FIFTY-FOUR

MOONRISE CAME and the woods were quiet. So was the house, though four people slept that night within its walls. Serena stirred first, which awoke Rune from his slumber. She thought he would squeeze the breath from her when he pulled her close to him, wrapping her tightly in his arms before he helped her to sit up. Rune gave her more water from a pitcher Lucy had left on the nightstand, when she told him she was thirsty after so many days of sleep.

She'd no sooner finished with her drink, then she was wrapped in his arms again. This time, he lifted her into his lap as he curled himself around her, almost afraid to let go. Serena didn't know how she would even begin to explain why she'd been gone so long and all that had happened. He was still there, the worry and the love in Rune's eyes so plain to see, it almost made her heart go to pieces even more than what she had to tell him was already breaking it.

"My love, what has kept you so far from me? Did I hurt you? I swear I do not, nor will I, love another," Rune whispered, kissing her forehead, his voice trembling as he spoke.

"I know. It was only fear that put doubts in my head, not anything you've done. I love you, Rune, and I've never stopped even for a single moment." Serena sighed, taking another deep breath, and trying to find the courage to continue, "I did not stay away because of anything that you did, or out of anger. I stayed away because I wanted something so badly, something we could never have had if I'd stayed here and not gone back."

"What do you mean, love?" Rune asked her, the confusion in his eyes plain to see. The things she was saying made no sense to him. What could she have wanted that badly to keep her that far from him?

Serena wasn't sure how to explain, so she kissed him softly. Her voice became unsteady as she told him, "Reach your hand underneath my pillow, and there will be small book there, just where I have always kept it. Open it, and look inside, you will see."

Serena was nervous that it would not be there until Rune found it just as she'd said. She sat, on the edge of tears, as she watched him open the cover to see the first photograph of their newborn son. His hands shook as badly as hers as he looked back at her.

"Rune, this is our son, Soren," She whispered, her voice shaking so badly, she was almost unable to utter the words. Tears breached her eyelids and cascaded down her cheeks as Rune crushed her against him, his expression one of surprise, happiness, and sadness all at once.

"This is our son? You stayed away so he could grow there as he could not here?" Rune asked, his voice still quivering. He held Serena against him while turning the pages of the album, seeing for the first time the very same photographs she hadn't been able to sleep without. "What has become of him if you are here?"

"He has gone to live with friends who will raise him as their own. I left books with stories about the both of us behind for him to read when he is old enough to understand," Serena told him, trying to wipe her eyes on the back of her hand as she curled against him. "I wanted him to know about you, about us, and that we love him. There's no reason to be afraid. I believe we'll see him again, maybe not in this realm, but in what comes after. I don't know why, but I can feel it."

"You gave me a son," Rune whispered again, as he reached the end of the album. He held it in his hands for a long moment, lost in thought before he leaned down to kiss her. He didn't let go of it until he slid it carefully back under the pillow once Serena was lying under him.

She missed Rune so badly, more than she ever thought she could. She hadn't felt complete until she was in his arms, and he was within her. She was ready to let go of her life before and be happy with him; Jane, Kendall, and the rest be damned. He loved her, and he'd waited, that was all that mattered.

The first night, they talked of their son as the others slept, lying in a warm bath together before going downstairs. The phonograph played their favorite records, as she lay wrapped in his arms, looking over the album of photographs together. They were still lying there when Lucy and Alec awakened, and she told her story over breakfast. They sat at the table together, like the family that they were, the family she'd always wanted.

CHAPTER FIFTY-FIVE

THREE DAYS PASSED and life returned to what had once been routine. The picture frame they'd placed Rune's favorite photograph of Soren in stayed on their bedside table. It was the last thing Serena and Rune looked at each night before they went to sleep.

The new council had been formed, and the rest of the members voted upon; Luke, Rune, and Martha were joined by four of the others that were chosen by the people themselves; William, Carol, Jacob, and Rosemary.

The decisions of the council would never be left in so few hands again. The council was larger, consisting of seven, so more opinions could be heard, and not just those of an inner circle disconnected from the people they were meant to serve.

Their first choice together was to consider what had to be done with Jane and the others, who were still confined to Iona's old home. Their fates would be decided on an individual basis.

Two women who had shown genuine remorse had been freed and allowed to go home, but three women and two men were still confined there together.

They couldn't just set them free and expect there not to be trouble, but none of them felt right sending them to the far side of the lighthouse gate. In the end, it had been decided to banish them instead to the unknown lands to the east of the river. None of them had ever crossed there, and no one had ever come from there.

There was no ford, and no bridge across, so one made of rope had been constructed carefully with the aid of a raft. It didn't need to be sturdy, because it would not be used more than once. The ropes would be cut away after Jane and the others were taken across; Jane's dismay was obvious once she realized where she was being taken.

"You can't do this! You can't just leave us here. There is nothing," Jane shouted at Luke and Rune as they stood at the end of the bridge. They had left them there; loosely bound with ropes they'd be able to work their way out of with only a little effort. Packs were sent that contained a good amount of food, clothing, blankets, and necessary supplies inside.

"But we have, and you've brought it on yourselves," Luke answered. "You can't live among us without hurting or trying to control the others, and that cannot be allowed to continue. It's far too late for promises of change. We all know that those promises would be nothing but empty ones. Jane, Kendall, Linda, Ivan, and Robert, the council has sentenced you to be banished to the east of this river. Do not cross it, or you will find yourselves taken back across again, in possibly not quite as friendly a manner as you were taken this time."

"None of us know what is to the east. You may very well find more people like us who might welcome you among them. Take what has happened here as a lesson so you do not repeat the same mistakes that found you cast out from us. Goodbye and good journey to all of you."

That said, Luke and Rune made their way back across the bridge carefully. Rune took the axe and cut the ropes, trapping the five that had been banished on the other side of the river. A good crowd of people had gathered around Rune and Luke to watch the sentence be carried out. The mood was somber when it had finished, and not quite the celebration of freedom one might expect as they turned their backs, and walked the path toward the summerhouse together.

The mood didn't lighten until after the evening meal had been served. They joined the children on the beach outside; Drew among them, laughing and playing among the waves. Even Lucy almost forgot her old age. She laughed and splashed in the water, much like the child she seemed to be, and would soon become again.

Serena smiled and clung to Rune as the waves carried her up and down in his arms as they floated together. For once the lighthouse was silent.

A distance down the beach, Lucy noticed a man sitting at the end of the pier. She did not know the newcomer from the last fog, who until then had stayed quietly to himself amidst the chaos of those last several days. He found his way there amongst the others on his own, smiling as he watched the children playing, even as he only sat there and watched from a distance.

"I'm sorry, I haven't introduced myself sooner, my name is Lucy Miller," Lucy told him, looking at him from behind dampened pigtails, her soaking wet dress clinging to her legs with a huge smile on her face. "Will you come and join us, sir? We've all been waiting to meet you, come on."

The man gave her a big smile, pulling his stocking cap down over his ears a little tighter, and scratching his beard before he stood and took her hand. He followed her off the pier and toward the beach as everyone rushed forward to welcome him home.

ABOUT THE AUTHOR

Aurora Wildey was born and raised in Marion, Ohio. Though Hereafter is her debut novel, she has had a lifelong love of music and the written word. She presently resides with her family in the small town of Oil City, Pennsylvania.

Learn more at www.aurorawildey.com.